The Spindle Chair

The Barn Church Series
Book One

by

SHELLIE ARNOLD

FIREFLY

The Spindle Chair by Shellie Arnold
Published by Firefly Southern Fiction
an imprint of Lighthouse Publishing of the Carolinas
2333 Barton Oaks Dr., Raleigh, NC, 27614

ISBN: 978-1-941103-87-6
Copyright © 2015 by Shellie Arnold
Cover design by Elaina Lee
Interior design by AtriTeX Technologies P Ltd

Available in print from your local bookstore, online, or from the publisher at: www.lighthousepublishingofthecarolinas.com

For more information on this book and the author visit: www.shelliearnold.com

Brought to you by the creative team at Lighthouse Publishing of the Carolinas: Eva Marie Everson, Ramona Richards, and Jessica R. Everson.

Library of Congress Cataloging-in-Publication Data
Arnold, Shellie.
The Spindle Chair / Shellie Arnold 1st ed.

Printed in the United States of America

PRAISE FOR *THE SPINDLE CHAIR*

In *The Spindle Chair*, debut author Shellie Arnold skillfully weaves together a story of longing and loss, fear and faith. At once beautiful and haunting, this is a book you won't soon forget.

~Ann Tatlock
Award-winning author of *Once Beyond A Time*

Author Shellie Arnold bursts onto the scene with an emotion-packed debut novel. Beautifully written. I was hooked from page one, and the story didn't fade away even when I'd finished it. Poignant and heart-stirring, *The Spindle Chair* is a must read!

~Ane Mulligan
Author of *Chapel Springs Revival*

I don't think I've ever read a novel quite like Shellie Arnold's *The Spindle Chair*. This story deals with tough issues and does so with authenticity and grace. I was touched on numerous levels, and I finished with a divinely-infused "hold tight to and fight" for lasting love. Though the particulars may change, every woman shares Laurie's need to be held close and loved deeply. Therefore, this novel is phenomenal book club material and should be on the shelves of anyone involved in women's ministry.

~Jennifer Slattery
Author, *Intertwined*, New Hope Publishers, 2015
Reviewer, Novel Reviews

Shellie Arnold is an excellent writer who captures life events, emotions, and moves to biblical conclusions related to real life situations. I believe readers will be encouraged to know that Shellie faces life's tough issues (loss, depression, loneliness, adjustments, communication, perception, family of origin issues, etc.) head on. I appreciate the biblical integration of *The Spindle Chair*, and endorse this book and wholeheartedly recommend it to couples.

~**Donald A. Lichi, Ph.D.**
Psychologist
Vice-President, EMERGE Counseling Services

ACKNOWLEDGMENTS

Until 2002, my writing goals sat squarely on the non-fiction side of the book market. Writing novels for adults was *the* farthest thing from my mind. I had been slowly building my platform as a speaker on marriage and family issues, and thought I knew what my next steps should be . . . until.

Boy, that's a word, isn't it? "Until" can be a lovely word if there's something wonderful on the other side, but it can also be quite ominous when one's future is uncertain. At the end of 2002 and beginning of 2003 my life had a definite *ominous* quality—after a severe anaphylactic reaction, I experienced unexplained neurological symptoms which worsened over time. By May 2005, intermittent episodes of right side paralysis controlled my life, and had all but destroyed my dreams of writing and speaking. More often than not, I couldn't write my own name, let alone write a book. And public speaking is out of the question when your head falls over, your mouth droops, and you can't talk.

On May 18, 2005, God healed my brain.

God. Healed. My. Brain. (deep, thankful breath)

My husband and I prayed for eleven months before I began writing again. During those eleven months, God gave me glimpses of a few scenes from *The Spindle Chair.* I had no idea what I was supposed to do with the pictures in my head *until* (there's that word again) God turned my head to fiction. That's when my writing journey broadened to include fiction.

So my first big *thank you* is to God, who not only gave me back my life and dream, but guided my steps to those listed below.

Thank you to the LPC team. All of you. For all you do, for all the tasks I don't even know about.

Thank you to the many professionals who assisted me with

research and answered my sometimes repetitive questions: Steven K. Abraham, Psy D.; Catherine L. Ballard, MA, LSW, PCC, CTT, TLC; John R. Ellington, Jr., MD; Mark Hancock; Patricia (Trudy) Sweat, RN; and Dr. William E. Broach III.

Kelli Mergenthaler, thanks for being my best friend, and for openly discussing your first-hand experience with infertility.

Eva Marie Everson, thanks again for letting me tag along to the Novel Retreat in North Carolina—a first for me—with you and Miss Betty (I miss her, too). I wouldn't even have made it through the airports without you! Being your critique partner is an honor I cherish. Your input is invaluable, your friendship worth even more.

To Larry Leech II and the "original" fiction group—there aren't enough words or commas to express all my thanks for your love, support, and encouragement.

To Deb Raney, Ann Tatlock, Ramona Richards, Cynthia Schnereger, and Steve Laube—you each encouraged me at critical junctures, and those encouragements convinced me to continue working on my craft.

To Davis Bunn, thanks for being patient enough to explain back story, without laughing at me.

To Mary Buckham and Dianna Love, your *Break Into Fiction* seminar put wind beneath my wings.

To Lon Garber who gave me my first chance as a writer.

To Word Weavers in Orlando, Florida, thanks for helping me start this book. And to Dory Stewart, the Medina County Writers Club, and Jessica R. Everson, thanks for helping me finish it.

Tamela Hancock Murray, I was about to give up looking for an agent. You were and continue to be a HUGE answer to prayer. I thank God for you!

To Susan Given, who convinced me emotional healing is within reach if I grab God's hand and hold on.

To my Biggest Fan (you know who you are).

To my children, for whom I write.

And finally to my husband. Stephen, I know we both remember you packing all my writing books into the attic at my request (constantly seeing them on my shelves hurt me so badly) when I thought my writing journey was over because of illness. Thanks for holding me and crying with me back then. Thanks for rejoicing with me now. Thanks for never letting me go.

For clarification: to my knowledge, Rowe City, Alabama, exists only in my head and heart.

Dedicated to

Geraldine Brady (Aunt Dean)

who first believed in me,
and helped me believe I could be a writer.

PROLOGUE

"Laurie, please be all right."

Laurie's mind was a black cavern. She heard Pierce's voice, but he sounded far away.

"Please don't die."

Die? Why would he think that?

"God, I can't lose her, too," he whispered.

Lose her . . . what?

The baby. They'd gone to an early dinner at Downtown Disney celebrating her new full-time position with one of Orlando's top interior design firms. Though she wasn't yet showing, she'd chosen to wear a maternity blouse. They'd returned home, and she'd taken a bath. She'd been thinking of little blue tubs she'd seen while shopping. How sweet it would be to swaddle a clean, wet baby. Hear him giggle and coo as she slipped his busy feet into tiny pajamas.

As she bent to towel dry her calf, a vicious cramp stole her breath, then tightened as a vice clamping her insides. Blood gushed between her legs.

Now, it was night. She was in the hospital. And the baby was gone.

"I'll be all right, Pierce." Laurie murmured through a pasty mouth. She blinked, fighting the sedative. But was that a lie? Would she ever again be all right?

He sat by her bed in the room's only chair and didn't seem to hear her.

"Oh, God. My wife." He rubbed his forehead against the sheet-covered mattress. "Our child."

The overhead light glared down on his head. She touched his hair. "Pierce?"

He raised his damp face to look at her. "Are you hurting?"

"Not really. Only inside." She swallowed past the dry lump. "I can't believe after almost six years of trying—our entire marriage—I miscarry." The deep ache squeezed her heart. Would she never experience motherhood?

She gulped again. "This can't be the end for us." How could she have miscarried when she'd felt so good, so healthy? She'd had none of the common side effects of pregnancy—no sensitivity to smell, no unusual tiredness, no morning sickness.

"I won't love you any less if we never have a baby."

She knew that. Deep inside she knew his love for her didn't depend on her ability to have a child, but . . .

Silence hung between them as she gazed into his eyes. "Thank you. I didn't know I needed to hear that, but I guess I did." What could a woman say when she'd failed at life's most basic, natural skill?

"Pastor Hammond told me to take a few days off to be with you, and Ella said to call if you need anything."

Pierce's boss and his sweet wife, Ella. "That's very kind of them." Tears threatened and she let them fall. "Mostly I just need you."

"I'm not leaving."

"Doesn't look like a comfortable chair."

"It'll do if it needs to."

She slowly lifted her head. Grief and sadness made one feel so heavy. "Will you raise the bedrail for me?"

He sat back and did as she asked. She scooted closer to the edge, then settled on her side.

"Want me to cover you up?"

Fresh tears fell again. "I want you. Will you climb in behind me? Hold me?" Her breath hitched. "This hurts me so bad."

He took off his shoes and padded around behind her. He lifted the sheet. The mattress sagged under his weight, and his jeans rubbed against her calves. Then he snuggled against her back and wrapped his arm around her waist. She laid a hand over his and pulled him tighter around herself.

"Pierce, I can't go home."

"What?"

"If they release me tomorrow. I can't go back to that apartment."

She imagined the blood-drenched towel still lying on the bathroom floor. She'd probably left a trail all the way to their parking space in the open lot and stains in their car. Cleaning up would be awful.

"I'll take care of it," he said.

"How?" The stench of dried blood. The *work* it would be. "Just throw away the towels I left on the bathroom floor." She didn't know what to do about the car.

"Ina Hood has always said we can have that apartment over her garage any time. I'll call her tomorrow."

"You mean move? How will you do it?"

"I'll take you to Ella's. I'll get church members to help me. No one should ever have to go back to any place that represents so much pain."

She pulled his hand to her lips, kissed it, and held it against her chest. So many men didn't even try to understand a woman's emotions. That Pierce understood hers, that he loved her this way, was a miracle in itself.

Her parents—especially her mother—would have loved him.

She touched her earlobe. "What did I do with my mom's pearl earrings? I put them in my purse, right after we got here, didn't I?"

"I can look to make sure."

She took his hand again. "No, stay with me."

"Dad called while you were sleeping. There's a board meeting at his church tomorrow, and he's anxious for an answer, you know? But after I told him about the baby, he said we should take more time to think about it."

She'd known her father-in-law would one day retire—though she couldn't picture Daniel Crane breathing, let alone talking, without preaching. She and Pierce had dreamed together of one day moving back to their home state of Alabama, so he could take over the church his parents had started so many years ago before adopting him.

But she'd always envisioned their children as part of that process.

She turned toward him, pressed her forehead to his. "I already loved our baby."

"Shh. I did, too. It'll happen one day."

Laurie closed her eyes. *Dear God, please, someday let me have this man's child.*

CHAPTER ONE

*I*n his new home, in his new bed, he turned away from the moonlight spearing through the tall window. He could get up. Go use the nice, inside bathroom, and then return to his new bed. His new mom and dad didn't mind him using the bathroom during the night. They had told him the one in the hall was his to use. He pulled up his knees, trying to hold it. No, he'd never get back to sleep needing to go this bad.

He slid back the covers. On bare feet he crept across the wood floor to the bathroom, clicked on the light, and squinted while closing the door. He barely reached the commode in time. The quiet flush reassured him he was indeed in a new home.

A fat, orange bar of soap rested on the sink's ledge. He lathered and washed as he knew he should, then opened the door.

The light cast a beam to his new parents' room. He gauged the distance, turned out the light, and tiptoed to the rug by their bed. He lowered to the floor and rested his head on his hands facing his new mom.

"Pierce?" Her kind voice soothed him. She turned on the lamp and knelt beside him. With gentle fingers she touched his cheek. "It's okay if you had to go to the bathroom."

He nodded and went into her open arms, snuggled in close as she rocked him and kissed his head. "My daddy didn't want me no more."

"Oh, honey, no. He just couldn't take care of you by himself." She continued rocking him. "Daniel. Daniel, wake up. Come help me hold our son."

Pierce opened his eyes to a serene Alabama sky peeking through

1

the mini-blinds. He blinked once, twice against the dream.

The scent of coffee and fried eggs mingled with stiffness and cramped muscles. Pierce rolled his neck and shoulders, banged his elbow on the side of his and Laurie's bed. He sat up.

Whoa. Why had he been lying on the floor?

Foggy eyes scanned the bedroom and focused. Small mountains of boxes surrounded their bed and pressed against the walls. Outside the paned windows, daylight draped around the old oak tree and soared to heaven. A large moving van filled with Laurie's and his belongings still sat at the street's edge, waiting to be unloaded.

"Laurie?"

"Be right there!" she called. "I'm making coffee. We should hang a big swing from a limb of that tree you and Gilbert played around when you were kids."

"That's an idea." He and his best friend Gilbert had played all over the narrow ten acres that held The Barn Church, the parsonage on the street corner, and the thick stand of trees between the two. Now, after all this time, he would be Gilbert's boss.

A garbage truck lumbered past and hissed to a stop at a neighbor's driveway. Pierce tensed as the truck started and stopped its way down the street. Air brakes. He always jumped at the sound, like that of the bus Daddy had carried Pierce to, set him on a green, vinyl seat, and sent him away to the Cranes.

Pierce rubbed his hands over his face. No, dwelling on his father's rejection helped nothing.

He rose and walked to the bathroom, brushed his teeth, dressed, and sat on the bed.

"Hey, sleepyhead." Laurie stood in their bedroom doorway, holding two steaming mugs.

"How long was I on the floor?"

"What?"

"I woke on the floor." He jerked a thumb over his shoulder. "By the window, right before the garbage truck drove by."

She leaned against the doorjamb, motioned with the cup in her right hand. "You were over there on the rug your parents left?"

"Yeah."

"You've had several nightmares these last eight months since I lost the baby."

"It wasn't a nightmare. I dreamed about the first night I spent here." He turned and stared toward the window. "Were you cooking eggs?"

"You don't eat eggs."

But he'd been certain as he awoke, he smelled eggs frying.

"Are you all right?" she asked softly. "Do you want this coffee?"

"Sure." He reached for the cup and looked at Laurie. He could concentrate on her, think only about her, and make the first five years of his life go away again, as he had many times during their marriage.

Her tousled, dirty-blonde hair. Her big, brown eyes. She thought her face was too round. Too freckly, though her "spots" had supposedly faded some since her childhood. He loved her face.

She was tall. Only an inch or two shorter than he, and he liked being almost eye-to-eye with her. This view of her bare legs that stretched below one of his old T-shirts wasn't bad either. He grinned at her and set his mug aside.

"What are you smiling at?"

He lowered himself back to the floor and prowled toward her like a hunting lion. "You got any shorts on under there?"

"I guess you're all right, then." She giggled and took a step back. "Don't you dare. Don't you even think about it."

"Think about what?" He crept closer.

"Pierce Crane." She set her mug on a stack of boxes inside the bedroom doorway and pointed at him. "There are boxes everywhere. We have less than two weeks to unpack before I start my new job as the senior pastor's wife."

He stopped in front of her, looked up, and wriggled his eyebrows. "I like pastors' wives." He pulled her down and pinned her to the floor.

"Don't you tickle me!"

He slid his hand up to her ribs while watching her try not to smile. Finally she laughed, pushed at his hands. "Pierce, stop!"

He pulled his hand back and braced himself above her.

Here was everything he could ever want. A job—following in his dad's footsteps as pastor of The Barn Church. A house—even if it was the old parsonage and his childhood home. But most of all, Laurie. "You are the most beautiful pastor's wife in the world." He kissed her. "And the only one for me."

She smiled as her eyes filled with tears. "You know you make me cry every time."

From the moment they'd met he'd been pulled to her compassionate heart, her huge, tender feelings. She was soft before God. Soft to him and others. Like a bee to acres of clover, he was drawn to her. Drank her in, fed from her. She probably didn't realize it, but almost every day she helped him forget that lonely bus ride.

"I love you, Laurie. Your sweet tears, your laughter, your ticklish places." He kissed her again, nibbled her lips and slid his hand back under her shirt.

"Pierce," she chided against his mouth. "We can't. The church board and their wives, everyone will be here any minute, and—"

The doorbell rang. Pierce groaned.

Laurie laughed again, pushed him aside. "Hold that thought for about twelve hours. They're here to help us unpack. We *do* need the help." She leaned forward and nipped his earlobe. "You can have me later, when we don't have all the deacons listening on the front porch. Besides, I have to change clothes before they see me."

"Can I watch?"

"No." She giggled. "Go answer the door."

"Fine." He stole a quick kiss. "But in twelve hours, you're mine."

***

Anxious to welcome folks to her home, Laurie dug through boxes stacked by their bed, searching for her jeans.

There was something to be said about folks who went out of their way to help someone new move into the neighborhood, even if that "someone" was their new pastor, a man they already knew and loved. The people of Rowe City were like that. She had known it from the first time Pierce brought her here to meet his adoptive parents.

This part of Alabama seemed frozen in time, almost decades removed from the years at the university in Montgomery, where she and Pierce met. The patch-worked, brown and green terrain rolled across soft hills and rich farmland. Long-slatted, airy fences edged dirt lane driveways. A water tower of cardinal red stood as a proud landmark near the railroad tracks. Humble outhouses dotted many backyards, not always elements of nostalgia. To Laurie's amazement, a few were still used.

Downtown, brick buildings meshed with uneven sidewalks. Matching streets wound their way past the courthouse, Downtown Diner, and Benson's Hardware, encircled the park, then yielded to the blacktop that merged with Highway 29. The nearest Wal-Mart was a twenty-minute drive, toward Dothan, home of the annual National Peanut Festival—a far cry from the tourist hype of Orlando. Laurie couldn't imagine a more wonderful place to live or raise a family.

A family.

Please, God, I know it might take a miracle, but I want to have a child.

She heard car doors slam. Laughter. High-pitched female greetings—the kind that made men's eyes roll. She knew Pierce would simply prop the front door wide open.

She found the box she needed buried in the corner, grabbed pants and a clean T-shirt, crawled over the unmade bed—and thought she heard a baby cry.

The familiar punch of grief hit her heart full force. The bitter ache trailed her to the bathroom where she leaned on the counter and struggled to take a deep breath. She looked in the mirror as she braced against a tidal wave of longing.

What was that verse in Proverbs? *Hope deferred makes the heart sick.* She believed it. Swallowing the bitter grief over her parents' tragic death ten years earlier had been very, very tough, but eventually the pain subsided. Especially after she fell in love with Pierce.

But this maternal longing in her soul throbbed like a fresh wound since the miscarriage. There were moments like those she'd just spent laughing with Pierce when she'd forget about losing her child. Then the pain would return, as if someone draped a dark cloak over her heart.

She missed a child she had never known.

Laurie struggled into her jeans and rifled through bags, looking for moisturizer and lip gloss. She could easily picture three or more blue-eyed children running in the yard and playing on a swing set outside the kitchen window. She could hear their whispers dancing across the dark wood floors, their laughter bouncing off the high ceilings.

The doctor had said she miscarried because the baby wasn't developing properly. "I can find no reason you shouldn't be able to carry a child," he'd said. Apparently, she was simply part of that thirty-or-so percent of infertile women whose inability to conceive remained unexplained. Which gave her hope.

She washed her face, ran a brush through her hair, and with stuttering breath shook off the yearning that clung like sticky scales. She tied back her hair and opened the bathroom door to find Pierce sitting on his side of their bed, staring out the window.

That same shadow had drifted across his face many times over the years, especially since her miscarriage. Whenever she saw it, she had a stomach-gripping sense that something hovered in the dark at the edge of their marriage.

He would be happy now, wouldn't he? Not just in pieces, but all of him. Even that one sad piece of Pierce he never wanted to talk about.

Then, like someone flipped a switch in his mind, he was back with her, reaching for her hand.

"Are you okay?" she asked. "About the dream? I know about your first night here, but is there more you need to talk about?"

"What? No. I simply forgot the truck keys."

"You're sure?"

"Of course I'm sure." He rose, grinning like a child. "You've met most of them already, but there's quite a crew out there. Ready to face them all?"

"Absolutely." She wrapped her arms around him and held tight. "I'm thankful for their help, and I'm happy as long as you're happy."

***

Laurie stepped into the hall and turned toward the front of the house. If she'd built her own home, she'd have designed it like this one, with a long hallway stretching from the bedrooms at the back to the centered front door. The large living area on one side, the dining room and kitchen on the other.

Pierce had indeed propped open the front door. He and the men stood surveying the contents of the open truck.

She continued around the corner, into the dining room where coolers and gallons of tea had been stacked, then peeked into the kitchen. Milly Newman, her mother-in-law's best friend, arranged her plates and little Ally Newman, Milly's kindergarten-age granddaughter, stacked her pots and pans.

"There she is! Hi! Hi!" Ally rushed over. "Granny says I wasn't born yet, but I've seen pictures of your wedding. You looked like a princess. When I get married, I'll look like a princess, too."

"I'm sure you will."

"Granny says it's crowded in here, but that's how a kitchen's supposed to be."

"She's absolutely right. It's wonderful." The adult orphan inside her reveled in this personal start. How she longed to have toddling children roaming underfoot and loud teenagers reaching into cupboards.

"Where's my girl?" Daniel set two boxes of Krispy Kremes on the counter and caught Laurie in a warm hug.

"Daniel, don't squeeze her so." Kay scolded from behind him. "Sorry we didn't get here sooner, Laurie. I didn't think retirement and sleeping late would agree with me, but it does."

Laurie kissed Daniel's cheek and then hugged her teenager-thin mother-in-law. "I think we've got plenty of help. How long can you, um, stay?" Her voice faltered as the room spun. Cold sweat skittered across her neck and scalp. She raised her palm to her forehead and blinked. "I think I need to sit."

Daniel grabbed a chair for her. "Did you eat breakfast? Have a donut." He reached into the box and pulled out a crème-filled, her favorite.

But Laurie's stomach recoiled at the sweet pastry's scent. "I don't think I can eat right now, Dad. Thanks, anyway."

"Daniel, go help somebody." Kay shooed him away. "Laurie, are you all right?" She called over her shoulder. "Milly, bring some water for Laurie."

"I think I'm fine. It's the move."

Kay raised an eyebrow. "The move?"

"Don't get your hopes up, Mom," she whispered. "My cycles are like clockwork." The room resettled, and the queasy feeling left as quickly as it had come. Laurie took a deep breath. "I'm more tired than I realized."

"Here." Kay handed her a cup. "It's cold. Sip."

"I think yellow for the kitchen, clear blue for our room. Like

Pierce's eyes. I love planning it all. I've got a list three pages long." Another loud thud came from the living room. "What are they doing in there?" Did she really want to know?

"I think we need some ice!" The call came from Pierce, followed by shushing sounds and stifled male laughter.

Milly turned to lean against the counter. "That'd be for my husband. If anyone's injured, it's him. He's so accident-prone, I hide all my tools." She bent and whispered loudly to her granddaughter. "He thinks we don't have any."

"But Granny, who fixes stuff when it gets broken?"

"I do, dear, before he realizes anything *is* broken," Milly said as Ally hid her giggle in her shirt collar. "That way he doesn't hurt himself. My Clyde can grow peanuts like a champ, but don't give him a hammer."

"Honey?" Pierce again.

Laurie stood and smiled at the knowing looks from the other women. She passed through the dining room into the small front entryway. "What do you need?"

There should have been a door on her right, the front door.

"Pierce, where's the door?" Slowly, she scanned to her left. Scattered around her living room, five men desperately glanced at one another in silent debate over who would be spokesman. Daniel, red-faced with suppressed laughter, nudged Pierce. But poor Clyde Newman, the focal point, stayed crouched by the center of the half-open sleeper sofa, his hand mysteriously hidden in its folds.

Abe Floyd, a church deacon and one of the largest men Laurie had ever met, cleared his throat and wiped his wide face with a handkerchief. "The couch wouldn't fit through the doorway. So we took the door off the hinges."

"Yeah." Angus Mann leaned his stocky frame against the back of the couch. "But the sofa got turned upside down, and the bed part fell out."

Clyde, a wiry little man with a white, military crew cut, spoke

9

with pride. "So I got under it, pushed it back in, and fixed it."

"O-kaaay." Laurie caught Pierce's gaze across the room and purposely avoided looking at her quaking father-in-law.

"We can put the door back, honey, that's not the problem."

Daniel coughed through his hand. "Give it up, Pierce."

Pierce shook his head. "Dad."

Laurie wished she had her video camera. "I'm sure you can."

Angus backed away from the couch, pointing and shifting up and down on the balls of his feet. "Then Newman got his hand caught. I told him not to stick it in there. But he did it anyway."

Deacon Floyd refolded his handkerchief. "Oh, Angus, we'll get him out."

Daniel straightened and wrapped an arm around Pierce's shoulder. "I believe God still works miracles."

Laurie's eyes rounded at Pierce. She bit her lower lip.

"Honey. *Please* get some ice. Or better yet, Milly."

"She's right behind me."

"I'm all right." Clyde didn't seem to be fazed. "Same thing happened when I fished a mangled spoon out of the garbage disposal. Got my hand stuck. Milly filled the thing with ice. After about ten minutes, I pulled my hand out. I'll be fine."

Milly stood with arms crossed. "I'm so sorry, Laurie. But maybe the rest of them can re-hang the door without his help."

"We just won't feed them until they do."

The room had gone silent, so everyone heard her comment. Daniel chuckled first, prompting Deacon Floyd's thunderous *hah! hah!* The dam of composure broke, and Laurie watched as laughter washed like a wave through the group. These people cared for each other, worked together, and loved each other like family.

"Excuse me," she said. Laurie went back to her room, closed the door with a quiet click, and leaned against it.

"Dear God," she whispered. "Thank you for bringing us here."

***

By early evening the rented truck sat empty, so Pierce and Daniel left to return it. Laurie stood on the porch and waved as the last car pulled away. She wandered back into the kitchen and stood across from Kay at the breakfast bar.

"Bet you thought you'd be a grandmother by now."

"I want what's best for you and Pierce. And I'll love grandbabies whenever they come."

"Can I tell you a secret? Something I think I'd only share with my mom if she were alive?"

"Of course."

"I love looking at baby clothes in stores and online."

"That's nothing to be ashamed of. I admit, my hands itch for an excuse to buy some. Daniel's forever looking in the toy department."

"I might be infertile, but I'm still regular as rain. Sometimes I feel like such a failure in the woman department."

"Laurie, you're not a failure. And there's nothing wrong with hoping for a miracle."

But how long would she have to wait? What if a baby never came? "Somehow I miss my mother more now than I did before the miscarriage. I'm so glad to be near you and Daniel."

"Only a woman who's endured a miscarriage can understand that pain. I lost three before God gave us Pierce. But we loved him like he came from our own bodies."

Laurie knew that as truth. They could not have loved Pierce more. Somehow the subject of adoption had never come up between her and Pierce. Was that odd? "Had you always considered it? Adopting, I mean?"

"Heavens, no." Kay shook her head. "Too expensive. We were both schoolteachers, and during that time we basically worked at the church for free. Though he was very poor, Pierce's father sought us out and arranged everything. Has Pierce talked with you about that?"

"He said his father simply put him on the bus and sent him to you. I know he remembers very little before being adopted, and he doesn't ever want to see his dad or his old home again. You know, he used to dream about his father and the bus ride. That nightmare became more frequent after my miscarriage. But, this morning, he dreamed of his first night here with you."

"I think he had bad dreams when he first came to live with us. The first few weeks, I'd get up in the morning and there he'd be, curled on the rug on my side of the bed, though he never gave a reason. I figured he did it because everything was new to him."

"New parents. New house." Could what happened this morning be that simple?

"That's what we assumed. He was only five." Kay sighed. "He was the most thoughtful, intentional child I'd ever seen. Seemed everything he did had a purpose. And everything had to be perfect. Never had to remind him to wash his face or brush his teeth before starting the day. He and Daniel used to have such discussions." She reached across and took Laurie's hand in both of hers. "You're so good for him."

"Thanks, Mom." Laurie stifled a yawn. All her energy was *gone*.

"A mother can't hope for more for her son. You love him, and he knows it. It shows. I see him smile at you, hear him laugh. He was such a serious child most of the time. It's his way."

Laurie blushed as memories of the morning's playful kisses flashed across her mind. If Kay only knew. Of course, she probably suspected. "I really do love him."

"And you make him happy."

"I hope so, Mom. I hope so."

CHAPTER TWO

Pierce lay fully awake in his favorite place, pressed against Laurie's back with one arm across her middle. He peeked back over his shoulder and through the slatted blinds.

The night rain had stopped, leaving behind a gray morning mist and a wet nip of cool. Perfect weather for staying in bed. The street in front of their new home sat quiet, as usual, on a Saturday morning in a community that still relied heavily on family gardens and farming for sustenance. There would be plenty of noise this weekend for Palm Sunday and a dinner-on-the-grounds farewell celebration to mark his parents' retirement.

Not that it would be Dad's last sermon. The man had preaching in his blood.

But the mantle would now belong to Pierce.

The bedside clock showed seventeen minutes after eight. Since he wouldn't officially begin his new job until Monday, he relished staying in bed and snuggling with Laurie. He closed his eyes and listened to her rhythmic breathing as he dozed.

She rarely slept this late, even on weekends. She rose early, always up doing something, reading something, planning something. Having her still in bed with him was a treat.

He smiled. She would start decorating with fervor. Wouldn't leave him alone about it until they completed every last detail. She planned to hang a swing in the tree where, one summer, he and Gilbert had built a fort.

Gilbert's father, Angus, had given them nails and scraps of wood from his shop, loaned them tools. They worked an entire Saturday—

cut boards for a ladder, hammered them up the side of the tree. They had planned a series of platforms among the branches with a hinged, drawbridge door that could be lifted with rope. Like a hideout.

But that night a terrible storm came. Tornadoes damaged nearby farms. Lightning struck the oak dead center, split it in two, and sent huge limbs crashing outside his parents' bedroom window. It was a miracle the house hadn't been destroyed, that none of them had been killed in their beds.

He remembered Dad holding him, his own skinny legs dangling, his feet almost touching the floor. His mother's arms wrapped around them both. "Thank you, God," Mom said through tears. "Thank you, God, for protecting our family."

What remained of the tree had grown, reaching out as if to balance itself. Yet the deep, dark gouge made by the lightning remained, the bark split clear through to the meat. The scar became the symbol of a truth his parents drilled into him: unexpected things happen every day, and sometimes they leave marks. But with God's help a person can grow despite his scars.

Waking every morning to see that tree had meant he was finally home, in a place with two inside bathrooms instead of a dark and scary outhouse. He'd been painfully afraid of that old outhouse . . . Pierce's heart sputtered and he squeezed his eyes tight. The old, dark outhouse on his father's farm. Why did he think of it now?

Laurie sighed in her sleep and rolled to face him, snuggled up to his chest. He kissed her forehead, her cheek, breathed in her scent, and relaxed.

"Go on, now." Mama patted his shoulder when he stopped on the tilted front porch. "There's a little moonlight. I'll stand right here while you go."

He wished he didn't wake in the middle of every night needing to go. And the outhouse was so far. The ground beneath his bare feet so cold.

The night so dark, but mama insisted he and Daddy not pee in the yard.

The Taylors' German shepherds barked viciously in the distance.

"Don't worry about those dogs. They're far away."

"But they always chase me, Mama."

"I know. That's why you don't go over there without me. But they're far away tonight. Go on, now, so we can get back to bed."

He stepped off the porch and—

Thud.

Pierce woke when his cheek hit the floor. He jumped up as a drowsy Laurie pushed her hair out of her face and looked at him.

"Are you okay? Did you just fall off the bed?"

His hands shook, so he rubbed them over his face. "Yeah." He forced a laugh. "I guess I did."

"How did you—"

"I'm fine. Really."

"You're sure?"

"I'm sure."

She studied him a moment, then threw the covers aside and headed for the bathroom. "Then let's go buy paint. I can't wait to get started on everything I've planned for this house. I'll take a quick shower. Promise."

Pierce lowered to the bed after she closed the bathroom door. He lifted a hand to his shoulder, where his mother's gentle touch had felt so real. He turned and looked at Laurie's Cheval mirror. In his face he saw his mama's eyes.

***

"You're going to make me wreck this car."

Laurie caressed the back of her husband's neck. "Naw, you're a tough guy." She laid her cheek against the headrest and studied his profile. "I liked sleeping in with you this morning. How did you fall out of the bed?"

"I don't know." He shrugged, turned into the parking lot. "And we're here."

Benson's Hardware occupied a coveted corner in the center of town. The hallowed landmark boldly displayed its three-generation history. To Laurie, the store was like a contained, uncomplicated country.

Benson's aged, wide-planked, wooden floors sloped up from the front entrance, then leveled out at the rear of the store. Battleship-gray rafters crisscrossed the high ceiling above a suspended maze of air conditioning duct. Ancient open shelves, with their old-metal smell, held both newly oiled and dormant tools and everything else from fertilizers to plumbing supplies. Small items hung on humble pegboard panels, which bowed and sagged from overuse and age.

Laurie tossed her purse into a shopping cart.

"I'll push," said Pierce.

As usual, Angus Mann, who proudly wore his assistant manager badge, stood behind the antique manual cash register. Its playful *ka-ching* could be heard nearly everywhere in the building and in the beauty parlor next door. Laurie watched as Angus struggled with the bottom drawer, then finally nursed it with WD-40 and slid it back into place.

He looked up. "Mornin', Laurie. You here to spend some of your husband's money?"

Pierce met Angus in the aisle and shook his hand. "She probably will."

Laurie excused herself, then wandered to the paint aisle to pick their bedroom color. She found Azure Dawn—the perfect hue—so she ordered it. She laid claim to a nearby chair, leaned her head back against a low wall stocked with drop cloths, brushes, and tape, and waited while the yellow-smocked clerk mixed the color.

"Laurie." Pierce's feathery whisper awakened her. Had she really dozed off? He placed a soft kiss on her cheek. Her eyes flickered open, and she spotted the airless paint sprayer securely planted in their cart. Apparently this would not be a simple project.

She shook her head and laughed as he loaded their paint into the cart. "That's what I get for leaving you alone with Angus."

Pierce helped her to her feet. "At least it's not the industrial sprayer he tried to talk me into buying."

"That's a plus."

For insurance, she tucked an extra roller and tray set into the cart. She could not only finish the trim but be half-finished with the room in the time it would take Pierce to read and reread the instructions for the sprayer. *Men.* He had the easiest part to do and still needed a new tool. He would probably call his dad to come over and see it. She wouldn't be surprised if Angus followed them home.

They checked out. "You're laughing at me." Pierce tossed her his keys as he loaded the car.

"No more than usual, *Pastor.*" She slid into the driver's seat and waited. Pierce climbed in, already reading the instructions.

She pulled onto the street and decided to test a theory. "Last night your mother told me they won Publisher's Clearing House."

No response.

"They're moving to Bermuda."

Nothing.

"Said they'll send you a postcard next year." She glanced at him. "So are those in English, or do you have to translate from Japanese as you go?"

"I'm using my time wisely."

"Yeah, right." She neared the turn for their street.

"You mock me? O, ye of little faith."

"My faith is fine." She motioned with her chin and let herself laugh. "It's you and that fancy sprayer thing that have me concerned. I mistakenly had high expectations about painting our bedroom today."

He shook the papers in his hand. "This thing works fast. Like lightning."

17

She parked the car in front of their home and took his face in her hands. "Like lightning, huh? Guess we'll see." She planted a loud, smacking kiss on his lips. "Can you unload this stuff while I run inside and fix us a quick lunch? I'm starving."

As she worked in the kitchen, Pierce carried the painting supplies to the bedroom, muttering to himself about her lack of appreciation for technology and innovation.

She chuckled as he brought in the airless sprayer and opened the box. "You know what that looks like, don't you? A sad laser gun from a low-budget, '80s sci-fi movie."

He grinned at her. "Every little boy wanted one, including me."

"I wanted every doll in existence—Cabbage Patch, Rainbow Brite, Strawberry Shortcake."

"Did you get them all?"

"Not all."

"It'll be fun to buy toys for our children." He paused and their eyes locked. "We will, Laurie. It's just a matter of time."

***

Pierce would not let this alien-designed, foreign-made contraption get the best of him. So while he and Laurie ate, he read the twenty-two diagrammed instructions for the third time.

Then he called Angus, who understood perfectly that every man needed an airless sprayer. This was serious business. Angus walked Pierce through the procedures for using the device, just as a surgeon would talk a truck driver through performing open-heart surgery by the side of the road. Grateful, Pierce took notes this time.

"You're laughing at me again." He peered up at Laurie as he knelt on their bedroom floor and opened a gallon of paint.

"No." She giggled as she finished the first coat on the window trim. "I'm laughing at you *still*."

When he pressed the trigger on the sprayer, he knew she held her breath. Some part of him did too, so he pretended he knew exactly what he was doing.

Boy, did that thing fly. And it used a lot of paint. Thankfully, they'd bought plenty.

"Hey, Bob Vila. Don't you have to let that first coat dry before you go around again?"

He released the power button and turned to her. "Bob Vila. Ha, ha."

"I was just asking, you were in your own little world there." She bent to open another quart of paint for the trim. "Ouch!"

Blood poured from the end of her finger. Fear squeezed the back of his neck as she wrapped the wound in the tail of her T-shirt. Still, the blood seeped through.

"I'd better go wash this out." She hurried to their bathroom.

His own blood ran cold. Slowly he laid the sprayer on the drop cloth-covered floor, then rubbed his hand over his face. "You okay?"

"I'll be fine. Don't know how I cut myself with a flathead screwdriver, but I guess it can be done." She exited the bathroom, held up her bandaged finger. "See? Good as new."

"I need something to drink."

"I'll get it."

"No." Was that panic in his voice? He had to leave this room. The house. And get away from the image of Laurie and blood. He cleared his throat. "I'll be fine. Take a break. I'll be back in a minute."

He marched to the kitchen and filled a glass with water, but couldn't stand still long enough to drink it. His breath had seized in his lungs. He left through the back door and kept going, straight across the yard to the barrier of trees between the house and the church lot. Why couldn't he simply exhale and catch his breath?

He glanced back once, expecting to see Laurie standing just outside the back door, worried. She was. But at least she didn't follow him into the woods.

Deep inside the leafy sanctuary, Pierce lowered himself onto a decomposing log. Nervous sweat broke out all over his body. He tried to gulp the water, but his shaking hands spilled most of it down the front of his faded T-shirt.

He dropped the glass to the soft bed of bark and leaves, braced his elbows on his knees, and gripped his head in his hands. "Dear Father, help me. What is going on?"

He raked his fingers through his hair, rose to pace, and looked at his hands. His wife had cut her finger. He saw her bleeding, and immediately his thoughts went to the miscarriage. How he'd wrapped her in a robe and carried her to their car. How she'd cried as he drove her to the hospital. How he'd wept at her bedside, certain she would die.

His wife cut her finger, and he'd become petrified to his bones.

He dropped to his knees.

"Dear God, you have given me everything I want. I don't need anything else, except for my life with Laurie to go back to the way it was before she miscarried our child. In Jesus' name. Amen."

The quiet came as he wiped sweaty tears from his eyes. He recognized the peaceful silence that often came during worship or after taking communion. A cool, cleansing breeze straight from God's throne—one that left him wanting to inhale deeply, fill his lungs, and hold the feeling inside. Looking through dangling moss and matted branches toward heaven, he breathed in and jumped up to pace again.

He will bring to light what is hidden in darkness.

The scripture from First Corinthians seeped through Pierce's mind like smoke winding through every crack and crevice. He wiped his sweaty palms on his shorts as the calm gave way to dread. How could he be uncomfortable thinking of that verse?

He loved the Bible. Loved to read it. Memorize it. Explain it to others and see them receive comfort and help, wisdom and answers. Why else would he have become a pastor? Learning the Word, loving the Word, was in him. Had been in him since Daniel and Kay first introduced him to the Scriptures when he was a child.

"Pierce, this is for you," Daniel had said the first night he was with them. They tucked him into bed and handed him a children's Bible. The cover showed a dark-haired man sitting on a hillside and surrounded by children.

Kay kissed his forehead and pulled a soft blanket up to his chin. "We'll read it to you any time you like, and when you get older you can read it yourself."

Then Daniel took one of Kay's hands in his, placed his other on Pierce's head, and prayed. He thanked God for bringing Pierce to them and asked God to put a love for the Scriptures in Pierce's heart and mind.

Pierce hadn't understood then what that prayer meant, but he liked the feeling he had when they prayed. When Kay mothered him. When Daniel spent time with him, talked to him, and answered his questions. So he kept the Bible close, slept with it under his pillow. Soon, he realized Daniel carried one everywhere. So he did, too. Even before he could read.

Then you will know the truth, and the truth will set you free.
What truth?

Light. Darkness. Truth. As he walked back toward the light and home, the verses chanted in his mind, pursuing him like an unseen monster in a child's nightmare. What waited in the dark would surely catch him.

Pierce lengthened his strides. He was a little shaken, that's all. A little stressed by the move, which provoked the dreams. Re-establishing a routine—studying and preparing sermons, preaching—would settle him down.

He returned to their bedroom and found Laurie with her back to him, finishing the second coat on the trim. He stood unnoticed in the doorway, watching her for a minute, getting his bearings.

Didn't a man sometimes need to plan what to say to his wife?

"Laurie?"

Long seconds passed before she faced him. Her splotchy face told him she'd been crying.

"I thought you'd be happy here." Tears fell from her eyes. "I thought that now, finally, you'd be happy. But there's still that sad place inside that you won't let me touch." She set down her brush. "I saw the tears in your eyes, the terror on your face. I don't know where they came from, but they were there."

"It's not important." He stepped toward her.

"Can't you share with me what's bothering you?" She shook her head, sniffed, and wiped her eyes with the back of her hand. Her voice dropped to a whisper. "Is it me?"

He closed the space between them, hugged her. "No. It's not you. It's never you." He smoothed the hair back from her face, lifted her chin to draw her gaze to his. "Believe it or not, I got really squeamish when you cut your finger." He slid his hands down her neck, massaged her shoulders.

"I still don't understand why you went to the woods. It felt like you walked away from me."

"No. Not from you." From something stupid in his head. "I don't know how to explain."

He held her tightly, not wanting her to see the desperation on his face. How could he tell her of his fear without making her feel guilty over losing their child or sounding like he blamed her for the miscarriage? He couldn't live without her. Couldn't breathe without her.

"I'm right here," she said.

He kissed her softly, to feel her close and—

"Yo! Pierce! It's Gilbert. You in here?"

He heard footsteps in the hall and quickly kissed her again.

Gilbert stepped into the doorway. "Hey! Sorry. The back door was open."

"So you walked right in." Pierce saw Laurie blush. He winked at her.

"I did knock." Gilbert stood with hands on his hips, rocked up on the balls of his feet much like his dad often did. "I met Dad for lunch in town. I was with him when you called. You know he gets lonely sometimes since Mom passed. Figured I'd come over and see how you're doing."

Laurie crossed the room. "Gilbert, would you like something to drink?"

"No, thanks. It's not like I want to help work or anything. Just sit and watch, heckle the new pastor a little."

Pierce took a deep breath. "My best friend."

"That's me." Gilbert laughed all over. "Laurie, how do you put up with him?"

"Oh, it's often a trial." She gathered her brush and paint, bent and poured the unused portion back into the can. "But you're hopeless. Why aren't you married? You need a wife, Gilbert. Someone who'll give as good as she gets."

"Got my order in. Haven't found her yet."

Laurie grinned. "And since I don't have a sister, you're stuck, right?"

Gilbert chuckled, and the tight band of tension around Pierce's chest released. "Laurie, let the man be."

She batted her eyelashes. "I'm just asking. There's nobody special?"

Gilbert looked at Laurie. "No, and I'm too busy working while the new pastor gets settled in his house. This summer I'm going to have the youth start doing community service projects. Take a Saturday and help out a nearby farmer Dad's done some work for in the past. Guy's got holes all over his yard. Thought we'd fill them in. Clean out his barn.

"He's only got one cow now, but there's enough old hay and mess in there he must've had more animals at one time. Stinks so bad, looks so bad, the county's providing a dumpster."

Laurie beamed at Gilbert and kissed him on the cheek. Gilbert turned beet red. "What was that for?"

"You might be marriage material yet."

"Sure." Pierce tossed him a brush. "Maybe the farmer has a daughter."

***

Gilbert stayed. Normally, Laurie wouldn't have minded the company or the help. She would've been happy Pierce enjoyed visiting with his childhood friend and co-worker.

But not today. Today she wanted to finish what she sensed was a very important conversation with her husband.

She could only relate this antsy feeling to what she experienced each month waiting to see if she was pregnant, paying special attention to every little nuance about her body.

They finished the second coat, then she fixed a quick meal while Gilbert and Pierce cleaned up.

"I should go," Gilbert said after they ate. "Big weekend coming up for all of us."

"No, man. Stay and watch the game." Pierce took his and Gilbert's plates to the sink, then headed for the living room.

Gilbert caught her eye and shrugged.

If she hadn't known better, she might have thought Pierce was avoiding being alone with her. *Was* he avoiding being alone with her?

She took a shower, scrubbed paint flecks from her hair, and rejoined them for the final innings. The chime clock struck midnight as

Gilbert helped them uncover and reposition the furniture in their bedroom, since the paint had dried. And finally, *finally* Pierce let Gilbert leave.

Then Pierce took a shower.

She sat in the living room. Alone. Flipped channels just to stay awake. When she could no longer sit still, she rose and paced. What was wrong with her? She never paced. *Pierce* was the pacer.

The unmistakable whoosh of water through the pipes finally stopped with a familiar squeak and shudder. Laurie stilled. Her heartbeat pounded in her ears.

You're being silly, she told herself as her mind reviewed Pierce's odd behavior that afternoon and evening. He really had looked frightened when she cut herself. Then he'd gone for a walk. She knew Pierce loved walking in the woods, but still . . .

Laurie heard their bathroom door creak open—on the next trip to Benson's she'd buy a can of WD-40. She shut off the television, turned out the lamp, and by the full moon's light found Pierce in bed, huddled under the covers. She readied for bed and climbed in beside him.

"I love you, Pierce."

"I love you, too." He turned to her, and she settled back against his chest.

"Are you okay?"

He kissed her shoulder. "I am now."

Normal, she thought. Everything as it should be.

CHAPTER THREE

Dr. John Bridges bounced down the long lane to his father's farm in his new, dove-gray F-150 4x4. He'd returned to Rowe City a few weeks ago to work at a local OB/GYN office, and had almost lost a few large pieces of his low-slung Dodge Viper along this cratered path. Buying a new truck was more fun than repairing the driveway or replacing his sports car.

He slowed as he neared the small farmhouse and scanned the dilapidated barn and house with its slanting porch. The disgusting pig-pen with its sinking fence, broken trough, and muddy occupants.

The acres he'd worked as a boy stretched before him. Ground that had seasonally disappeared under fluffy white tufts of cotton or twining peanut plants now lay barren. Somehow each time he visited, the place seemed older, more pitiful. Much like his dad.

John walked up the steps and knocked. He eased open the creaky screen door and entered. A single lamp glowed in the living room where his dad slept on the faded, torn couch.

Dad was filthy. Dirt caked his hairless scalp, ringed his neck, and had formed a crust on his hands and fingers and clothing. In short, he reeked. John wasn't sure the stench was human. Being a doctor, he'd experienced pungent smells during his career, but this aroma wasn't all Dad's. It smelled like pig and mud and rot.

He held his breath, crouched, and gently shook his father. "Dad."

No response.

"Luther," he tried his father's given name. "It's me. John."

The house needed cleaning almost as much as his dad. When the old man didn't wake, John decided to deal with the house first. Thank God he had spare rubber gloves in his truck.

He tackled the kitchen first. Cleaning the bathroom before Luther bathed would be a waste of time. Maybe, if the man slept well enough, he could wash himself this time.

He quickly washed the dishes and counters. A mountain of unopened mail covered the table. He tossed flyers and junk mail into an open garbage bag placed on the floor. He stacked the few bills—and several certified letters from an attorney that expressed a client's interest in purchasing the farm—to the side.

Why wouldn't Dad read his own mail? Bathe himself? John wasn't sure if Luther was becoming senile or was simply stubborn. Possibly depressed. He pulled out his cell and noted on his calendar to schedule a check-up for his dad.

John glanced at the sleeping man. Luther looked fairly fit for his age. Walked well. Apparently he still tended the small vegetable garden, on occasion. And the last, single cow in the barn. Then there were the pigs.

John shook his head. Whatever attachment his dad had to the pigs could only be deemed weird. Maybe the man had a "thing" for pigs like some people did for dogs or cats.

But Luther's bizarre propensity for digging holes around the pig shed was difficult to understand. That's why his dad was so dirty. Obviously, he'd spent the night digging again instead of sleeping.

The last envelope was from Rowe City Gospel Church and specifically addressed to Luther Bridges. Odd. John couldn't remember his dad ever talking about church or God or anything like that, let alone attending. Next Sunday was Easter, wasn't it? John read the letter and stacked it with the bills.

After Luther bathed and ate, John finished sanitizing the bathroom, a huge job in itself. Then they sat together on the crooked front porch.

"Dad, I can arrange some repairs. Get someone to mow the weeds behind the house." They reached higher than the windowsills.

Silence.

"That lawyer's been sending letters for awhile now. His office isn't far from mine."

"Not talking to him."

John sighed. "Okay."

Minutes passed.

"That church group offered to clean out the barn." Manure and old hay—probably dating back to John's teen years—filled the structure, leaving barely enough room for the cow under its leaky roof. "They also offered to work in the yard." Like filling in the holes.

"They can clean the barn."

"But Dad, the holes are *dangerous*. You could fall—"

"The barn. Nothing else."

John looked toward the dormant fields. This was one of the longest conversations he had ever had with his dad—the man who had given him a roof over his head, chores after school, and one-sentence orders on weekends, but never affection. The subject? The barn and some holes in the ground.

He clearly remembered applying to college, seeking a full-ride scholarship. Being only sixteen at the time, the forms required a parent's signature. Luther had scrawled his name, grunted, and told him to stay out of trouble. Two months later, John boarded a bus waiting at the end of the driveway and took his first plane ride, leaving behind the farm where he had lived since his fourth birthday.

"Dad. Let them clean up the yard a little."

His dad simply stared over the land, now golden in the setting sun. "No."

"Why?"

Silence.

"Dad, I can't come every day. Let me take care of some things. Let these people help."

"The holes stay." His dad rose, snapped his fingers at the saggy russet cow, and walked to the barn.

John stayed seated. As the barn door eased closed behind his dad and the cow, a steady, soaking rain began. It washed the air, removing the gritty, tickling dust that coated the countryside. With each drop, the land seemed to breathe a sigh of relief. Maybe, if it persisted, the lullaby from the tin roof would help Luther sleep through the night instead of rising to dig in the dark.

Finally the rain faded to a drizzle. John rose. He walked to the end of the porch and looked toward the pig shed. The drenching rain filled in the holes as if healing the land of its scars.

CHAPTER FOUR

Pierce grinned like a kid on the first day of summer vacation. His perfect world all but burst with sunshine. And that flawless perfection started with Laurie, who sat at his side for the Palm Sunday morning service in The Barn Church as they listened to his dad speak.

As usual, laughter rippled through the crowd. And, as usual, Deacon Floyd—whose booming *hah!* could be heard above everyone else's chuckle—received the standard elbow-jab from his wife. Which, of course, did *nothing* to stop his outburst.

Dad could have been a stand-up comedian. More than once, Pastor Daniel Crane had lured in new members with dry humor and self-deprecating stories. The tales had multiplied over the years and often involved Pierce. Now Laurie appeared to be a target—she'd looked so bewildered two days ago when she discovered the front door was missing. Couldn't we all relate to expecting one thing, then getting another?

Pierce's dad delivered the perfect segue. ". . . and that's just how the disciples felt between the Triumphant Entry on Palm Sunday and the Crucifixion that same week."

Laurie nudged Pierce. "Give me a few weeks before you use me in any stories," she whispered.

She didn't have to worry. Pierce didn't thrive on humor like his dad did.

He remembered in vivid detail the first time he entered a church. He'd been living with his new parents for only a few days. One bright morning, when the sun was high and the sanctuary empty, Daniel had pulled open the heavy double doors and taken him inside.

The big barn building, with its dark, knotted wood, smelled familiar. A little musty, with a heavy tang of polish. Support beams stood straight as soldiers, their bases splinter-free, smooth from innumerable animal hides and human hands brushing against them through the years. Stains dotted the clean-swept, concrete floor, its surface pitted and chipped from animal's hooves and men's boots.

It was a barn, but it wasn't. The building seemed special and held a different kind of quiet.

With one hand cradled in Daniel's, Pierce walked up the center aisle between long, wooden pews. Their slow footsteps and low voices echoed, gently bouncing off the arched ceiling.

"Pierce, have you ever been in a church before?"

Pierce shyly shook his head. As they walked, he trailed his loose hand over the ends of the pews and peeked up, wondering if Daniel would stop him from doing so.

He didn't.

"This is where I work," Daniel said. "It's quiet in here now, but during a service there's lots of music and singing. Then I preach. I talk to everyone about God and His love, how He wants to help people and be a part of their lives."

They stopped at the front behind an upright wooden box with a big, flat top that Daniel called a pulpit. Pierce couldn't see over it even when he stood on his tiptoes.

"This is where I stand," Daniel said from behind him, then pointed to the first bench on the right. "That's where you'll sit with your mother. Everyone will want to meet you. You may have to shake hands with some folks you've never met. Then we'll walk back home, across the church yard, down the trail through the tall trees, the way we came today."

Pierce looked up and stretched his neck back as far as he could to see the thick rafters and pitched ceiling. Daniel lifted him as the sunlight shone through the loft windows over the main doors, producing a shimmering rainbow spotlight all the way to the floor beside them. Pierce raised his little arms, reaching with spread fingers, trying to grasp the brightness and colors.

Daniel held him there, raised him higher as dust motes swirled and danced, until the sun moved and the rainbow disappeared. Several minutes must have passed. Daniel's arms had surely cramped.

This was Pierce's first memory of church. Of peaceful quiet. Of being held by loving arms in beautiful, warm light.

Daniel had carried him past the small fenced cemetery at the building's edge and continued toward home.

"Does God know where people go when they die?" Pierce whispered, not sure what to make of the grave markers jutting up from the ground.

"Yes." Leaves and pine needles crunched under Daniel's steps. "Yes, He does."

"Does He know where I am?"

Daniel kissed Pierce's head, pulled a stick of Juicy Fruit from his pocket, and tore it in half. "Yes, He does. Want some?"

Pierce smiled at the memory. Daniel hadn't changed much. He still preferred the same sweet gum, often popping and snapping it on purpose when Kay was near. The building's exterior had also remained the same. Kay had insisted they keep the original colors and textures. The original gray-brown looked welcoming, she'd said. So the iron hardware for the broad double doors had been painstakingly restored. The wavy-glassed windows that sat crooked and low on the slatted walls had been salvaged, too. Even the horse silhouette window in the loft had been preserved. Daniel's only stipulation: a cross to replace the weathervane—every person needed a point in the right direction now and then.

Thankfully, the inside of the main building had gotten lots of attention. Air conditioning. Carpet. Offices and a hall sectioned off at the back to include a nursery. Padding had been added to the unforgiving pews.

True to form, Daniel slipped in a final joke before ending his sermon and handing a microphone to Deacon Floyd, who looked straight at Pierce and Laurie.

"When Pastor first told me of his plan to retire, well, frankly, I didn't want to hear it. I mean, I'm older than he is, and God hasn't let *me* retire yet! But as those of us on the board prayed about a new leader for our church, it became clear there was only one right choice. Pierce. Laurie. We'd like to welcome you and pray for you two this morning."

Laurie squeezed his hand. "Pierce, I feel so much love from these people."

The congregation stood. The deacon raised a large, pink-palmed hand to heaven and prayed aloud.

***

Laurie entered the smaller, barn-turned-youth building and stopped in stunned amazement beside Pierce. Enough food to feed a small village, possibly a large one, covered rows of tables. She grabbed a plate.

Smoked hams with thick, deep-garnet skin covered a dozen platters on tables placed end to end. Roasts, which must have been rolled in black pepper before baking, filled deep serving dishes. Seasoned fried chicken overflowed cast iron pots and foil-lined buckets. Literal *buckets* of fried chicken. She speared a breast and thigh and continued moving down the tables.

Vegetables dotted the buffet, a culinary color wheel. Bowls of orange yams. Corn both yellow and white. Green broccoli swam in cheesy sauce beside darker collard greens. Bottles of vinegar rested alongside. Jars of hot peppers—red, yellow, and green—beckoned the unaware and dared the brave to taste a blistering sample. Laurie's stomach rumbled. While loading a second plate, she almost drooled on herself.

And Pierce, God bless him, directed her to his parents' table while he went straight to the desserts and got her a slice each of two different chocolate cakes.

"You're going to love this one." He set the slice slathered with a decadent cherry sauce before her like an offering. "Milly Newman makes it. It practically drips off your fork."

"Then maybe I'll eat it first."

"Of course you can eat it first." Daniel beamed a smile at Laurie. "Sure didn't eat much the other day."

"I'm fine, Dad. I was just tired." She leaned toward Pierce and whispered, "Can you help me out here? Get the attention off me?"

"Sure. Watch this.

"Hey, Dad." He glanced around the table. "The other day I told Laurie about the time you and I camped in the woods between the house and here. You know, when you left me out there and snuck into the sanctuary to sleep on a pew?"

"Son, you were supposed to keep that between you and me."

Kay turned to Pierce. "What did you say?"

Daniel groaned. "What are you trying to do to me?"

In that moment, Laurie saw Kay barely contain her wrath, Daniel his dignity. She chuckled at Pierce's mischievous grin. Is this what he'd been like as a child?

"Now, Kay, it's not what you think. I—"

Kay lowered her chin. "Daniel Crane. You left Pierce by himself?"

"I'm toast and I know it." Daniel waved his fork at Pierce. "You, mark my words. When the day comes that your future with the woman you love is at stake, do the smart thing. Beg." He winked at Laurie. "Besides, son, you'll undoubtedly be the one at fault."

Laurie expected Pierce to give a smart retort. Instead, he appeared to be staring at a random spot just over her shoulder. She blocked out the activity around them and looked right into his eyes. "Are you okay?"

"Of course," he answered. "Why wouldn't I be?"

Why indeed.

***

A hand landed on Pierce's shoulder, and he turned to see Rick and Julie Matthews. They'd been several years ahead of him in school, but he remembered Rick playing football and them always being a couple.

He stood and shook Rick's hand. "Great to see you, Rick. Julie. "

"Sorry we couldn't get over to help you move in," Julie offered. "Spring break for the kids, we were out of town."

Laurie rose from her chair and spoke to Julie. "Oh, we had plenty of help. I enjoyed your solo this morning so much. Pierce still remembers you singing at the high school football games."

Others also chose that moment to greet them. Pierce relaxed more and more as he shook each hand, while Laurie met and conversed with folks she'd never met. She was so good at making people feel welcome and valued. He'd finally come home and, God willing, they'd get to stay here and live their lives.

The noise level rose with conversations and laughter as men headed back to the food lines. Children pulled reluctant mothers to the desserts and grabbed cookies, brownies, slices of cake, or pie. Gilbert approached, plopped two overloaded plates onto the table, and dropped himself into a seat beside Pierce. "These chairs get smaller every year. Hand me a biscuit."

"Got enough to eat there, Gilbert?"

"Your concern warms me." He leaned toward Pierce. "Help me out in a minute, will you? We've got something special for your folks."

"Sure."

After eating, Gilbert rose and walked to the center of the converted barn with members of the youth group who held large, odd-shaped garbage bags. He put both pinkies in his mouth and whistled, silencing the gathering.

"In case you're wondering, Pastor Daniel, Miss Kay, we really love you," Gilbert said. A collective cheer ended with applause. "And to show that love, we have a few things for Pastor Daniel. Miss Kay, you're perfectly safe. You can sit and watch. But Pastor Daniel, we need you right here, right now."

Daniel tossed his napkin onto the table. "Pierce, did you know anything about this?"

"I did not. Get up there."

Applause erupted again as Daniel joined Gilbert, who motioned him to a seat in the center of the room.

"Do you know what he's going to do?" Laurie asked.

"I haven't a clue. And I'm not responsible."

"Pierce, I love it here. I love these people. I love you."

He kissed her temple as Gilbert spoke.

"Some of us have been here a long time. We've grown up hearing Pastor Daniel preach and tell jokes. And to show our appreciation, we have a few gifts for you, Pastor, to help in your retirement."

Expectant laughter drifted through the crowd, along with a stifled cackle and Deacon Floyd's abrading *hah*! Daniel's face turned red and his shoulders shook, clearly in anticipation of the coming jabs.

Gilbert lifted a bright red T-shirt out of the first bag. "The first item we have for you reads, 'Help! I'm a retired preacher, and I can't shut up.' That way, when you're just wandering around, Ms. Kay can find you."

The laughter grew. Dad didn't have a chance.

"Next, we have a toothbrush." This was easily two feet long. "We figure you can use it whether you keep your real teeth or not."

Dad accepted it graciously and mimed brushing, which sent the crowd into another round of laughter and applause.

"And finally, new sunglasses." They, like the toothbrush, were terribly over-sized. "You can take these with you while enjoying the cruise we're giving you."

Silence swept over the room. Kay's eyes misted. "Oh, my," she said.

"Ms. Kay, the Board and I know that all these years you two have never had a real vacation. We wanted to give you one. Everything's paid, it's a package deal. A two-week Caribbean cruise, you pick the date. Gives you plenty of time to plan and pack."

Daniel stood and walked to Kay. He spoke only to her, then gave her a quick kiss. "I asked her to marry me. She said yes!" They held each other for a long moment as cheers rose to the beamed ceiling.

Pierce watched, marveling at his parents' example—years of ministry and sacrifice, mutual support and stubborn love. They'd taught him about God, forgiveness, acceptance, sin, and grace. Somehow they'd perfected the skills to surviving life in the ministry, one that all too often stole family time, required endless energy, and held numerous crises and inconveniences. He and Laurie would duplicate that union. They were already on their way to doing so. His previous position as assistant pastor in Florida had merely been practice for their future.

Laurie's hand slid to his. He scanned the crowd as the whistles, cheers, and laughter faded. These were the people God wanted them to serve.

He breathed deeply. Something inside him clicked into place.

***

His first Monday as pastor of The Barn Church. In Pierce's opinion, there was no finer job, and no finer way to go to work, trotting along the path through the trees, enjoying the fresh smell of morning dew. Expectancy bloomed as a rosebud opening in the sun. God stirred his spirit. He rested in the certainty of being open to God, ready to listen, and willing to learn. He wanted to grow.

He planted himself behind his desk and read Matthew 26 and 27, the week from Palm Sunday to Easter. While eating lunch he took notes, yearning to rediscover the story and see details he hadn't noticed before.

When he finished the section regarding the Crucifixion, he went to his knees.

Change.

Most would say Jesus' death was the ultimate change because it appeared to be such an ending. But His sacrifice ripped apart the isolating temple veil and removed the barriers between God and man. Every person now had access to forgiveness. All because Jesus chose to submit to the Father's plan, despite the changes He was required to face.

Life held many frightening or painful changes. Like the ones he and Laurie had gone through for him to accept this job. They'd left friends and security in Florida. Took on new responsibilities, new problems. Moved. Yet changes proved one phase of life ended as a new phase began. Relocating here to guide this church was a God-directed change.

"Father, make us new. Start by changing me."

A wave of apprehension, which he couldn't ignore, fluttered through him.

Christ, if given the choice, would not have chosen change in *that* form—death. He'd prayed as much in Gethsemane. But Jesus recognized mankind's access to forgiveness, reconciliation, and reunion with the Father rested on Him. To Jesus, the potential payoff was worth the price.

If Pierce submitted to the changes God wanted to make in him today—and tomorrow, and the next day—the pain would be more than worth it. He simply had to follow the path, through obedience, to *change*. If he refused, he would harm himself and others.

What if Jesus had refused? Impossible to comprehend, but what if?

Pierce would not refuse. He would yield, and he needed God's help leading the congregation to do the same.

He rose, sat in his chair, and wrote a one-page summary. Everything he had just prayed and seen for the first time.

"Father, make us new. Start with me," he said again.

I am.

He called Laurie to let her know he'd be working late, then stayed in his office and prayed through the evening. He walked home by starlight past the quaint, ever-expanding cemetery and through the still trees while night creatures scurried around him. The street and house stood quiet. The light by the back door shone as a beacon guiding him home. Later, he went to sleep beside Laurie, covered in a blanket of contentment.

He woke on the floor shivering with cold, curled up like when he slept on the bus.

***

Laurie and Kay meandered through the fabric store.

"This is perfect." Laurie unrolled a swath of yellow eyelet. "Exactly what I wanted for the kitchen." She set it in the shopping cart. "You know, Mom, it's really sweet the way Dad repeatedly asks you to marry him."

"Often he does it in front of people to embarrass me, like at the dinner last Sunday." Kay laughed. "Sometimes after reading in bed at night, he asks me again right before we go to sleep."

What would she and Pierce be like after so many years of marriage? If they had no children? If it was just the two of them?

"Pierce reads in bed, too."

"He picked that up from Daniel. But Pierce isn't messy like Daniel. My Daniel can destroy a bathroom in two seconds. Pierce was a meticulous child. Changed out of his pajamas, brushed his teeth before he ever came to the kitchen or spoke to us in the morning."

Laurie knew. Pierce did *nothing* before brushing his teeth.

"They all have their quirks, Laurie. We do, too. Daniel can't preach without telling jokes. He says it makes a hard truth go down easier. Like Mary Poppins and a spoonful of sugar, or some such thing."

Maybe Pierce's quirks were those occasional, quiet-sad moments he had. But nothing really explained him sleeping on the floor. It just didn't make sense.

"What's your quirk, Mom?"

"Oh, I'm organized on the outside, but my emotions are usually a cluttered mess."

They rounded the corner and there, in huge displays, found rolls of material with matching wallpaper and borders. Classics with Victorian roses. Retro checkered patterns. Whimsical prints for a child's room or a nursery.

"Well, look at this," Kay said. "It'd be perfect for a boy or a girl."

Laurie sighed. "Yes, it would."

The long, wide border depicted a sun-drenched farmyard complete with a red barn and a silver silo. Chickens, with their fluffy yellow peeps, walked beside pink, pointy-eared pigs. Polka-dot cows grazed with a toffee-colored horse whose silky black forelock lay to one side, exposing large, kind eyes. Laurie envisioned herself at her dining room table sewing matching striped curtains.

"Every woman in your position still watches the calendar, even if she doesn't talk about it. I should know." She squeezed Laurie's hand. "No harm in keeping hope alive."

Laurie squeezed back, then released. No, she couldn't keep the yearning to become a mother from resurfacing, but she could put it in its place. In the parlor of her heart, she offered the longing a seat next to her other cherished dreams.

"I have to set it aside, Mom, for a while anyway, or it's going to control my life. I'm not going to sit around wishing for a baby. I'm going to make our house a home, even if it's for just me and Pierce."

Kay gave a nod. "Good for you."

Laurie spied an olive-green damask, lay the bolt across her cart, and spread out the sample. "Mom, this would be perfect for your new living room."

"You have such a great eye, Laurie. Will you try to find a job like you had in Orlando, with an established design firm?" She winked at Laurie. "Or try being your own boss?"

"I haven't quite decided. Am I that easy to read?" In her mind, she was already designing the logo—Designs by Laurie, maybe with a color wheel for the "D." "How did you know I was considering it?"

"Because I'm a mom. Because I love you like my own. By the way, the other day I unearthed a shoebox of Pierce's things from when he was little. It was buried in Daniel's study. It's in the car. You can take it home."

"He's been really busy all week. I've barely seen him. I think he's worried about Sunday."

"Worried? About Easter?" Kay re-rolled the damask, tucked it into the cart, and pushed toward the checkout lane.

"He thinks I don't know, but twice this week he's left our bed and slept on the floor."

Kay stopped. "You mean Pierce sleeps on the floor? On purpose?"

"No, Mom. It's happened a few times since we moved here. He goes to sleep beside me, but he doesn't stay in our bed."

"I'm going to say something to Daniel."

Laurie touched her arm. "Please don't. Not yet anyway. He says it's nothing."

"But if he's having second thoughts about taking over the church—"

"It's not second thoughts. I don't know what it is exactly." Though she had a feeling it wasn't as simple as nervousness over a new job. "He doesn't want me to make a big deal out of it. Let's give him time. If we need help, I promise I'll ask."

Kay shook her finger. "I've got your word?"

"Yes. If we need help, I'll ask. You've got my word."

Chapter Five

Pierce stood in his office, adjusted his tie. A cool Easter Sunday morning was the best possible time to preach a first sermon as a new pastor. The church should be full today. Even prodigals darkened the doors on Easter Sunday, if only to please their mamas.

Mama.

He eyed his double-breasted suit in the mirror, thankful he hadn't dreamed of Mama in several days. His heart ached when he dreamed of her, thought of her or the bus ride.

At least today he'd start giving back some of what his adoptive parents had given him. After coming to live with Daniel and Kay, Pierce had been a celebrity of sorts. Every elderly member served as his surrogate grandparent, every child in the congregation his friend. His was a large family where hugs were given at the church altar and prayers in the aisles. He never got away with anything, not that he'd tried. He'd strived to make his new parents glad they'd adopted him.

He ran his hands over the large walnut desk Dad had used.

Pierce had cut his teeth on this desk, spiritually speaking. Watched Dad study. Heard Dad pray. Dad's scent still lingered—worn leather Bible, Juicy Fruit gum. Dad never left home without both. Pierce glanced under the desk, half expecting to see Matchbox cars and tan army men—he hadn't liked the green ones. Instead, he found worn carpet and a gum wrapper.

Mom's influence showed as well. A lace doily under the candle on a side table. A gold-framed print of Jesus praying in the Garden of Gethsemane. But mostly the room spoke of his dad, who'd patiently answered all his questions, no matter how small or insignificant.

"How big is heaven?" Pierce once asked while zooming cars around the room.

Daniel set aside his Bible. "How big?"

"Can you stand up there?"

"Yes, of course."

"Then how come everybody gets buried lying down?"

"Come here, Pierce." Dad opened his arms. Pierce slid onto his lap and rolled a truck along the desk edge. "Only the body stops living when someone dies. The part that thinks, feels, and loves—the part that can know God—lives on. That's the part that gets to go to heaven, and God gives the person a new body that won't get sick or die again."

"Ever?"

"Never."

"Kind of like if you go to sleep in one place and wake up somewhere else?"

"Kind of like that."

Now, Pierce ran his hands across the grooved desktop. He glanced at his watch as the old seat creaked beneath him. Service wouldn't begin for two more hours.

He yawned as exhaustion rolled in like morning fog in a dark swamp and wrapped him in its weight. He laid his forehead on his folded hands and closed his eyes.

Mama sat in her chair on the porch, the one missing a spindle. It was daytime, and she smiled at him, her eyes sparkling with love.

Then it was night, and a five-year-old Pierce stood with his ear pressed to the door of Mama's room. He looked through the keyhole.

Suddenly he was on the bus—Set it aside, boy—the loud, rumbling motor hurt his ears.

Then he was back at the door, listening. Mama was crying on the other side. He peered through the keyhole—

Pierce jerked awake. He jumped up from the chair and gulped huge breaths. He pulled a handkerchief from his back pocket, wiped the back of his neck, and checked his watch. Almost thirty minutes had passed.

His clothes, even his socks, clung to his sweat-drenched body as if he had run a mile.

He called Laurie at home. "Hey. Will you bring me a different suit?"

"I'm almost dressed now," she said. "See you in twenty?"

"Great." He shed his jacket and tie, unbuttoned his shirt, and waited. Soon Laurie tapped on the door. Pre-service worship music followed her inside, then silenced when she closed the door behind her.

"I brought a black suit, white shirt, two gray ties. One solid. And the one with the diamond pattern." She took steps toward him, raised soft fingers to his face. "What's wrong? Are you sick?"

He stiffened at her approach. He didn't want her to touch him. Which didn't make sense.

Shame rose like bile in his throat. For the first time ever, he wanted to tell a bald-faced lie. He wanted to say yes, he was sick, and he needed to go home.

And, for the first time since choosing to become a pastor, he didn't want to preach. The desire to run, to hide, gripped him. He wanted to crawl under the desk and stay there.

Or lock the door behind Laurie, seal them inside together forever. Just the two of them. No past, no present. No demands.

No memories.

"I'm not sick." He watched her wait for him to say more, but he had nothing further to say. Something bubbled up inside him, dangerously near to exploding all over both of them. Somehow Pierce knew whatever "it" was would devastate Laurie.

Don't think about it. Don't think about the past.

No, he'd think about Easter . . . and preaching . . . and Laurie.

He forced a smile.

***

Laurie had watched a chameleon once, fascinated by its ability to change from green to brown to green again, moving from leaf to branch to another leaf. As a child, she'd marveled at the creature's ability to adapt by altering itself.

Watching Pierce now, Laurie's heart winced. She knew her husband's heart had just taken a step away from hers.

She'd never sensed a distance between them like she did in that moment. Right in front of her, some part of him closed off, like a vault sealed by a thick, steel door. As she watched him change into clean clothes, she all but heard the tumblers drop.

A suffocating sadness bore down on her. The sinking sensation she'd experienced their first morning here had been true. Real. Their marriage was threatened, but not from the outside. Did Pierce not notice the unnamed, unidentified issue that had wedged between them, pushing them apart?

She needed to pray, talk to Kay, do *something* to discover a way to stop the chasm from growing wider and deeper.

Pierce chose the solid tie and looped it around his neck. She turned away before he could see her tear-filled eyes reflected in the glass and saw the sheet on his desk entitled "Change." With a shaky hand, she lifted the paper and cleared her throat. "Is this for today?"

She recognized the silence that followed. He was stalling. Or picking what to say. Why?

She turned to him, still holding the paper, and decided to wait him out. This time, she wouldn't be the first to speak.

Pierce yanked at the crooked Windsor knot, untied the whole thing, and began again. "Yeah," he said. "I was, uh, reviewing my notes."

His uncomfortable glance in her direction said he didn't want her to read what he had written. Again, why?

She put the paper back on the desk. "Was there something wrong with the other suit? A stain?"

He retightened the tie, straightened the ends. "No, but thanks for bringing these over."

His tone was one he might use with a stranger. On second thought, no, he was friendlier with strangers.

"You're more nervous than you realized?" She kept her tone calm, her face motionless, but her heart pleaded. *Please, please talk to me.*

"You could say that."

He walked to her, wrapped his arms around her. Did he not feel the separation?

Finally, she closed her eyes. "You'll be great," she said quietly. "This is where you're supposed to be."

***

Julie Matthews' angelic voice rose and fell with the choir. The notes flowed smoothly, seamless as a rainbow and just as pretty. No matter how many times Pierce heard Julie sing, his thoughts always went to heaven and what worship around God's throne must sound like.

But today, the melody brought little comfort. Laurie's words echoed in his head as he waited to begin his sermon. He was where he was supposed to be, doing what he was supposed to do, wasn't he?

Last Monday he'd tasted something wonderful in the newfound truth about change, something that brought a hunger for spiritual growth like none he had ever experienced. Yes, he'd awakened on the floor the very next morning, but he'd been fine until today.

So what was this frightening sensation of being out of control, like he had turned a corner and there was no going back? Or someone else was driving the car, and the road always returned him to his first five years, to his father's rejection?

When the choir's last song faded, Pierce took his place at the pulpit.

"Happy Easter, everyone." Several hundred people sat shoulder to shoulder in the rustic building. "I know most expect a traditional Easter sermon every year. We usually hear about Jesus' prayer in the Garden of Gethsemane, the Trial, the Crucifixion, and the Resurrection. Instead, I want to tell you about my prayer time last Monday."

He shared what he'd read and prayed. The perspective that Jesus' death was the biggest, most difficult, and painful change He could have been asked to experience.

"Change and the pain it brought were not Jesus' enemies. Rather, these were essential tools that the Father used for our benefit. Without Jesus' death, our sins couldn't be forgiven."

He descended from the stage, stopped directly in the center aisle.

Without warning, his lungs clamped shut. His fists clenched at the idea of nails penetrating Jesus' flesh.

Breathe, he thought. *Finish. So you can leave.*

His feet itched to run. Yet a part of him wanted to stay right there, suspended in a familiar place, safe from the unknown path ahead.

"There's a particular change I'm praying about for myself. Something I want God to resolve in me once and for all."

All eyes, including Laurie's, focused on him. "Maybe some of you feel that way. You need change. At your job, in your family. Maybe the change you need is salvation, simple forgiveness so you can begin a new relationship with God.

"Maybe the change you need is like mine. It's personal, inside you. I'm inviting you to come forward and let me pray with you, for you. I appreciate your prayers for me. I know God will work with all of us right where we are." He waited, sweat dripped inside his collar as the pianist took her cue and played softly. Would anyone respond?

"Please consider yourselves dismissed," he said. "But I'll wait here in case anyone needs prayer."

A muscular young man seated halfway back stood and walked forward. Then an older gentleman. A woman. A family. More than a dozen more came forward and waited their turn.

"God, please heal," he prayed. "We ask You to intervene. Bring the change we desperately need to follow Your plan."

Sensing their desperation, he wept as he prayed. For some, asking God for help was a last-ditch effort. Their troubles shook him, an unexpected earthquake in his soul.

Or was that his own gripping fear, despair, and hopelessness?

After he prayed with the last person, Pierce crossed behind Laurie, who talked with Julie and Rick Matthews.

"Your voice is so beautiful. I love to hear you sing," Laurie said.

Pierce tapped her shoulder. "I'll walk home. See you in a few."

"Great sermon," Rick offered as he nodded in his direction.

"Thanks."

A heaviness settled in his chest, making breathing difficult. If he stopped moving, he might not be able to take another step. He continued out the side door, forced his body to slog through his own emotional quicksand, across the parking lot, and into the canopy of trees.

If only he could be alone. But solitude wouldn't be possible until much later. His parents were coming for Easter lunch.

If only he weren't wearing a suit. He could lie down and sleep on the soft, pine needle-covered ground.

And then he remembered. Remembered when he lived on the old farm with Daddy and Mama, before being sent away to live with

Daniel and Kay. Remembered that, after going to the outhouse at night, he used to lie down and sleep on the rug by Mama's bed.

***

Laurie tidied her kitchen as Pierce walked his parents to their car just before sunset. While she'd enjoyed talking with Kay all Easter afternoon, she couldn't help noticing how little Pierce had spoken at all. She'd hoped he would talk with Daniel about whatever was bothering him.

She stood alone in the kitchen, squeezing her eyes tight as worry bubbled inside. Her taut nerves tightened like a stretched rubber band. If Pierce came back and tried to pretend nothing was wrong, she'd shatter into a million pieces.

Exhausted, she leaned back against the kitchen counter. "Heavenly Father, I know this is supposed to be a day of new beginnings and celebration. Instead, it feels like an ending, because my husband turned away from me today. You know he's struggling with something. He even told the whole church. Please help me know what to do."

Pierce came through the front door and spent an inordinate amount of time closing it, checking the lock, then repositioning the dining room chairs. Laurie raised her brow.

The phone rang. She watched him answer, listen, and nod, all the while avoiding her gaze.

He hung up, reached for his keys. "That was Gilbert. Something's wrong with Angus."

"Do you want me to come too?" She stepped toward him.

Part of her hoped he would say yes and that he needed her to be there. Part of her wanted him to say no because she wasn't sure she was ready to address the widening distance between them.

He turned from the door and watched her, waiting. "Only if you want."

Great. Why wasn't he this agreeable when she wanted him to talk about what was bothering him?

"Or I can call you if it's serious."

That's what she figured. Neither of them wanted to be alone with the other. Happy Easter.

"Yeah. Call me."

She heard his car leave as she went to shower. Later, she re-entered the quiet kitchen, noticed the message light blinking on the phone, and pushed the button.

Beep. "Laurie. Doctor says Angus is fine. Probably had indigestion from eating too much for Easter dinner. I'll be a while."

She sat up in bed reading Psalm 91. *He will call on me, and I will answer him; I will be with him in trouble.* Any other time the passage would have offered comfort and peace, but not this time. And she was so horribly tired. Staying awake until Pierce came home? Not possible.

She sank into her pillow as tears over the distance between her and Pierce threatened to fall, her body so heavy she wondered how she'd managed to stay upright through the day. Her shuttered eyes barely registered the sweeping headlights from Pierce's car as he parked it in front of their home.

***

Pierce found Laurie asleep.

The bedside lamp shone on her beautiful face, now blotchy from crying, with a tear-dampened tissue crumpled in her hand on her open Bible. She lay curled up on her side of the bed, on top of the covers, shivering from the chill the showers and cold front had brought to Easter evening. He covered her gently with the quilt and took the tissue from her hand.

"Shh," he whispered as she warmed and relaxed. "I love you."

He stripped to his boxers, silently slid into bed, and wrapped an arm around her. He pressed his face to her hair. *God, these feelings came after the miscarriage. I'm afraid if I tell her that, I'll hurt her*, he prayed.

You already are hurting her.

He lay with her in the dark and tried to relax. He would never hurt her on purpose. She knew that, didn't she?

He inhaled her scent, told himself to calm down and concentrate on enjoying the feel of her against him. Finally, he slipped into sleep the way he always did, with Laurie in his arms.

CHAPTER SIX

Laurie's eyes popped open to Saturday morning's dawn. Her career and her marriage were back on track.

Pierce had woken her Monday morning with kisses. Later, he'd called from the church saying the board wanted her input on designs for renovating the youth building. Then, he'd surprised her last night, taking her to a quaint Italian restaurant outside of town, near Daniel and Kay's condo, to celebrate the church being her first client in Rowe City. After reviewing her proposal, the board wanted her to handle the renovation. The focused attention had brought blessed relief to her wounded heart. Maybe the move had simply gotten them out of sync.

She rose and padded to the kitchen. Dinner had been delicious. And the way they had loved each other late into the night . . . Her skin still had a warm, silky feeling. What they had done together was so beautiful, so complete, as if they'd reaffirmed their love without words.

She made coffee, sat at the kitchen table, and opened her Bible. She leafed through her prayer journal, noted the dates and scolded herself for not re-establishing this morning habit sooner. Moving was so disruptive. She scanned the dates again, flipping the pages.

Her period was late.

She glided her pen over the calendar, once again counting the days. Was she really eleven days or more late? Somehow she'd lost track or inadvertently attributed the lateness to stress. Then she had forgotten about it, completely.

Until this morning. Could it be true this time? A miracle after all the disappointments?

She laid aside her pen. Spread both hands on the table to steady herself.

"Dear God, if I'm pregnant—finally, truly pregnant—please keep my baby safe. Let me carry this child to term."

Laurie placed a hand on her belly. "Are you in there, little one? Are you really in there? If you are, I already love you so very, very much."

She should take a pregnancy test. She knew she should, but she almost didn't want to know. If it was positive, for the next eight or nine months she'd battle dread that at any moment she might miscarry again.

She walked to the bathroom. Her hands shook as she opened a twin-pack box of pregnancy tests she kept under the sink, and followed the instructions.

Pregnant. The little plus sign said so. *Oh, God, when did You do this?*

She. Was. Going. To. Have. A. Baby.

Pierce's baby. Seven . . . No, by then, eight years after becoming his wife.

Suddenly, she understood. The unusual tiredness and strange energy bursts. The random bouts of nausea and ravenous hunger—symptoms she hadn't experienced the first time. The fact her pants felt tighter over the past several days.

She was pregnant. Pregnant!

Don't be scared, she told herself. They had waited so long.

Laurie blinked slowly. The little pink cross was still there. She rose and splashed water on her face. How far along was she? A few weeks? A month?

It seemed impossible. Yet, at the same time, hadn't she sensed something had changed?

She eyed herself in the mirror above the sink, noticed her face was a little drawn, her eyes sunken. She turned sideways to view her profile, pulled her nightgown tight from behind. Yes, her regular clothes would have to be put away for a while. How fun!

Maybe that's what the little episodes of emotional turmoil between her and Pierce had really been all about. Maybe he wasn't really having as many moments of sadness as she thought. Instead, maybe her own feelings of upset and unbalance had created the distance between them.

Pregnancy could do that to you, couldn't it? Make you extra sensitive? Yup, being pregnant explained it all.

"Heavenly Father. I am in awe of You and Your timing."

She splayed both hands across her stomach. "Dear God, thinking about this baby makes me love You even more. Please protect this child."

She couldn't wait to tell Pierce their dream had finally come true. Tell him and see him smile, maybe laugh, grab her and hug her. They would pray together, thank God together, talk about names. They would call his parents. Kay would be so excited and rejoice with her. And Daniel? He would baby her, fuss and bother, drill her about what she should and shouldn't do. He would be absolutely incorrigible.

She drew a deep breath. Pierce would be the most wonderful father. He would be fun and loving. He would care for her, make her take care of herself, and then it wouldn't be long before they would go to the hospital and have their baby together. Then they would bring him or her home and—

A nursery. Finally she'd get to decorate her child's nursery. She'd locate her books about pregnancy, a baby's growth, and that first year of life and read them all again.

She stood, lifted her mother's pearl earrings from a silver dish on the countertop, and inserted them with a smile as joyful tears spilled out. *I miss you, Mom. Today, I miss you and Daddy so much.* She would honor them by striving to be as good a parent as they were.

"Oh, Jesus, thank You. Thank You!" She could practically feel God pour joy into her, like that verse in Isaiah—God gives the oil of joy instead of mourning.

She left the bathroom and crawled across the bed to where her husband still slumbered.

"Guess what?" She tried to hold in the giggles, but couldn't. "Pierce." She laughed even as more tears rolled down her face. "Wake up!"

***

It was Saturday. Yes, Pierce knew it was definitely Saturday, which meant he should have been allowed to sleep unhindered.

He had been dead to the world. Completely comatose, as usual at this time of the morning. His deepest sleep always came right before the alarm clock sounded each morning, of course, because the bed always felt softest, warmest, and most comfortable when he needed to get up.

But it wasn't the irritating clock. No. Today it was Laurie, his wife, who he loved with all his heart and with whom he looked forward to sharing his entire life. She was interrupting the glorious haze of sleep that followed a particularly fantastic night together.

He moaned. Opening his eyes took too much effort and wouldn't matter anyway, since he lay on his stomach with a pillow over his head.

She laughed. Simultaneously shook his shoulders and the bed. Like she had lost her mind. Maybe if he pretended he didn't notice, she would leave him alone.

"Pierce. Honey." She jostled his torso, lifted the edge of his pillow.

Something crawled on his nose, or up his nose, or in his nose. He opened one eye as she pulled the pillow away, blasting him with bright daylight. She held a small, white tube in his face.

He rolled onto his side. "Okay. Okay. I'm awake."

"You're also a *daddy*."

He bolted upright, and somehow she still held that thing right in his face.

58

"Look!" Like a kid with a long-awaited and much-loved present, she managed to kneel and jump on the bed at the same time and still show him her surprise. "It's a plus sign. Do you believe it?"

Daddy. She said "daddy."

And that little white stick. He had seen those before. She had used them before. Not for a while, but . . . *oh, boy.*

"Laurie, you're pregnant?"

"Yes." She threw her arms around him, which toppled both of them dangerously close to the edge. She lay on top of him and laughed, raining kisses all over his face, and saying "I love you" over and over.

"Hug me. Kiss me. Oh, I'm so happy." She pulled his arms around her. "Pray. Right now. It's a miracle, Pierce. We have to thank God."

Some part of him wanted this moment to be perfect for her. Knew that she needed it to be.

"Father God," he said. "Thank You."

Another part stood aside, holding back dread. Why?

"We've waited a long time for this."

Hadn't they?

"We've wanted this."

Hadn't he? Of course he had. Laurie was so happy. But—

He took a deep breath. He wouldn't let anything ruin this for her.

"Thank You, Lord, for blessing our love. For answering our prayers. Please keep my wife safe, and bless our child."

He looked at her, took her face in his hands, gently brushed away her sweet tears with his clumsy thumbs, and called himself an idiot. He would do anything to keep that look on her face.

"I love you, Laurie. You're everything to me."

She sat up, straddled his hips, and lifted her nightgown over her head.

"Love me again. Now." She lowered her mouth to his. "Make

the morning perfect."

"I haven't brushed my teeth yet." He tried to sit up.

She ran her hands down his torso. "I don't care."

Again he searched her brilliant face. He wanted to give her this perfect moment, savor her expression of pure happiness. He would let nothing, *nothing* take that happiness or mar their future.

"Okay," he said. And he loved her.

***

Dark dust swirled across the church parking lot as Pierce sat alone in his idling car.

Three weeks. For three weeks he had known he was going to be a father.

His parents were, to say the least, thrilled. His mother had cried. So had his father.

Laurie battled morning sickness. Actually, more like all-day sickness, which curbed her excitement. Who could remain thrilled during days dominated by nausea and vomiting?

She'd already lost weight. Their normal morning chatter had ceased. Laurie rose each morning in silence, looking frail and moving as if she battled the flu.

He rubbed a sweaty palm over his face, glanced at his cell phone, and shook his head. If he canceled lunch with his dad again—as he'd done each week since learning Laurie was pregnant—both his parents would corner him until he told one of them what was wrong.

What could he say? That every time he thought of Laurie delivering their child, he remembered the miscarriage and how he'd been afraid she was going to die?

He put the car in gear. Drove past newly plowed fields on his way to town. Spring had battled winter with showers and wind and

60

heat. Now everything turned green.

Life grew. Like his child inside his wife.

He waited to turn left at the Downtown Diner and wished his cell would ring with an emergency. He parked beside the vintage eatery, whose interior dated back to the 1950s—fountain drinks and root beer floats were still served in tall, ridged glasses—and watched the door close behind his dad. Once inside, Pierce wound a path across the black-and-white checkerboard floor to the booth where Daniel sat, and he slid in.

"Laurie goes to the doctor this week, doesn't she?" Daniel poured sugar into heavily sweetened tea, stirred. "How's she feeling? Breaks my heart to know the girl's throwing up like that. Can she keep anything down?"

Pierce knew his father expected a response to each question and comment. "Yes, we go to the doctor this week. She's feeling puny, throwing up, and doesn't want to eat. Mostly she nibbles on crackers."

"Are you taking care of her?"

"Yes, I am." Pierce knew better than to be offended. Dad loved Laurie. "And it's good that Mom comes over in the mornings. Keeps Laurie from getting lonely or bored or doing too much. Sometimes people from the church stop by. Julie Matthews from choir. Milly Newman."

"That's good. The church folks will help you if you let them."

"She wants to start decorating the nursery, but I'm telling her to wait until she feels better. She doesn't like that idea. She wants to do everything right now." His voice dipped. "I just want her to be okay."

"Of course she'll be okay." Daniel pinned him with a sharp serious stare. "This baby's a gift, Pierce. Every child is. A miracle from God. Like you were, boy, and don't you forget it." Daniel motioned for the waitress to come take their orders. "Lots of women who have miscarriages handle pregnancy fine later on. Or so your mother says, although that wasn't the case for us. God had another way for us. He gave us you. Don't be afraid because of the miscarriage."

After Pierce left Daniel, he drove back by those same furrowed fields. Like a camera flash he saw an image—fields like those beside the road, bathed in shadowy moonlight and silence.

His heart pounded. He flexed his hands on the wheel, checked the rearview mirror, and sped back to his office. Yet, sitting at the desk that used to be his dad's, he couldn't help remembering their earlier conversation. Maybe this is what men whose wives had miscarried felt when their wives became pregnant again. Maybe this was normal, understandable anxiety because of what he and Laurie had been through less than a year ago.

He'd grieved, hadn't he? They'd grieved together.

He did a Google search—"fear in pregnancy after miscarriage"—and learned that some fathers got stuck in grief, some lost interest in sex, and many, many men experienced a marked increase in anxiety if their wives became pregnant again.

Pierce leaned back in his chair and took a deep, deep breath. His emotions were perfectly explainable. Normal, even.

Of course, it made complete sense. He'd simply have to manage it until the birth, *without* saying anything to Laurie.

That evening he sat on the sofa and persuaded Laurie to lay her head in his lap.

"I can't believe how bad I feel," she said. "All over."

"Shh. Close your eyes and rest."

He massaged her head. Long strokes through her hair. Small circles over her brow. He brushed his fingertips across her eyelashes. Just to keep her there beside him. Just to feel her next to him.

***

Laurie knelt on the bathroom floor hugging the commode. Yesterday, she was sure she had vomited up her liver. Twice. A small price to pay for her long-awaited child. Could extensive morning sickness adversely

62

affect the baby? Hopefully the obstetrician could prescribe a medication that would stop the spasms. As a new patient, she'd had to wait a month to get an appointment, but after today she'd have immediate access to an obstetrician.

She wiped her face with the damp cloth Pierce handed her. "Thank you, honey." No matter what, by Christmas it would all be over. The nausea, the vomiting, the weakness. And then—according to the endless caring folks who had already offered her unsolicited advice, harrowing delivery, and humorous parenting stories—the fun would begin. Sleepless nights. Sheer exhaustion. And infinite love.

"Laurie, we need to get you to the car. I know you don't want to be late." He helped her sit on the edge of the tub.

"I'm still in my nightgown." She plucked at it and glanced at his face—he hadn't even noticed. She half-laughed at his expression. "I'm sorry. I know I'm a mess. I know I'm high-maintenance right now."

He knelt before her, his tall frame sandwiched into the small space so he could put his arm around her. "It's okay. I love you."

"I love you, too. Could you get my denim sack dress? It's loose."

She took a breath and managed to slowly stand, then leaned against the wall she had planned to paint pale gold. That would have to wait. Everything would have to wait.

Except the baby. And the doctor.

While Pierce drove, she reclined the seat as far as it would go and closed her eyes. An endless freight train stopped them at the edge of the city square. She could hear it but didn't dare open her eyes. Watching the passing cars would pitch her stomach again.

The metal cars clattered by in a slow, steady rhythm. Pierce took her hand.

"You've been doing that a lot lately," she said.

"What?"

"Holding my hand." Caressing her face. "Massaging my scalp and babying me. Sometimes I actually forget how awful the rest of me feels."

She turned in the seat and looked directly at him. "Asking Kay to come sit with me during the day was a very sweet thing to do." She paused. "Pierce, you're amazing. You know that, don't you? I get so scared sometimes. I worry I'll miscarry again. What you did for me after I lost the baby, the way you loved me . . . all I have to do is look in your eyes and I know I'll be fine during the pregnancy and delivery as long as you're with me."

The crossing gates lifted and he pulled across. She shifted back in her seat and closed her eyes again. They arrived at the medical clinic with minutes to spare. She sat up gingerly as Pierce slowed and waited for an SUV to move from a parking space near the front entrance.

"Wait here." He parked and turned off the engine. She watched him round the hood, enter the lobby. Seconds later he came out smiling broadly, pushing a wheelchair.

He opened her door and bowed. "Your chariot awaits."

"Oh, Pierce." She eased into the wheelchair. "I think I just fell in love with you all over again. Did I tell you they use first names here? Dr. Jordan isn't Dr. Jordan. He's Dr. Nate, for Nathaniel."

"Got it. Dr. Nate."

Thankfully, they waited only a few minutes. "Laurie?" A nurse called from the doorway.

She and Pierce rose and followed.

"I'm Deb Jordan, doctor's wife, Milly Newman's daughter, little Ally's mother." Laurie smiled to herself at the typical small town introduction. "Come on back," she said, and escorted them down a brightly painted hall to an examination room decorated with equal cheer.

No drab off-whites and putrid greens here. Sunny yellow-topped, white chair rails and bead-board. A floor-to-ceiling window centered on the far wall overlooked a small, walled-in garden. Caricatures of the physicians and staff hung in silver frames. Someone had done an excellent job decorating the place to make it feel warm and private, yet open and airy.

"I'll be your nurse for most of your visits." Deb winked at Laurie and grabbed a gown and sheet out of an overhead cabinet. She stopped, folded her arms with the gown and sheet still in them. "Hmmm. You're weak. Green. Hollow-eyed. Means you've been sick a lot."

Deb turned to Pierce. "Daddy, do you want to help?"

***

Pierce blinked as he realized Deb was speaking to him.

"Mr. Crane, would you like to help?" she asked.

"Sure," he said as she handed him the gown.

Deb laughed. "Are you a nervous daddy? You look as green as your wife." She offered an arm to Laurie, helped her turn to sit on the low bed. "Everything off. Gown snaps up the front. Open the door when you're ready. We'll perk you up before we have you filling out forms or anything else."

By the time Dr. Nate came in, Laurie was almost asleep on the bed and Pierce wanted to jump through the picture window and gulp the fresh air. *This is real. Laurie's going to have a baby.* Though he knew she needed him, he desperately wanted to leave.

As he offered a damp, shaking hand to Dr. Nate, Pierce looked at his wife. The need to protect her, to soothe her, surged through his chest then settled in a clump at the base of his throat.

"Can you give her something?" Why was this guy still standing there looking at him? "Make her feel better so this isn't so hard on her?"

"I'll do my best." Dr. Nate's half smile was placating at best. "If you'll let go of my hand."

"Sorry." Pierce let go. He put his hands in his pockets. Then planted them on his hips. Finally, he folded them behind his back.

"Hi, Laurie. Tell me, when was your last period?" Dr. Nate asked and sat on a rolling stool. "No, don't sit up. You can lie there while we talk."

"About nine weeks ago, maybe. But it wasn't normal." She reached for Pierce's hand, laid her other forearm across her forehead.

"What do you mean, not normal?" Dr. Nate continued scribbling notes.

Sweat dripped down Pierce's neck.

"Pierce, honey, you're squeezing my fingers."

"Sorry." He dropped her hand, stuck his own in his pocket.

Dr. Nate tapped his pen on Laurie's chart and pointed. "Yeah, you've got a grip there, Pastor."

But his grip was slipping, as if something unraveled inside him.

Deb squeezed by her husband's wheeled stool and patted Pierce's arm. "Mr. Crane, why don't you sit? Here." She scooted a chair over by the bed, then returned to her husband's side.

Pierce lowered to the edge of his chair.

"About that last period," Dr. Nate said.

Laurie rested her hand low on her stomach. "It was shorter, spotty, I guess."

"And the one before that? Spotty and short?" Dr. Nate continued.

Laurie nodded, "Now that I think about it, yes."

Deb helped Laurie scoot down on the bed.

"How long since your last exam?" Dr. Nate asked. "Pressure here. Breathe."

The procedure was nothing new. During her previous pregnancy Pierce had accompanied Laurie to an appointment such as this. He knew the doctor was speaking to Laurie, but he couldn't help breathing deeply, too.

"It's been a little over a year. I never miss." She flinched. "Ouch."

Dr. Nate rolled back. "We're done. Deb, finish up, let her dress, then we need to get some fluids into her. She's dehydrated."

"Right." Deb took over with Laurie, and Pierce stepped away to again look out the window.

Get a hold of yourself. Laurie was already scared. He had to be strong for her. He couldn't fall apart.

Through an IV, Deb gave Laurie fluids, vitamins, and a medication for nausea. She also loaned them a DVD about pain management and delivery. Pierce couldn't understand any woman refusing pain relief, and he did not want Laurie to suffer.

"I feel sooo much better," she said as they neared home. "Maybe we could watch the delivery video tonight."

"We'll see."

"Don't you want to?" She paused. "I know this is scary after the miscarriage. But this time feels different."

"Yeah." He pulled into their driveway where his mother waited. "Mom will want to hear all about the appointment."

Laurie smiled. "I know. That's part of the fun."

"I need to go to the office," he said as he stopped the car.

Laurie looked at him with confusion. "Okay." She searched his face. "But don't you want lunch first? Then walk through the woods like you normally do?"

"No time to walk today. And I'm not hungry."

She looked at him as if trying to figure out a puzzle. "Then I guess I'll see you tonight." She kissed him and left.

Within minutes, he entered the quiet refuge of his office, but he couldn't sit. He paced, reading through sermon notes as his hands shook.

Just seven or eight more months. It would all be over in seven or eight months.

***

"Laurie, I bought you something. For the baby, really. Be right back." Kay went to her car and returned to the living room with a large gift bag.

"Mom, what did you do?" Delighted, Laurie smiled and accepted the surprise.

"It wasn't me." Kay joined Laurie on the couch. "Or it wasn't *only* me. Daniel started and we just couldn't stop."

Her baby's first gifts. If her lunch stayed put, this would definitely be a red-letter day.

Laurie lifted out the multi-colored tissue paper. The bag contained a striped baby blanket, tiny bibs, a chocolate-colored teddy bear whose softness rivaled a down-filled pillow. And a white book—a little, silver-edged Bible, engraved on the front with the words "Our Miracle Grandbaby."

She hugged Kay while dabbing at tears of joy with the back of her hand. "Oh, Mom. They're lovely."

Kay shifted. "So, what's your due date?"

"Early December for now, though the doctor says I might be farther along. We'll know more next week when the blood test results are back."

"You look better, sweetheart. And so far you haven't lost your lunch."

"I hate throwing up. Last evening was dreadful. Dr. Nate said I should eat small, healthy snacks, even if I can't handle a real meal."

"We'll make a list, and I'll go to the store for you."

She reached for Kay's hand. "Pierce is scared, Mom. I can feel it."

"He's probably concerned about you. We've all been concerned about you and the baby. Being pregnant can be quite an ordeal."

When Kay left for the grocery store, Laurie carried her Bible to the porch and picked up where she left off in Philippians 1. She lifted her face to the warm afternoon sun and breathed in the crisp, fresh air. Her baby would toddle here. Learn to walk here. Someday run and play here with a ribbon-tailed kite. A child with eyes like her daddy's.

Pierce. He had looked so uncomfortable during the appointment. He hadn't even stayed in the room with her when Deb drew her blood. And he'd looked horrified when she suggested they watch a delivery video tonight.

He wasn't being cute. He wasn't being funny. She'd seen that look in his eyes whenever he skirted around what was really bothering him. Or when he was afraid.

He who began a good work in you will carry it on to completion until the day of Christ Jesus.

"Dear God, I know I haven't been my normal self lately because of the pregnancy. But I know something's not right with Pierce. Work in me. Work in us. And thank You again for this baby."

CHAPTER SEVEN

"I'm late. Sorry."

Laurie swallowed the last bite of shepherd's pie as her husband closed the front door, and told herself her shaky stomach was due to pregnancy rather than the fact that Pierce hadn't shown up for her appointment today—even though she'd reminded him of the time—where she'd learned that some women did indeed endure morning sickness all day, every day, for their entire pregnancies. Though hers seemed to have shifted. She was pretty good most mornings, but if she didn't eat in the middle of the day her evenings were tough.

Today she'd forgotten to get lunch after her appointment.

He tossed his keys on the front console table, washed his hands in the kitchen sink, loaded a plate from the dish on the stove, and joined her at the table like nothing was wrong.

"School's out for the summer next week," he said as he dug in. "Gilbert says the youth will have a ball tearing out walls and getting ready to reconfigure the youth space from your drawings."

"Getting permits here is brutal. It's taken much longer than I imagined. I've made connections with suppliers and think I've found some good deals. I can stop by anytime to go over them with you and Gilbert."

"You shouldn't be there when they start demo. Too dusty."

"Why? Because I'm pregnant?"

Their eyes met, and he lowered his fork. "I'm sorry I missed your appointment."

"Pierce, what's going on with you? We don't talk much anymore. You leave early in the morning, work until evening, then walk in the woods without me."

"I'm sorry. I've got a lot on my mind."

"Won't you share it with me? I watched for you as I sat in the waiting area. When they took me back to a room, the receptionist asked if you were coming and said she'd send you back. But you never came. The due date's off, Pierce. The two spotty periods threw off my due date. I'm halfway through the pregnancy. Our child is due November 2." He looked away, and she wadded the napkin in her hands. "Will you please look at me? I heard our baby's heartbeat today. Doesn't that mean anything to you?"

He rose and carried his dish to the sink. "Of course it does. I texted you, told you I couldn't make it, and I was sorry."

"Yeah. I got that message as I was leaving. I'm to return the videos at my next appointment." He'd never directly refused to watch them. He simply always found a way to not be available.

He walked to the back door, reached for the knob, and stopped. "I'm sorry I missed the appointment. Why don't you bring the samples or whatever by the office tomorrow after lunch. Gilbert and I can take a look at them."

"Right," she said, as he confirmed her suspicions. He had made an art out of changing the subject from the baby to the youth-building renovation or some other subject.

She watched him leave. Part of her fought against anger at the strange rejection and wanted to throw something. Yet she knew breaking every dish or even screaming for an hour would help nothing. Change nothing.

Still, most mornings he woke wrapped around her.

What could be the problem during waking hours? She couldn't think of a single thing she'd done to deserve being shunned in this manner.

She loaded and closed the dishwasher, set the dial. The instant hum vibrated her very bones, but at least it masked the sound of her solitary heartbeat.

"God, I can't stand this. At first I thought I was mistaken, but now I see the pattern. I feel like he's tearing his heart away from mine at the roots."

And she was grieving the loss. She recognized the bitter-bile tang—she had swallowed enough of it when she lost her parents and after the miscarriage.

Somehow this was worse. Children were meant to grow up and leave their parents, so she supposed that losing them both in an auto accident soon after she graduated from high school wasn't as life-altering as it might have been. And the miscarriage? Well, some statistics showed as much as twenty percent of pregnancies end in miscarriage, or so she'd read. But Christian men weren't supposed to tear themselves away from their wives.

She flipped off the kitchen light. In darkness, she walked to their bathroom. She wiped away tears as she ran water in the tub and added foaming bath salts. Her face ached from crying so much over the past weeks.

This was not how she had dreamed a pregnancy would be. They weren't shopping for baby furniture or decorating the nursery. They hadn't talked about names. They didn't *talk* about anything.

She sank into the lavender-scented bubbles in her yet-unpainted bathroom. She couldn't call a new friend. Everyone she knew in town was someone from church. Besides, she'd barely begun making friends within the congregation at last Saturday's Ladies Luncheon. She couldn't call Kay. What would she say? That Pierce was withdrawing from her in every way that mattered in a marriage? And she couldn't call her friends in Orlando—they would all expect her to be happy. If she didn't understand what was happening in her own marriage, how could one of them?

Attending Sunday services proved beyond difficult now. People wanted to congratulate her and Pierce, which was sweet, but it put her in an impossible position. She had to accept their hugs, prayers, and squeals of joy alone—and answer vaguely if someone mentioned Pierce and his feelings about the pregnancy.

She couldn't lie. Wouldn't lie. But it was a fine line to walk, and it left her isolated even as she was surrounded by others who obviously cared.

Her mother would have known what to do. Mother . . . how she needed her mother right now.

She took a deep breath and tried to relax. She'd started writing him letters, a string of them, a journal account of her feelings and prayers and what his withdrawal was doing to her. A spiral notebook, partially filled, sat on the nightstand. She had considered hiding it but figured if he did peek and read, then the time had come for him to know how she felt.

She stroked her slightly rounded belly.

"I miss him, God. His body's near sometimes, but his heart is somewhere else." He hadn't touched her since the morning she learned she was pregnant and they'd made love.

The morning she learned she was pregnant. Did Pierce carry the same worries as she did at times, that she'd miscarry again? He'd been brave enough—or sentimental enough—to give her a Mother's Day card as well as Kay, and Laurie had already purchased one to give him for Father's Day next week. Should she give it to him? How could she know what he needed, what he wanted, if he wouldn't talk to her?

She bathed and then reclined in the frothy water. The miscarriage had been horribly traumatic. What was it he'd said at her bedside? *Please don't die.* Maybe he was simply staying busy, occupying his mind, until she was farther along.

But he was in agony. She could see it, feel it. Was it possible he didn't even realize—

She felt a flutter in her womb.

Laurie sat straight up in the water, gently pressed her hand where she had felt the sensation.

She held her breath. Waited. Wished to feel the movement again.

Thump.

The unexpected kick brought her such joy she scrambled out of the tub. She grabbed her robe and ran, barely remembering to turn on the outside light, and let the back door slam behind her as she headed for the woods through the wet, heavy air.

She was dripping wet, but she didn't care. She had to find Pierce. Her happiness was too big to contain, the feeling too wonderful to keep to herself. She smiled so wide her cheeks almost cramped. Surely if Pierce experienced this, if he felt their baby move, any concerns he had may be set aside. Maybe he would change back into the man she had fallen in love with and married.

Hope burst inside. Her heart and lungs swelled. If the baby was a girl, Hope would be a great name.

She stopped to catch her breath then continued walking. "Pierce! Pierce!"

His footsteps pounded as he exited the woods. Concern etched his face as he approached. "I heard the door slam. Are you okay?"

She laughed. "I'm fine." She threw her arms up to hug him.

He held her away. "You're wet," he scolded. "What's wrong?"

"Our baby moved." She grabbed his hand and pressed it against the damp robe over her belly. "Here."

She looked into his eyes, willed their child to move under his palm.

Please feel what I'm feeling. Please stay with me like this, like we used to be.

He tried to pull his hand away, but she kept her grip firm. Seconds ticked by without any movement under their hands.

Please don't back away from me. Please don't walk away.

Didn't Pierce know? Didn't he see in her eyes everything she felt, every way she needed him? She had to tell him.

She hooked an arm around his neck and kissed him.

At first he responded. Then his hands fell away, his arms at his sides. She might as well have been kissing stone.

She closed her eyes and let him back away. "I simply wanted you to feel the baby."

"You should go dry off." He looked away. "I'll come inside in a minute."

"But—" She stepped toward him and heard his cell phone ring. She turned away at the relief on his face as he welcomed the interruption, and closed her eyes in defeat. What did she have to do to build a bridge between them?

He ended the call. "Angus is having trouble again. Gilbert called an ambulance. They're on the way to the hospital."

"Should I come, too?"

For the first time in weeks he touched her. Her heart sighed with relief as he laid his palm on her hair and let his open hand slide down the side of her face to cup her cheek.

"Laurie, I realize I've been quiet lately. I do love you. I've done some research. I think . . . maybe I didn't realize how much the miscarriage affected me."

He looked terrified as he spoke. Heavy tears sprang into her eyes, and she held his hand in place. "Pierce, we can work through anything if you'll talk to me."

"I have to go."

She nodded, still cradling the sweetness of this momentary touch and the familiar warmth of his breath.

"Call Mom and Dad. They can meet me there."

He studied her face. If only he would ask her to go with him.

"If you feel up to it, get dressed and come on. I'm sure Gilbert would appreciate it."

She pressed a kiss into his hand. His touch felt wonderful, and she needed it, needed him so much the words practically jumped out of her mouth. "What about you? Do you want me there?"

He swallowed. "Yes. You should be there." He stroked her cheek with his fingers. "I want you there."

She smiled. "I'll help you in any way I can."

***

The murky haze cleared by the time Laurie arrived back home. She stepped from the car, reveling in the silence. The stars had multiplied and twinkled brightly. She could actually see the Milky Way.

After the emergency room doctor informed them that Angus likely hadn't suffered a heart attack, Gilbert had insisted they leave the hospital. He'd call if the prognosis changed.

Laurie yawned even as excitement grew inside her. Pierce had sat beside her in the waiting room most of the evening. Twice he had reached for her hand.

She readied for bed quickly, hoping he wasn't too tired to spend a few minutes together without the tension that had been between them. She wouldn't mention his dreams or prepared childbirth classes. No, maybe they could talk about baby names. Maybe hold each other. Maybe more.

She opened the bathroom door to find Pierce propped up in bed reading. Love swelled in her heart, and the baby kicked again. Perfect.

She climbed into bed, laid her head on the end of Pierce's pillow, and shifted so her belly pressed against him. If the baby moved again, he would probably feel it. That should change everything.

Timidly, slowly, she moved her hand from her thigh and laid it like a feather on his warm chest. He didn't seem to notice, didn't react.

Trepidation rolled over her in waves. Should she move her fingers, stroke his chest, kiss his shoulder, or say something? Or should she settle for this tiny bit of contact and the fact that for the first time in weeks he wasn't pulling away from her?

No. Something rose inside her, lifted its chin in defiance. They had less than five months until they'd become parents. Their child deserved better than a home where the parents didn't even touch each other. Whatever had him in its grip, she'd help him deal with it.

She kissed Pierce's shoulder, flexed her fingers on his torso, slid them slowly up to his neck, and caressed his collarbone.

Please come back to me. Love me again. The way we used to.

***

Pierce hadn't turned a page for several minutes. He couldn't focus on the words.

How could he have forgotten the perfection of Laurie's touch? How could he have deprived himself, deprived them both, of the closeness they once enjoyed without reservation?

He lowered the book. Closed his eyes. And enjoyed.

She scooted up to kiss him on the mouth. His eager hands quickly found her face. Together, they slid down on the bed as he wrapped his arms around her, his torso pressed to hers.

Thump.

He jerked away from her as his heart raced like a thoroughbred's. He sat straight up and searched her confused face. "What was that?"

Her eyes rounded bright and flashed with her smile. "Did you feel it? Did you feel the baby move?" She reached for him, threaded her fingers through his hair, pulled his head back for another kiss. "Isn't it wonderful?"

He jerked back, scrambled off the bed, and rubbed his hands over his face.

Her voice trembled. "I can still make love with you. We won't hurt the baby." She reached for him again.

Anguish ripped his throat. "I didn't know it would be like this." He jerked on a pair of jeans and grabbed his pillow. "I'll sleep on the couch."

"Please, don't go." She extended both arms. "Pierce, I don't understand . . ."

"Neither do I." He turned and left the room.

Pierce tossed his pillow on the living room couch. He was sick, absolutely sick thinking about Laurie giving birth. Which was understandable given the circumstances, wasn't it? But why couldn't he set it aside?

He flipped on the TV. Channel surfed. Turned it off, leaving the house silent.

He paced, trying to ignore the guilt, the shame of leaving her. Then he lay on the couch, tried to read his Bible, but couldn't concentrate. He attempted to pray, but his stumbling efforts only increased his frustration. He finally turned off the light, his body throbbed with exhaustion, but his heart raced with panic and his brain searched for scriptures, ideas, anything to relieve the awful pressure pounding through his system.

For hours he stared into the darkness, giving Laurie time to fall asleep. He shouldered his shame, gathered his pillow, and trudged back to their bedroom.

She looked exactly as she had on Easter Sunday. Curled up on their bed, tissue in hand, her cheeks damp with tears.

Unable to deny himself the feel of her or the sweetness of going to sleep with his arms wrapped around her body, he eased into bed behind her. He draped his arm over her and finally he, too, fell into sleep's blessed oblivion.

***

Before Laurie opened her eyes the next morning, she felt behind her to Pierce's side of the bed. She knew she'd find Pierce on the floor.

She went to the bathroom and returned as the alarm sounded. Her husband avoided her gaze as he stood. "Pierce, you need to talk with someone. You should call your dad."

"I'm not calling my dad."

"You never once left our bed and slept on the floor until after we moved here. Doesn't that tell you something? Your parents would help us."

"Only if I knew what to tell them, which I don't."

"You could try telling them the truth."

He looked at her. "That I remember the bus ride but not what happened before it? That I remember my mama's face? Remember looking through a keyhole and wetting my pants?"

"You never told me that part."

"Because I dreamed it last night."

"If we tell your parents about the dreams, they will help us."

"No. Not yet."

"I know you're tore up inside. Sometimes it rolls off you in waves."

"I'm fine. I'll be fine. I can sleep on the couch if it bothers you."

"That's not what I meant."

He passed her on his way to the bathroom and closed the door behind him; she pressed her forehead against it. A part of her wanted to pound on the barrier shouting, *Don't shut me out!*

She clenched her fists at her sides, considered using one when he came out, then remembered the look on his face when he spoke of wetting his pants.

Dear God, what happened to my husband when he was a little boy? And what does it have to do with us having a child now?

CHAPTER EIGHT

Laurie stood in her kitchen, scanning her list of fabric suppliers while vegetable soup simmered on the stove. She and Julie Matthews had worked in the nursery until just after lunch. After Julie left, she'd spent two hours tracking down a delayed order supposedly misplaced over the Independence Day holiday, only to learn the material was out of stock.

She leafed through swatch books, found an alternative, then placed an order online as the July late-afternoon sun speared through the kitchen window.

Next she called the electrical contractor. Part of his work hadn't passed a preliminary inspection. He must redo the work immediately, so a re-inspection could take place by week's end, or the entire renovation schedule would be derailed. That she couldn't have. The work must be completed well before her due date.

She leaned against the counter and sipped cold sweet tea. The last weeks of June, these early days of July had thankfully passed as a blur. She'd been able to distract herself with work.

But the baby was growing. She was growing. Maternity clothes had become a must. Anyone glancing in her direction could see she was pregnant. She was bonding with her child, talking to the baby, daydreaming about the baby, but she seemed to be losing her husband.

Pierce's emotional withdrawal from her continued like the slow amputation of a limb. If their paths crossed during her frequent visits to the youth building to monitor the renovation's progress, he might ask if she was okay, but he never seemed to look directly at her. At times, she was reduced to email to keep him updated, or simply to know if she should expect him home for dinner.

Rather than reading in bed like he used to, he stayed in the family room—supposedly working—until well after she'd fallen asleep.

On several mornings, she'd found him on the floor. She didn't ask for an explanation, just to see if he'd offer one. So far he hadn't.

He wasn't cruel. He wasn't angry. He was simply . . . absent. How could she reach him?

She heard Pierce's car pull up out front and then his key turn in the front door's lock.

"Laurie?"

Sweet baby, that's your daddy's voice.

"Honey? Can you come to the door?"

She hurried to him. "What is it?"

He turned, pointing to the box. "I found it on the porch. UPS."

"If they knocked or rang the doorbell, I didn't hear them. But I've been expecting this." She ignored his puzzled look. "Will you bring it back to the nursery?"

He lifted the huge, awkward package and motioned with his chin for her to proceed. "What is it?" he asked.

"It's for the baby." She hoped he would follow her and entered the nursery first. "I figured if we opened it in here, we wouldn't have to fit it through the door after it's assembled."

He stood in the doorway and scanned the room. She'd painted the top two-thirds of every wall the same sky hue as their bedroom, the lower sections a soft brown, like freshly tilled earth.

"I found a great wallpaper border. It's over two feet tall, if you can believe it. It's a continual farm scene. Barnyard, animals, a silo. If we put it where the colors meet, it'll be great, don't you think? There are even little grass sections we can place at random."

He cleared his throat. "Should you have painted? I thought the fumes were bad for both of you."

She smiled at him. "I'm well past the first trimester. Julie Matthews helped me. The windows are big, so we opened them and kept fans going. We did it this morning. It's already dry."

She had paint under her nails, and specks still dotted her hair. "Would you help me open the box?" Her voice shook.

His mouth tightened and he cleared his throat. He pulled a pocketknife from his front pocket. "What is it?"

"A crib." She held her breath when his hand stilled. She had always wanted to make this memory with him—assembling their baby's crib. "Ina Hood sent it. She used it for her own children. I'm sure it's a cherished family heirloom, but she wanted us to have it."

"You called her?"

"Your parents did. I think they called everybody." She paused. "She's happy for us, Pierce. Everybody is."

Panic scampered across his face.

"Pierce, please? Don't eat and leave tonight. Do this with me." She watched him debate.

"It's exciting! It's what we always dreamed together."

Then, he looked at her as he used to, as if she were the answer to every question he had.

He lifted out the first piece of the blond, antique crib and laid it on the floor. "Guess we should put it together."

Laurie laughed. "I guess so."

To Laurie's amazement, the clear fragrance of a fragile, unspoken truce hung in the nursery air.

They laughed together more than once as they worked to construct the crib without instructions. While Pierce attached the casters, Laurie ladled vegetable soup into two bowls. With cracker crumbs on their hands, they picnicked on the floor and decided to place the bed near the door. The opposite wall's trio of tall windows obviously needed shelves on both sides and a window seat with storage underneath.

"Laurie, you're really making this room nice."

"Thanks. It's important to me."

"You'll make a great mom."

She looked at her beloved, threw her arms around him, and burst into tears.

With tentative, gentle hands he patted her shoulders and hair. "Shh."

She clung to him, starved for his company, his voice, his touch. She wiped her eyes with the back of a hand and burrowed against him to whisper against his neck. "Thank you."

"For what?"

"For sharing this with me. I feel like we've drifted apart lately. And we've hardly talked about the baby." She felt him swallow. "Will you do something for me? For us?"

"If . . . if I can."

"Will you lie down with me tonight like we used to? I'm not asking for anything else. Just, please don't go to the couch. Let me go to sleep with you beside me."

He kissed her temple, then the top of her head. "Sure."

***

For the first time in many weeks, he wasn't sneaking into bed after Laurie fell asleep. Rather, Pierce fully intended to fall asleep pressed against his sweet wife's back.

Her tentative hand crept over her hip and twined his fingers with hers. He actually relaxed and drifted into a deep, sound sleep.

Mama sat in her chair on the tilted porch. She had clear, blue eyes and brown, wavy hair that matched his own. The sun shone down, and she smiled at him as she brushed his hair out of his eyes.

Then he saw Mama in her nightgown. The way it hung over her body, grazing the top of her small, tanned feet. How she draped her hand over the side of her bed, resting it on him when he slept on the rug. He heard her soft voice, with its quiet southern drawl, calling his name as he wrote in the dirt with a stick.

Next, he was standing with his ear pressed to the door of Mama's room. Mama was crying on the other side. He peered through the keyhole.

Then he stood on the bus steps. "Mama's gone." Daddy grabbed him by the shoulders and shook him. "You hear? Your mama's gone."

Pierce woke before dawn, facedown on the floor. As he rose, the familiar anguish rushed over him like a tidal wave, and it nearly drowned him.

As his eyes adjusted to the darkness, he clicked off the pre-set alarm clock. Laurie slept on her side, the outline of her back defined by the light quilt she'd claimed in the night. His hand quivered, then reached for her as if drawn by an unseen force. The whisper of her name stuck in his throat.

She shifted in her sleep, rolled in his direction, and kicked off the covers. Her rounded belly strained against the nightgown she wore. She laid her arm across her stomach, cradling their baby.

Pierce closed his eyes but could block neither the new, graphic remembrance of his mother, nor the visual evidence of his child growing inside his wife. Both images seared his eyelids.

Numb, he brushed his teeth. Dressed, left, and walked to his office through the woods. Yet this time, the familiar path held no comfort.

Several times during the day, he'd almost called Laurie. Just to hear her voice. Just to know she was all right.

He'd reach for his phone, be ready to make the call, and freeze. He couldn't think of her without thinking of the pregnancy. And every time he thought of the pregnancy, fear threatened to swallow him whole, as it had the evening she miscarried.

Last night's reprieve, induced by her excitement over the crib, had been only that—a reprieve.

He worked late, almost until midnight. Left his office and walked back through the familiar woods. He found his wife in the kitchen, standing at the counter, eating a container of yogurt.

"You're finally home," she said. "I had leftovers. I can heat some up for you if you're hungry now."

"No, thanks," he said, looking at her.

"What?" she asked as she licked the spoon. "Do I have food on my face?"

"No."

They stared at each other. Terror seeped from his pores and almost caused his knees to buckle. He turned and walked to a dining room chair and sat. She followed and sat also.

"Pierce, what's wrong? You've got to tell me. I've watched you turn white as a ghost. You pull away from me. I've lost count of how many mornings I've found you on the floor. I thought we'd turned a corner last night putting together the crib."

"Stop." He held up a hand. "I can't talk about it."

"Why can't you talk to me? Or is it that you won't talk to me? We used to talk about everything."

He rose. "Not this!"

"What haven't you told me?"

He banged his fist on the table.

She jumped as if he'd slapped her. "You're scaring me, Pierce."

"No, *I'm* the one who's scared." He slumped back into the chair, his face in his hands. "And I don't know why."

"Is it because of the miscarriage?"

"I was so afraid you were going to die."

"I remember you saying that. I woke up in the hospital, and you were begging God not to let me die. Why would you think that?"

"Because of all the blood. Because you looked half dead lying there asleep from the sedative they gave you."

She blanched.

"I'm sorry." He took her hand. "I can't figure this out."

She pulled back to look him squarely in the eyes. "What are you dreaming when you leave our bed and lie down on the rug?"

"I dream about the bus ride."

"When your father sent you to live with the Cranes."

"Yes."

"You were five, you were scared, and you didn't understand what was happening. I know that. But there's got to be more. What did he say to you?"

"He said, 'Mama's gone. Your mama's gone, and you're not staying with me.'"

"Anything else?"

"I don't remember."

"You don't remember anything else he said, or you don't remember anything else you've been dreaming?"

He rested his head on her shoulder. "I'm dreaming about my mother. I'm a little boy, and I see her sitting in her chair."

"And?" She rubbed his head, her bulging belly between them. "Tell me the rest, Pierce. The fact that you don't want to proves it's important."

"I'm standing at her bedroom door. I'm listening, and I hear her crying. Then I'm looking through the keyhole."

"What do you see?"

"That's where it always ends. I have no idea what's on the other side. Please don't ask me any more questions right now. I need time to figure this out."

He heard and felt her sigh. "Only if you promise to tell me anything else you remember."

"Okay. I will."

***

Pierce pulled in front of his home as the last orange rays of sunset disappeared behind the trees. He shoved the car's gear into park and slumped over the steering wheel, leaving the engine running.

Earlier that day he'd finished his sermon, then sat in his office because he hadn't wanted to come home. Why did he feel this way?

The memories he'd shared with Laurie last week scrolled through his mind.

A chill went through him—cold, colder—until he wrapped his arms tight around his stomach and huddled in the driver's seat. A shadow, an image, danced in his peripheral vision.

He turned his head—

And remembered his mother's death.

The vision punched him in the chest. He barely stifled a cry of shock. Did it happen that way? Could it be true?

Oh, yes, he thought. It happened exactly that way.

Pierce covered his face with his hands. Mama, his sweet mama. How he'd loved her. She'd had the gentlest touch. The kindest smile. How could he have forgotten her death?

He would no longer be able to think around the random pieces of memory, weave through them like one might a bizarre emotional obstacle course. Having the whole picture changed the rules.

The two will become one flesh. You gave her your word. Tell Laurie what you just remembered.

The command hit Pierce like a slap. He put his head back against the seat.

No, no. He had to be mistaken. Telling Laurie this, now, would devastate her.

He waited and waited, hoped he'd come up with a justification for keeping the memory to himself. Instead, he grew certain he had no choice but to tell her.

He found Laurie in the family room.

"I've already eaten," she said, the television remote in her hand.

"It's okay. I'll fix myself a sandwich later."

"Pierce, I was too nervous to watch the delivery videos with Kay, even though she offered. I have to return them soon." She paused. "A healthy birth isn't like a miscarriage. I'm starting to get nervous about the process, too. Maybe if we watch a normal birth, we'll both feel better."

He loved her so much, maybe she was right.

"I'll give it a shot." He lowered himself to the couch. Her small smile offered encouragement as she pressed PLAY.

The introduction didn't bother him. It just contained a lot of what most would consider good, useful information. Then a birthing scene came.

Laurie reached for his hand and squeezed. Pierce closed his eyes.

The narrator called it natural childbirth. Which meant the woman labored without pain medication. Pierce turned to face Laurie. She looked better than she had in several days, her expression hopeful, with a little pregnant glow shining through the dark circles under her eyes. He took a snapshot with his mind, to have, to save, because she had never looked more beautiful. Then he slipped his hand free of hers. He knew he was about to break her heart.

"Laurie, turn it off."

She didn't hear him at first.

On the screen, the baby crowned. The mother gave a long, groaning push. Another. The head and shoulders came first, then the newborn all but slid out, screaming like a banshee. The mother cried tears of joy. So did Laurie.

"What, honey? What did you say?" She wiped her eyes.

He couldn't repeat the words. His throat had closed.

A second birth story began. This time the mother on the screen needed a C-section. Laurie concentrated on the video.

Pierce sat perfectly still beside her. Quiet, contained, staring at the floor.

Finally, she looked at him, turned down the volume. "Pierce, what's wrong?"

"Laurie, I have to tell you something." Despair coated his words. "About before I came to live with Mom and Dad."

CHAPTER NINE

Hazy moonlight fluttered across his closed eyelids that night long ago.

As it had many times before, a dull cramp low in his belly woke Pierce from a fitful sleep. He blinked, grateful for faint stars rather than a pitch-black night. But then he heard a sound like a whimpering animal. He crept out of bed and over to Mama's room.

With his ear pressed to the thin wooden door, he heard her. Crying. Panting. Groaning.

Somehow he knew he shouldn't be there listening.

But he had to know. He had to know what was happening in there.

Mama never shut him out. Her door stayed open at night.

More often than not, he greeted the day from the braided rug by her bed. The soft cotton of her ankle-length nightgown always brushed his feet as she rose to greet the day. Then she made Daddy breakfast and coffee. Pierce knew from the smell when she'd overcooked the fried eggs.

But tonight, Mama's door was shut. Shut and locked.

His tummy hurt. And he needed to go to the outhouse. But Mama always said to tell her before he went out there at night. He couldn't go without letting her know.

He danced in place outside the closed door. Listening. He heard more groans and strained not to wet the thin, too-small underpants he always slept in. He couldn't hold it much longer.

Risking a scolding—or worse, a switch—he angled his head, squinted, and peeked through the metal keyhole.

When he did this during the day, he had discovered he could see all the way around the narrow room, across the bed, and out the window to the pig shed. He often thought that when he was bigger and had his own house, he would never put his bed on the same side of the house as a stinky pig shed. Tonight the room should have been dark, but Daddy had turned on both lamps. Something was wrong.

Mama lay on the bed, her face out of view. Across the tops of her bent knees he saw Daddy. He stood at the window, his back to Mama and the door. Maybe Daddy wouldn't know he had looked through.

Mama's knees shook.

Now he *really* had to go. If he sneaked out, Daddy might not see. He could ease the screen door shut real quiet and tiptoe across the porch on the opposite side of the house. He could be back without Daddy knowing he'd left.

Pierce turned away.

"Luther. Luther, please. Ohhh," Mama said.

He heard her and peered back through the long slot below the rusty, round doorknob.

"Luther. Hold my hand. Luther." She panted.

But Daddy just stood there. Feet spread. Arms crossed over his chest, hands flat against his sides. He didn't even look back at her.

Mama screamed. Like Mrs. Taylor, their neighbor, had screamed when her husband accidentally chopped off his finger while helping Daddy in the barn.

"Mama! Mama!"

Pierce twisted the doorknob, beat on the door with his fists as tears pooled in his eyes.

"Go back to bed, Pierce. Now!" Daddy yelled. "Do it, boy!"

"Mama!"

Another groan.

With one dirty foot pressed against the door jam, Pierce pulled hard on the knob. Even as the yellow wet trickled down his other leg, he twisted the knob and tried to get to her.

"Luther!"

"Mama!" he cried through the keyhole, then pressed his cheek flat against the door to see more.

Daddy finally came to Mama. He stood between her knees at the bed's edge.

She sat up, grabbed his forearms. "Promise me you'll keep Pierce." She grunted the words. She panted and gasped, her body rocked and jerked. "Promise me you'll keep both of them! Luther!"

Mama screamed again. She lay back, perfectly still. Daddy reached between her knees.

Then something dark dripped onto the floor, found a groove in the old, scarred wood, and seeped under the door to reach Pierce's bare, damp feet.

Blood.

"Mama!"

Daddy jerked the door open from the inside and sent Pierce sprawling to the floor. "Move."

Daddy held a screaming, kicking baby. He pushed past Pierce and staggered down the hall.

"But what about . . .?"

Daddy walked out the front screen door, let it slam behind him, and stepped into the night.

"Mama," Pierce whispered.

He didn't want to look. But he had to.

Lamplight flickered over the room, bathing it in a soft glow. On the floor, blankets and rags coated with blood lay in piles. The room stank.

And there was Mama, silent.

Deep-red stains covered her soft, threadbare gown. Blood dotted her hair and face and her limp hand hanging over the side of the bed.

He knew where she kept her handkerchiefs, had always liked the soft, thin ones with lace edges. So he crawled quietly across her room and took one, softly closing the drawer. He knelt by the bed and wiped her hand.

She'd be better in the morning. Sure she would. She was really tired, that's all. He would lie here on the rug beside her, like he always did.

He woke up freezing, his underpants still damp, balled up on the rug by Mama's bed. He didn't smell breakfast. He heard no murmurs from the kitchen—only a crying baby.

He raised himself on an elbow, peeked around the foot of the bed, and saw no one. Not Mama, not Daddy. Until he sat up, looked out the window, and saw Daddy digging.

Just like when his puppy died.

His breath caught. He hurried to his room, changed his clothes, hid his dirty ones under the thin mattress. He didn't brush his teeth—though Mama'd taught him that his day must always start with a washed face and brushed teeth. Instead, he ran to the front of the house.

He stood at the porch door, face pressed against the filthy screen, in pants too big and a T-shirt too small.

"Pierce," Mrs. Taylor whispered behind him. "Don't you go out there."

He glanced quickly in her direction. She sat in one of the three chairs at the kitchen table. Mama's chair, the one missing a spindle. She was feeding the baby a bottle.

"Are you staying with us, Mrs. Taylor?"

"No, Pierce. Your daddy fetched me last night to care for your baby brother. Seems he's hungry all the time."

Pierce didn't look at the baby. Rather, as he watched Daddy work, tears dripped down his face and his heart beat frantically in his chest.

The shovel hissed with each thrust into the ground. Despite the cool air, Daddy had sweat through his undershirt. Usually when Daddy worked outside, Mama sent Pierce to take him some tea.

But there was no tea today. And Mama lay wrapped in a blanket on the ground beside a dirt pile that kept getting higher and higher.

Why would Daddy put her so close to the stinky pig shed? Did the hole have to be that deep? Why couldn't they just leave her in the bed, give her time to sleep and get better, like last summer when *he* had a fever and Mama made him rest?

"Mama," he whispered. "Please wake up, Mama."

Then Daddy dropped the blanket in the hole and covered it up.

Pierce's stomach lurched. He didn't eat that day or the next. He couldn't, though Mrs. Taylor brought meals she'd cooked in her own kitchen. Daddy asked her to come every day to care for the baby so he could still work in the fields. If Mrs. Taylor hadn't come, Pierce would have spent every day alone in the farmhouse, peering through the screened door at Mama's fresh grave.

The next afternoon, Daddy came in early from the fields. He spoke to Mrs. Taylor, then paced on the porch.

"I'll put the baby down in your room," Mrs. Taylor said to Pierce. When she returned, he saw she carried a paper sack.

Daddy came back inside. Mrs. Taylor wrapped a piece of bread in a napkin and placed it in the bag. Daddy spoke to her. "Is that all of his things?"

"Yes, sir," she answered. She didn't look at Pierce.

"Daddy?" Pierce's voice shook.

"Fine. You stay. I'll be an hour."

"Daddy?" he asked again.

"I'll clean up some," she answered.

Daddy pulled on a jacket, grabbed his hat and keys and the paper bag. "Pierce, get in the truck."

That's when he knew. He cried, screamed, and begged as tears streamed down his dirt-streaked face. "No, Daddy, please. Please let me stay."

But Daddy grabbed his arm and hauled him onto the porch and around the house.

"Let me stay. I'll help. I can."

But Daddy walked faster, practically raising Pierce off the ground as they rounded the house and neared the rusty pickup. Then Daddy lifted him, set him in the seat, threw the bag in the floorboard, and slammed the door.

"Why, Daddy?" He pushed the words out as his chest heaved in panic.

Daddy cranked the truck. They pulled away from the house.

"Why? Why?"

Daddy slammed on the brakes. "I can't take care of two of you and work. Now hush!"

"Why are you keeping the baby? He can't help you. I can work. I'll work hard."

The old pickup rattled over the dirt lane, dipping in potholes and jarring Pierce's teeth. The window on his side of the truck only rolled up partway, so he wrapped his twig-thin arms around himself. The bitter, slapping wind beat his face dry, forced his sobs back into his throat. Through sniffs and dry tears he tried to reason with Daddy all the way to the bus station. He wouldn't eat much. He could help more. He would even take care of the baby.

"I heard Mama ask you to keep me!" he cried. "I'll be good, Daddy. I promise."

But Daddy kept driving.

Finally they stopped. Daddy pinned an envelope with Pierce's name to his shirt, carried him to the bus, and placed him and the paper sack on the narrow stairs by the driver.

"Hush. There'll be no more out of you," Daddy said.

"But Mama said . . ."

Pierce shook his head. Maybe Daddy didn't really want to send him away. Maybe Daddy thought he missed Mama too much and just didn't want to stay without her here.

So Pierce tried one more time. He turned on the step, eye to eye with his father. "Daddy, please."

"Mama's gone," Daddy grabbed him by the shoulders and shook him. "You hear? Your mama's gone. Frettin' don't change nothin'. Set it aside, boy."

Then Daddy picked him up with his big, hard hands and carried him to the second green vinyl bus seat.

"Don't move," Daddy said. He left Pierce there and never looked back.

***

Pierce now stood at the window. Still as a statue with his back to Laurie, much like he described his father had while his mother labored. He didn't turn, didn't move, didn't speak or look at her.

She waited for long seconds, hoping and praying he would come back to her, reach for her. Her heart tore open. She pictured it bleeding for the little boy Pierce had been.

Their living room was silent as a grave.

The DVD had ended, leaving only a black screen. Although the table lamp in the corner still shone, the room seemed darker to Laurie, as if the evening itself seeped through the rest of the house, nibbling away the light.

The tears she shed while Pierce spoke had dried and left her face tight. Her legs, though she stayed seated on the couch throughout his story, quivered like Jell-O. She knew she couldn't stand, and her limp arms refused to move. She couldn't reach for him.

A chill seeped through her mind and snaked its way around her heart. She now knew the secret she'd sensed, the wall that had been between them since the day they married.

"I can't be with you in the delivery room, Laurie."

His words scraped her wounded heart raw, but he wasn't looking at her. He didn't see he'd just smashed her dreams.

"I'm sorry, but I can't." He left the room without a backward glance.

She watched him walk to the front door and grab his keys from the console table holding her mother's chime clock. Then he walked out, locked the door, and left her alone with their child.

***

He'll come back, Laurie thought. Of course he'd come back, and talk to her, let her help him grieve. Whatever he needed, she'd do it.

But seconds passed to minutes. Laurie's heart dropped bit by bit in her chest as the minutes became an hour.

Unsteady, she rose and turned out the lights, then readied for bed. What else could she do?

She called his cell. The voicemail engaged. "Pierce? I . . . will you let me know you're safe?"

Maybe he'd ended up going to see his parents. Or Gilbert. She could call them and ask.

She started to dial, but something—like a gentle hand on her shoulder—made her stop.

Laurie slipped under the covers. Hugged her husband's pillow to her chest and stared into the darkness.

"Dear God. I feel like I'm living in a whirlwind. I'm pregnant. Finally pregnant, which should be wonderful. I'm exhausted. I have deadlines with the renovation; for the next two or three days, I have to be hands-on at the site for the final touches. I've got a husband who's suffering. What he went through was so awful! Listening to him say it—even if he'd let me—I don't know how to help him."

She fell asleep praying. Woke an hour later and left another message on Pierce's phone.

Their home was so dark. So quiet. So empty. *Pierce, please come home.* How long could their marriage last like this?

She slept again, on his side of the bed.

She woke to sunshine. Vibrant, scandalous sunshine so bright she winced, and the scent of freshly brewed coffee.

She turned. Her husband stood in the doorway, dressed for work, holding a mug and avoiding her gaze.

"I, um, made this for you." He offered the cup.

She accepted. Opened her mouth to speak, but he cut her off.

"I thought I had it figured out. I thought I was one of those men who was significantly affected by the miscarriage, one of those guys who has a tough time when his wife conceives again. I told myself I could handle it, that thinking about you delivering would get easier."

"We can work on it together." She reached for him.

He stepped back, raked a hand through his hair. "Last night I left here and drove, just drove through town, ended up back at the church parking lot, and I kept thinking about the night we put the crib together, you know? That was a happy night. Something we'd talked about doing, looked forward to doing together." He paused. "I can't *do* this, Laurie. I'm so sorry. You deserve better. Our child deserves better. You need someone with you during delivery who will help you, not someone who's not sure he can be there!"

The agony rolling off him slapped her heart. He stood there shaking, breath heaving, and she simply wanted to reach for him, comfort him. But how?

He took a deep breath and finally met her gaze.

"Will you please talk to your parents?"

He shook his head. "No. They're . . . it's . . . they're too close. I don't want to hurt them, too." He covered his face with his hands. "I'm already hurting you and I'm about to hurt you more."

She glanced at the clock. If happiness were sand, life was pulling apart her fingers so every grain fell away, lost. "I have to be at the youth building in less than thirty minutes. You have responsibilities as well. We should table this, reorient our thoughts, and talk tonight."

"Tonight I want you to go see my parents and ask my mother to be your labor coach."

"Why?" She scurried off the bed, set her mug aside, and searched in the closet for pants and a blouse. "We have time to work on this before our baby comes."

"With no guarantee I'll be able to do it. No. *No*, Laurie, you need someone dependable."

"We can get counseling."

"I can't talk to a stranger about this."

"Then at least let me tell your parents. We need their support."

He turned away. "Fine. Tell them."

She closed her eyes. She wanted to scream at him.

Then she remembered the look on his face after he woke on the floor the first morning in this house. The day they painted their bedroom. Easter Sunday in his office before the church service. At her first visit to the doctor. The night he felt their baby move inside her. How sad! That such a beautiful thing could bring him that kind of pain.

She opened her eyes to see he'd gone, then sat on the bed and braced her forehead with the heel of her hand. She wanted to be understanding. To support him. To give him the benefit of the doubt.

And right then, there simply weren't enough minutes to deal with it all.

She showered and dressed, then drove to the youth building, dialing her in-laws.

***

You're broken.

You're unfit to be a pastor.

The words punched Pierce with each step through the woods toward his office.

Unfit to lead others. You know your recent sermons have been pitiful. You can't help anyone.

Pictures of his mother's death, her grave, the ride in the truck to the bus stop—like still shots from a movie—pulsed through his mind.

How screwed up was he?

He exited the woods and neared the cemetery. Why hadn't he known? *How* could he not have known?

A little reaction to air brakes had been explained away—loud noises sometimes bothered him. His aversion to eggs—a simple dislike of taste. Being unable to participate in his wife's pregnancy, a baby they'd waited for, tried for since the beginning of their marriage? What other buried memories waited to be remembered?

He entered through the back, went straight to his office, and shut the door.

Liar.

But he couldn't tell a truth he hadn't known. And he hadn't known until yesterday.

Yesterday? Had it only been yesterday evening that he remembered?

Pierce sank into his chair. Lay his head in his hands on the desk.

He was a pastor. A believer. He knew what to tell himself—about God, and forgiveness, and fear, and how Jesus bore the sin and burdens of all mankind. Still, he was failing as a husband, failing in his fight against fear.

101

Yet, he knew God had opened the door to this job for him. He hadn't asked for this position, he'd been offered it.

Surely that meant something.

"Dear God, it's like there's two of me. The one that loves Laurie, the one that loves our child and has wanted our child. He's lost. Or paralyzed. Or hidden. Behind a guy who is afraid of what the next minute might reveal."

He rose and paced. "I have responsibilities here. People depend on me. Laurie *should* be able to depend on me."

An ache came around his heart, a piercing pressure like a terrible bruising. Disappointment and profound sadness.

His cell beeped, a text from Laurie. "Need you at youth building."

Set it aside.

His father's command from the bus ride made his stomach pitch, but he could do it. He could stuff his feelings, walk across the grounds, and do what needed to be done for the church body.

Pierce left his office. In this little part, he could do what Laurie needed him to do.

CHAPTER TEN

Laurie's feet throbbed. So badly she removed her shoes at the end of the day and drove barefoot through town to her in-laws.

Warm summer rain pelted the ground as Laurie parked in front of their condo. She grabbed her umbrella and sprinted for their door. Daniel greeted her at the door, wearing his new red T-shirt. He pointed at the "Help! I'm a retired preacher, and I can't shut up" logo on his chest. "You saw this, didn't you?"

She gave a reluctant laugh as he hugged her. "Yes."

"It's my license to talk to anybody, any place we go."

Kay approached from the hallway. "When have you ever needed a license?"

"Want some gum?" Daniel smacked Juicy Fruit and offered her a piece.

"No, thanks."

Kay swatted his hand. "Put that way. Don't you ever run out?"

"They sell this stuff everywhere."

"Come sit, Laurie." Kay ushered her into the kitchen and served her a glass of iced tea. "You're upset. Are you and the baby okay?"

They all sat and Kay gripped Daniel's hand.

"Yes. Physically we're fine." She paused while Kay and Daniel exchanged a look.

"Laurie, we know something is wrong. It's Pierce, isn't it? He's been avoiding Daniel and me. He always did that when he was upset."

"Yes." Laurie took a deep breath. "Something's definitely wrong." But where to start?

She wept as she told them everything—Pierce's mother's labor, his brother's birth, his father's rejection—with as many details as she could remember and ended with him saying he couldn't be with her in the delivery room.

She rested her head on Daniel's shoulder and closed her eyes. "The miscarriage made him abnormally afraid for me, but he didn't tell me. Every time he had a weird, sad mood, I thought he was grieving like anyone would. He developed an uncanny ability to turn away from everything, including me, like he had an on/off switch inside. The move brought out some memories, but my pregnancy unleashed a flood of them. I don't know what to do."

Daniel spoke first. "If you hadn't come to us, we would have tracked down both of you."

"We're always here for you," Kay added.

Laurie dried her face. "Pierce didn't want me tell you or anyone else, but he gave in because he wants me to ask you, Mom, to be my labor coach."

"Of course I will, if it comes to that."

Laurie searched their faces. "I don't know what to do. He won't talk to me. He won't even talk about the baby."

"Is this why he sometimes slept on the floor by my bed?" Kay rose, removed a pan from the oven and spooned casserole onto plates.

"I believe so."

Laurie looked at Daniel, who sat uncharacteristically silent. "Dad, what are you thinking?"

"I remember when Luther first came to me." He rubbed his chin in thought. "He found me in the church in the middle of the day, weeks before he sent Pierce to us. He had spoken with an attorney that morning, someone he knew. He said he couldn't take care of his son alone. I thought that meant Pierce's mother had already died. Although he looked hard, rough, and labor-worn, I could tell he cared about Pierce. Why else would he have tried to find a new home for him? But from what you are saying, she was still alive and pregnant with another child."

Kay set plates before them and returned to her seat. "Maybe they were too poor to care for two children, or maybe he expected her to die in childbirth. Did Pierce say anything about his mother's health? But he was only five. He wouldn't know, would he?"

"I have no idea," Laurie said.

Daniel sat back. "Luther came to see me twice. Kay, you met him when we went to the lawyer's office."

"When I saw him, I felt so sorry for him. He looked lost and defeated, I guess. Like he no longer had a reason for living." She turned to Daniel. "I can't believe Pierce never told us. But this means he has a sibling somewhere. Doesn't he want to find his brother?"

Laurie reached for her glass. "I don't know what he wants." She shook her head. "He hardly talks to me, except about the youth building renovation. He won't talk about the baby." Her voice lowered to a whisper. "Except for the night we put the crib together, we're not even sharing a bed."

Daniel rose and left the room.

"Is he angry with me for saying that?"

"No, no. Of course not." Kay shook her head. "You should eat, you know, even if it's just a little bit."

She wiped her eyes again. "I . . . don't think I can."

Daniel returned with an old manila folder and spread its contents on the table. "Here." He picked up a thick stack of stapled papers. "The adoption was between us and Luther Bridges—no mother listed. We received signed copies days after he sent Pierce to us. We had already completed our part with the lawyer. There was nothing more to it."

"I thought it odd," said Kay. "The way Pierce's father contacted us, handled all the arrangements. Then only called once—I think he used a pay phone—the morning he sent Pierce. He never gave us a number to reach him."

"What about the lawyer?" asked Laurie. "Maybe he knows something."

Daniel returned the documents to the folder. "The lawyer died years ago. Luther arranged the adoption. We simply signed and paid the fees."

Kay looked at Laurie. "He didn't seem like the kind of man who would just give a child away. I think he was heartbroken."

"If he thought his wife was going to die and he wouldn't be able to take care of his older son, a newborn, and his farm, he *would* be." Tears slipped down Laurie's face again. How many had she cried over the last several weeks? Enough for a lifetime. More than when she lost her parents.

"We never asked him about his mother." Kay walked to the sink. "We thought she had been dead for a long time, too long for Pierce to remember her. He never told us any different. No wonder, even as a teenager he didn't mind me taking him to school rather than riding the bus. Daniel, how did we miss this?"

"That's what Luther led us to believe. And he cut off all contact after he sent Pierce."

Kay ran water, then shut off the faucet and closed her eyes. "I remember that face. A dirty, tear-stained face on a stinky little boy I scooped up into my arms. He was so quiet. Probably shocked by the grief. The shock of losing his mom, watching his dad bury her in the yard . . . how could a child hold that inside? Then being swept away from all he knew to a new home, a new family?"

"He didn't know what living with an inside bathroom was like," Daniel turned in his seat. "Remember, Kay? He used to play with the light switch, turning it on and off two or three times before he went inside and closed the door. That switch is low on the wall and clicks so loudly, we thought he liked being able to reach it or was fascinated by the sound."

Kay braced her arms on the counter. "He was thankful it wasn't dark. Oh, Daniel."

"He didn't want me to tell you," Laurie said. "He doesn't want you to make him talk about it."

"But we love him," Kay argued.

"To Pierce, that's not the issue." Daniel rose and went to his wife. "It's not personal against us. He's just surviving."

"He's surviving by pulling away from me," Laurie said. "I think he's afraid I will die while having our baby. How could he believe that?" Her shoulders fell as she remembered the night she miscarried. What started out as an evening of celebration ended with Pierce's strange, mumbled prayer at her bedside. "We've waited for years for this miracle. We both wanted this, talked about it, dreamed about it, and planned for it. But maybe a hidden part of him hoped I'd never get pregnant again."

Daniel barely swallowed his mouthful before he spoke. "Did you really think that because you're married to a preacher, everything would be easier?"

"Well . . . " Yes, she supposed she had.

Daniel stuck one, then a second piece of Juicy Fruit gum into his mouth, popped and smacked. "Honey, he's a Christian, he's a minister, and he's our son. But he's not perfect. No one is. Just ask Kay."

"Daniel, be gentle." Kay sighed. "Laurie, he means well. You don't have to tell us anything you don't want to."

"Have you suggested he talk to a professional? A counselor?" Daniel asked. "I know someone. But, this has all been revealed in the last what, twenty-four, thirty-six hours? He's probably still in shock."

But she did want to tell. Not just for sympathy, for insight. "He barely speaks to me. He won't talk to you two. I suggested seeing a counselor, but he says he can't talk to a stranger."

"Maybe he's not ready yet. You can't fast track this for him," Daniel said.

"So, what am I supposed to do?" She pointed at her belly. "I'm on a deadline here."

Kay leaned forward. "And a beautiful deadline it is. Let yourself get excited, Laurie. Let yourself feel the joy of this baby, your long-awaited miracle. What Pierce does or doesn't do, doesn't change the fact you're going to be a mom."

She looked at them both. If there was ever a day she missed her parents, it was today. The way Daddy's eyes twinkled when he called her *baby girl*, and wrapped his arms around her like the sweetest blanket. The way Mama listened as if enthralled by every wish, daydream, *what if*, and heartache Laurie shared. But at least the orphan inside her had Daniel and Kay.

"I never thought I'd be married, and except for you two, facing a pregnancy alone." She rose. "I'm okay. I mean, I'll be okay. I should go home."

Daniel walked her out and watched her leave.

Give him the journal.

The thought hit when she reached the highway. Adrenaline surged through her as she passed the red water tower, Benson's, and the Downtown Diner. She caught herself pressing the accelerator, looked down, and hit the brakes. Sixty-five in a thirty-five mile an hour zone—she'd never speeded like this in her life!

She adjusted her speed, rolled down her window, and re-settled her hands on the steering wheel. Hot wind slapped her face, snapping her hair, and pushing its way into lungs that had cramped this morning when talking with Pierce about renovations at the youth building. Would he ever again look at her the way he used to?

Give him the journal.

Usually she avoided confrontation. She didn't like conflict. Compassion had been strengthened by her grief from losing her parents. Having experienced pain herself, she recognized it in others.

But sometimes pain was a good thing. Her sickness, nausea, and vomiting confirmed someone wonderful grew inside of her.

Labor would be the same way. There would be pain, but there would also be a pay-off. Enjoying the second required embracing, or at least enduring, the first.

Oh, yes, she thought, pulling in front of their home. If she wanted her marriage to change for the better, she had to act. With wisdom, with love, with God's leading, but she had to act.

After all, of the two people in this marriage, *she* was one of them. *Dear God, please help me.*

***

He'd thought his parents would call. And Pierce couldn't decide if he was happy or unsettled that they hadn't. What did they think of him now?

You're damaged.

Would they have adopted him if they'd known how damaged he was? Would Laurie have married him?

He wouldn't have asked her if he'd known. He wouldn't have married at all.

She was sitting outside in her car, the headlights shining straight into the dining room where he sat having just finished eating a sandwich. He wanted to go to her, but felt he had nothing to offer.

The headlights went out. She turned off the engine and came inside, passing by the doorway without looking in his direction. He didn't blame her.

Moments later she approached, placed a notebook and an opened envelope on the table between them.

"Laurie, we need to talk."

She sat. "Yes, we do."

"Did you tell my parents?"

She opened her mouth to answer, closed it, and simply nodded.

"Thanks for doing that. I didn't know what to say."

"The truth is always a good place to start." She took a breath, set her chin. "I told them exactly what you told me. And they listened because they love you and care about you. Shutting out people who love you damages you and them.

"See this?" She pulled a card from the envelope and slid it to him. "It's from Ina Hood."

The "Congratulations! You're expecting!" card showed a smiling pregnant woman in profile.

"There's a check in there for $1000. You know Ina. It's not enough to her to send the crib. She wants us to start a savings account for our child."

He held his breath for a moment, exhaled, focused. He reached for her hand and saw the thrill in her eyes when he did.

"Laurie. Look. This is new territory for both of us. And again, I'm sorry I can't give you . . ."

You're broken. You're damaged.

Confusion etched her face as she crossed her arms on the table. "I . . . accept your apology?"

He ran a hand across his forehead where sweat beaded like dew. "I grew up watching my father be a minister. I learned some scripture in college, but mostly I learned theology and the logistics end of being a pastor. I had one pastoral counseling class. One. Nothing I learned touched on anything like this."

You hurt like no one else. You can't be what she needs.

"So now you understand why I can't be with you during the birth, right? Why I can't talk about or get excited about the baby?"

She cocked her head. "What?"

"I've always loved how deep your feelings are. Your tender heart, so sensitive to others."

She answered with a narrowed gaze.

He wanted to get up. To move, to pace. But something held him in the chair.

"If someone came to you and told you the same story—my story—you would understand immediately why they couldn't handle certain things, couldn't do certain things."

"Let me get this straight. You think that because I'm tender-hearted and have soft feelings, I'll understand how upset and uncomfortable *you* are about *me* having *our* baby."

He opened his mouth to answer, but she held up a hand. He closed his mouth.

"And since I understand, I'll accept the fact that you can't be there for me, *won't* be there, actually. We won't talk about our child, and we won't enjoy this pregnancy together." She shoved her chair back, rising as her voice did. "Am I supposed to tell you when I go into labor, Pierce? Do you even want me to bring the baby home?"

A flood swept down her face. Her breath heaved. Her body shook.

"You know what?" She raised a hand again. "Don't answer."

He knew better than to try. And he was glad he hadn't stood. "I'm not going to fight with you, Laurie."

"Fight with me? *Fight* with me?" She almost stepped away, then turned back, slapped her hands on the table in front of him and braced herself on the surface. "I want you to fight *for* me. *For us.*"

"This is what's best for us. You can be happy about the baby. Go shopping with Mom. Have her be your labor coach. Do whatever you need to do."

"Do you even hear yourself? You won't talk to me. Won't go to sleep with me. You've barely touched me in weeks."

"Laurie, I'm sorry. I know my limits. I *can't* do this."

She sank like a deflated balloon back into her chair, reached for a napkin and dried her eyes. "I knew something was wrong. Every time I asked, you brushed over it and denied it. And I let you! Because it was easier. So, I'm sorry, too."

"I didn't *know* what was wrong."

"But you knew *something* was wrong." She took his hand in both of hers, stroked her thumbs over it and lowered her voice. "I'm not mad at you for not telling me before now. You didn't remember before now, is that right?"

"That's right."

"But we need to handle this together. Remember that 'two become one'?" She paused. "I miss you. I miss us. Don't you miss me?"

Yes, he missed her. He hadn't felt this unattached since his mother died.

He looked at her sweet, round face. In her red-rimmed eyes he saw the woman he'd fallen in love with, married, and vowed to cherish "'til death do us part."

She'll die. You'll be there to see her die.

And having his baby could kill her.

He shuddered as cold, black dread clenched his heart. What would he do if she died?

No. He could not deal with her pregnancy. If he stayed busy enough, the next few months would fly by, she'd deliver, and the acid eating up his insides would subside.

She searched his face. "I love you so deeply, so much. I never thought I could love anyone as much as I love you. You're my best friend, yet I feel by refusing to get help, you're willingly killing my dreams right in front of me. Pierce, please. I want to look into your eyes when I have this baby. I want to share this with *you*."

He slid his hand free.

"I know you're going to say no. You're pulling away from me. You've done it before, and you're doing it again."

"I don't even know who I am anymore! Don't you get it? I'm not who I thought I was. And I won't lie to you. I won't make a promise I don't know I can keep. My father promised my mother he'd keep me.

He broke his word and it destroyed me."

"You need to know what your pulling away has done to us, to me." Her voice was a gravelly whisper as she slid the notebook to him. "It's all in here."

Pierce stared at his plate.

She'd be better off without you. You're too messed up to be a pastor.

The notebook, with its glossy red cover, lay before him like a still pool of blood.

The chime clock struck midnight. A second later his cell rang—Gilbert. The only person whose call he'd answer right now.

"Pierce! Oh, buddy. The EMT's think Dad had a heart attack. I know this is the third time in just a few months, but man, I think this is real. Can you come?"

"Sure." He hung up. "Gilbert called an ambulance for Angus. I need to go."

"*We* need to go. I'll call your parents. They'll probably beat us there."

Chapter Eleven

L aurie wondered if Pierce realized he was driving her to the place where she would deliver their child.

After arriving at the hospital, they went upstairs while Angus underwent an immediate procedure—his cardiologist happened to be on duty. They found Gilbert, Daniel, and Kay in the large waiting area on the second floor, a space shared with the labor and delivery unit. Nervous families paced anxiously or huddled together counting minutes beside expectant fathers and excited grandparents.

Laurie shook her head. She could almost picture the evil one himself prying at her fingers, diligently working to loosen her grip on God and peace and her dreams of having a family with Pierce.

She didn't want to let go of God or Pierce, but if Pierce continued in the opposite direction, how could she possibly hold onto both?

Gilbert, who sat alone in a corner, gave her half a smile and reached to shake Pierce's hand. "Thanks for coming."

Laurie watched as Pierce hugged his friend.

"Anytime."

She turned away from the tenderness, from the compassion her husband showed Gilbert. But no matter how she tried to control it, jealousy, sharp and strong, seared her heart when Pierce bowed his head right there and prayed aloud with Gilbert.

Gilbert was only a friend. She was his wife.

And, at this very minute, she was pregnant with his baby. But he hadn't prayed with her in weeks. As far as she knew, he hadn't prayed for their child since the day she told him about the pregnancy.

"I'm going to the restroom," she turned around and mumbled to Kay.

"He doesn't realize what he's doing to her," she heard Kay whisper to Daniel.

"Maybe he doesn't want to," Daniel answered.

Laurie darted down the hall with Kay following. She eased the restroom door open, bee-lined for the closer of the two stalls and locked herself in. She couldn't squelch the sobs.

Kay gently knocked on the metal door. "Laurie."

"Mom, I don't know what to do." Laurie talked through the door and blew her nose. "It's like we take one step toward each other and six steps back. Eventually, we won't be in the same country."

Laurie opened the door, unfolded and refolded the soggy tissues in her hand. "We just had the worst—and I mean *the* worst conversation."

She lifted her eyes to Kay. "He's hardly touched me since the day we found out I'm pregnant. And he won't let me touch him. I cook his food, wash his laundry, and I'm carrying his child. But we're living as roommates. I might as well be a piece of furniture."

Kay pushed herself away from the wall and wrapped both arms around Laurie. "Lord, the woman in me wants to slap him. The mother in me wants to defend him. The part of me that trusts You knows You're at work. Please speak to Pierce."

Laurie threw away her tissues and walked to the sink. "How do you know God's hand is in this, Mom? I've been a Christian almost all my life. I'm a pastor's wife, and I'm struggling to see how any good can come from our situation."

"It's like Pierce has been walking on a broken leg that healed wrong," Kay said. "And God wants him to be fit enough, healthy enough to dance with you. You are the daughter I never had. And that precious baby you're carrying is my grandchild. I'm praying for you, and I'm praying for Pierce."

Laurie's bulging belly touched the edge of the counter. She quickly turned back to Kay.

"Here, Mom." Laurie took her hand, gently pressed. "Feel it?"

A soft push. New, precious life.

Kay's eyes watered.

"I think he's stretching," Laurie said, "or she. There's a lot of movement this time of night." Tears spilled out of her eyes again. "Weeks ago. We were going to bed. I thought . . ." She glanced in the mirror and saw her own blush. "I thought we would be together, love each other. I kissed him and he kissed me back. I wanted him to love me so much. Then his stomach pressed against mine. The baby kicked, and Pierce jumped away like I had the plague.

"He left me, Mom. He left me and took his pillow to the couch. I was so humiliated, I was nauseated. And that was before he remembered exactly how his mother died. Now he just climbs in bed after he thinks I'm asleep."

Kay took Laurie by the shoulders. "And he won't talk to you."

"Hardly. It's like he tries and then something stops him from opening up to me. He expects me to read between the lines of his feelings—which he won't talk about either—and just accept that he can't be there for me when our baby's born. I know he's afraid. But if he would just talk to me, we could face this together, couldn't we? I'm so disappointed, Mom. I'm angry and hurt. I always thought this would be such a happy time for us, for me." Laurie shook her head. "I want things from him, Mom. And this is the only time some of it will mean anything."

"Because you're pregnant."

"Yes. What if this is the only baby we ever have? My heart's getting hard. I can feel it. Tell me what to do."

"Be diligent to study scripture, Laurie. Dig in and follow it. You won't get through this without staying close to God."

"You're right. I know you're right."

"The next part might be one of the toughest things you'll ever do," Kay said. "Offer Pierce every possible chance to be part of your life and pregnancy. Don't withdraw from him, even in reflex, the way he withdraws from you."

Laurie stiffened. Why should she keep trying to reach out to him, including him when he obviously wanted to avoid her pregnancy?

"I know what you're thinking," Kay continued. "That you have every right to protect yourself by putting distance—emotional, even spiritual distance—between the two of you. I'm begging you not to do it. Not for him, but for you. I'm sure you won't get any closer to the solution you want, the marriage you want, that way."

Laurie blurted her response. She had thought it so often, it stayed on the tip of her tongue. "But he won't let me help him. Every time I try, it's like he slaps my hand away. That gets old after a while." Her heart had been wounded in the same places over and over again.

"That kind of treatment does get old. I've left a couple of messages on his phone and had no calls returned." Kay wrapped an arm around her. "But here's two things I've learned. First, God's the only one who can change Pierce, or anyone else for that matter. Not you, not us, not even our love for him. Second, you're not responsible for how Pierce reacts to what you do, you're responsible for what you do. If you maintain the distance and feed the dissension between the two of you, you're sure to get more of the same.

"But if you show him you love him anyway—and that does not mean you can't tell him when he hurts you—you have a chance of growing together instead of growing apart. Then you have nothing to apologize for, no mess to clean up on your side."

Laurie shook her head. "I wasn't perfect either. I knew something was wrong, and for too long I refused to confront it. I guess I just didn't want to lose him."

"Laurie." Kay spoke with a tenderness Laurie imagined her own mother would extend. "Now that you've seen something you shouldn't have been doing, you're repentant and you're trying to change it, right?"

"Yes."

"Oh, sweetie, Pierce deserves the same opportunity. God's giving you the chance to change, and He's not pulling away from you. Treat Pierce the same. Pierce just needs more internal renovating than you do right now."

"Renovating. I understand. But I'm tired, Mom. I'm really tired."

***

After his wife left and his mother followed her down the hall, Pierce counted the minutes.

Gilbert knew nothing about Pierce's predicament, and his concern for Angus further distracted him. More than once, a doctor wearing mint-green scrubs came out of the maternity unit to talk with another group in the waiting room, family members and friends obviously hoping for news about a new mother and a newborn baby. Pierce heard whispers, *this is taking too long*, and speculation, *maybe she'll need a C-section*. He tried to ignore the mounting tension in the room. He couldn't imagine a worse place to be.

Gilbert stood, ran his hands down his thighs. "I'm going to get some coffee. Daniel?"

"No, thanks. I'll wait here with Pierce."

"Me neither," said Pierce, and Gilbert left.

"If you want a weekend off, I can preach some Sunday soon," Dad said. "Maybe you and Laurie could go somewhere together."

"Look, Dad. I know you're trying to help. But no. Thanks anyway."

Dad put a hand on Pierce's shoulder. "Son. God can heal you. At some point you will need to talk about your mother and father."

Pierce's eyes darted around. Was anyone watching? Did anyone hear?

He gave a slight shrug away from his dad's hand. "Leave it alone, Dad."

You're broken. You've no business in ministry.

"Excuse me, Pastor Crane?" A thick, athletic-looking teen nervously cleared his throat and approached. "I'm sorry. You are Pastor Crane, right? The Barn Church?"

"Yes," Pierce answered.

"I, um, I went there with my mom. On Easter." He pulled his hands out of his pockets, shook Dad's hand, and stood before Pierce like a defendant on trial. "I prayed. You prayed. With me. I'm Luke."

What else could Pierce do? He patted the seat next to his. "How can I help you, Luke?"

"You see, sir . . . it's like this. My girlfriend's having a baby. My baby. And I'm scared, you know what I mean?"

Yes, he did know.

"She's getting an epidural now. I know we shouldn't have, you know, been together without being married. But I'm going to marry her."

Pierce knew, he *knew* what Luke was going to ask. It's what everyone asked of a pastor, what would always be expected of Pierce. But this must be his last. No way could he ever make himself do this again.

Poetic justice, he supposed—praying for a young couple and their unborn baby would mark the end of his career.

Someone behind Luke called his name. He answered over his shoulder. "I'll be right there. Please, Pastor Crane, will you come pray for Isabella and the baby?"

To Pierce's surprise, his dad stood. "We'll both go."

They found a beautiful young girl with tousled, long, dark hair lying on her side in the hospital bed. Luke rushed over to her. "What happened?"

"I'm fine," she said, a tired smile on her face. "The epidural worked. Who are they?"

Embarrassed, Luke stepped back, and introduced Pierce and his father. "I thought they could pray with us. For the baby."

She motioned Luke closer. "Do they know we're not married?"

"Yeah, but it's okay. On Easter Sunday I heard the pastor say that God will start working with you right where you are. Right now, you're in labor, so we start here."

"Maybe he'll marry us, after," she said.

Daniel nudged Pierce forward.

A machine at the bedside beeped, beeped, while emitting a rhythmic whirring sound. Perched on top, a video screen showed a pulsating picture of a tiny heart.

The room grew smaller, smaller.

The sounds grew louder, louder.

Birth was about to happen here.

Pierce cleared his throat, then prayed aloud hoping Isabella wouldn't have a contraction before he finished. His dad offered a second *Amen*.

Dr. Nate entered, walked quickly to the young mother-to-be's side. "Feel better?"

Isabella shifted to her back, reached for Luke's hand. "Much."

"Hi, Pastor." Dr. Nate smiled as he grabbed a pair of gloves from a box on a shelf by the bed. "Didn't know you knew Isabella and Luke."

A nurse swung the door open. "Dr. Nate, we need you in the next room, please."

"I'm coming." He followed her out. "Be right back," he said over his shoulder.

Daniel patted Isabella's arm. "Luke, let us know what happens. Just call the church number and leave a message."

"Yes, sir. I will."

Pierce all but ran back to the waiting area. He looked at Gilbert, who sat flipping through a sports magazine. "Where's Laurie?"

"She took Kay home. She said Daniel could give you a ride later."

"I'll be back in a minute." He walked away as if he had a purpose, as if he had somewhere important to go. He rounded the corner, and took advantage of the privacy to sag against the wall.

No, he could never, ever do that again.

You shouldn't be in ministry.

And Laurie. He'd failed her—he knew it to his core. He had and would continue to fail her, because he'd never be strong enough to be there when she had their child.

Pierce closed his eyes. He was no better than his father.

***

"Laurie. Your hands are shaking. Do you want me to drive?"

Laurie watched her speed the last mile to Kay's home. "No. I'm . . . I need to hold onto something."

"I understand. Just, just know that I'm here if you need me."

But for how long? People who loved you, despite their best intentions, didn't always get to pick to stay forever, even if you needed them. Laurie knew that firsthand, from losing her parents. Neither of them would have chosen to leave her alone the way they had.

Inside her, a sickening, dark certainty grew that Pierce would leave her, too. That he would leave by choice. Before these last few weeks she'd never have expected it.

Laurie parked in front of Kay's door, Kay reached out and rested a hand on Laurie's tightening fingers. "I'm sure you really miss your parents right now. I can't replace your mom, but I do pray for you like I think she would if she were here."

Laurie nodded briskly, the knot in her throat blocked any verbal response.

Kay patted her hand. "You don't have to answer. Be safe driving home."

Rural Alabama didn't exactly boast an abundance of streetlights in its farming communities. The dark roads home demanded she use her high beams. The temptation to drive, just keep driving somewhere, anywhere, simmered and boiled like hot lava through her stomach. She hadn't vomited in days, but her frayed nerves might end that streak.

She parked in front of her home. The sweet frame house stood dark and empty as a tomb. Would it mark the spot where her marriage died?

The baby kicked. "Oh, God." She folded her arms across her middle as grief shook her body. "I love Pierce. And I love this baby. How can having one cost me the other?"

She waited. Listened. A single pair of headlights approached behind her, then passed.

Pierce hadn't followed her. Did he even know, even care, that she'd left?

***

Pierce stared out the passenger window as Daniel drove him home.

"I can preach in your place this weekend if it'll help you."

"Yeah," Pierce said. "You should do that."

"As long as you want me to. Son, you've isolated yourself and you're depressed. You're just now remembering a past no child should face."

And realizing how very flawed and damaged he was. Pierce pressed his palms to his temples. "I'm sorry, Dad. I wish this didn't hurt you . . . or Laurie."

"Hurt me?" Daniel patted Pierce's shoulder. "My concern is for you and Laurie and the baby you made together."

"I can't be who I promised Laurie I'd be. I can't do what we dreamed about together."

"Casting your cares on God means handing them over. That requires looking at them, touching them. Which isn't fun or easy. Don't let your past dictate what you will and won't do. God's brought your memories to the surface to heal you. Now it's up to you to walk through the process."

They reached Pierce's home. He got out of the car, then spoke through the open door. "I know you're trying to help, Dad. Maybe I'm not really cut out for being a pastor." He held up a hand. "No, don't say anything else, just take care of the church this weekend."

Pierce went inside to the living room and sat on the floor in the dark.

***

Her hair mussed, her face puffy from exhaustion, Laurie found Pierce the next morning standing in their living room and staring out the window. Looking at what, she didn't know, and couldn't imagine. She had absolutely no idea what was going through his mind. She might never know.

Sorrow, dry and gritty as the desert, scraped against her heart and made her wince. She could do nothing more to persuade him to open up to her.

Whatever is true.

But she had nothing more to give him.

Think about such things.

He was leaving her right then, in every way that counted. In his heart and mind he was walking away.

She leaned against the doorway and forced raspy words through her tear-roughened throat. "If you don't love me anymore, don't want me anymore, I wish you'd just tell me."

Still he didn't face her. "I think I should resign my position as pastor."

Tears she didn't think she had sprung into her eyes. So . . . what? They'd move again? Or had he considered her at all?

If not, where would she go? What about the baby?

She squeezed her eyes tight. Drew a shuddery breath. "Will you look at me?" Fury, fresh and full, spun through her like a tornado and she clenched her fists at her sides. "You at least owe me *that*."

"Go ahead," he said. "Fire away."

He turned, and the desolate look on his face broke Laurie's heart again.

"I have another OB appointment this week." She walked to him. "I don't know if you care, but I'm still doing everything I should for our unborn child."

"I don't know what else is inside me, Laurie."

She stopped, drew another shaky breath. Fat tears dripped down her face. "The pain that's been hidden inside you, it's immense, I know. But how, *how* could you pray with another woman in labor, when you won't even talk to me about our baby?" Her heartbeat pounded in her throat. "We dreamed together of having a child. What happened to our dream?"

Sorrow sliced her heart repeatedly, leaving long, fresh gashes. Pierce didn't know it, but the blood of their marriage was all over his hands.

The phone rang, but neither of them moved to answer. She tried to stand there, watching him, waiting, hoping he'd reach for her. But nausea rose high and rolled strong, forcing her to flee to the bathroom.

***

He followed her. What else could he do?

She'll never forgive you.

He sat on the edge of the tub while she heaved into the commode, then handed her a wet cloth when she simply sat on the hard

125

wooden floor, her forearms folded over the toilet seat and bracing her head. When her stomach had emptied, she simply curled up on the floor.

The phone rang again. Neither of them moved to answer.

"I'm sorry, Laurie. I'm so sorry." He slid to the floor beside her and sat in his own shame. He had the strangest feeling of hanging in mid-air, as if suspended in a weird limbo-land, dangling between worlds and realities.

"Sorry doesn't help me. Leave me alone, Pierce." She stood, and turning her back to him, reached into the shower and turned on the faucets.

He left her there, closing the door behind him as the phone rang yet again. He hurried to the kitchen and snatched it up. "Hello."

"Pierce. So glad I caught you at home. It's Isaac Hammond in Orlando."

"Pastor Hammond."

"I've only got a moment here, Pierce. But I wanted to get in touch with you as soon as possible. Ina Hood died yesterday. She left specific instructions for you to be contacted at her death. She wanted you to handle part of the service. Airfare, rental car, everything's paid. You can stay at your old apartment over her garage; I have a key for you. I know she was important to you and Laurie, and I know Laurie's pregnant, but can you come? Today?"

"Sure."

He stayed in the kitchen debating how to tell Laurie about Ina's death and funeral. The water pipes were still humming, so he called his parents and asked them to stay with Laurie while he was gone, then quickly packed and slid a note under the bathroom door.

A cowardly action, probably selfish, and would confirm to her that he was only slightly higher than slime. On an impulse, he shoved the notebook she had given him into his suitcase, then zipped it closed.

***

Laurie turned off the shower. A second later, the house shuddered, the unmistakable ripple of the front door opening and closing.

She stood in the tub in silence, knowing the house was empty, knowing she was alone except for the child she carried. Had Pierce gone to his woods to pray?

A chill forced her from the damp enclosure. In the steam, she donned a robe and sat on the lowered commode lid and tried to calm her pitching stomach. She slowly dried her hair and gingerly brushed her teeth to remove the bitter taste of vomit.

The doorbell rang. As she opened the bathroom door, a piece of paper flitted across the floor; she grabbed it, and headed for the front of the house. Her in-laws stood on her front porch.

She opened the door. "Mom, Dad, what's going on?"

Daniel hugged her, released her.

Kay hugged her, and held on. "Good. You found the note. No arguments, we're staying with you. No matter how long this takes."

"What?"

Her eyes scanned the paper in her hand.

Ina Hood died . . . funeral . . . called my parents . . . flying to Flor-ida . . .

But the last two lines most caught her attention.

I don't know what the future holds for me. I don't think I can be what you want and need.

Pierce had indeed left her.

CHAPTER TWELVE

Pierce was thirty-five thousand feet above the earth, and he had never been lower in his life.

The short flight took a quick curve over the Gulf of Mexico and down the Florida peninsula to Orlando. He drove the rental car to Pastor Hammond's home and arrived as the entire family—all eight of them—shared their evening meal.

He had known Isaac and Ella Hammond since beginning his pastoral internship at their church. Back then there hadn't been quite so many of them in this mid-sized home. Over the years their brood had grown, yet the couple had obviously kept their relationship strong, their love fresh. On more than one occasion he wondered how they accomplished it.

"Pierce, how good to see you!" Ella hugged him tight as Isaac approached from his other side.

"Ella, you look great. Isaac."

"I've got the key to the apartment at Ina's. But you're welcome to stay with us and visit for a while."

"Sure," he said, though he didn't know why.

Ella tugged on his arm. "Come on. I'll fix you a plate."

He didn't feel hungry, but he hadn't eaten since yesterday. He followed her to the kitchen and picked at the plate she sat before him. After the meal, one by one the children left the kitchen.

"How do you do it? Keep up with them all?"

Ella smiled. "They're ours."

Isaac reached for his wife's hand. "You'll be getting a crash course soon enough. That first one changes your world, your focus." He raised his wife's hand to his lips, gently kissed it. "Until you become a parent, you really don't know what love is."

"I'm not sure it'll be that way for me."

Ella raised an eyebrow at Isaac, then rose. "Coffee, Pierce? Dessert?"

"No, thanks."

"Honey?"

"Did the kids eat all the ice cream?"

She opened the freezer. "Looks like we'll get the last of it." She set three bowls on the table and seated herself across from Pierce again as Isaac turned to him.

"Want to talk about it?"

Where to begin? Maybe the end. "I'm not sure I'm cut out to be a pastor."

"You've prayed about this?"

Pierce didn't respond.

Ella shifted in her chair. "Why?"

"I just learned something about myself, and I don't know what to do about it."

"What does Laurie say?" Ella prodded.

Isaac gave her a look that said, *Easy, honey, easy.*

Ella smiled sweetly. "Well?"

"Look. I know you both mean well, but a Band-Aid won't fix this. She's thinking I'm a jerk and a coward." He pretty much agreed with her. "My congregation deserves a better pastor. Laurie definitely deserves a better husband."

"What if I told you that no problem you have is too big for God? You'd laugh, right? It's what I'm supposed to say. You've told others; you've preached it. You've prayed with people who were devastated, encouraged them, told them God would work everything out."

Isaac leaned back in his chair, polished his spoon with a napkin, and continued. "One of the biggest problems of being a minister, a Christian for that matter, is if you've been one long enough, you know all the answers." He set his spoon beside his now empty bowl and leaned forward as if sharing a secret. "Or you think you do, until something comes along that flattens you, leaves you lying in the dust with a big, fat footprint on your head. Until then, all you've done is repeat what you've studied. Only after facing your own battles can you truly empathize with others and minister from the heart instead of from some book or sermon you memorized."

Pierce pushed his bowl away. "Are you telling me God's allowing this, this, *trial*, so He can use it to help me minister to others? That's a crock and you know it."

Isaac's eyes narrowed. "No. I'm telling you that life is hard. Stuff happens. Trouble is always present, and God is always there. He always *has* enough, always *is* enough to help you overcome anything, so the hard stuff doesn't control your life."

Pierce stood, then paced, shaking an index finger at Isaac. "See? *See?* That's where you're wrong." He didn't want to be rude to his friend, but . . . "He *doesn't* always help."

"What help did you ask for that you didn't get?"

"It doesn't matter now."

"Did you know that Ella is my second wife?"

Pierce stopped and grasped the back of his chair.

"Get your attention? At twenty-one, I married a beautiful, petite blonde named Paige. We were so in love, or so I thought. Her dad owned a mortgage company and was training me as a loan officer. I thought we had it made. She got pregnant. Long story short, I was thrilled but she wasn't. Turns out, she didn't want to be a wife or a mother, or even alive for that matter. Instead of having the baby and letting me keep the child, she killed herself, taking my baby with her."

Pierce watched Ella take Isaac's hand, and remembered all the times Laurie had taken his, in love, in support, in comfort, or play. How much he would lose if he lost her.

"How did you get over it?"

"I don't think you ever get completely over something like that. But it's God's love through Ella and my children—not amnesia or forgetting what happened—that helps heal me every day. Whatever you and Laurie are going through right now, you need to know that she is not the enemy. Sometimes God heals you through a person, and the life the two of you live together day in and day out."

Ella got up and stood beside Pierce, wrapped an arm around his shoulders. "Pierce, why don't you tell us what this is all about? I tell my children that if I don't know what's wrong, I can't help fix it. But if you tell me, I might be old enough, smart enough, to know something that will help."

The refrigerator hummed. The clock on the wall ticked.

Something cracked inside him. Suddenly he wanted to tell them. Isaac had been his first mentor, Ella had always looked after him and Laurie. And they had nothing to do with Alabama or his childhood.

"After Laurie's miscarriage here in Florida, a nightmare I've had all my life became more frequent. The same dream, when my birth father sent me away to live with the Cranes. After we moved, I've had more dreams, which are really bits of memories."

He grabbed Ella's hand on his shoulder. "Then we learned Laurie was pregnant. I couldn't figure out why I was so afraid. At first, I thought it was because of the miscarriage. But then, what, two days ago? I remembered my mother's death."

The words came like an avalanche. He'd not watched Laurie's expression when he told her his story. He couldn't. It was too horrifying and he could barely get the words out as he described the sounds, the sights, the smells.

This was harder, telling it now to these friends. Seeing their faces, hearing Ella's breath catch, watching Isaac shake his head in compassion as he ended with his ride on the bus.

Pierce crumbled, curling up in his seat.

Here was pain he had never imagined. Slicing, searing pain that scorched his lungs and blacked out the edges of his vision. If sorrow could kill, surely he had just taken his last breath.

"After going to live with the Cranes, I was thankful everyday for my new home, my new parents," Pierce whispered. He took a deep breath and hung his head. "I was happy—Laurie and I were happy—before the memories surfaced. Now I'm not sure I know who I am. Or who God is. I don't like the questions I have when I think about Him. And I'm paralyzed thinking of Laurie having my child. What kind of Christian and husband and pastor does that make me?"

"Quit thinking about Him and keep talking to Him," Ella encouraged.

"The kind of trauma you faced can leave deep wounds," Isaac said. "You can refuse to deal with the memories, and you'll feel the same as you do now. Day after day. But if you want to hold on to Laurie and your love, if you want to hold on to God, you have to do it with both hands. Which means you have to let go of something else."

Pierce looked up at his friends. "My head's messed up, Isaac. I'm completely broken. I've wounded Laurie and I've been really stupid."

"Mostly, you've been hurting," Isaac said. "I'm curious. What did you preach about on Easter Sunday?"

"Change. How change is needed for breakthrough."

"I'm guessing you used the passages about the Crucifixion. You should read them again, Pierce. Did you forget that our Lord was broken first?"

***

Our Lord was broken first. Our Lord, was broken first.

Pierce's heart beat hard in his chest as he drove through dark, dormant Orlando streets to the apartment over Ina's garage. He entered, flicked on the light, and remembered bringing Laurie to live here right after the miscarriage.

He sank to the floor, right there inside the door. His whole body ached as if he'd been beaten.

He'd been so scared when he knew his father was taking him away. So scared of what lay ahead.

But even worse was the rejection. The one person other than his mother he thought he could depend on, had betrayed him.

He grabbed his computer from his suitcase, accessed the Book of Matthew and read as Isaac had advised.

Afraid. Rejected. Betrayed. He'd missed it. He'd totally missed it.

He'd seen the change, seen the benefits of Christ's work, but he'd overlooked the brokenness that preceded it.

You asked me for change.

He will bring to light what is hidden in darkness.

Now Pierce understood. The scripture wasn't a threat, it held a promise. Everything that hid in darkness—even the darkness inside himself—would most assuredly be brought into the light.

Yes, he was broken. He'd always been broken. He'd simply been ignorant of that brokenness.

But being broken was the prerequisite to being changed.

He'd been ashamed of his brokenness. Ashamed of his pain. As if mistreatment by others somehow devalued him and made him less.

The shame became his prison. Keeping him in, and keeping others like Laurie out.

The fear, a whip. *Fear is about punishment. Fear brings torment.*

And he'd buckled. He'd buckled and cowered in the corner as if the remembering was an evil thing. He'd swallowed the lie that, since remembering caused pain, it must be bad.

He set aside his computer and lay face down on the cool ceramic tile.

"I repent." The words bubbled from his heart like acid and scorched his throat. "Dear God, I repent. I should have known better. I know scripture, I *knew* this. But just like Isaac said, it wasn't real yet inside me."

He'd tried to figure out what was happening on his own, through research and reason. He'd tried to control his emotions with determination and willpower.

"I let fear punish me. I let it torment me. I let it slant the way I looked at my life, my marriage, and my ministry.

"I want this change. I want it. However you'll give it to me."

The weight was lifting.

More relief. Pierce wanted more.

"I give you everything, God. My past. Stuff I haven't remembered yet. All the hurt I don't even know is there. "

And a clean, refreshing presence filled the room.

"Take my fear. Fear I don't even know I have."

He raised to his knees. Lifted his hands.

His heart cramped and tears flowed. Lips trembling, he whispered. "Have thine own way, Lord, have thine own way. Thou art the potter, I am the clay . . ."

***

Pierce woke on the floor. But this time was different. He'd sung himself to sleep inside the apartment doorway. He had a kink in his neck, but his spirit was lighter than it had been in months.

He sat up. Checked the time. Three-thirty a.m. was not the time to call Laurie.

Who would have thought that now, after almost eight years of marriage, he'd be trying to win her back.

He stood. Love for his precious wife burst through him. He refused to give up and let her go. The desire to love her, to make her smile surged through his system, as if shocking his heart back to life.

But having left the way he did, how could he reach her? How could he begin to understand all the damage he'd caused?

The journal.

He dug the notebook out of his suitcase, stretched out on the

135

couch, and opened to the first page.

***

Dear Pierce,

I've been praying about what you told me, trying to figure things out. I don't think it's the memories that cause you problems; it's how they make you feel and how you think because of them.

You can't see beauty in my delivering our child, so you won't participate in the pregnancy with me. You pushed me away and pulled away from me at a time when we should be rejoicing over a miracle. I know you're in agony. I don't pretend to know the depth of it, but if you won't talk to me, how is there any future for us? Please talk to me.

***

Hi, honey.

It's early afternoon and a sunny rain shower has just stopped. It made me think of the day we met. Do you remember?

I was running to my dorm when a quick rain burst from the sky. You pulled me and my roommate Shawnie under the overhang outside the cafeteria. There was barely enough room for two, so you stood at the edge while a stream of water from a leaky gutter filled your backpack and ran down the back of your pants into your sneakers. I can still hear the squish-squish sound as you walked me to my room under a beautiful rainbow. Your books were ruined. Are we ruined now, too?

***

Dear God, I'm feeling the baby move regularly now.

Pierce has only felt it once. When he did, he jumped away from me, repulsed and horrified. How could that look on his face come from feeling our baby? Every time I think I don't have any tears left, more come. I love our baby. And I love Pierce.

How can a miracle cost me my marriage?

***

Pierce read page after page, over and over, until he thought his eyes might bleed. Memorizing parts and pieces, tucking them inside his own breaking heart and re-learning Laurie's. Her tender, soft, compassionate heart, which he had fallen in love with long ago and depended on over the years. Knowing he had crushed that precious heart left him horribly ashamed.

"Dear God, I've been so messed up. And I've messed up so many things, I probably don't see them all."

He will bring to light what is hidden in darkness. Then you will know the truth, and the truth will set you free.

"Father, wash my mind where these memories live, and my heart where my love for Laurie lives. Make my love for her strong enough. Help me depend on Your Spirit enough to do whatever You ask to fix my marriage and to heal."

He set his alarm to call Laurie later that morning and fell asleep clutching her journal to his chest.

***

Laurie poured herself a cup of coffee.

Stars still twinkled outside her kitchen window as if everything in the world was as it should be. She stood in the silence, in the almost dark of the last minutes of night, and watched the sun begin its slow, determined rise.

Wouldn't it be nice if she—like the sun—knew exactly what

she should do, and exactly how to do it? Should she look for a job, in case Pierce didn't return? Look for an attorney, in case Pierce wanted a divorce? She knew women, Christian women, who'd dissolved their marriages when faced with less than what she and Pierce now faced. What if, deep down, Pierce wasn't as committed to their marriage as she? He'd already left her in every way that mattered. His going to Florida was merely a geographical manifestation of the condition of their marriage.

She heard Daniel groan from the sleeper sofa bed in the living room.

"What time is it?" he said.

"Quiet," Kay answered. "Time for me to get out of this bed."

"Sorry excuse for a bed, you mean. I might not be able to stand up straight until Wednesday of next week. I smell coffee. I *need* coffee."

"Then you better start trying to stand up now, because we've got stuff to do today." A quick smack of lips. "We're making Laurie breakfast."

When Kay rounded the corner, Laurie raised her mug. "Sorry, but it's decaf."

"He'll live," she said. "Sit, Laurie. I'll make French toast and bacon."

"Standing's better for me right now." If she sat, she might never move forward in her life again.

Daniel trudged to the table to sit. "Did I hear someone say *bacon?*"

Kay set two pans on the stove. "Some help you are."

"I'm here for moral support."

"You're a mess is what you are."

"Yes, but I'm cute."

Laurie took another sip from her mug. "We used to tease like that." She didn't look at them, but she knew she had their attention.

The phone rang, a shrill interruption. She set aside her mug. "I don't want to talk to anyone."

Kay answered for her, before the third ring. "Pierce Crane residence. Hello, son." She listened. "We stayed with her last night, and it's a good thing. She couldn't keep food down yesterday after you left."

For a moment, Laurie worried Pierce might wish to speak to her. Then she flashed hot with anger when that didn't appear to be the case. Everything she thought she knew about being married to him, had it all been an illusion?

Laurie's hands shook. She carefully lowered the mug to the counter.

"Yes," Kay continued. "We can stay, and yes, I can go with her to her doctor's appointment."

Was that it then? Was he handing her off to his mother?

"Hold on," Kay said and offered Laurie the phone. "He wants to speak to you."

Laurie held the phone against her shoulder, bit her lower lip. "Is this how it's going to be now? You leave when you want, I leave messages you don't return, then you call when you feel like it?"

"I didn't *leave* you. Not like that—"

"Don't you see, Pierce?" Could she take any more wounds at his hands? She took a fortifying breath. "Because you are afraid, you've been leaving me since I found out I was pregnant. We vowed to face life and everything in it, together."

"You're right," he said. "I read your notebook. I see now, honey. Please let me try to fix the damage."

She watched Daniel peering over Kay's shoulder as she turned the bacon strips. They were the closest thing to parents she had now. She didn't want to lose them, too.

"Laurie?"

She could hear the trepidation in Pierce's voice. The angry part inside her wanted to hang up on him. Make him sweat. Something to make him understand how much damage he'd done to their marriage.

"Laurie, please."

But wasn't it Pierce's deep, hidden anguish that had created the rift in the first place? Did she really want to add more to his life? Honestly, no. If they were truly *one*, ultimately she'd be hurting herself, too.

She had had enough—between losing her parents, the miscarriage, and now feeling like she was losing Pierce and their life together. What she wanted, what she *needed*, was for the pain to stop.

"Laurie, honey, *please* . . ."

Pierce might actually be crying. Would their life together always be plagued by tears?

"I love you," he said.

The baby kicked Laurie's elbow pressed against her side. "What about our child?"

"I'll talk to Mom and Dad. I'll pray. I'll do everything I can to show you how much I love you. If I have to stand there with my eyes closed, I'll find a way to be with you when you have our baby."

"Do you really mean that?"

"I was scared, Laurie. The fear grew too big and swallowed everything else."

"Please don't say it unless you mean it. It means too much."

"Mom can go with you to the doctor. I love you, Laurie. I'll go next time, I promise. I love you and, yes, I love our baby."

Her knees gave out at the words she'd longed to hear. In silence she set the receiver on the counter and shrank into Daniel's soothing embrace. "He's saying all the right things. Everything I've wanted to hear for months, but I don't know how to believe him."

Daniel pushed the speaker button. "Son, you're on speaker now."

"Dad, Mom, I'm sorry for how I've behaved."

"I think it would help Laurie if you told us what's happened," said Daniel. "Pierce? You still there?"

"I'm here. And this is hard to admit. Dad, have you or Mom

ever been so scared you couldn't breathe, but you didn't know why?"

"Fear can control a man, Pierce. It can make you do things you wouldn't normally do, make you believe things you wouldn't normally believe."

"Isaac and Ella helped me see that. I spent most of the night praying and reading Laurie's journal. There's more to tell, but I'll have to fill in the details later. Dad, I want you to take over the church for a couple of weeks at least. Tell the board everything that's happened. Tell Gilbert. I need them praying for me and Laurie."

"We'll do it."

"Mom, go with Laurie to the doctor. It's important. I don't want her to be alone."

Daniel kissed the top of Laurie's head. "If she wants, we'll stay with her until you come back."

"Is Laurie still there?" Pierce asked.

"Yes," Daniel answered. "But she can't talk right now."

"Go help her, Dad. I'll call again later."

The line went dead. "I need a minute," she said to her in-laws. Trembling, she moved to the dining room table and sat. The baby moved again; Laurie rubbed the side of her belly.

"You're my miracle," she said to her unborn child. "The miracle I prayed for, the miracle your daddy needs."

CHAPTER THIRTEEN

"Thanks for driving me today," Laurie said to Kay as they left the doctor's office.

She had not told Pierce, but a sonogram had been scheduled for today's appointment. She'd postponed it, telling Deb Jordan that Pierce was away, and she didn't want him to miss it.

"Let's get some lunch," Kay suggested. "You feel up to it?"

"I guess."

"Pierce mentioned you liked the Italian restaurant near our place."

"That's fine." The location of their last date. They had held hands over the table. Pierce kissed her in the parking lot before driving home. Later, by lamplight, they had taken their time in bed. They had laughed—gotten more than a little sweaty—and loved each other as if they hadn't a care in the world. For one long, fantastic moment, time had stopped. They gazed into each other's eyes, suspended in a place of total intimacy and union. She'd thought she'd seen her dreams in his eyes that night.

She had to admit, the good parts of their marriage usually outweighed the bad. The bad was just awfully bad right now.

She wrestled with anger—at the situation, at Pierce for letting his past control him, for shutting her out. In some ways, the anger felt good. It held energy. Power. Fuel, to help her make plans. She had a baby to think about.

But holding on to anger would cost her the future she wanted and had been journeying toward with God before this whole disaster. If

Pierce did heal and she carried anger, wouldn't the wall between them then be of her own making?

The heavy scent of garlic and the welcoming aroma of fresh-baked bread greeted Laurie as she and Kay entered Patrini's Italian Grill.

Lunch was served the same way her dinner date with Pierce had been, on elegant, white china, and accompanied by burgundy linen napkins. Although the building sat near the highway, it was surprisingly quiet at midday. Strategically placed indoor waterfalls camouflaged traffic noise and scattered conversations.

Kay whispered to Laurie. "It smells wonderful, but a little strong. Are you sure you're okay with this?"

Laurie nodded. "I'm fine. I'll eat slowly."

They followed the hostess to a rear booth; in moments their waitress appeared, a curvy young woman. Her flowing black hair reached her waist and her nametag read "Mariabella."

"Hi. Welcome to Patrini's." She looked from Kay to Laurie, motioned to Laurie's belly. "Got enough room between you and the table? We can shift a little to give you more space."

Laurie couldn't help but smile as Kay and Mariabella repositioned the table.

"That's better. What would you ladies like to drink?"

They gave their orders. Mariabella took two steps away, then spun back around. "I know you. You were at the hospital Saturday night."

Laurie's smile faded. Kay answered. "That's right."

"My sister, Isabella, was having her baby there. Well, my whole family was there." She shrugged, then focused on Laurie. "And your husband prayed with her and Luke. That was really nice."

Laurie stilled as a pang of jealousy left her feeling immature. "How, how is she doing?"

Mariabella, glowing with joy and wonder, squatted at the table's end and produced photos from her uniform pocket. "They're great. She had the most beautiful baby boy. Look at that head full of black curly hair." She blew identical bangs off her forehead. "What's that about, right?"

She stood, slid the photos from the table. "Our parents were so mad at her when they found out she was pregnant," she whispered. "And at Luke, of course. I guess not every baby is planned, huh? But your husband was so sweet. He never once said anything about, you know, them not being married yet." She rolled her eyes. "But it's okay. Now I'm an aunt. I get to help plan their wedding and be my sister's maid of honor. Do you think your husband would marry them, let them have the wedding at your church?"

Laurie swallowed hard. "He's out of town right now. Why don't you call the church and leave a message. I'm sure you'll hear from him next week sometime." She lowered her menu. "I'll have the lasagna. Mom?"

"Sounds good to me."

"Perfect. Won't be long."

Laurie waited until Mariabella was out of earshot.

"I thought we were so close. I thought we had a strong marriage. I don't know what we have now."

"A strong marriage."

"How can you say that?"

"Because you two have grown strong in every other area, despite this huge weakness in your relationship."

Mariabella returned, set steaming plates before them and left again. Laurie cut into the lasagna. "I don't know what to do."

"Laurie, I believe your pregnancy is divinely timed. None of this has happened outside God's plan for your lives and marriage."

"I feel that in my heart." Laurie pressed her fist to her chest. "I do."

"Then everything that goes with it is in God's timing, too."

"And what does God require of me?"

"To help—not hinder—His work in Pierce."

"How do I do that?"

Kay leaned toward Laurie. "That's what you have to find out."

"I feel like all I do is complain to God. I sound whiny even to myself. I don't mean to be impatient." She looked down at her rounded belly, then back at Kay. "But we're on a deadline here."

"Laurie. You have enough hormones right now for three or four women. That's how pregnancy is. And yes, it magnifies a woman's joys and sorrows. Don't you think God knows that?"

Laurie's eyes watered. "I know I'm a cliché. I cry over Hallmark commercials."

"God gave you that soft heart."

"I obsessed over having a child, Mom. I did." Even to Laurie's ears, the confession seemed anti-climactic. "I think I still am."

"Put all that energy, all that effort into hearing God. You can have a soft heart and still be strong. Jesus was."

***

Laurie wanted to walk.

Kay expressed concern about her getting overheated in the afternoon sun, but Laurie needed to feel her body moving as her spirit restlessly stretched and stirred. So after they returned from lunch, she chose to go alone into the woods that always lured Pierce, and promised her in-laws she wouldn't stay in the pressing heat too long.

She walked under the branches, sat several minutes, then walked more. Where was Pierce? What was he doing?

She purposely hadn't mentioned it to Kay, but August was only days away and would mark one year since the miscarriage. One year since she'd thought her life was near perfect, then, in a matter of seconds, a nightmare began that continued to this moment.

Standing under the leafy canopy, she lifted her eyes to heaven.

Dear God, I'm alone and I'm afraid to weep over that child. If I give into the grief now, on top of everything else, I'm afraid I'll lose this *baby. Pierce isn't here, I don't even know if he realizes the date. Reminding him might set him back. Please protect this child. Let this baby live. And show me what to do about my marriage.*

As she meandered back home, the sun shone bright, so bright the sky stretched out forever, all the way up to heaven. The cloudless dome with its sea glass cast reminded her of Pierce's eyes. *Your daddy's eyes, little one.* She loved the child within her so much already, at times she thought her heart would burst. She wondered how more love could fit there. Grow there. Come from there.

But it surely would, she thought as she climbed the porch steps.

I know the plans I have for you . To prosper you. To give you hope.

She stopped mid-step and grabbed the handrail. God's plan.

God was indeed using her pregnancy to push Pierce to face his past. To let God heal him.

What was her part in God's plan, as she and Pierce faced their first real marital struggle?

Whatever is true.

The verse propelled her back to her bedroom. She wrote the verse at the top of a page. "Finally, brothers, whatever is true, whatever is noble, whatever is right, whatever is pure, whatever is lovely, whatever is admirable—if anything is excellent or praiseworthy—think about such things."

She tapped her pen against the page.

God, please help me see. Help me understand.

Her spirit was willing, but her mind had to be ready, too. Thinking right would help. It would keep her from making mistakes that hindered God's work.

So she wrote again. This time placing in columns the key words the verse encouraged readers to "think about." True. Noble. Right.

Pure. Lovely. Admirable. She asked God to reveal what she needed to know about each.

True. She loved Pierce. Even though loving him right now wasn't easy.

That's like Me. I love you, even when you're not perfect, even when you do things that hurt you and Me.

Noble. What did noble mean?

She looked it up. Noble meant honorable or of great value.

Working to change her marriage was of great value to her. She truly believed God would help her actions be right, be pure, so she wouldn't make a bigger mess. Not having so much to apologize for was certainly a lovely thought. And what a testimony it would be some-day—to her child and to others—if she shared how God helped her avoid bitterness, rebuilt the trust between her and Pierce, and made her marriage better than it had ever been.

Dear Father, show me how to do this.

When he asks, tell Pierce everything.

Everything. What she needed. What she wanted. Her feelings.

Tell Pierce everything. The encouraging words came as a loving mother's caress, soothing the wounds in her heart. As if someone opened a window, peace flooded her, drenching her spirit in a newborn-pink glow. If she listened to God and obeyed, the peace would stay deep inside, no matter what Pierce did or didn't do.

Love him like I do, like I love you.

But what, exactly, did that look like?

Watch me.

With head bowed, she prayed. For Pierce. Herself. Their baby. Their future. And she knew she must ask Pierce to do the same.

＊＊＊

Ina's family swarmed inside her opulent home. Though they'd assured Pierce there was plenty of room for him, too, he opted to stay in the garage apartment. It reminded him of easier days. Of Laurie. He could almost smell her there.

He could best describe his daily experiences over the next few days as having major surgery without anesthesia.

Visiting the funeral home with the Hood family to complete the arrangements brought to mind his own grief as a child. That hollow, sore-all-over feeling that made you want to curl into a ball and hide in a corner. He watched the tears, heard the quiet laughter as each remembered Ina in his own way, as they planned the service and chose a casket.

The sad and beautiful scene struck a chord within Pierce. Maybe he could try remembering his mother's life and her love for him, instead of dwelling on her death.

He excused himself after dinner with the family and retreated to the apartment. He just wanted to sit alone, in the quiet, and call Laurie.

He dialed, she answered softly, then neither of them said anything for several moments.

"Are you still there?" he asked.

"Yes. I'm here."

"How'd your doctor's appointment go?"

"Okay." A pause. "Kay got to hear the baby's heartbeat."

Wow. "Wow. I . . . wish I'd been there." It was true. He did wish he had been there. He loved their baby, too. "Can you ever forgive me?"

Long seconds ticked by.

"I'm working on it," she said. "I keep telling myself you were reacting, rather than trying to hurt me."

"Do you still love me?"

"Yes. And I hope you mean everything you're saying to me."

"Tell me what you need."

She sighed. "Honesty. Your love. More. Your dad—"

"My dad what?"

"Your dad knows someone, a professional." She paused. "Can we get counseling?"

We. She still loved him, and they were still a *we*. "Yes, I'll go see a counselor. Anything else?"

He heard her take a really deep breath and exhale. "Love our child with me."

He knew she was holding back from him. Something she didn't want to ask, wasn't ready to say, or was afraid to say . . .

Who did that sound like?

"You know, we used to pray together all the time." She paused. "We used to laugh together all the time, too," she added quietly. "Watching you pray with others on Sunday mornings, with Gilbert the other night, with another woman in labor . . . Will you pray with me?"

He'd been praying all day.

Not with her you haven't.

"For our baby? Pierce, it's just me. And God. We both love you."

"Dear God." Words stuck in his throat. What if Laurie changed her mind and didn't want him to come home? What if worse memories surfaced? Sweat broke out across his shoulders. "God, I've been so afraid. Until recently I didn't know why." He closed his eyes, squeezing back tears. "Honestly, I'm still afraid. Lord, please protect my wife and my child."

His child. He wept with gratitude over God giving them a child. He cradled the phone in one hand, wiped tears with the other as they fell off his chin and onto his T-shirt.

Finally he got his breath back, his voice back. "Laurie, are you still there?"

She cleared her throat. "Heavenly Father, Pierce needs You."

Her tender words broke him again, and he shook his head at the way he'd isolated himself from her.

"Please wrap him in Your presence."

He hated that he'd listened to lies and pulled away from her.

"I'm asking You to heal his heart. Complete the work You've begun in him. In us."

"I love you, Laurie. I love you so much."

"I love you, too, Pierce. And I'm really tired. Work at the church has produced two new potential clients. I've got two meetings tomorrow as well as a stop by the youth building."

"Then you should get some sleep. Good night."

"Good night, Pierce."

He hung up and lay in the dark as midnight approached.

"Dear God, I open every locked door inside myself to You. Show me everything I didn't see before. Teach me. Change me."

Then you will know the truth, and the truth will set you free.

***

Laurie couldn't sleep. She could remember only one other instance she'd been this uncertain about her future. It was the morning of her parents' funeral, when she'd numbly dressed in black and driven to the church. To this day, at the sight of lilies and carnations, she remembered that dismal morning, and the graveside service, as she stood under the canopy while the saddest rain she'd ever heard pelted the overhead canvas.

Standing at the window, she glanced back at the clock, just after four a.m. Rain fell outside, the heavy drops beat the ground with such force she thought she saw the earth wince at the bruising.

Much like her heart was feeling now.

Was Pierce sleeping peacefully there in Florida? Was he awake, thinking of her?

She leaned against the window frame, all her energy gone. She turned at a soft tap on her door. "Come in."

"I thought you were awake." Kay stepped into the room. "Can I get you anything?"

"No, thanks."

"You talked late with Pierce tonight."

151

"Yes. Yes, I did."

"I don't mean to pry, Laurie. I just want you to remember that Dad and I are here to help."

"I know, Mom. And I appreciate it. I do." She paused. "I think about Pierce as a little boy. He connected with you and Daniel. Many adopted children have problems with trust and feelings of abandonment. You should know he never mentioned anything like that to me about his relationship with you. He knows he's loved."

"Thank you for saying that. Truly." Kay turned to go.

"Mom?"

"Yes."

"Do you think I should actively pursue more clients? Our lives have been such a whirlwind since we moved here. Except for the one project at the church, all my energy and focus have been on Pierce and the pregnancy. But what if he doesn't come back? What if I'm left to figure out life on my own? I trust God, I do. It's just . . ."

"Pierce you're worried about."

"Yeah."

"You're afraid to trust him. Afraid to get your hopes up that he really is changing."

"Yeah. I feel so wounded. Like he's kicked my heart in the same place over and over. I think I was really spoiled. Back at the church in Orlando, I saw other couples who faced problem after problem. I guess I mistakenly thought we lived above all that."

"Everybody faces something." Kay paused. "Laurie, what's your biggest concern?"

"That even if I continue listening to God, Pierce won't."

"You're afraid in a week or two he'll revert back and pull away from you."

"Yes. I'm trying to treat him like he's sincere, still, I don't know that I trust him. It feels like lying."

"Isn't it really that you're choosing to give him the benefit of the doubt? You're both learning new things right now. You'll both make mistakes. But if you learn together, you'll end up closer than before."

***

Ina's oldest grandson couldn't arrive for at least two days, which pushed the funeral back. Pierce called Laurie as soon as he found out.

"I've been alone a lot, here in our old apartment." Had it only been a few months since they'd left this place? "I spend most of the time praying."

"Tell me what you pray," she said in her hopeful dreamer voice.

"I pray for your safety and our baby's health. That God will make me strong enough to love you the way you need to be loved." He paused. "Ina has about twenty grandchildren. They play, they aggravate each other, they cry at different times when they remember their Grandma Ina's gone. I see myself in some of them, as their parents and other family try to explain why Ina isn't here any longer. I understand that kind of bewilderment, you know?"

"Of course you do."

"I need to tell you something. Remember the day we painted our room?"

"When you went into the woods."

"When you cut yourself, I ran. But I didn't know why I reacted that way, so I asked God to make our marriage like it was before the miscarriage. He answered me with a scripture instead."

"Really? Which one?"

"First Corinthians 4:5: 'He will bring to light what is hidden in darkness.' It shocked me."

"I imagine it did."

"Laurie, I still want you to have your dreams."

"Pierce, every dream I have has you in it."

Every dream I have has you in it. He reminded himself of Laurie's words the next morning when, after days of postponement, the viewing and funeral service finally took place. Pierce stood outside the church, watching the long string of cars form around the building for the processional. Isaac peered over the roof of his car and motioned Pierce inside. "Pierce. We're supposed to be at the front of the line."

"Sure."

Isaac pulled behind the hearse and family cars. "You okay?"

"I don't know."

"You miss Laurie."

"Yeah. I miss Laurie."

They drove through Orlando to the cemetery where the moments passed like scenes in a movie. The interment with rows of family dressed in black. A daughter whose body shook with grief. Adults' eyes clouded with tears while bored children shuffled their feet.

For the first time, Pierce wondered about the man his mother left behind. And let himself picture his father as a grieving husband. A devastated father. A stunned, poor widower who had no money for a proper coffin, burial plot, or headstone. Had his life ended that day, too?

At the family dinner, relatives embraced. They reminisced over pictures and recounted memories. Pierce stood to the side near Isaac and Ella, and wondered about his own baby brother. A screaming bundle whose fate was unknown to him. A child who never felt their mother's touch.

Between the two of them, Pierce might still have gotten the better life, if his father had kept the baby but hadn't loved him.

A quiet, curious yearning entered Pierce's heart. To know what had happened to his brother.

Still, that same heart shuddered at the question standing like a dark shadow at the back of his mind. What had happened to his mother's grave?

CHAPTER FOURTEEN

John slowed his truck, parked beside the barn, and strode to the house.

Lately, he'd spent his days off with his dad, rather than visiting after long days in the office or sleepless nights in the labor and delivery unit. The lazy afternoons spent together on the front porch could almost be called pleasant. He and Luther had even shared a couple of real, if short, conversations.

The morning sun beat the ground, its heat bouncing up in waves. With no breeze and pea soup humidity, before noon the heat would be stifling. What would it take to install an air conditioner in the cracker box home? The hottest part of summer had arrived; adding a window unit shouldn't be difficult. Not nearly as tricky as getting his dad's permission.

"Dad?" John stepped onto the porch.

He heard a groan, but not from inside. The sound came from behind him, to his right, past the pig shed.

Not again.

John found his dad amidst a Swiss cheese-like configuration of holes, facedown in muck and mud, shovel in hand. No telling how long Luther had been there. He took the shovel and tossed it aside, knowing he'd have to refill some of the holes before leaving today or the shed would fall over the next time it rained.

What was wrong with Dad? Three, four times now, John had found him like this, or seen evidence he'd been out here working during the night. Luther Bridges, demented digger.

"I can't find her," he said as John rolled him over.

155

"Can't find who?"

His dad raised a knee, blinking and coughing. John checked his forehead for fever and took his pulse.

Luther batted away John's hands. "I have to tell her about our boys."

"I'm your boy. How many fingers am I holding up?"

His dad looked straight at him. "But John's a baby."

"Not anymore. Let's get you cleaned up."

He stood behind his dad, hooked his arms around the old man's chest. On the third try John got him up and shuffled backward, dragging him toward the house.

When had Luther begun shrinking? Not his height, his limbs were still long, his hands and feet still big. But he lacked meat and muscle, his bones looked like a skeleton wrapped in tissue paper. Even his boots sagged on his narrow feet.

"Why are you pulling on me?" Luther complained.

"To get you inside." He thought back over his limited geriatric training. "I should've taken you for a physical weeks ago."

John's heels hit the bottom porch step. He dragged up, up, while Luther's feet struggled for purchase. When they backed to the doorway, Luther's hand went out. "Put me down, boy."

"Dad, you need to get cleaned up."

Luther grunted.

"I'll cook lunch while you shower." John glanced behind him, noticed the kitchen stank in its normal state of "slum meets the south." Mud, hay, heaven-knew-what coated the floor. He would gladly pay someone to clean weekly if Dad would agree.

Luther pushed away and straightened. "You cook. I've got work." He walked down the steps swaying like a drunk, then headed for the pig shed.

John followed, debating whether to argue or watch. The trained physician in him followed his "patient," ready to observe, listen, and diagnose. The son wanted to speed up the process, get out of the suffocating heat, and take his father straight to the best neurologist in the area.

"Work. Okay. How can I help?"

Luther poked the ground with the shovel as if testing the holes, then dug between to form a ditch.

"Dad, what are you doing?"

No answer. No surprise there.

"Dad." John's hand went to Luther's straining shoulder. "I'll help if you tell me what we're doing."

"Where is she?"

"Where's who? Dad. Will you *stop*?"

Luther stopped. He sunk the shovel into the ground then braced himself on the long handle. His deeply grooved face fell. "Your mother. I have to find her. She's here, and I have to find her and tell her about our boys."

Boys? There were no *boys*.

"I'm fine, Dad." An eerie wave of apprehension swelled inside him. As a physician—an OB/GYN, but still—he'd been trained to look beyond symptoms such as the desperation and grief on his father's face, to understand their source.

Seeking to soothe, he lowered his voice. "Why are you looking for Mom out here? She's been dead since the day I was born."

Luther grabbed John's shirt. "I buried her here," he whispered through trembling lips, as he surveyed the ground. "I buried her, I sent you to live with the Taylors, and I gave away your brother."

John barely remembered living with the Taylors. He knew they weren't his parents, they told him so. Not unkindly, just matter-of-factly. When he turned four, they brought him back home and he met his dad. But he had never heard anything about his mother being buried in the yard, or a brother being given away.

"Will you help me find her?" Tears merged with the mud on his dad's cheeks.

Could all this be true? John had never seen his dad cry, never seen anything but quiet, stern reserve in the man. Luther was either delusional, or having a nervous breakdown, or . . .

The most peculiar feeling washed over John, that there might be someone who could remember their mother and talk with him about her. John didn't know what she looked like, had never seen a picture of her. As far as he remembered, Dad had never spoken of her, until today.

"Dad, is this the truth? Do I have a brother?"

Chapter Fifteen

After a full eight-hour day, Laurie unlocked her front door. She went inside, dropped her purse on the console table, kicked off her shoes, and wished for a pool. Even a small one, where she could float and for a few short moments enjoy *not* feeling her ligaments and tendons pulling with her child's every stretch. If this baby's in utero behavior was any indication of after birth activity, Laurie was about to be run ragged.

Thankfully, the youth building renovations had been completed today—she'd actually marked the final item off her list. If all went well at next week's inspection, an occupancy license would be issued and Laurie could add another completed job to her portfolio.

She'd prayed off and on throughout the day and reminded herself of verses she'd studied, in preparation for tonight.

Her husband was coming home. To her. And their unborn baby.

She supposed in some ways she'd been preparing for battle—or, rather, a new beginning.

If Pierce was truly changing.

She moved toward the kitchen and caught the scent of roses. A bouquet of yellow blooms filled a cut glass vase. She read the card. "Because we love you. Dinner's in the oven." The kitchen curtains she'd sewn last night had been pressed and hung. Even the fabric she'd measured and cut for the dining room chairs was ironed and neatly stacked on the bar beside the vase.

Whatever would she do with herself? She'd indulge in a bubble bath.

She ran the water deep, let herself doze and dream as the soft lavender-scented bubbles soothed her body. When her skin was wrinkled and pink, she hauled herself out of the tub.

She worried a moment, just a moment as she dried her body, about her baby's health. After all, the miscarriage had happened right after she'd bathed. But the little thing was practically dancing around in there, which obviously meant all was well. She was right at twenty-eight weeks, which meant only twelve to go before she'd get to hold her baby. She'd soon have a sonogram. Would Pierce keep his word and share that with her?

Wrapped in her robe, she ate supper while standing, then returned the simmering meat with its juices to the oven, where it would stay warm until Pierce arrived. On an impulse, she dug out photo albums, perched on the couch, and let herself remember.

She scanned snapshots of early college days. When her hair had been longer, her face thinner. Her heart lonely, having lost her parents. She traced a fingertip over herself on the page. Yes, she had been lonely. She knew God then, had a few friends, but no family. When she met Pierce, her whole world changed.

She remembered wondering why he had picked her. He could have easily chosen someone more beautiful, smarter, more talented. But he chose her. And courted her quietly, in a determined, methodical manner. Almost like he knew and understood he was winning her heart one day, one moment, one word at a time.

On her first trip to meet Kay and Daniel, she had been so nervous her teeth chattered. Pierce held her hand as he drove, rubbing his thumb over hers until it was almost sore. "They'll love you, Laurie. Because I love you," he'd said.

She opened their wedding album and studied her pearled gown, his tailored tux. Pierce had looked so sure of himself then. So steady. It almost didn't seem possible this was the same man with whom she had been living for the past few months.

She had considered him perfect. She had neither expected nor been prepared for his flaws. That had been both naïve and unfair.

Now they had a baby on the way.

Would she only accept her husband back now if he was perfect, when she herself still had so much to learn, as Kay had graciously hinted? About being a wife. Being a mother. Even being a Christian.

Did you plan on being married to him for the rest of your life?
Of course she did.

Did you think you would be growing together during that time?
Yes, of course.

Changing? Learning? Creating a family?
Yes.

Then you have exactly what you wanted, don't you?

***

Pierce couldn't move. Wedged in the center seat, he tried to relax as the plane descended, but the aircraft's stale interior nearly suffocated him. He just wanted to see Laurie, touch her, sleep beside her. He'd barely slept while in Florida.

He rubbed eyes he knew were bloodshot and looked out the window to the evening sky. Laurie wanted them to get counseling. Maybe a professional could help him, so he could be with her during the delivery.

Dear God, please show me how to make things right with Laurie.

And what should he do about his brother he'd seen only as a newborn? His father, who might be dead?

Finally the plane landed. Pierce wanted to call Laurie, but his cell didn't have a signal. Urgency demanded he keep moving, closer to Laurie, closer to home. He hurriedly lined up to exit the cabin, and got stalled in the aisle.

Finally he made it to the terminal and wove through the crowd, only to wait in line at the parking lot elevators. Hunger clawed at his stomach, but he didn't want to take the time to stop and eat. He dialed Laurie and got voicemail. "Laurie, I, I'm really thanking God for you

161

right now." He watched a smiling couple slide into the backseat of a taxi outside the main doors.

His phone beeped. Low battery. He'd better talk fast.

"My phone's dying. I actually reached for your hand during the funeral yesterday." He laughed self-consciously. "I even caught myself listening for your voice in the crowd at dinner. All those times before that, when I wouldn't talk to you, you thought I wasn't paying attention. But I was listening. I heard your conversations with our baby, your prayers—"

Beep.

". . . for me." In frustration he hit END and shoved the phone in his pocket.

Pierce drove, bumper-to-bumper between cabs, buses, and harried businessmen, fighting his way toward home. Laurie had left the light on for him. He hurried up the steps.

"Pierce, is that you?" Laurie's sweet voice drifted out to him.

"Yes, honey."

She turned off the outside light, leaving him temporarily blind and in the dark.

"Laurie?"

She whipped open the door and, hiding behind it, motioned him in. "I'm getting your supper." She planted a quick kiss on his cheek and darted away.

He dropped his suitcase to the floor and spotted flickering candlelight in the dining room. The table was set for one; obviously she had already eaten, as she should have. For her, an empty stomach equaled a queasy stomach.

Food. Thank God.

And Laurie. Double thanks.

He sat. Then he noticed the music. Classical, though he didn't know the composer. She'd also closed the blinds. He smelled the roast and mashed potatoes before she set the plate in front of him.

"Your mom cooked dinner and left it in the oven."

He reached for her hand, but she returned to the kitchen. His frustration, short-lived but potent, evaporated into the soft mist of steam rising from the hot rolls she brought back with her. She sat beside him.

He reached for her hand again, rubbed his thumb over her lovely fingers. Holding her gaze, he let her see the frightening darkness that had threatened to consume him. "Laurie, I love you."

***

"I'm not going anywhere." Laurie reached for a roll, buttered it, and handed it to him. "Take your time."

Even if Pierce spent the next eight, ten years or more working through his pain, wouldn't it be worth the time and effort? If the situation were reversed, she hoped he would stick with her, too, no matter how long it took.

"Welcome home," she said.

She waited while he ate. When he'd finished, she rose, rounded his chair, and massaged his stiff shoulders while her heart sent pleas to his. *Please keep your promise. Don't pull away from me anymore.*

"Did you get my message?"

She rubbed harder, deeper, the way she knew he liked. "Yes." She had listened to it, listened again, and saved it. "Roll your neck."

She wanted him to reclaim her, re-establish the beautiful physical intimacy they had enjoyed before. How she needed to feel wanted. Desired. Loved by him.

In silence, she removed her outer robe and draped it over the back of a chair, revealing a black silk-and-lace gown that flowed over her curves and her rounded belly. Despite her pregnant state, she felt a little sexy. She bent to whisper in his ear while the corners of her mouth lifted in a flirty smile. "Ready for dessert?"

He rose, turned to her, and clasped his hands at the small of her back. "I guess you went shopping."

"There's a new maternity store in town." She smiled, sliding her hands up his chest, and enjoying the sensation of touching him without being rebuffed or rejected. "I bought this, introduced myself, and invited the owner to church. I think she'll visit, if only to see what kind of church has a pastor with a pregnant wife who buys black lingerie."

She waited for him to kiss her. Didn't he want to kiss her?

"Your baby's dancing. He or she's happy you're home, too. But right now I need you. I need you to love me."

He pulled back, obviously uncertain and nervous. "Are you sure?"

"Dr. Nate said I am fine. We can be normal."

She turned her hips, rotating her belly to the side so she could hold him close. "We won't have much time alone after the baby comes."

"We're okay then?"

"We'll have tough spots, I'm sure. But if we keep going like we are now, we'll be fine, don't you think?" She searched his face. "Will you do something for me?"

He nodded.

Trembling with hesitation, she placed his hand on her stomach. "Just stand here a minute."

Finally, the baby pushed and kicked Pierce's palm. She watched as surprise and recognition brought a smile to his face. With tentative fingers she stroked through his hair, the thick brown waves she hoped their child would have, and consciously clicked a snapshot of his priceless expression for her heart's box of treasures.

His fingers twitched against her belly. Laurie's breath hitched. "Pierce, please don't pull away."

***

Pierce dropped to his knees, splayed both hands across Laurie's stom-

164

ach, and gently pressed his face to her belly. "I love you, little one. I love you and your mama."

And to think he had almost cut himself off, completely, from both of them. Thank God Laurie didn't hate him—this beautiful woman, who was going to have his baby.

"What are you thinking?" she whispered.

"I'm thinking how I'll feel if you decide to breastfeed. Part of me wants you to. I think it would be the loveliest thing I could ever see."

"Oh, Pierce."

He looked up at her. "And part of me doesn't want you to, because I want to feed the baby, too. Then I think you need to nurse, or you'll never get to hold him, or her, because I'll never want to let our child go. How could my father let me go, Laurie? How could he send me away? He had to know it would hurt me more than a newborn who didn't know any better. It tore me apart."

The baby kicked Pierce's hand again, hard. And again, then must have flipped. Laurie's belly rolled like a shifting waterbed under his palm.

"Does that hurt?"

"It feels strange. Even if it did that wouldn't mean it's bad. Some things that hurt aren't bad."

"Tell me you'll have an epidural right away." Tears gushed from his eyes, he wiped them with the heels of his hands. "I picture you in labor. Crying. Hurting. Bleeding. And I can't decide whether to throw up or run."

Laurie managed to lower herself to the floor beside Pierce, quite a trick with the long gown and her heavy, about-seven-months-along belly.

She thought she heard a seam rip, sacrificed her attempt at being sexy, and hiked up the gown so she could kneel and wrap her arms around her beloved. All she could do was hold him.

She'd envisioned a much different homecoming when she'd

bought the negligee, when she'd bathed and slathered lotion on her skin earlier this evening.

But his weeping broke her heart. She had never seen him cry like this. Like a broken, abandoned child. Chest heaving. Breath catching. His entire body shook. His tears soaked her gown.

She would have to be careful. She must be gentle and easy with him. She didn't have to push; God was obviously doing that.

"I'm here, Pierce. I love you." *Father, help me say what You want said, and do what You want done. Tell me.*

Love him.

Don't we need to talk now? I want him to talk to me.

He will. Love him.

Minutes passed and her knees ached. Gingerly, she lowered herself to a cross-legged position, facing him. Gradually, his tears ceased.

She knew how he must feel. Exhausted and heavy-headed. She'd cried just like this so many nights. Still, gratitude filled her.

Finally, there was honesty between them.

***

Pierce could fall asleep right there. On the floor, with Laurie's arms around him, his head on her shoulder.

Then he realized. He'd soaked her neck, the ends of her hair with his tears.

He had no idea how long they had been there like that, how long he had cried. The fact that she had stayed with him through it all—his secrecy, his withdrawal, his poor treatment of her, his tears—humbled him. And sealed his love for her inside a furnace-forged steel resolve.

You wanted change. This is only the beginning.

He could barely speak. "Laurie."

The tips of her fingers stopped his words. "Shh. You don't have to say anything right now."

The music stopped. Their eyes locked. In hers he saw the love he had always needed. He simply hadn't known how to let it reach the places inside his heart that he hadn't let God or himself or anyone else touch.

She whispered, "You'll have to help me up. I think my leg went to sleep."

He helped her into a chair, then sat at her feet. "Which one?"

"Both?"

He began with her toes. Small, slender, soft. He rubbed them, kneaded them. He slid a palm around her heel and cradled it, while massaging her arch.

She twitched and giggled, running a hand down her thigh.

"Does that tickle?"

"Yes. My legs feel like bugs are crawling all over them."

He grabbed both calves and pulled gently, slid his hands down to her ankles. How he had missed touching her.

She closed her eyes. "I don't want to move. But I have to go to the bathroom." He helped her stand, she held their hands between them. "If you'll lock up, turn off the lights, we can go to bed."

He replaced the chair at the table and rinsed his dishes, surprised that he could still move, still function, despite his atypical meltdown moments ago. Apparently, she thought no less of him for it. Amazingly, neither did he.

When he entered their bedroom, he found her gown on the floor. He stripped to his boxers, slipped in bed behind her like he always did, and was surprised to find her wearing one of his old T-shirts.

She turned out the lamp, settled back against his chest. "I've been sleeping in this since you left because it smells like you."

He buried his face in her hair, breathed deep. "I'm sorry I left you. I'm not just talking about going to Florida."

She reached back for his hand, pulled his arm around the baby she carried. "I know."

For the first time in weeks, his entire body relaxed.

"Wake me if you need me." She raised his hand to her lips and kissed it.

"I'll always need you."

He felt her smile first, then her whisper. "We'll sleep tonight and love each other in the morning."

He kissed her shoulder, answered with slurring words. "Anything you want. I love you, Laurie."

"I'm glad you're home."

***

The bus driver, a skeleton-thin black man who smiled a lot, kept watching him in the wide mirror above the steering wheel.

Hunger pangs rumbled in his stomach, but Pierce didn't know if eating on the bus was allowed. So he sneaked a few finger snatches of bread out of his bag and slipped them into his mouth one at a time when the driver looked elsewhere. Then he used the paper sack for a pillow and lay facing the dark-green back of the seat, because looking out the big window in front of the driver made him feel like he was falling and needed to hold onto something.

The bus stopped. Had they driven him back home?

He sat up and looked around, recognizing nothing. The farm was nowhere to be seen.

Then the bus made a loud hissing sound—just like Daddy's tractor—and continued on. Which made him more afraid because he knew Daddy and Mama and the farm were very far away.

With a dry crust of bread crumbled in his fist, he silently cried himself to sleep.

He woke in Daniel Crane's arms.

CHAPTER SIXTEEN

When morning came, Laurie left Pierce sleeping in their bed. She crept out of their room and called her in-laws to let them know Pierce had arrived home safely. Then she went to the nursery to stand by the crib. She stroked her hand over her belly.

Joy and relief shot through her heart, almost taking her breath. Pierce was home, he was willing to go to counseling and work on their relationship.

Soon they would bring their child home to this house, this room. They needed to hang the border, purchase a rocking chair, build the shelving and a window seat. Julie Matthews and Milly Newman wanted to plan a baby shower, which meant she needed to make a list of things she needed and give it to them.

Time would fly now that she'd reached the final trimester. At her next appointment she would finally have a sonogram. They needed to decide whether or not they wanted to know the baby's sex.

Laurie wanted to know. She wanted to pick a name and use it when talking to her child. But they hadn't discussed names. They hadn't discussed anything.

Urgency. One wave, two, crested in her heart and crashed into her mind.

There was too much to do—finish the nursery.

Too much to learn—Lamaze.

Too much to handle from Pierce's memories. She hoped he didn't change his mind about seeing a counselor.

When would there be time to enjoy being pregnant? To think about the baby? To do all the things she had kept herself from even thinking about?

She turned to see Pierce standing in the doorway.

"You dreamed all night," she said.

His eyes stayed on hers.

"I held your arm tight around me every time you started to pull away."

***

Pierce could see Laurie was worried and a little scared. It showed on her face and in the way her hand trembled as she pushed back her hair.

"We, um, still have things to do in here. Will you help me?"

"Sure." He pushed away from the doorframe and stepped to her. "You left the bed."

She fidgeted with the hem of the T-shirt she wore. "We meet with the counselor at five o'clock today. Okay?"

He caught her shoulders in his hands and rubbed. "Laurie, I don't know everything I'm supposed to do."

Her damp eyes glowed, her breath and words came fast. "Can't we just love each other? I don't mean pretend that you're not going through something, pretend *we're* not going through something. But can't we simply love each other? Can't there be moments we *enjoy*, times we talk about the baby? And if we cry, we cry. But we might laugh, too."

She closed her eyes, stood rigid and took a deep breath as he had seen weightlifters do. Her voice faded to a whisper. "I feel so disconnected from you. I have for weeks. Now I know why." She opened her eyes, and looked straight to his soul. "But I can't stay mad at you. Every time I pray, it's like God says, 'No, don't concentrate on anger; be thankful you know what the problem is. Now you can fix it.'"

"I do want to fix this, Laurie. For us." He pulled her close, pressed his forehead to hers. "For our baby."

"Watching you cry last night, I didn't know what to do. I didn't know how to help you. Then when we went to bed, I didn't know what you were thinking, and I didn't want to pressure you. We used to make love all the time before this happened. I feel like I need you even more now. I need the good times to balance out the bad. I always thought we could face anything if we faced it together. Can't we just be together? Do your memories have to be a wedge between us?"

He looked into her eyes as her tender hands traced his jaw line, his cheekbones, over his brows.

Be transformed by the renewing of your mind.

The scripture swirled through his heart, as if bringing fresh air and sweeping through cobwebbed corners.

They will become one flesh.

The choice he would have to make over and over again for days, weeks, possibly the rest of his life, waited before him. To share his struggles with her as he had last night. He would be a better husband because of it. A better father.

He covered her hands with his, kissed her fingers, and slid them from his face. "Come back to bed with me."

He led her back to their room. "I don't know why," he said. "I don't know why I pulled away from you, even after telling you what I remembered. In some ways it's just as scary to be honest, but at least when I'm honest, I get to be close to you. And I have to be close to you."

***

There was no music, as Laurie had planned for last night's reunion. No sexy nightgown and dim lights to camouflage her form. Instead, raw daylight wove its way around the blinds. She could hide nothing.

Pierce had touched her silk-covered stomach last night, feeling

171

their child inside her move. But he had not actually seen her belly for weeks. Until now.

Her heart pounded as they stood facing each other by the bed. He kissed her. The baby kicked and rolled.

With quiet reverence Pierce gently stroked her stretched skin. Laurie watched his expression as wonder changed to tenderness, then surrendered to possessiveness. She could almost read the words on his face, *this is mine.*

"I love you, Pierce." Her heart sighed with contentment. Had they ever been this open, this transparent with each other before?

She lay on the bed and opened her arms to him in welcome. A shimmer of anticipation danced across her skin, followed by his hands, then his lips. How she needed his touch.

By unspoken agreement, the pace stayed slow and intentional. She kept her eyes open, loved looking into his as grateful tears blurred her vision.

Finally he braced himself above her. "I shouldn't put my weight on you." His breath danced across her mouth. "How do we . . .?"

She smiled up at him. "I think we can figure it out."

Later, when she laid her head on his shoulder, she let her eyes drift closed and whispered, "Wake me at three o'clock."

Laurie thought she'd sleep, but she didn't. Pierce relaxed, she heard his breathing go deep and even. But rather than rolling over and turning her back to him, she stayed beside him, her head on his shoulder, an arm draped across his chest, their unborn child between them.

If only they could stay like this, right here—just the two, no, three of them. But life didn't work that way. Hadn't she noticed yesterday, when looking at their wedding pictures, how much she had changed? How much Pierce had changed?

How naïve that she'd never considered—while planning their wedding, choosing a gown, even during their honeymoon—that moments like these wouldn't always happen easily.

At three o'clock she woke him with a kiss on the cheek and dressed for their appointment.

Later, Pierce drove with one hand, held hers with the other. She hadn't been out of his sight or his reach—literally—since he found her in the nursery that morning. Now his tightening grip, his sweaty palm, revealed his struggle to her.

"I'm fighting, Laurie. I'm really fighting to make myself do this."

She turned his hand, rested it on their baby. "Thanks for fighting for us."

***

"It's nice to meet you, Pastor Crane." Dr. Eric Goodnight, a trim, balding man with wire-rimmed glasses, extended a hand to Pierce and motioned him and Laurie to an over-stuffed couch. They sat.

The room didn't feel like a doctor's office. Probably because the dark-paneled space with its deep shelving resembled a library and occupied the main floor of the man's restored, hundred-year-old home.

"Your father and I met in seminary. I'd originally planned to become a minister, then continued on to medical school. Now I minister to ministers, and others, of course."

"And you stayed in touch with my dad?"

"We had a very successful arrangement. He referred to me those he thought needed more than he could give. I sent him those who had no clue about God. Maybe you and I can continue doing the same."

Didn't Dr. Goodnight realize why he and Laurie were here?

The doctor stood up. "Laurie, trade seats with me," he said.

Now Laurie was to Pierce's right, in his peripheral vision. He couldn't see her directly without looking away from the man now occupying the other end of the suddenly shortened sofa, a man who was way too observant for Pierce's comfort.

"I'm pretty good at reading people," Dr. Goodnight said. "And you're wondering what I think of you, if I've already judged you." He paused. "I've found that most Christians, particularly ministers who find themselves in a situation like yours, have done more than enough judging of themselves. In most instances, it usually doesn't occur to them that God still has a plan for them, is still orchestrating their circumstances, and wants to continue using them in ministry. They tend to let their imperfections blind them to their potential." He looked directly at Pierce, stood and headed for the door, calling back over his shoulder. "Excuse me for a moment. And call me Eric."

Pierce knew he was being given an option. To leave or stay. To try or give up.

But when he looked at Laurie—his sweet wife, pregnant with their child, the woman he had made love with just hours ago—refusing help didn't seem like such a good idea.

He grabbed Laurie's hand. "Laurie, I need us to pray. Right now." She barely nodded her agreement before he bowed his head.

"God, Father. Thank You for not leaving me. Thank You that Laurie didn't leave me." His voice broke. He opened his eyes and studied her shocked face. "I thought we had a great marriage, God. I thought we were really close. But now I see that we can be closer, and I want that more than I want my past to stay buried. Help me. Help us."

He held her until Eric returned.

"So. What do you want to tell me?" The doctor placed three bottled waters on the coffee table and sat.

Pierce shifted. "Well, this is all my fault."

"Not all—"

Pierce raised a hand to stop Laurie, and faced Eric. "Yes, it is. Laurie simply reacted to what I did. She believes she reacted wrongly, but nevertheless, if I hadn't done what I did, there would have been absolutely no reason for her to do what she did."

A slow smile came to the counselor's baffled face. "Okay. What did you do?"

Pierce told him everything, from the way his mother died to

being sent away. "To me, I went to sleep with one life and woke up with another. I didn't remember my mother's death, specifically. My new parents were good to me, and I wanted to be good so I wouldn't be sent away or given away again. Sometimes I didn't want to go to sleep at night. I was afraid I might wake up somewhere else and have to start all over again. Their home was fancy compared to the farm. Inside bathrooms, air conditioning, they even had a television.

"When I did wake up alone at night, the only thing I thought to do was go by their bed. They had a rug, like the one I used to lie on by my mama's bed." He shook his head. "It seemed like my place, you know? That's probably crazy."

"No, it makes perfect sense." Eric opened a water, handed it to Laurie.

She rose slowly, blushed. "Actually, I think I need a restroom first."

"That way." Eric motioned with his hand as Pierce continued in a low voice.

"I'm still completely afraid when I think of Laurie in labor. The fear is . . . inexplicable."

"It controls you?"

Pierce nodded. "Yes."

"We'll need to talk more, of course." He paused, waiting until Laurie returned and seated herself. "You've described several responses to trauma. Compartmentalization, memory suppression, and memory repression. What happens is that memories of this type can be triggered— opened or revealed, if you will—by other events. In your case, Laurie's miscarriage, then the move, and now the pregnancy. The emotions connected to those memories return also, and can cause problems."

"I feel so flawed. Can I even be a good father?" He looked at Laurie then back at Eric. "What does this mean for my credibility as a pastor? I have a wife to provide for."

"As I said, we'll need to talk much more. Some folks with this issue isolate themselves. Harm themselves. Develop addictions or have any number of negative responses. You, on the other hand, seem willing to face your trauma and deal with it. Since you're a believer, what I'm about to say should bring you comfort and hope: God wants to heal you. To do that, He has to reveal the pain and its source. If you trust Him to guide the process and utilize the help He provides—Laurie, myself, His Word, your parents—you will heal."

"I dream a memory almost every night now, sometimes repeats. Last night I dreamed more about the bus ride."

Laurie placed her hand on his shoulder. "I knew you were dreaming. Why didn't you wake me?"

Pierce shifted in his seat. "Eric, should I wake her every time? Isn't that a bit ridiculous?"

"Not if it's how God chooses to orchestrate your healing. Why don't you tell us the latest memory?"

***

As Pierce recounted last night's dream, Laurie listened.

Would she ever know the difference between his quirks, his personality, and his coping mechanisms? Did it matter? She'd thought he simply didn't like the taste of eggs, but his retelling of his mother's death explained why the smell distressed him. Now he'd revealed a clear aversion to the color green, because of the bus seat.

She felt her eyes widen with comprehension. Pierce didn't own one green shirt. They'd never owned a green chair, a green rug, even a green bath towel. He'd always suggested other colors when she'd asked. Come to think of it, years ago she'd exchanged a green kitchen rug for a different color, because he hadn't liked the one she bought.

"Laurie. Let's talk about you," Eric said.

She took a breath. "All right."

"When you scheduled this appointment, you shared your background both personal and professional. You live your life proactively.

Putting yourself through college right after your parents' death. You're an interior designer—you take other people's wants and needs, turn them into ideas, and change their environment to accommodate those wants and needs."

"I never thought about my life that way, but, yes, I suppose you're right."

Pierce looked at her. "She can absolutely make things happen. Not in a bad way, in a good way. She sees a need and she's right there." He reached for her hand. "It's one of the things I love about her."

Eric smiled, then folded his arms and leaned back. "That will probably be your biggest obstacle in this situation, Laurie. You're a very compassionate person. You get joy from relieving others' discomfort." He shook his head. "But you can't fix this for Pierce. In my opinion, more memories will surface—in God's timing—some happy, some not so happy."

She swallowed. "And we'll have to deal with them as they come, with no guarantee I'll have Pierce in the delivery room with me."

Pierce rubbed her hand. "Laurie, I'm going to try. I really am."

"Listen to me," Eric said. "In a situation like yours, the goal can't be about a timeline or delivery date. The goal has to be staying open to God and open to each other."

Stay open to God and each other. Eric's words looped through Laurie's mind as she and Pierce drove away from Eric's office. She thought of their lovemaking earlier that morning. It had been so complete. Lovelier, better than ever.

She raised her fingers to her face. She didn't look the same as before. She was fat. Pregnant fat, but still. At least one pink sliver of a stretch mark edged her belly button. He had to have noticed.

Of course he'd noticed. She almost rolled her eyes at herself.

"Can I ask you something?" How could talking about this be so difficult? She had not been self-conscious about her body since their first delicate weeks of marriage. Not that her physique had been perfect before. But she couldn't tell if her insecurity came from the emotional distance that had been between them or the physical changes in her.

His beautiful eyes, so intense, glanced at hers and held a moment. She saw the brighter specks that sparkled like diamonds, then he looked back at the road. What did he feel and think now when he looked at her?

"Was everything, um, all right for you, earlier I mean? I don't look the same."

"You're pregnant."

She saw the wheels turning in his brain. Then concern etched his face.

"Did I hurt you?"

"No," she whispered. "It was wonderful." And different.

They passed thriving peanut fields that rustled in the hot evening breeze. A huge, swirling, pink-and-orange sun hung low in the distance, a beautiful beacon guiding them directly to Daniel and Kay's home.

What if Pierce went through all of this—facing his past, talking through it, the counseling—and remained crippled inside? She'd seen marriages crack because of a disappointment, then crumble as the crack became a canyon.

If Pierce couldn't be with her in the delivery, would she be able to forgive him? Would he be able to forgive himself?

She couldn't afford to think that way. Pierce had come a long way in the last week. Hopefully this was indeed a new beginning for them.

"It's good that Eric gave us direction, a place to start. Don't you think?"

She waited.

"Pierce?" What was going through his mind? "I think it's a good idea to get more details about the adoption from your parents."

She bit the inside of her bottom lip. If she invested all of her energy in him and their marriage, would she have any strength, any moments left to think about her baby? To actually enjoy being pregnant?

They drove on. Almost thirty minutes in the car together, and Pierce had spoken maybe ten words to her. She gently pried the hand closest to her off the steering wheel and held it in hers on her stomach. Still he said nothing as he parked in front of his parents' home.

"Pierce, honey, you're squeezing my hand again."

"Sorry. What kind of soap do you buy?"

"What kind of soap?"

"Yeah."

"For dishes, clothes, or us?"

He paused, obviously not understanding her response. "Us."

"Whatever's on sale, I suppose. Although you said you don't like Ivory."

"Is that the white one?"

She couldn't help but laugh. "Yes, it's white. You told me it made you itch."

"I think that's what my mother used. The smell makes me think of her."

"Oh, Pierce. If only I'd known."

"Will you tell my parents about our appointment with Eric? I really don't think I can talk anymore right now."

"Of course," she said. "I'll do whatever you need."

***

At dinner, Pierce ate in silence while Laurie shared with his parents the details of their meeting with Eric.

"This is a little weird for me," he finally said to Daniel and Kay. "Coming over to talk with my parents about my father."

Kay lowered her fork. "Why?"

Reluctantly, he looked at her. "Well, doesn't that upset you? Being reminded that you're not my real parents?"

Daniel swayed back in his chair, motioned to pictures of Pierce displayed on every possible surface throughout the room. "We *are* your real parents. We have been since you were small."

"But we've never talked about this before," he said, and noting Kay's distressed gaze, he didn't want to talk about it now, either.

"Pierce, we told Laurie," his mom said. "We thought your mother had been dead for a long time, and that you were too little when she died to even remember her. It never occurred to us to ask you. We owe you an apology for that."

"But he contacted you before she died."

Daniel answered. "Yes, Luther came to see me weeks before he sent you to us, after church one Sunday. Later, we met him at a lawyer's office. We didn't have personal contact other than that. The lawyer was reputable and explained we'd have to pay the appropriate fees."

Pierce's throat clenched tight. "And you signed papers, never having seen me." He closed his eyes.

There had been a wall inside his mind, which had separated that life and this life. That time and the time after he came to live with Daniel and Kay. The barrier now lay in ruins, but the idea of joining the two time periods, merging them into one lifetime, terrified him.

His mouth went dry. Maybe kids from broken homes felt this way, as if someone turned their emotional equilibrium upside down. Once someone's parents divorced, once he separated his parents in his mind, how difficult it would be to see them together, talk to one about the other.

He wiped his hands across his face. "I don't know what to say. I don't know how to look at this."

"You were an answer to prayer for us, Pierce," Kay said. "For me. A miracle. I know it might seem strange now, but we'd been trying to have a child for years, much as you and Laurie. We didn't know you, but we already loved you. We couldn't possibly say no."

Daniel leaned in and pinned him with a dead-on glare. "Not

knowing what happened to your brother and father, this is just my opinion. But you can still choose to look at us and see God's provision for you." He cleared his throat. "Son, what's your biggest worry?"

Pierce grabbed Laurie's hand. "That I'll never get past it all. That I'll watch Laurie die while having my child." He hung his head. "Sometimes, I just want to know if Mama's still there, buried by the pigs."

He struggled not to fidget under his parents' concentrated attention. He'd never said those words to anyone, had barely admitted them to himself. A part of him even wished he'd never told Laurie. Couldn't he have gritted his teeth and forced himself to be there when she gave birth?

"I don't want to talk about this anymore," he said. His wife and parents exchanged looks, then they all nodded and finished the meal in silence.

They left shortly after dinner and drove home. "Do you have to pull away from them simply because of what you've remembered?" She hung her blouse in the closet. "They love you the same, treat you the same way they always did."

He paced at the foot of their bed. "How many people know?" What had he been thinking, talking so openly about a past he himself still didn't understand? "Who knows, Laurie?"

"You asked them to tell the church board and Gilbert. Everyone supports you and is praying for you. No one wants you to throw away your ministry simply because—"

"Because what?" He stopped, planting his feet like a warrior braced for battle. "Because I don't know what I'm doing? Because my whole world's gone haywire?"

"Not your whole world. Not us. We—" she waved her hand between them, pointed at the baby. "We don't have to lose everything between us. Change only cost Jesus what was no longer needed. That's what you said on Easter Sunday. The time to send the Holy Spirit had come, so Jesus didn't need to live here on this earth any longer. God is changing you and restoring your memory so you can deal with it."

She slammed a drawer and slid a nightgown over her head. "If we lose *us*, it will be *your* doing, because I'm not leaving you."

Frantic, he grabbed her shoulders. "Why do you still want to be with me?"

"Because I love you," she said. "Even when life's not perfect, or you're acting like a jerk." She shrugged away from his hold. "Excuse me, I have to go to the bathroom. Again."

If we lose us, it will be your doing, she'd said. He sank to the bed.

"Don't you think I know how you feel?" she said softly, from the bathroom doorway.

His eyes narrowed. "How?"

"I've lost people too. I lost my parents. The baby I miscarried. You think I don't know what it's like to grieve? To feel lost? I was alone for three years before I met you. No parents, no family. No one. It insults me that you think I can't relate and won't understand."

"I'm sorry," he said. "I wasn't thinking about it that way. I never knew when I'd have another dream, and I didn't know what they meant, only that they made me afraid."

He stood. Reached for her, feeling as if his fingertips barely grasped the edge of a cliff. She stepped into his embrace, and his hands trembled as he held her against him.

"This morning in the nursery you asked me if we could love each other anyway, even when we are hurting."

She nodded against his shoulder. "Life won't always be easy, and we need each other even more when it's not."

"I was miserable without you, when I was pulling away from you, and when I was in Florida."

"Please don't pull away now. You promised me you wouldn't."

He had promised he would love her.

She wrapped her arms around him. "Why do you always think

you're alone?"

Because in the hidden parts of yourself, you felt alone.

"That I will reject you?"

Because those parts have been draped with a cloak of rejection.

"Don't you know you're my life?" She pulled back, pointed at her burgeoning stomach. "I'm pregnant with your baby. What more proof of my love do you need?"

None. Absolutely none.

His heart beat hard in his chest as it had after he'd left Isaac and Ella's—a sign he was at a critical crossroads. She'd always given herself fully to him. What if he chose to concentrate on loving her instead of how he felt, instead of his turmoil?

He needed to do this. He needed to love her. Despite every worry, every unknown about his future, his certainty that his heart and head might actually explode if he met his brother and faced his father.

"Will you lie down with me?" he asked, straining against shackles he now knew were attached to his childhood. "Will you let me love you?"

Her expression softened, but he sensed her wariness. It had been a long time since he'd loved her simply to give.

He coaxed her to the bed, to lie on her side facing him. He wedged a pillow at her back, a second under her stomach, and knew he'd made a good choice when she sighed with relief. Then he turned out the light. Switched on the bedside lamp. Climbed under the sheets with her and raised her hand to his lips.

"Do you know I love your hands?" He placed a kiss on each finger, held her soft skin to his stubbly cheek. "Your hands give care, they serve, they carry kindness. I've been the recipient of that care, service, and kindness. What can I do for you?"

He looked at her with all the focus he could muster. Long seconds passed, and she looked away, almost shy.

"I don't know what you want me to say."

"It's not about what I want."

He kissed her hand again, longer, lingering kisses with his eyes locked on hers. This time, this act with her, was how they created their own world. Hiding from her had made him feel horrible, because they were meant to hide together, with each other, in each other.

"What do you want?" he asked.

"I think my hand's getting all your attention."

He let himself grin. "That I can fix."

He shifted closer to her, slid one arm under her pillow and caressed her face with the other as if she were spun glass. He followed his fingertips with his lips, kissing her brow, her nose, her cheeks, her chin, and finally settling on her mouth.

His hand slid over her shoulder, down her arm to her side.

She giggled. "No tickling," she said against his mouth.

He stilled his hand. "Tell me how to love you, Laurie. Tell me what you need."

She turned her head and whispered in his ear.

Her request made him feel like a king. He granted her wishes, gave her all she asked.

Mysteriously, his heart opened, joined Laurie's and locked into place.

CHAPTER SEVENTEEN

Pierce Crane. That was John's brother's name.

As John sat on his father's porch and watched the midday sun burn its way across the sky, he let the knowledge sink in. The shock of it still shook him, rocked him as if he were in a small boat on a choppy sea. He wondered where his brother lived, if he was educated. If they shared the same affinity for knowledge, sports cars, and the uninhibited laughter of a beautiful woman.

Did his brother's eyes match his own? Did he remember their mother? Did he know if their father had actually buried her on the farm, near where John himself sat at that exact moment?

Would he care to meet, or did he blame John for their mother's death?

Since learning of his brother's existence, John had visited Luther more frequently and often brought meals. Getting more details from his dad had been time-consuming and frustrating. No one would ever accuse Luther Bridges of talking too much.

But late last week, John hit pay dirt. Apparently the nutritious food and consistent company had helped his father become more coherent. More *there*. Although he still wouldn't talk about John's mother, he had finally told John his brother's name. Pierce Crane. He'd been five years old when their mother died.

The screen door whined open as Luther—freshly showered—stepped out to stand by his son's chair.

John stood. "Are you going somewhere?"

No response.

"Dad?"

His father's eyes fastened on the driveway. John turned to see a slow-moving dust cloud that could only be from an approaching vehicle. "Are you expecting someone?"

Silence.

His dad descended the steps, took his customary shoulder-width stance, and crossed his arms. He was either angry . . . or waiting.

The dirt-coated sedan slowed to a stop, and a man the size of a refrigerator squeezed out of the driver's-side. With his plate-round face he threw Luther a smile that said "nice to meet you," and stepped forward. "Mr. Bridges. I apologize for being a few minutes late."

"Old Man Dawkins driving his tractor on the highway again?"

John's eyes widened. Had his father just welcomed a stranger and offered more than a three-word sentence?

The visitor laughed. "Yes, sir. He sure is."

"Thought I heard it sputtering in the distance. My son," Luther said, indicating John.

John quickly extended his hand. "John Bridges."

"Gilbert Mann. Rowe City Gospel Church. Thanks for seeing me today."

The church offering to clean the barn.

John returned to his chair and sat. Watched his dad play host, walk toward the barn, talking and using small hand gestures—not the same man who had raised him.

A slow tour around the house brought them back to the front.

"We appreciate the opportunity, Mr. Bridges."

"Sure."

"We'll be here a week from Saturday." Gilbert glanced at John. "I'll warn you. Teenagers can be loud. But they're good kids, sir. We'll do good work for you."

"Sure."

The visitor returned to his car. His dad went inside, the porch door slammed behind him.

John bounded down the steps, trotted over to knock on Gilbert's window. "Where's your church?"

"Just outside of town. Most folks call it The Barn Church."

"Oh. Yeah. Are you the pastor?"

"No. I work with the youth. Pastor Daniel retired a few months back," he answered with a cherubic smile. "His son just took over. Pierce Crane."

CHAPTER EIGHTEEN

Laurie walked with Pierce the short distance from their car to Eric's office door. "Do you think I've gained weight since we left the house?"

"I might not be the smartest man in this county, but I know better than to answer that."

"I thought maternity clothes were intended to be used throughout the pregnancy. But I will not be able to wear this dress again. It's too tight when I sit." At thirty-two weeks she looked like she was about to pop, or that's what she thought whenever she looked in the mirror.

They entered, and the contrast from September's broil to air conditioning brought a smile to her face. She dropped—there was no other way to describe it—onto the soft couch cushions and welcomed the goose bumps.

"We're a little late because of me," she told Eric. "I don't move as quickly as I used to."

Eric chuckled. "And I'm afraid that won't change for a while yet." He listened as she and Pierce filled him in on their progress. "You've gathered a lot of information in a short time." Eric wrote notes as he spoke. "That can help tremendously, Pierce."

Laurie felt Pierce stiffen, so she shifted closer to him on the couch.

Urgency simmered inside her. She fought the urge to fidget, to be impatient with Pierce. She'd determined to help him however she could, yet she fervently wished she could speed things up.

Which was exactly what Eric had warned her about. Somehow her greatest strength had become her biggest weakness.

She tapped her belly as Eric handled an interruption from his secretary.

Had they told Eric all they'd learned? That Luther had contacted Daniel and Kay before Annabelle died, and had not told them she was still alive. Kay had described Luther as "sad." Broken, worn, and sad. He must have loved his wife, and he must have believed she wouldn't survive giving birth a second time.

Had the darkness of grief swallowed up Luther, even before he lost Annabelle? The thought of losing her, the possibility of raising two children alone, maybe it was more than he could bear. Maybe his actions weren't indicative of a malicious man—as Pierce had first described him—but rather a devastated husband, a reeling father.

She wished she could snap her fingers and fix Pierce, so he could be happy about the baby. She needed him to be with her in the delivery room. Not just in body, but really *there*, emotionally, both for moral support and so they could experience the moment together. This might be their only child.

"Pierce. I'm going to the restroom." She stood. "Whew. When I'm sitting I forget how heavy I am. Be right back."

She gratefully leaned against the sealed door, then ran cold water over both hands in the sink. Too much was happening, and not enough was happening.

She wished she knew what God had planned for Pierce. For her and the delivery.

Why?

Well, she needed to be prepared. Her parents' deaths had been so unexpected, so final. The miscarriage, another awful reminder of how uncertain life can be.

Trust me.

The sonogram would soon be performed, wasn't every pregnant

woman nervous before having a sonogram? *God, please don't let anything be wrong with my baby.*

My baby. My miracle.

Trust me.

Her racing heart skidded, then slowed to a normal speed.

Six months ago she hadn't known she was pregnant—but she was. Less than six months ago she hadn't known about Pierce's mother's death or his brother's birth. Did she not trust God to finish His work in both of them?

Heavenly Father, I'm sorry. Forgive me for forgetting to trust You, and not trusting You even when I remember I should.

She returned to the couch and took Pierce's hand.

***

Today, Pierce did not want to be in Eric's office.

During their first appointment, he'd appreciated the homey atmosphere. The rich wood, the small bin of toys and plastic Legos shoved into the corner. For young patients? For grandkids?

But not this time. Today he felt boxed in. Trapped in a place and a process he was too far in to get out of, and not far enough in to be excited it was almost over. Because he hadn't had any new memories since their last meeting?

Laurie had scooted over closer to him when Eric's secretary entered the room. Then she went to the bathroom, came back, and took his hand. Pierce expected her to say something. He *wanted* her to say something—anything to distract him from the issue at hand.

But that would defeat the whole purpose, wouldn't it?

Laurie whispered in his ear. "Did you see that?"

"Hmm? What?"

"The long look that Eric gave his wife. It was sweet."

Eric's wife. And secretary.

"I didn't recognize her at first, either." Laurie pointed to a photograph on the desk. "But look. It's her. Lighter hair, shorter, too. Pretty."

Once again, Eric took the chair across from them. "My wife just got her hair done."

Laurie beamed a proud grin at Pierce, then spoke to Eric. "It looks great."

"That's what I said." The doctor re-opened his notes, looked at Pierce. "Now, where were we?"

"You said knowing everything that happened will help me." But how? A noose of frustration wrapped around his mind.

"You don't agree," Eric said.

"I don't know." Pierce released Laurie's hand and lifted both of his.

Eric set aside his notes, leaned forward to brace his forearms on his thighs like he and Pierce were two friends simply having a conversation in his living room. "My friend, knowing the truth won't change your experience; but it might change how you interpret your experience. You see, a five-year-old can't understand adult issues like a husband grieving the loss of his wife, but you can almost understand that now because you're married to Laurie and you're afraid for her, right?"

"Yes." Every muscle in Pierce's body tightened.

"Makes your skin crawl, right?"

"Yes."

"A five-year-old can't understand a father who would send him away from the only home he had ever known, but as a man you can understand a father who wants a better life for his child. Isn't that why you're here?"

Pierce spread his fingers across Laurie's stomach and locked his eyes on hers. "I'm here because I love you. Because I love our child. Because God insisted I tell you and won't let me keep this part of myself from you." He included Eric with a quick glance as he rose to pace.

"Here's something you need to know: I can't stand this emotional roller coaster I'm on. One minute I think 'Yes, I can do this. I can be the husband and father, the minister, God wants me to be.'

"Then a tidal wave of anxiety crashes into me and I'm drowning, gasping for breath. I'm ashamed to say part of me wants to get out of the water and forget it. But now that I've started this process, I really can't stop. I have to finish it."

He stopped in front of them, feet spread, arms crossed. And immediately grieved leaving Laurie's side. He sat beside her, took her hand and gently massaged her fingers.

"I get some of it right." Like the way he'd reconnected with Laurie and managed to stay close to her. "Then I crash and burn like an idiot." Like his attitude when he walked in here today.

"Pierce," Eric said. "Repeating old habits is easy; changing them is hard. It's work to behave differently. We're not looking for perfection here."

"I'm looking for relief!" Embarrassed, he lowered his voice. "I don't want to find my father. I don't want to see him." He kissed Laurie's hand. "I don't know what to think about my brother."

Beside him, Laurie sighed heavily. "Your father may be the only one who can tell us exactly what happened to your mother, if your brother lived, or any number of—"

Eric held up a hand to stop Laurie, and looked at Pierce. "But you'll do whatever you need to, won't you. You'll do it for yourself and you'll do it for her."

Pierce nodded. To his surprise, Laurie laid her head on his shoulder. His chest ached at the simple gesture.

Sometimes loving someone was hard. Laurie loved him, even when doing so was difficult. She let him love her, even if their circumstances weren't perfect, even if moments before they had shed tears together.

Now he knew that sometimes loving God was hard, too. Sometimes obeying God was scary. And sometimes, as Jesus experienced, something—or Someone—had to die a long public death, so necessary changes could take place.

"Sometimes I can't believe you love me like this," he said.

She pulled his hand back to their baby. "I've always loved you like this, you just couldn't feel it before. I'd always thought there was a part of you I couldn't touch. I think that part is your memories. They wrapped around you like an old, ratty blanket."

Hadn't he sensed it, too? A shadowy wall. A mysterious barrier, first between him and his adoptive parents, then between him and Laurie?

"I think you're right. I hate it, but I think you are right."

"We might find that locating your father and brother won't be as terrible as you think it will," she said. "Yes, you lost your mother, but other reasons you felt rejected could be untrue."

Eric glanced at Laurie. "She's right. There could still be parts you don't remember. Not that your feelings aren't real, but you don't know any of the motives behind the actions. You feel betrayed because you believe your adoption by the Cranes is proof of your father's rejection. Maybe that's not true. The result, yes; but not necessarily the reason.

"Bridges is an extremely common name around here. You're probably related to half the occupants of the next three counties. But your father could be dead, too, Pierce. Have you considered that?"

"No." Did Pierce hope his father was dead, so there would be no opportunity to face him? "I've tried not to think about him." He paused. "What should I do now?"

"Keep doing whatever brings you closer to God, closer to Laurie, and you won't go wrong. You might never have all the answers, Pierce. Some of the pain, some of the questions, you may have to give to God every day for the rest of your life."

***

In some ways, Laurie thought, everything had changed. She knew more about her husband's struggles as a person, as a man, than ever before. While often difficult, hearing him connect emotions with his memories under Eric's direction appeared to help Pierce. Yet inside, she couldn't help weeping for the child her husband had once been.

In other ways, like the way he snuggled up to her back in bed and wrapped his arm around her waist, or the fact that she could feel him lay there completely awake and practically vibrating with mischief, everything was the same.

"You need to get some sleep before morning," she whispered.

"I know. The kids and youth love their building. Gilbert told them all to thank you every time they see you." Through her gown, he caressed her belly. His fingers met the bump of her belly button and lingered there.

"I'm glad they're enjoying it." She brushed his hand away.

He moved it back.

She rolled to face him.

In the darkness, he kissed her cheek and happily placed his hand where it had been.

"Why are you so fascinated with that?"

"What do you mean?" He traced his fingers over the pinkie-sized bulge.

She giggled. "I'm embarrassed for you to do that."

"It's dark. No one can see. I can't even see, well, barely."

She nudged him in the ribs.

Pierce continued to play. "Does that happen to all pregnant women?"

"You're not going to sleep now, are you?"

He rose on an elbow, braced his head in his palm. "Probably not. I like this better." He kissed her cheek again.

"What's gotten into you? If this is what my dumplings do to you, I won't make them again."

"Sure you should. Now let's pick names. What do you think about Daniel for a boy?"

"I think that would make someone very happy. I heard you call them today and tell them you'll preach this weekend. I'm sure part of you is nervous, but the more I've thought about your Easter sermon, the more I'm sure you've made the right decision."

"Because?"

"Because maybe this is just like Jesus' crucifixion. It was more than a little change for Him. It was total humility, total exposure of His struggle between life and death, between righteousness and sin. Everyone watched Him and some believed because of what they saw. Mankind hasn't changed. What if the greatest change that can happen for people watching you, happens *because* they're watching you?"

"Thanks, and you're right about the nervousness. My hands are sweating right now just thinking about it. But my spirit is relieved."

"I'm proud of you. But." She huffed at him. "Will you stop rubbing your fingers over my poor, deformed belly button?"

He didn't. "Only if the middle name can be Boone. Daniel Boone Crane."

"You have to be kidding."

"We'll buy him a furry, raccoon-tailed hat and a toy rifle."

She shook her head, with groans she rolled back onto her other side, and spoke over her shoulder. "It's after midnight. I have to meet with a client tomorrow. No more dumplings for you."

"I bet Daniel Boone liked dumplings."

"*What* made you think of Daniel Boone?"

"I just remembered. On the farm, we didn't have a television. But Mrs. Taylor had an old black and white, rabbit ears and everything. Sometimes I watched it if Mother and I went for a visit. I guess that's kind of a good memory, huh?"

"I think so. Ouch."

Pierce froze behind her. "What?"

"Baby kicked my bladder. Be right back. Push."

With a gentle helping hand, he nudged her off the bed.

"I have a girl's name picked," she said minutes later, climbing back in bed and pulling Pierce's arm back over her middle.

"Tell me."

"Hope. I like Hope."

"Hope Elizabeth Crane." He murmured against her shoulder.

"Elizabeth was my mother's name."

"I know. Now hush. I need to get some sleep."

"Pierce? Thank you."

"I love you." He kissed the back of her neck. "I hope it's a girl."

"We can find out next week. The sonogram."

"Right. The sonogram."

She clamped her hand around his retreating wrist, sang her next words. "You promised. You're going."

"Yes. Yes, I am." He patted her belly. "Maybe it's twins."

Laurie elbowed him in the ribs. "That should take the grin off your face."

***

The music seemed extra loud in the rustic church. The dresses, ties, and lights extra brilliant. Pierce was hyperalert, hypersensitive to every-thing—including the welcoming handshakes and hugs he received—as though he had been gone for months instead of weeks.

Time ticked slowly, sprinted, then slowed again.

The choir sang about God's divine plan—yes, there was a plan.

The offering was collected—almost time for him to speak.

His ears buzzed so loudly as he stood at the pulpit scanning the crowd, he half expected someone to run to the window and watch for an approaching tornado.

Instead, all eyes stayed fixed on him. Laurie's. His parents'. Gilbert's.

Those of Deacon Floyd and his petite, white-haired wife with her hand-crocheted shawl—she must have one in every possible color.

Rick and Julie Matthews. Had she sung a solo that morning?

Luke—what was that kid's last name?—sat near the front. His girlfriend hadn't accompanied him, probably still recovering from childbirth. But another girl sat with him, and an older woman. Both had eyes as black as night, and hair to match. Luke's future in-laws?

Clear sunlight speared between the creaking double doors at the back of the room. They eased shut as a young professional-type, in dark pants and a stiffly pressed white shirt, entered and took a seat with a bald-headed old man.

"Good morning, everyone."

Deacon Floyd led the response. "Welcome back, Pastor."

As the applause dwindled, Pierce couldn't help feeling ashamed. Just weeks earlier he had considered leaving these folks. They knew nothing of it. They loved him.

He supposed despair and fear could almost blind a man. Narrow his sight to pinhole size so his spiritual vision was reduced to nothing.

A thin thread of truth, like a delicate, gold filament, weaved its way through Pierce's mind from where Laurie had planted it in his heart. She was right; all eyes were on him.

A baby squealed. Someone coughed. Expectant gazes wavered as bodies shifted in their seats.

How long had he stood there saying nothing?

He took a deep breath. "I have no notes for you today."

Sweat greased his hands. He shoved them in his pockets and stepped back to pace across the stage. "My wife is responsible for what you'll hear this morning." He raised his chin in Laurie's direction and stopped short. "And my parents. Who could ignore them, right?"

He paused while knowing laughter rippled across the congregation.

"Easter Sunday was the first time I preached with myself in mind. Remember I talked about change? The change that Jesus faced to fulfill His destiny as our Savior. That change was death, of course, but nevertheless, divinely orchestrated by our Heavenly Father, so that we could have our sins forgiven and our relationship with God restored. I prayed with some of you about changes you needed God to work in your own lives."

He stepped off the platform, stopped at the base with feet spread, arms crossed.

"God's answer for me on a personal level was no."

Across the room, heads cocked and brows furrowed with silent questions.

"I didn't like that answer." As if in thought, he rubbed a palm over his jaw line, then placed it over his heart. "I'm sorry to say I almost resigned my position here because of it." Again he paced, then stopped to face them. "I'm ashamed of that. I apologize to all of you, and ask your forgiveness.

"Right now, I'm stumbling through obedience to God. I suppose I feel a lot like the children of Israel when God parted the Red Sea. The Egyptians followed, hot on their heels. And yes, God performed quite the miracle standing the waters up that way."

He walked to Laurie on his right and placed a hand on their unborn child. "But sometimes walking through a miracle is more frightening than staying where we are. Our feet don't expect dry ground where there should be mud. The shock of seeing God's handiwork up close makes us realize how truly vulnerable we are. How needy we are. How big He is."

He stepped back to the foot of the stage. "Next week I'll speak about miracles. Not how to get them, but how they impacted different people in scripture. My father and I will rotate weeks after that, so Laurie and I can prepare for our new baby.

"Today, I'd like to end the service by offering prayer. Not mine.

Yours. As I said, I'm learning as I go. So, I'll wait here for you to come take my hand and pray, because you need to talk to God and listen to God for yourself—not hear me talk to Him. But I'll agree with you now, and continue to pray for you this week."

A little red-haired girl, in a worn pink dress and dirty sandals, slipped into the aisle. Pierce bent to hear her whisper. "God told me no, too. The doctor says my daddy is dying of cancer."

His mouth went dry as he crouched in front of her. What could he possibly say?

But she had already taken his hand. Already squeezed her eyes shut and begun to speak. "Dear God, so far You haven't healed my daddy. I need him. My mommy needs him. If Your answer is still no, please don't be mad if we cry. We need money. Tell us what to do." Then she smiled big, hugged him, and scampered back to her seat.

Through watery eyes he saw that no one else had moved. Had he been wrong to do this?

Deacon Floyd raised a hand, standing and looking around. "Pastor, there's too many of us to line up in front of you. Maybe we should all just stay and pray together for a while."

"Sure." Pierce answered as he stood again. "I'll stay as long as anyone needs."

He heard weeping. Faint, racking weeping.

It came from the far left, rear corner of the building. From the old man—bald head bent, thin frame shaking—who sat near the polished professional. Pierce watched, quietly amazed and thrilled as several people walked over to pray for the distraught stranger.

Across the congregation, some knelt at their seats. Others stood and approached the altar area. Small groups formed, grasped hands, and murmured needs.

It was all God. It was only God.

Pierce couldn't have made it happen if he had sent letters, made announcements, and passed out instructions at the door. God didn't need his help, only his participation.

More, Father. Show us more. Show me more.

Rick Matthews approached, then shook Pierce's hand and held on. In a soft and tired voice he said, "My son, Lord. He believes You're leading him to military service. We wanted direction for him, but this, this means he'll leave in less than a year. He's the glue in our family. Oh, God, keep him safe." He raised his head. "Thanks, Pastor."

"Sure."

Many minutes passed and a comforting quiet filled the vaulted room. After a short benediction, Pierce proceeded to the heavy, ancient doors to greet folks as they left. His gaze locked with the well-dressed newcomer's. He watched the visitor follow out the old man, the one who had wept.

Chapter Nineteen

Withering fall heat blasted John as he opened the truck door. Sweat trickled across his scalp as he jammed his key in the ignition and drummed his fingers on the steering wheel, waiting for his father to fasten his seatbelt. He flipped the AC dial to blizzard and pulled onto the street.

"So. That was my brother."

Luther sat like a scolded child, silent, with folded hands.

"He stands exactly like you." Feet spread, arms crossed.

Pierce had the same medium build as John, though not as wiry. They both had thick, dark-brown hair, which must have matched their mother's. His dad's hair—when he'd had hair—reflected Luther's Cherokee heritage. Straw straight and raven black.

John bought a bucket of fried chicken at a drive-through, drove to the farm. What kind of childhood had Pierce had? What supposed miracle was he experiencing, and what had God told him "no" about?

"Does he have Mom's eyes?"

Perfect sky blue. And John thought those eyes had followed him and his dad, *their* dad, right out the door ahead of the quiet, meandering crowd.

"Yes."

Minutes passed. John slowed and turned onto the long, unkempt driveway. "You gave him away." The truck lurched and rumbled along the rutty lane. "When?"

"Days after you were born."

What? "The Taylors wouldn't keep two of us?"

"Didn't ask."

"Mom died here, having me."

He looked ahead at the pitiful farm. She'd bled to death. Partly during labor, partly a postpartum hemorrhage. Probably due to uterine atony, he hypothesized—more commonly known as a boggy uterus. Or, a partial placental abruption—a tearing away of the placenta from the uterine wall—might have been a contributing factor.

If she'd been in a hospital, she might have lived. She definitely would have needed blood, possibly an emergency hysterectomy, but she would have survived. Although she might not have been able to have any more children.

John suspected she probably shouldn't have had *him*.

He glanced at his dad. "Do you blame me?"

No answer.

"How old was I when you sent me to live with the Taylors? Days? Weeks?"

"Couldn't tend you and the farm."

"Newborn, then."

One son given away. Another, a baby, sent away for years.

"Did you love our mother?"

Luther answered with a grainy whisper. "She died because I loved her."

John stopped the truck in the usual spot by the barn and shoved it in PARK. He raked a hand through his hair. "I was what, four, when you brought me back here? Why did you want *me*? For help? Free labor?"

His dad looked out the broad windshield over the waist-high weedy fields, and seemed to age right before John's eyes.

"For the company."

CHAPTER TWENTY

This time, Laurie sat in the front seat next to Pierce as he drove to her mid-week doctor's appointment. And again, a train stopped them. The ten a.m. freight certainly ran like clockwork.

Clickety-clack. Tick-tock.

The passing boxcars marked time itself, mimicking the count-down to her delivery and highlighting the "to-do" list in her head.

Accompany Pierce to appointments with Eric, listen and learn, pray for Pierce. *Check.*

Be patient when he walks in the woods at night to pray, instead of staying with her and talking non-stop about the baby. Difficult, but *Check.*

Wait on God's timing—the hardest item on her list.

Could the worst be over? Pierce hadn't had a nightmare for more than a week. He'd preached last Sunday. And, most important, he would be with her this morning for the sonogram. Maybe he didn't need to track down his father and brother after all.

"Pierce, honey, the crossing gates are rising."

"So is my blood pressure." He eased over the tracks and took Laurie's hand. "But better to be nervous about doing the right thing than the wrong one."

"I'm so excited," she said. "And a little nervous. The baby must feel it. He or she's doing somersaults."

Laurie strolled into the office with a happy, expectant bounce in her step. She couldn't help throwing a huge smile at the petite, redhead receptionist. "Hello, Pam."

"Sonogram day for you," Pam said. "Very exciting."

"I can hardly wait."

To Laurie's surprise, Pam reached over the desk and grabbed her husband's arm. "Pastor Crane, that service was so good Sunday. I just love the way you preach. And you were so sweet to my niece, Gracie. That was her first time in church, ever. She's staying with me while her parents are at a cancer treatment center out of state. She's been telling everyone that the preacher held her hand and hugged her in front of everybody. Thank you."

"Pierce. That little girl . . ." Laurie said as they sat in the waiting area. "I knew I'd never seen her at church before."

Pam called them back a minute later. "Slight change of plans," she said as she led them to a room. "Dr. Nate had to leave for the hospital. Dr. John, the cute new guy, will see you today." She wiggled her brow and Laurie laughed. "You would have to meet him anyway, eventually. You know the drill. Designer gowns are on the shelf."

Laurie turned her back to Pierce, slid her hair to one side. "Unzip me?"

"Sure." He eased down the zipper. "I've always loved the freckles across the back of your neck and shoulders. They glow like a sunburst." He pressed a soft kiss between her shoulder blades.

A quick knock sounded at the door and it swung open. "Sorry," the young doctor said. "I'll give you another minute." He closed the door.

She laughed, leaned back against Pierce, and pulled his arms around her. "I know you're mortified, probably blushing like a teenager caught making out in the church parking lot. But at this precise moment I am *so* happy."

***

"This is the spine. You can see the rib cage. Looks like a busy little thing." The young Dr. John—had Pierce seen him somewhere before?—moved the ultrasound Doppler over Laurie's gel-covered stomach.

Pierce likened the pictures on the screen to a black and white movie, though not as grainy. His child's spine was seashell white; it curled, wriggling as the baby rolled and kicked. The rhythmic, whirring sound—interrupted by the occasional thump—indicated a sure, strong heartbeat.

"Now here's the head." The doctor pressed some buttons on the keyboard and froze the picture. "I'm taking measurements. And here is a front view of the face."

Pierce actually saw the features.

Laurie laughed. "That's my baby's face?"

A miracle happened inside Pierce, a sharpening of focus, as if the gears of his mind slipped into position. He snatched up every precious detail.

Laurie, so happy. Pregnant, laughing with joy, love shining on her face.

His baby inside her. Whose growth and movement stretched her skin. Whose very life came from Laurie's sweet heart that Pierce loved beyond reason or words.

Then God let Pierce glimpse his future.

His life spread before him. Full of wonderful possibilities, unexpected problems, certainly some sorrow. And, God was giving him a family, creating it right in front of him. They meant more to him than anything.

"Pierce, we want to know, don't we?"

"What?"

"We need to tell him if we want to know the sex of the baby."

He kissed Laurie's cheek. "Sure."

"Let's see." Dr. John slid the device around, stopped and pressed more buttons, then did it all again. "I'd say you have a daughter."

Laurie's high-pitched squeal almost burst Pierce's eardrums, but he didn't care. And there would be many more ear-splitting screams, from his little girl who would grow and play and call him Daddy.

"It's Hope, Pierce. Our little Hope. I can't stop crying." Laurie sat up, giving him a loud, smacking kiss, right in front of the young doctor.

"Hope Elizabeth Crane," she said. "I can't wait to tell your parents."

***

Dr. John Bridges turned off the machine, handed Pierce and Laurie some black-and-white photos, and ejected the DVD they had brought so they could have their own copy of the sonogram. "Consultation Room 2 is right across the hall; come over after you get dressed."

He lifted her chart and paused at the door. The way they were looking at each other, he wasn't sure they knew he was still in the room. "Mrs. Crane?"

"Yes?"

She still wasn't looking at him. "Come across the hall after you're dressed."

"Yes, of course. Thank you. Oh, Pierce . . ."

John exited the room, closing the door behind himself. With Laurie's records in hand, he went straight to the empty employee lounge and chugged a coke in three big gulps. He needed caffeine. He needed air.

He needed to think.

When he'd first opened the door and realized who his patient was, he'd been grateful Laurie wasn't quite ready. Giving her the extra minutes had also given him time to switch completely back into professional mode and make himself concentrate on his patient.

He squashed the can and tossed it into the recycling bin. What had Laurie said? She couldn't wait to tell Pierce's parents.

What if Pierce had never been told he was adopted? What if he didn't know? What if he didn't remember their father, the farm, or their mother?

John flipped open her chart.

Laurie Crane. Husband, Pierce Crane. The same man who had preached on Sunday at Rowe City Gospel Church, where John sat in the back with their weeping father.

His patient's husband was his own long-lost brother.

There were only two options, weren't there? Identify himself, or not.

If he was on-call when Laurie went into labor, he would deliver his own niece. Would Laurie be comfortable with that? Would his brother look at him and see the person responsible for their mother's death?

He should say something to them.

But first he had some investigating to do.

John searched through Laurie's demographic information, locating the emergency contacts. Daniel and Kay Crane were listed, Pierce's adoptive parents. He'd call them as soon as he had a minute.

He composed himself. Met with them like any other expecting couple. His little break had put him behind, so he caught up on patients, then closed himself in his office and called the Cranes.

The call was answered by a female voice before the end of the first ring.

"What is it, Laurie? Did you forget to tell me something? Daniel and I are thrilled it's a girl. A girl!"

"Mrs. Crane?"

"Yes. I'm sorry."

A male voice belly-laughed in the background, the woman spoke away from the phone. "Hush, you." Then back to John. "So sorry. I thought you were someone else."

"Mrs. Crane, this is Dr. John Bridges. I'm an obstetrician at Dr. Jordan's clinic. Is your husband available also?"

"Yes." She paused. "Our daughter-in-law, Laurie Crane, is a patient at your office. She's expecting our first grandbaby."

"Yes, ma'am. If I could speak with you and Mr. Crane."

"Just a moment." Then he heard, "Daniel, it's Laurie's doctor. He wants to speak to us."

A gentleman came on the line. "This is Daniel Crane. My wife is Kay."

"Mr. Crane, this is Dr. John Bridges. I'm an obstetrician at Dr. Jordan's clinic. Do you two have a moment?"

"Certainly, Dr. Bridges. We've got you on speaker. How can we help you?"

"Well, sir, and ma'am, does Pierce know he was adopted?"

"Is something wrong with Laurie?" Kay asked.

"No, ma'am. Laurie's fine."

Daniel spoke next. "Dr. Bridges, exactly what is this about?"

"Well, sir, ma'am, I just learned of Pierce's existence . . . I'm Pierce's brother."

CHAPTER TWENTY-ONE

The phone rang right after Pierce and Laurie entered their home. Laurie opened the refrigerator. "I'll make lunch."

Pierce lifted the receiver. "Hi, Mom. Oh. Sorry, Dad."

"Son, we received a call from Dr. John at the clinic just moments after you and Laurie left there. Dr. John *Bridges,*" his father said.

Pierce sank against the counter. He suddenly remembered being a little boy, jumping out of the huge oak tree in the front yard and pretending to fly. With a towel tied around his neck, and a Superman figure in hand, he leaped off the branches—thrilling at the weightless feeling—and hit the ground running. He was a superhero. Invincible. Pain and peril couldn't touch him.

Both pummeled him at once.

Pain. The face of his dead mother, dotted with traces of fresh blood, hung in his mind like filmy gauze. He couldn't look at anything in that moment without seeing her.

Peril. He had been found and was trapped. Like a child who had seen an approaching tornado and run for the cellar, only to find that when the storm passed, heavy debris blocked the doors from the outside.

"He found our number in Laurie's chart and called us first, concerned you might not know you were adopted. He's your brother, Pierce. He and Luther came to church Sunday. He says he didn't know about you until recently."

His father had been at church Sunday? And his brother. That's where he'd seen Dr. John before.

"He wants to meet you. He even asked if I thought you'd meet him for lunch, like, today. I don't think you should wait on this, son. I believe this is an answer to prayer for you."

***

One look at Pierce's paling face, and Laurie knew that her actions in this moment would have a lasting impact on her future. Their future.

Like the day she'd arrived home from school and discovered a stray dog hiding under the back steps. She didn't touch it, but simply backed away and scampered to the front door instead. Later, a neighbor had been bitten by that same dog, and contracted rabies.

A second time was the night of her best friend's sixteenth birthday party. Laurie had looked forward to it all week; she and her friends had planned a midnight picnic while camping at the nearby reservoir. But her friends, including the "birthday girl," decided to swim in their birthday *suits*, when some boys showed up bringing liquor to share.

Laurie had refused to participate, and instead locked herself in her best friend's new car and slept in the back seat.

One of the boys had drowned. The police found his body the next morning.

This event—this *happening* and how she handled it—was a pivotal moment. *Father, what should I do? What should I say?*

Carry each other's burdens.

She went to Pierce and wrapped her arms around him as he stood frozen with the phone pressed to his ear. She rubbed his back, gently moving her hands up and down, as his heart pounded against hers.

Finally, he relaxed enough to breathe. He gulped air.

"It's all right. I'm here. It's all right."

Dear God, please shroud my husband in peace. Give him strength, help him, and heal him. Give me wisdom to know what to do, what to say.

"Yeah, Dad, I heard you. I'll talk to Laurie, let you know what I decide."

He replaced the phone in its cradle and clung to her.

***

Pierce clutched Laurie tightly, desperate to hold onto her and his new perspective, the new vision of his family that God had given him during the sonogram.

Laurie and their baby girl, Hope.

He was not alone. He was five years old. On a bus—the likes of which he had never before ridden—clutching a small paper sack to his chest, his head bobbing against the bottom of the bus window's hard metal frame.

He was not curled up on and facing a dark-green seat, waking to find that his old life and everything he knew before was gone, swept away as unwanted dust.

I know the plans I have for you. To prosper you.

The adoption had been arranged before his mother died.

God will meet all your needs according to his glorious riches in Christ Jesus.

Daniel and Kay had been waiting for him at the bus stop.

The Lord your God is with you, he is mighty to save. He will take great delight in you, he will quiet you with his love, he will rejoice over you with singing.

Pierce remembered waking as Daniel lifted him in cradling arms and carried him down the bus steps to their car. Kay held him in the back seat as they drove home.

She sang to him.

Pierce was tinier than most five-year-olds, small-framed. He was dirty. He probably smelled.

He remembered them taking him home, showing him this kitchen. His room, the one Laurie was now making into a nursery.

Where the bathrooms were. Two of them, inside, with lights.

Kay had continued to hold him while sitting at the table that day, Daniel sat next to them. In the quiet house, they spoke softly, coaxing him to eat.

He remembered hearing the sharp crunch of a fat pickle in his own mouth. The tart smell of vinegar from a big, glass jar filled with them. The sticky juice that trickled to his chin.

They had kept him and loved him and made him their own.

If his father had kept him, would his life have had the same love, the same laughter, the same opportunity to grow up knowing God?

Pierce doubted it.

And there was the rub.

"Laurie, do you believe I can be thankful for God's provision of my parents, and still grieve my mother? What I mean is, I don't have to be glad Mama died in order to be grateful for Mom and Dad, do I?"

"Of course not. One doesn't have to exclude the other."

"It's work to think this way." He paused. "You won't believe what's happened."

His brain spun as he told her about John. He watched her eyes go round, her face light up. When she bit her bottom lip, obviously torn between trying not to say words he might not want to hear, but probably needed to.

"Tell me, Laurie."

"Okay." An instant, huge smile appeared on her pretty face, and she tightened her hold on him. "If he's your brother, he might be able to tell you everything we want to know. What happened to him, to your father, and how your mother died."

"I know how my mother died." Pierce closed his eyes, tried to shake the image from his mind.

Laurie lowered her voice. "We need to know the *why* behind the *how*—maybe there was something wrong with her, something that's not wrong with me—so you won't be scared I'll die the same way."

She had just said aloud his biggest obstacle. That when she went into labor, he would stand helplessly beside her, unable to do anything except watch her die, as he had his own mother.

Daddy hadn't helped Mama. He had turned his back on her when she needed him most. When she called his name again and again. *"Luther. Luther!"*

Yes, Pierce's fear was irrational; it didn't make sense in light of technology and reality and every other piece of common sense or fact he could think of. Still, it had control. After all he'd remembered, all he'd told Laurie, everything he'd discovered and discussed with Eric—fear spoke loud and clear: Run. Escape. Hide.

Then you will know the truth, and the truth will set you free.

"I want to be free, Laurie. But I don't know how many more steps I have to take, or how to take them."

Laurie bracketed his face with her hands. "Pierce, open your eyes. Look at me."

He complied.

"I am so proud of you. When our daughter gets old enough to understand, I want to tell her what a brave, godly father she has."

"I don't feel brave. I feel desperate."

"Just take the next right step, Pierce."

"Right," he said. "I have to go meet my brother."

***

Laurie wanted so badly to go with Pierce, she almost couldn't keep from demanding he let her accompany him. But something inside her knew he needed to meet with his brother alone. She didn't like it, but she knew it to be true.

And what was she to do with herself after she prayed with him, prayed over him as he drove away from their home?

How she wished her mother was near. Or at least available via phone.

Kay. Laurie dialed her mother-in-law and got voicemail. Pierce had probably called them as soon as he left.

She walked down the hall to her bedroom and lay on her side. Despite her husband's fragile emotions, he continued to take baby steps every day. Still, how tentative those baby steps were.

Dear God, couldn't he have a little more time to get stronger? More sure of himself before he faced John?

She'd thought they could simply concentrate on healing now. Rebuild. Continue their counseling with Eric, yes, but focus on each other, on their child.

Lord, I'm trying to trust You. Couldn't we have more than an hour to rejoice over having a daughter?

She reached for her Bible. Opened again to Philippians 4:8. *Whatever is true.*

Had her ideas and expectations—about marriage, about starting a family, her pregnancy—been based on misperceptions? In some ways, lies?

You've measured every life event against those expectations, much as Pierce measured every life event against his past.

No wonder her disappointment was so profound. And she'd fussed at God, hadn't she. Fussed at Him because her life experience didn't meet those Laurie-invented expectations.

Dear Heavenly Father, I'm sorry. I know I need to give You my future, but I find that, just like Pierce, I'm afraid of what might be asked of me. Please, no matter what Pierce does, no matter what happens, help me do the next right thing.

She dialed Kay again, and this time reached her mother-in-law. "Mom? I think I just discovered something about myself. I need to ask your opinion."

***

Pierce flexed his hands on the steering wheel as he drove to the Downtown Diner to meet his brother—the "cute new doctor"—again. How weird was that?

During the sonogram, time had moved as slowly as thick molasses. The long moments coated with sweetness had spread, one after the other in a beautiful, long line. He had savored them, knowing he could hold onto them when life became difficult.

But he hadn't expected the difficulty to come so quickly, or to be of such monumental importance.

Was he thankful or sad he hadn't recognized his father and brother on Sunday? He had noticed them, but he hadn't "known" them. They left as the service ended without him learning their names.

Which might have been a good thing.

Sunday wasn't the right time.

This morning Pierce had been in the same small room with John. Yet he'd felt no connection to the man.

This morning wasn't the right time, either.

No, the time was now. In the next two minutes.

Yet a part of him wished time would stand still. He wanted more minutes before seeing his brother, thinking anymore about his father, and becoming a father himself.

Pierce pulled into a parking space and adjusted the sunglasses he hoped would provide a minuscule amount of privacy. Heaven only knew how many people would be at the diner, watching.

He didn't want to think about it. He wouldn't think about it.

He walked to the glass door. The familiar smell of grease, burgers, and fries, the expected clang of silverware against dishes and counters as patrons consumed their meals, all were muted by the nerves jangling in his head.

Before he realized it, Milly Newman blocked his path. "Do you know what the baby is yet?" She clapped her hands together. "I've got to call Laurie and plan her baby shower!"

Mr. Newman stood military-stiff behind his chair, tossed bills on the table. "Milly, let the man eat."

She hugged him. "Sorry, Pastor. We're all so excited and happy for you."

She let him pass, but he knew others watched and wondered why Daniel wasn't meeting him for their usual Tuesday lunch.

Pierce stopped at the end of the booth. John stood and extended his hand. "Pierce, thanks for meeting me."

"Sure."

He supposed he expected a shock at the offered contact, but his hand met his brother's without event. A small step.

He should . . . sit.

He sat.

They should . . . talk.

"Laurie says hi." Could he possibly sound more ridiculous?

"She seems like a great lady."

Silence stretched. The waitress approached with two small glasses of water in hand, took their orders, and left.

He could do this. He *could* do this.

"You married?"

"No. Almost, once. But no."

Okay. What now?

"Sorry, but I only have a short time before the next patient." John shifted in his seat. "Have you had a good life?"

How to answer that, when he was only beginning to recognize it himself? "Yes. Yes, my life is great."

"Because of Laurie?"

Pierce gulped his water. "Yes. Laurie."

"I didn't know you existed until a short time ago. Did you know Mr. and Mrs. Taylor?"

Mrs. Taylor. Kind woman, quiet, who came to help when Mama died. She packed the paper sack with clothes, and bread wrapped in napkins. "I remember them."

"I lived with them until I was four. Then Dad, our dad, took me back to live with him. I guess they moved away; he never said."

"You're kind of young to be a doctor, aren't you?"

John laughed. "I graduated early. Full scholarships to med school. Left the farm at age sixteen, just returned this year."

"Really?"

Just in time.

"I became an OB/GYN because of what happened to our mom. Dad and I went to your church Sunday. Is it always like that?"

The gears of Pierce's mind ground with confusion, shifting from his life with Laurie, to memories and grief, to church last Sunday.

"Like what?"

"Do you always talk like that? I went to church for a few months, with the girl I almost married. The minister talked about everything we shouldn't do, threatened us with Hell, and bragged about everything he did right. You said you're not perfect. You even asked the congregation to forgive you. What's that about?"

Pierce wasn't sure how to answer. Was he in the role of brother or pastor?

You're my child.

His cell rang. "Excuse me a moment." Laurie—thank God. "Hello."

"Pierce, are you okay?"

"Yes."

"Is John there with you?"

"Yes."

"Ask him to come for dinner tonight."

His throat tightened. "What?"

"Invite him to our home. You two can talk without being interrupted or rushed. And you'll have me for support. It's a good idea."

John was paying the waitress for a to-go bag and glancing at his watch.

"Pierce?" she asked.

"Yeah. Okay. I'll be home soon." He ended the call.

John's cell vibrated across the table. "My alarm." He snapped it in the clip at his belt. "If I don't set it, I'm always late."

His brother was leaving. Pierce could pretend it wasn't a big deal. Say they would talk soon, then never follow up. He could dismiss this meeting as having little consequence, let Laurie handle asking questions and making connections, and never speak to his brother again.

But that was not the right thing to do. He didn't like it, but he knew it.

"That was Laurie. How about coming for dinner tonight? We'll talk more."

He saw the surprise in John's eyes. "Okay. I'm on duty, I have to be at the hospital by eight o'clock. But I can come around six."

"Sure."

John paused. "Out of curiosity, what did God say 'no' to you about?"

Pierce's blood first ran cold, then hot with shame. "I asked God to help me forget my father, forget everything from before. So I could have my life with Laurie back the way it was before her miscarriage."

"And He told you no? I mean, does He talk to you often?"

Pierce laughed derisively, thinking of recent difficult conversations. "All the time."

John processed, then the ghost of a smile played about his lips. "That's really cool."

CHAPTER TWENTY-TWO

Laurie had four and a half hours to prepare. Four and a half hours to clean. Four and a half hours to plan. No matter what Pierce said, they *were* making a plan.

"I'm making a casserole," she said when he arrived home. "I need you to do the floors. I simply can't bend to do it."

"Sure thing." He accepted the rag and mop she'd already hauled out of the kitchen closet.

She layered ham, diced potatoes, and sliced green pepper for their dinner, added cheese and slid the dish into the oven to bake. She would top it with more cheese and croutons later. She set the timer.

Then she joined Pierce, dusted while he vacuumed. She wanted to make a good impression. Getting ready for company was so much fun.

She followed Pierce to the kitchen. "We need to make you a list."

He gulped a glass of water. Poured a refill. "A list for what?"

"A list of questions. If we have them written down, you won't lose track or forget anything that's important to you."

"Laurie, I . . ."

She could see the war behind his eyes as he fought to keep the doors of his heart open. She walked to him, placed his hand over their baby, and wrapped her arms around him.

"John is your brother, and he's coming here for dinner. I know you're not entirely comfortable with that, but we both know that talking to him is probably the best way to find out why your mother died the way she did."

The baby kicked Pierce's hand.

Laurie smiled at him. "I'm *so* proud of you! For meeting with John today, for inviting him here tonight. Everything will be fine. You'll see."

Pierce simply pressed his forehead to hers. "I hope you're right. I really hope you're right." He paused. "I think a list of questions is a bad idea."

"But how will you—"

"Maybe, if you see me get stuck, you can kind of guide the conversation. You can probably say it all better than me anyhow."

"I'll do whatever you need me to do."

Later, when she added the finishing touches to her table, she critiqued her handiwork. From her best dishes, to the crystal salt and pepper shakers, to the floating scented candles centerpiece, everything was in place for a cozy dinner for three.

She heard Pierce's footsteps on the creaky floor, then his arms wrapped around their baby from behind her. She let her head lie back on his shoulder, breathed in the remnants of his shower. He kissed her cheek.

"Can we just stand here for a minute? Moments like these with you are what I thought I'd lost," she said.

God, please don't stop pulling my husband toward healing. Little about my pregnancy is the way I had envisioned, but don't stop Your work in us.

"He asked me about God," Pierce said.

"Hmmm? I could sleep here in your arms, but it's time to make the salad. Want to help?"

"Sure." He followed her to the kitchen, where she gathered the ingredients and handed him a knife.

"If you'll slice, I'll mix the dressing." Her hands stopped in midair as his previous statement registered. "Did you say he asked about God? What exactly?"

"First, he asked me about the service. He's only been to one other church, but didn't find it very friendly. He was surprised I admitted my mistakes and confessed my short-comings in public."

She gave the long-necked glass bottle filled with fresh herbs and olive oil a good shake, and stared balefully at him.

"I know. I know. You were right," Pierce admitted.

"And?"

"Then he asked me what God said "no" to me about."

She set the bottle on the counter, wiped her hands on a dishtowel and squeezed it tight. "Did you tell him?"

He stuck his nose in the air, sniffed, and grinned. "Of course."

She snapped the towel at his thigh.

He reached for her, and the doorbell rang.

***

Pierce had to admit, as he listened to John and Laurie talk, if he had met John as a boy or recently as a man on the street, they probably would have been friends.

John was smart. Very smart. He cared about his profession and his patients. He lived modestly except for his custom vehicles and an obsessive attachment to very expensive designer boots, an appetite cultivated during his years at a private medical school where shoes were the only form of self-expression allowed. Apparently, the habit was not only difficult to break, he had no desire to do so. Any future wife would have to accept and accommodate this; she would get the small closet. Laurie had laughed when John shared the fact.

With Laurie's perfect performance as hostess and her sweet laughter drifting across the table, Pierce almost forgot who John was and why he was there. Almost.

When the antique clock chimed seven, reality hit Pierce like a furnace blast. Instant heat, sweat, the desire to close and shield his eyes. He struggled not to cower in a corner.

John wiped his mouth and lay the linen napkin beside his plate. "Laurie, that was really great. I might make it through the night without my customary two a.m. vending machine raid."

"Thank you." She answered their guest but looked at Pierce, locking her eyes on his. She must have sensed that ripple of panic. She reached for his hand and he squeezed hers—an unspoken *go ahead*. "We were hoping you could help us, tell us about Luther. Or maybe Annabelle. Do you know why she died?"

John shifted in his chair, instantly transforming into "Mr. Physician." "Well, I only know she died immediately after having me, or that's what I was told. I was born, she passed out, Dad didn't know what to do for a newborn, so he took me to the neighbors. He returned home, bringing Mrs. Taylor. But Mama had already died."

Laurie continued in her friendly, gentle way. "Do you know why he didn't get help before that? Call a doctor?"

"No time. I came early and fast. Most likely premature, precipitous labor, less than three hours. Probably thirty-five, thirty-six weeks gestation—about a month early. The hard contractions came quick and close together from the start. But there's no way to know if her labor started because of infection, her water breaking, or placental abruption, which is when the placenta begins separating from the uterine wall. The latter often results in infant fatality, the mother's as well if there's no immediate medical intervention.

"That's how I became interested in obstetric medicine. As a kid, after school I went to the library and read medical journals, researched possible scenarios for what had happened.

"It fascinates me. How a woman's body can do that, actually grow a person inside, then deliver a healthy, totally self-supporting life." His expression filled with wonder at the miraculous. "It's amazing, don't you think?"

Pierce couldn't breathe. "Excuse me," he said.

***

Laurie watched Pierce leave, knowing that John saw the long, loving look she sent after her husband. She heard their bathroom door close.

"Everything you described and talk about so easily?—he's only recently begun remembering. His mind blocked out the trauma. Those memories almost cost him his ministry and us our marriage."

"You're kidding. He looks totally calm, totally in control."

"He's not."

"He would make a great doctor. Solid under pressure."

"No. He just hides things well. Too well."

"Right. Like Dad." With calm, quiet eyes he looked at Laurie. "What does Pierce think about me? I want to get to know him better, learn about our mother. It's more than obvious this invitation was your idea."

She must tread carefully, choose her words wisely.

"I don't think he knows exactly what he thinks of you. He's trying to keep an open mind about you, and an open heart to God. Both of you have questions only the other can answer. You're happy just to talk with him, be in his company, get to know him." She sighed as the weight of the day rested heavily on her shoulders. "Remembering why and how his mother died hurts him."

***

Pierce stood in the bathroom, arms braced on the vanity, staring into the mirror.

His mother's eyes looked back at him.

But she wasn't his mother only; she was their mother, his and John's. And apparently John was neither scarred nor damaged by his childhood and history. It didn't bother him to know, to remember, or to talk about any of the same things that had crippled Pierce.

He shook his head. If his mother—their mother—had lived, he would have had to share his room, his toys, share her. His entire life would have been different.

What kind of big brother would he have been?

Tears flooded his eyes. Grief squeezed his chest tight, and he sucked in a sob.

What was this terrible ache around his heart? Like it had been seized by a large, menacing hand.

The walls of the bathroom closed in. The room became smaller. The light brighter. The fan louder.

He stood there paralyzed.

He couldn't break down. Not now. He needed to leave the bathroom, go shake his brother's hand, and get the man out of his and Laurie's home. Out of his mind.

He scrubbed his face with both hands. Patted it like a prizefighter does before stepping back into the ring. He rounded the corner to the dining room as John neared the front door.

Laurie caught his eye. "Honey, John has an emergency at the hospital. He has to leave right away."

"Laurie, Pierce, thanks again for dinner. Sorry I have to eat and run." He stopped on the front porch, turned back. "You may not want to have a relationship with him right now, Pierce, but in the future I might need your help with Dad."

John wanted his help. With their father.

Concern tinged Laurie's voice. "What's wrong?"

"His sense of reality comes and goes. It's a little better right now—" His cell rang again. "I gotta run." He jogged to his custom truck, then looked back as he opened the driver's side door. "By the way, your church youth group will be at the farm this weekend. Seems they're cleaning out the barn."

"Good old Gilbert," Laurie said as they watched John drive away.

Pierce exhaled heavily, marveling at the irony. The day they'd painted their bedroom, the time he'd freaked out over Laurie cutting her finger, Gilbert had indeed said the youth group would be helping a nearby farmer.

"Yep. Good old Gilbert."

He helped Laurie with the dishes, then convinced her to go to bed early, when he saw her yawn for the fifteenth time while loading the dishwasher.

In their quiet room, he massaged her feet.

"I'm really proud of you, Pierce. You did great with John tonight."

"He's a pretty smart guy, isn't he?"

"You're smart, too. You both have the same care with others, as well. John for his patients, you for your congregation."

He hadn't considered that. What else did they have in common?

He placed her feet under the sheet and sat in the near-dark watching her sleep. Despite her peaceful countenance, chaos reigned outside of him and Laurie. In the past, that chaos would have controlled his relationship with Laurie and his relationship with God.

He pressed the heel of his hand to his heart. But Laurie and God were on the inside now. He didn't push them away anymore and wasn't pushing them out. They were his lifelines.

Although it didn't make sense, he had never felt safer. Even though Laurie was asleep, and he wasn't. Even though he knew he wouldn't be able to avoid John. Or box up the memories that had recently been unpacked.

He considered walking in the woods, but didn't want to leave her. So he went to bed, too. The bed sagged under their weight as he lay against her back. He raised up, kissed her soft, cool cheek. Listened to her steady breathing, then settled behind her. He placed his hand on her belly, patted his baby goodnight. Hope kicked back.

"The Lord is my shepherd." He whispered the psalm, until his breathing matched Laurie's, until his body and mind dangled in the place between waking and sleeping.

"The Lord is my shepherd, I lack nothing. He makes me lie down in green pastures."

Can I have another dog, Mama? Can I, Mama?

They sat together on the porch like they always did—Pierce on Mama's lap—watching Daddy drive the tractor far across the pastures and into the fields.

Mama kissed his head. "We have to be careful now when you sit with me."

"Why, Mama? Are you sick?"

"No. Your baby brother or sister is growing in here." She pointed to her stomach.

"Really?" He wiggled off her lap. "Can I see?"

Mama smiled sweetly, brushed her hand through his hair. "Not 'til he's born."

"Tomorrow? Is it a boy?"

She gave a little laugh. "No, not tomorrow. It's going to be a while. And I just think it's a boy. We won't know for sure until he's born."

"Can I hold him? Will he play with me?"

She cupped his face in soft, gentle hands. "Yes, and yes. He'll have to grow some first, but you two will be best friends. And you'll always have somebody, no matter what happens."

"I have you, Mama. And Daddy."

"Yes, Pierce, you'll always have us, too."

Pierce woke with a start. As a long-submerged swimmer surfacing and gasping for air, he sat straight up in the bed, his eyes wide and his chest heaving.

Laurie reached for him as she rolled to face him. "What is it? What's wrong?"

The tears traveled from his toes. Up, up, coursing through his heart with such force he thought the sorrow might drown him.

"I loved him before he was born." The tears gushed forth as he stammered. "My brother. I loved him because Mama did, and she taught me to do the same."

"Oh, Pierce. Honey, let the grief out."

He wept in her arms, remembering the little farmhouse, his mother's spindle chair, the feel of his little boy cheek against the soft cotton of her dress, as he tried to hear his brother moving inside her. The gentle stroke of Mama's hand through his hair.

After long minutes his sobs ended. "I can't reconcile them showing up at church last Sunday. I don't know what's worse: that I didn't recognize them, or that I'm glad I didn't recognize them."

"There is no *worse*, Pierce."

He relaxed in her embrace, their unborn daughter between them. "I never saw my dad shed one tear when Mama died. Last Sunday, he cried like a child."

"Not all tears can be seen, Pierce. Yours weren't visible for years."

Chapter Twenty-three

L aurie had not seen a more desolate place in Alabama or anywhere else.

Pierce hadn't wanted to accompany her to the farm, he simply wasn't yet ready to see it or his father. Instead, he'd asked her to be his eyes and ears today, and she'd gladly agreed.

Now she wasn't so sure she was ready either.

She slowed her car and turned onto the long dirt drive, passing a tilting mailbox that bore the name Bridges. This had to be the place.

The first bump jarred her bones. Dodging all of the dips proved impossible. The burning sun speared through her windshield, penetrating her sunglasses and warming her skin despite the AC blasting in her face. A barnburner of a day, some would say, but pretty standard for late September.

As she traveled the long lane, several years worth of untrimmed weeds scratched the sides of her car, and she took a deep breath, fortifying herself.

"God, I know you have led me here. I'm about to meet Pierce's father. Help me know what to say."

The weeds didn't really stop. They crept into the yard and surrounded the most pitiful farm, or what remained of a farm, she had ever seen. The barn leaned, its doors hanging crooked as the structure settled toward the house. Someone had braced a shovel there, no doubt to keep the door open, make entering and exiting easier as the youth group hauled buckets and bags to a waiting dumpster. The rotting home with its sagging porch looked like it belonged in the dumpster, too.

Her husband was born here. And John.

Laurie parked behind John's truck and took advantage of a few extra seconds of cool in the confines of her car. Gilbert, followed by John, came through the screened door and bounded down the steps. They caught sight of her and waved, then sauntered over.

She exited the car. The stench of animal dung and rot assaulted her nostrils and made her stomach twinge.

"Laurie, I know you brought food. Don't lift anything. I'll get it."

"Thanks, Gilbert. Backseat's loaded."

She'd brought five dozen donuts, a cooler of drinks, and another of sandwiches, which Pierce had loaded for her before she left this morning.

"I'm thinking maybe it's a good thing the city fell through scheduling the dumpster before now. Not even teenagers could've handled this kind of work in July or August."

John approached and offered his hand.

"I'd rather hug you," she said. "If that's okay."

"Well, yeah." He lowered his voice. "Just can't promise what kind of reception you'll get from Dad. Okay?"

She nodded. "I understand."

John led her to the porch and called through the screened door. "Dad. Laurie's here."

She stood beside a spindle chair and tried to keep her hands from fidgeting. How awful could this man be?

She heard shuffling steps, then a man who looked as worn as the land around her eased out the door and gently pushed it closed with a squeak.

His eyes were black, darker even than John's. His skin leathery, the term "red man" came to mind. Prominent cheekbones manifested his obvious Native American heritage. If he'd been young, in another time, another place, she would have thought *warrior*. He stared at her,

232

as if studying her face, then noticed her pregnant state. Tears bubbled at the corners of his eyes.

"Dad, this is Laurie. Pierce's wife."

He didn't move, but she just couldn't bring herself to settle for an impersonal handshake. She stepped to him, raised her palms to his shoulders and drew herself against him.

His whole body seemed to sigh. He only allowed himself to be held a few seconds, but in those precious moments she felt his bony shoulders under her fingers and knew his over-burdened heart was as frail as his aging body. This man oozed sorrow, the kind that made young eyes bleak and old bones sag. The same grief her husband battled.

She pulled back, made her gaze as gentle, as compassionate and non-threatening as she possibly could, and tried to hold his. "It's lovely to meet you, Mr. Bridges."

***

Laurie cried all the way home. The grief, the absolute agony Luther carried had set off all her empathetic radar. The story was just so sad she almost couldn't bear to think about it as a whole. Still, she opened her heart to embrace it, to catalogue what she'd learned from John about Annabelle, her pregnancies and her death, because she knew Pierce needed that from her.

Grief she thought she'd conquered bubbled up fresh and new. A week before she left for college, her parents had gone on a date, and she'd gone to bed. The incessant ringing of the doorbell, and a somber-faced policeman woke her hours later. Her parents were gone.

Then she'd faced infertility. Most women didn't think to appreciate their ability to have children until that ability was questioned. When Laurie learned of her infertility, she'd grieved from her core. She'd waited—until Pierce was gone to work and she was alone at their first apartment—then wailed and wept, wishing her mother was there to comfort her.

When she lost the baby, she'd suffered loss again. To her, the miscarriage was a death just like losing her parents. And she'd had to cry it out, over and over. Holding the grief inside would have suffocated her.

Was that what had happened to Luther? Had he never grieved, never let it out, and now it crippled his body and his mind?

Returning home, Laurie pulled into their driveway and dried her face. Pierce, their home, Daniel and Kay, her unborn daughter—she had a lot to be thankful for. God really did give beauty for ashes.

She found Pierce in the nursery, talking on his cell and pacing by the trio of windows.

"No, Angus, no, you don't need to come over here, I don't care how good you feel. I'm just measuring and wanted your advice. Floor to ceiling shelving is what Laurie wants, and I want to do it right. But if the baby's a climber—"

She stood, yet unnoticed, in the doorway and listened to him try to get in a word.

He scratched his head. "A laser-level. I'll have to get one of those."

Which meant another two-hour trip to the hardware store. She almost laughed. At least Benson's had vending machines, if she got hungry.

"A table saw? That'd be great. Yeah, Gilbert can leave it by the back door. No, she won't mind."

Obviously, the conversation would continue for a while.

She went to the kitchen, poured a big glass of iced tea, debated between leftover meatloaf and ordering a pizza. The latter won, no contest. A large, thick-crust pizza with extra cheese, pepperoni, ham, and green peppers. She calculated thirty minutes until delivery, practically drooling on herself as she dialed and placed the order.

Ice cream. Ice cream would tide her over while she waited on the pizza.

Tomorrow she would reach the thirty-four week mark. During

the sonogram, John had measured the baby and confirmed her due date. November 2 was so close. All the more reason to let Pierce know what she had learned today. Maybe it would ease his mind.

***

"Thanks, Angus. I'll let you know. Sure. Bye."

Pierce heard Laurie puttering in the kitchen. The freezer door slammed, which probably meant she was getting ice cream.

If it were just the two of them, just them and their baby, no other concerns or complications, his would be the happiest life. He could love her and enjoy their time together.

You have been loving her.

He could look forward to their baby.

You are.

He could work on projects and get excited about being a father.

You are.

Yes, he realized, he was.

He smiled as he measured again. If they added thick moldings like Angus suggested, the final product would indeed blend with the home's original architecture.

Maybe he should build identical shelf and toy box units in both extra bedrooms. He and Laurie might have another baby one day. Two children. Siblings who could laugh together, run and play like—like he'd thought he and his brother would.

John. Laurie had seen him today. And the farm. And his father.

He heard the doorbell ring, heard Laurie answer. He slid the tape measure into his pocket and retreated to the kitchen. Panic trailed him. Black, ominous. Picking up speed and brushing the hair on his neck. In his mind he was running to escape the terror that had always overtaken him.

Then he heard Laurie's sweet voice. "Hope, I just can't wait for you to be here." He rounded the corner to the dining room, caught her before she sat. He pressed a kiss to her belly, then tickled her sides.

"Pierce." She jerked, stifled a giggle. "Don't tickle me."

"I just want to hear you laugh."

"Why?" A giggle escaped, then she really laughed. "Stop. Please stop."

He stood and held her. "Somehow it changes me. It changes everything. Making you laugh heals something in me," he said.

She pulled back to look at him. "You're serious."

He kissed her nose. "As serious as you are about pizza. A large?"

"I'm starving," she said.

"Guess I'm hungry, too." He sat, opened the box, served her a slice. "So, how'd it go?"

At first she hesitated. Then she told him how proud she was of the youth group for working together to help someone in need. She talked about Gilbert, who had been so sure they could finish all the requested work in a day, and the look on his face when he realized he was greatly mistaken.

Then she reached for his hand, stroked her thumb over his.

"I met your father, Pierce."

All morning he had known this was coming, and wasn't that part of why he needed her, part of why he depended on her? She was his cushion, a way to soften the blows.

She choked back tears. "Honey, I looked at that farm, a sad, lonely piece of ground, and I thought it looked just like your father. He's a sad, broken man, Pierce. Like grief has hollowed him out and left only a shell." She paused. "I felt sorry for him."

"What?" He shoved his chair back so hard it fell. He stalked from the dining room to the front door and back.

"I'm sorry the idea of me having sympathy for him distresses you."

He stopped. No, Laurie was not the problem. She was not the enemy. Her compassion was part of why he loved her.

She faced him. With silent tears streaming down her face she looked him square in the eyes. "I love you. I'm right here, and our baby's coming soon."

She waited, watching him. But never, not once did she berate him or correct him. She simply sat there with love in her eyes.

He hung his head.

Pierce lifted his chair, placed it directly in front of her and sat, bending until his head rested on their child. She stroked his hair and let her tears fall unhindered onto his bowed head.

"You feel how badly I hurt, don't you?" he whispered.

"Yes." A pause. "And I learned some things that should make you feel better."

Did he want to know? Did he dare try to learn more, remember more?

Then you will know the truth.

"She loved you, Pierce. She loved you and your brother. And your father."

He tensed and she paused again.

"You were early, too," she said, lowering her voice. "Probably more than a month. You were born in less than two hours, and you were so little they weren't sure you would live. She had bleeding problems after you were born, but eventually it stopped.

"She—they—tried to be careful after that. So she didn't get pregnant again. Do you understand what I'm saying?"

Yes, he understood. His mother had almost died having him. And she probably shouldn't have had any more children.

"You're a miracle three times over, Pierce. You were born, and you lived. And you are the answer to Daniel and Kay's prayers."

"Did, um, did my father tell you all this?"

"No. John's pulled pieces of it out of him over time. He and I put our heads together before I came home today."

He wrapped his arms around her and held on. "She made him

promise to keep me. To keep both of us. He sent both of us away, then he took John back." He lifted his head, searched her face. "Tell me how that's a miracle. Tell me how that's God's hand at work."

She took a deep breath. "I'm not saying what he did was right. I am saying you being alive is a miracle. And if he had kept you, if you stayed on that farm, it's highly unlikely we would have met. You wouldn't have had the childhood you did. You probably wouldn't know God the way you do."

He didn't want to make her mad. Didn't mean to argue. But— "John turned out okay."

She continued stroking his hair. "John didn't know he had a brother. He never had a mother, and he doesn't know God." She kissed his cheek. "And, honey, you're not John." She took a weary breath. "Pierce, the house."

"Dilapidated?"

"Worse. It was pitiful. The barn . . ."

"That thing's still standing?" He'd been as scared of its dark corners as he was of the outhouse.

"Barely. There's one more thing you need to know."

Pierce gritted his teeth and stood. "Does my father still have pigs?"

"That's what I need to tell you."

He shook his head. "No. No more today. I can't take it."

She closed the pizza box. "Okay. All right. What do you need from me?"

He looked at her tear-stained countenance, her sweet, round face growing more round from the pregnancy. She looked tired. And all morning she had been out in the sauna-like heat.

"I need you to go take a shower, then let me rub your feet."

"But—"

"No arguments. I'll clean up. Go."

He shooed her away with kisses and pats. He swept crumbs into his hand and thought of the dust on the farm. He pushed his chair under the table, and thought of his mother's chair, the one missing a spindle. He glanced around the tidy kitchen with its sparkling counters, its toaster placed just so, and thought of the mess Mrs. Taylor cleaned up the morning his father buried his mother.

Rattling pipes signaled the end of Laurie's shower. Pierce got two thick towels from the hall closet, carried them to their bathroom, handed her one for her hair, and dried her back with the other. Loving her, taking care of her, was so much better than sulking and sinking into a dark, lonely pit of isolation. "Come lie down."

He rubbed her feet, her calves. When he worked on her hands, she sighed with pleasure and her voice came slow and sleepy. "How can my hands be tired? Don't we need to go to Benson's and buy a laser level?"

He laughed. "Benson's can wait." He moved up her body to her scalp, massaged through her wet hair. She moaned as she had over the pizza.

"But I need to tell you more."

"Another day. Shh. Go to sleep."

The idea of joining her, of lying beside her to comfort himself, tempted him. But the wheels of his brain—or was it his spirit?—kept turning. They urged him to research, to learn, verify, and understand.

Then you will know the truth.

He left her a note on the kitchen counter, jogged to his office at the church, and searched the Internet. Premature labor. Bleeding during labor. Placenta—placental abruption.

Hearing Laurie use the terms was one thing, but he needed to understand them before he could discuss them with John. He printed pages of information, then hurried back through the woods and settled at the dining room table to study.

He poured over the data, so much so the terms swirled through his mind during sleep and through the next morning as Julie Matthews and the choir sang about God's amazing love.

Laurie leaned toward him, and smiled. "Heaven must sound like this."

He should be celebrating. While reading last night, he'd discovered no legitimate reason to worry about Laurie. She was healthy, happy, and would most likely stay that way. But according to what he had learned, labor complications couldn't be accurately predicted.

He knew in his spirit what he needed to tell himself: God was in control. But his tortured mind argued, and that was the battle. Actively, consistently choosing to listen to his spirit rather than his mind.

They ended with an a cappella chorus that brought the crowd to its feet. As one church body, choir and congregation raised their voices in worship, shaking the barn's vaulted ceiling. When the hymn ended, all the participants erupted in thunderous, spontaneous praise to God. Worship surrounded Pierce. People clapped or raised their hands. Some stood. Some knelt. Others voiced their love for God with silent words, as the Holy Spirit personally interacted with each one.

And Pierce watched. Watched as a hungry child, face pressed against a display window. The good stuff was on the other side, but he couldn't reach it. He couldn't join in. Even after the praise ended, the invisible barrier remained in place.

He stood behind the pulpit as the congregation resettled themselves. Scanned the crowd twice, looked for his father or his brother, but he didn't see either of them. He glanced at his parents, feeling guilt that he had looked for John and Luther first.

He didn't feel like preaching. Didn't feel like encouraging and teaching others. *My grace is sufficient for you, for my power is made perfect in weakness.*

He didn't really want to talk, at all.

Pour out of yourself, Pierce. Simply share what I'm doing in you.

"If you were here last week, you know I'm beginning a series on how miracles affect people's lives. This week, I'd like to concentrate on

Moses. After he learned his true identity, after he fled to the desert and got married. I want to begin with his burning bush experience.

"I've heard people reference this story and say something like, *I'm not going back to Egypt*, implying once you're out of something, it's never right to revisit any part, at any time or for any reason. I disagree. God ordered Moses to return to Egypt. And I want you to notice two things. One, his return was the answer to many prayers. Two, he didn't return with the same mission, the same mindset, or as the same man. He didn't go into bondage, he returned as a deliverer."

Deacon Floyd raised his hand. "Pastor, would you repeat that? That was really good."

Across the room heads nodded. He heard papers rustle, pens click as they took notes.

"I said, he didn't return to go into bondage. He returned out of obedience. God sent him back to do a job. To deliver the Israelites from slavery, and to help them take the next step in their relationship with God. He went back with a new mission. He had left as a prince of Egypt, but returned as a spokesman for God."

He cleared his throat.

"Learning the truth of his lineage changed him. As a man."

He caught Laurie's eye. Then drank water from the cup that was always left on the pulpit—something he had never done before—and cleared his throat again.

"Excuse me."

He coughed.

"What I mean to say is—"

The irony was almost laughable. His original intent had been to talk about the impact Moses' experiences—the burning bush, the miraculous plagues, the parting of the Red Sea—had on Moses as a person.

When preparing his sermon, he hadn't seen the similarities. He was Moses. A man who was adopted, who viewed his family in a par-

241

ticular way. He learned part of the truth, did something really stupid and almost ruined his life, then God revealed His plan and confronted him with his past.

God, You got me. You really got me. He shook his head.

"I . . . just realized I'm preaching to myself." He once again caught Laurie's eye. She winked.

After Pierce finished his message, he closed his Bible. "I think many of us can relate to Moses. We have a view of our past that reaches into our present. We make decisions based on our past. We embrace and we shun things because of our past. All the while battling things we believe—possibly true, possibly false—because of our past.

"Eventually, God will intercept our chosen, planned path. He will orchestrate a detour that reroutes our journey. Ultimately, His plan is that we not be controlled by our past. Rather, He wants us to put Him in control of our lives, which requires us recognizing both His presence and His influence, in our past."

Pierce descended from the platform, motioning to Laurie. "Honey, come here."

He took her hand in both of his. "I love Laurie. As you can see, God is growing our family. Most of me is happy about that. But because of some things in my past, part of me isn't happy. Even though I know this baby is a miracle, even though I love my wife, even though I know God is leading my life in the direction of fatherhood. Part of me is still struggling not to let my past control my present and my future.

"If you're in the same place—you know God's hand is on your life, you know He's doing things, but some part of you is unhappy about what He's doing—ask yourself if that hesitation, that frustration, has anything to do with your past. Being happy about God's current plan for you may begin with a shift in your perspective on your past."

He planted a soft kiss on her cheek. "Thanks, honey."

After the service, he greeted every person as the building emptied. His parents, his friends, the church board, people who loved him and had watched him grow up. They filed by, extended their hands, offered their love. They rejoiced with him over the coming baby.

As Laurie had said, he had been surrounded by love and support since being adopted. He had indeed avoided a motherless childhood, possibly a loveless home.

Yet a part of him still wanted to hold on to his resentment for being permanently given away.

Even though he had walked over to the church early that morning, he drove Laurie home in her car, just to be near her.

He changed into jeans, and helped her heat leftovers. They carried their plates to the nursery, ate standing, and re-planned the shelving project. It reminded him of the night they assembled the crib, how tense their relationship had been then, how uncertain she had been of his love.

How uncertain he had been of everything.

"Laurie, where's the shoebox of my things Mom gave you?"

She looked at him for several long seconds. "Are you sure?"

"No." He shook his head. "But I think it's time."

"It's in the trunk of my car. I'll get it," she said.

***

Pierce sat against the nursery wall, waiting for Laurie to bring the box. Brilliant sunshine pushed through the bank of tall windows, shooting shafts of light across the old wooden floor to his bare feet, much like the moonlight that had shone across his body the night his mother died.

Laurie waddled into the room carrying the old shoebox, then sat in the rocking chair beside him. "Your mother said she found this while unpacking. She gave it to me around Easter, I think."

He took the box from her, still warm from baking in the trunk. "I don't know what's in here."

"It doesn't matter. We'll face it together."

243

"This might be nothing."

"It doesn't matter. And I'm not," she motioned to her belly, "we're not, going anywhere."

His insides shook. He could practically feel his heart vibrating. He lifted the lid.

The smell of old metal hit him first. His hand closed over the miniature silver convertible resting on top. He held it to his ear and shook it, grinned like a child finding buried treasure. "I hid pennies in the ones that had working trunk lids." He opened it, and several blackened pennies fell into his open hand.

He found baseball cards, a busted yo-yo. A rusted railroad spike and three arrowheads sealed in a plastic bag. Luke Skywalker and his buddies Han Solo, R2-D2, and C3PO.

Dead silverfish lay in the bottom with a battered red Cream of Wheat semi. "I got this truck as a gift, right after I came to live here. I thought the trailer was for hiding things."

"More pennies?" Laurie asked.

But nothing jingled.

He reached in with his fingers, pulled out a wadded woman's handkerchief.

His lungs seized. *Mama's handkerchief,* and something was crumpled inside. Carefully, he opened the cloth. "Laurie?"

"It's okay. I'm here."

The creased picture was a thumbnail, black-and-white, photo booth type. In it Pierce saw the young faces of Mama and Daddy. Kissing.

Laurie sat forward in the rocker. "Have you seen that before?"

"I, I don't know." He shook his head. "I remember finding the handkerchief in the paper sack Mrs. Taylor packed for me. But I didn't want to lose it. So I shoved it in the truck right after Daniel and Kay, you know, gave it to me." He looked at Laurie. "I don't remember seeing this picture." His voice fell to a whisper as he studied the old photo.

"They look happy, don't they?"

"You need to know," Laurie said. "You wouldn't let me tell you before, but you need to know about the holes in your dad's yard."

Holes? Right. Gilbert had said the youth group was going to help a farmer with holes all over his yard. "What about them?"

"Your father's been digging, mostly around the pig shed."

"Why?" But as the question left his mouth, he knew the answer.

Then you will know the truth, and the truth will set you free.

"He's searching for your mother's grave."

***

He was shirtless and barefoot. A little, dark-haired boy in floppy overalls. Tan lines bridged his shoulders. He wore a frayed hat the color of wheat. A piece of straw dangled like a toothpick from his slightly parted lips. On a self-made path, he trod around and around the small farmhouse, holding his breath every time he passed between the putrid-smelling pig shed and his parents' room.

Then he heard Daddy's truck coming home.

Daddy had been gone all day, but before leaving he washed and shaved his face smooth. The sound always reminded Pierce of an ax being sharpened.

Pierce had smelled the soap, heard the peculiar scraping sound of blade on beard. And wondered where Daddy was going.

From the hall Mama had spoken to Daddy. "Your shirt's hanging on the bed post." But she did not look at him.

Pierce peered in their room and saw Daddy shining his boots. The tangy odor made him think of oil mixed with sugar.

"Can I go with you?"

Daddy's hands paused mid-stroke. He hung his head, then he shook it like he had when the horse kicked him flat. His voice was hoarse and hollow. "Not this time."

When Daddy left, Mama did not kiss him goodbye. She did not wave or watch his truck disappear down the lane. Rather, she sat in her chair at the table and rubbed her watermelon belly.

"Can I listen, Mama?" Pierce knelt beside her chair. "Can I hear the baby?"

Mama let him press his ear to her stomach. The baby kicked his cheek.

"Will it be a boy, Mama?"

"I don't know. It's a surprise."

Then Mama said she was tired. She wanted to lie down. But he could go out and play.

Now Daddy was back. He parked his truck in its place between the house and barn. But he didn't get out. Instead he sat there for a long time staring over the fields.

Then Daddy draped both arms over the steering wheel and dropped his head. His shoulders shook first, then his arms as he slowly turned his head back and forth.

Maybe Daddy hurt himself.

Or maybe he had come home and since Mama wasn't sitting on the front porch, he thought she was gone. Because, lately, Daddy had been asking her to stay. Telling her he needed her. Begging her not to leave.

Mama would never do that. Mama loved them.

So Pierce went to Daddy's truck. Rising on his dirt-covered toes, he grabbed the ledge of the open window for balance. "Daddy, Mama's here. She didn't leave."

Daddy's face was red and wet. His eyes looked like you felt when you spun around and around and around, then fell to the ground.

"Want me to get you one of Mama's 'kerchiefs?"

Daddy stared at him.

"I found a gopher turtle hole."

Pierce's fingers slipped. He fell hard on his bottom.

Daddy opened the driver's door, stepped out, and stopped.

"I'm okay," Pierce said, dusting off his legs.

Daddy nodded. Then he shoved a thick stack of papers under the front seat before going inside to Mama. Pierce followed, and from the front porch heard their bedroom door close.

So he walked around the house again, kicking up stones, tossing them, while his insides shook like a cold puppy. Something was wrong—with Daddy, or with Mama. Or maybe both.

He boosted himself up on an old stump and peeked in their window as the thin lace curtains hung still in the breezeless air. Seeing them hugging, kissing for so long, filled him with both relief and embarrassment. Daddy's hands kept moving over Mama's back. Hers were in his hair. Daddy said, "Don't leave me, Annabelle."

Pierce stood watching them and wondered where Mama might want to go.

CHAPTER TWENTY-FOUR

J ust before noon, John handed the Labor and Delivery reins over to Dr. Nate as three mothers-to-be were wheeled in. He'd dodged that bullet by the skin of his teeth.

John hopped into his truck, drove out of town under a fire-bright sun. Today he'd install the window unit he'd bought yesterday at Benson's. He didn't care if October was almost here, he couldn't stand one more sweltering evening at the farm without air conditioning. Then, he'd call sweet Rebecca—with her long, dark hair and green, Greek eyes—a fine specimen of a nurse he'd charmed into offering her phone number before his shift ended.

John faced three glorious days off. No appointments, no hospital duty. He might drive his Viper to Montgomery—he'd hardly driven it lately—get a fancy hotel room with excellent room service. Maybe sweet Rebecca had time off, too, and would join him.

He passed huge fields covered with hordes of peanut plants sunning themselves in the early fall heat. He heard Old Mr. Dawkins' tractor before he saw it. Being behind it added twenty minutes to the drive, but he didn't care.

He puttered along, remembering the weekend's flurry of young arms and laughter. One thing was sure, with an army of good-natured teenagers and enough food, a lot of work could get done. Some stuff they tossed out had probably been in the barn since his childhood.

Dad hadn't spoken again of church, even while the kids had worked. Yet his expression changed when Laurie introduced herself. His eyes softened around the edges. His voice grew humble—*here, let me carry that for you. Sure, you can set that over here*—a tone John had never before heard from his father. Most unnerving were the tears Luther had blinked away as he later retreated inside the farmhouse.

John parked. Lifting the box out of the truck bed, carrying it to the porch where Luther sat left him covered in sweat. Twenty minutes to install the unit and stand, another hour and his father's one window living room would be a cool haven. Maybe Dad would sleep better at night if he weren't so hot.

"Dad, I'll fix lunch as soon as I get this in."

He sat the box near the living room window, aside the old recliner. Parting the curtains scattered dust, but the unit's HEPA filter would soon take care of that. The cord did reach the outlet; however, the room's single lamp was already plugged into the only working outlet. John called out. "Dad, where's an extension cord?"

No response.

He walked to the front door. "Dad. I need an extension cord for the air conditioner. Do you have one?"

Luther rose slowly, eased down the front steps, and stopped. "Inside the barn."

"The kids found one in the barn?"

Without looking back, Luther walked into the untended fields.

CHAPTER TWENTY-FIVE

Laurie lay her head against the seat rest, folding her arms and closing her eyes. She should have been thrilled she and Pierce were getting away for their anniversary—a trip Eric had suggested before they last left his office. Wasn't their anniversary October third, and hadn't Daniel offered to fill-in for Pierce if needed?

She'd read about energy bursts many women experience during the end of pregnancy. Apparently she'd missed out on that phenomenon, as *exhausted* seemed to be her new normal. From counseling appointments with Eric which drained her emotions. From gently trying to keep Pierce in bed with her at night when he had dreams and awakened her—yes, she wanted him to awaken her, to talk to her, but did it have to be in the middle of every night?

Pierce had been quiet for days. Not depressed, simply quiet and contemplative.

Every few hours he stopped Laurie with a touch, or called from the office, and asked her to pray with him. His petition was always the same, "God, please help me."

She knew he was processing something. "I can't put the words together. It's too much," he said. "Keep praying for me."

So she had prayed. She continued to pray. But she wasn't seeing any results.

He didn't appear to be hiding anything. He simply couldn't explain. Which left them in a strange holding pattern.

Believing that helped her be patient with him. To a point. Unfortunately, her patience was wearing thin. Pregnancy, indigestion, hormones, *something* was making her cranky.

"I'm hungry," she said. "Anything close with a drive-thru."

"You want a burger?"

"Yeah. A big one with extra pickles." She opened her eyes. They'd stopped at a traffic light. She scanned signs lining the street ahead of them. "There." She pointed to a small Mom-n-Pop hamburger joint.

He swung in behind several cars. They ordered and continued their journey to the southern Alabama coast. She inhaled the burger, wished she'd ordered two.

"I need to tell you about another dream," Pierce said.

"Honey, you woke me last night." He'd dreamed of being given a puppy. He'd kept it by his bed in a cardboard box he'd lined with newspapers.

"Not this one. It's from a few nights back."

"Must have been Wednesday, am I right?" The one night she'd slept entirely through.

He told her of Luther dressing in what his mother had called "uptown clothes." How his father had seemed so tired, so burdened, and for once, Mama hadn't kissed Luther before he left. That after Luther returned, he'd sat in the pick-up, crying, then stuffed a large manila envelope under the front seat before going inside.

"I think he'd seen the attorney. Didn't you say my parents showed you a large folder filled with the adoption papers?"

"Yes."

"I think my father had been to see the attorney. And I think my mother knew. She knew he was afraid she'd die, that he was considering giving me up. That's why she begged him to keep me and John."

"I . . . I don't know what to say." She glanced at her husband. "You're supposed to wake me. And if you don't wake me, you're supposed to tell me right away." She stared out the window as they traveled through yet another small town. "I wish you'd told me sooner, rather than keeping this bottled up inside."

"I have a lot of pictures running through my head, even at night."

"I can't help you sort through them if you don't tell me."

"We're almost to the hotel. We can finish talking about this there."

"You want to wait until we're in a room with people listening on the other side of the wall?"

"It's a nice place, Laurie. We'll have privacy."

Perfect. Privacy. A lot of good that would do while she fought being so irritable.

No, downright snarky, she admitted. Controlling her ping-pong emotions grew more and more difficult as her due date drew near.

They crested a hill, and the world opened before them. White sand. A cloudless sky over an endless sapphire and gray ocean. Diagonal waves lunged at the shore.

Pierce drove into the first public parking area they saw, and leaving the A/C on, lowered the windows. At the smell of sea and salt and sand, Laurie wished she could wade in and float, if only to let the water bear her belly burden. As for the other burdens . . .

She stared at the floor, knowing she couldn't keep what she was thinking inside. "Pierce, if you keep secrets from me it'll put your past right back between us."

He turned to her. With a tentative hand, he traced his fingertips across her brow. "Look at me, Laurie. Please." With a soft hand he stroked her hair. "I'm sorry what I did upset you."

"More than that. It scares me."

"Because it feels like I kept a secret from you and secrets become walls."

"Yes, and—"

"I'm asking you to acknowledge that I wasn't trying to put distance between us."

She turned to him. "But Pierce—"

He kissed her softly then pressed his forehead to hers. "Do you remember why Eric encouraged us to learn the truth about my past? Do you remember what you said to me? That maybe some of my pain was based on lies.

"I'm trying to let the truth do what Jesus promised. Set me free. I'm trying to let the images of a cruel father's rejection be replaced with a caring father's decision. He hurt me back then. He may not have meant to, but he did. Knowing that helps it not hurt so badly now. Since I wasn't trying to pull away from you, and I did tell you when I was ready, can't you do the same? Can't you step back and let some of it go?"

She pulled back and looked into his eyes as the sea breeze tousled his hair. A part of her—the snarky part—told her he was getting away with something. She told that part to hush and shoved it aside. Why waste their time alone?

"It's a misunderstanding, Laurie. I wasn't hiding things from you. I was thinking, and I was praying." He kissed her again. "Please understand. I was trying to stand on my own two feet. Work with God myself, like I've seen you do to love me these past months."

"Like you've seen me do." Shivers jolted along her spine as he nibbled her lips. Her breath caught.

He grinned. "You're my hero."

"Your hero." She strained to keep herself from laughing. "In maternity clothes."

He wiggled his brow. "And out."

Her laugh rang out, then stupid, *stupid* tears filled her eyes. Would she be pregnant forever? Part of her almost wanted it to last longer, to give Pierce more time to deal with his past, but—

"My feet ache. They're swollen, and I have to wear soft, ugly shoes."

"Okay. You're my hero even though you have swollen feet?"

She wiped her eyes with the back of her hand. "Stretch marks have exploded across my stomach. My skin has reached its limit. *Overnight.* And I crave Snickers bars. I might actually kill for them. And fish sticks. Who in their right mind craves fish sticks?"

"I don't think it's a question of 'right mind,' I think it's just being pregnant."

"I'm gaining weight by the second. I'll be wearing tents by the time our baby is born. Ugly, flapping tents special ordered from some tentmaker." She sniffed and leaned against him. He put his arms around her. "I've been really trying to be loving and sweet and understanding."

"You have been. You are."

"I don't think I can be much longer. I don't want to be pregnant anymore." She laughed again, wiped her cheeks with her fingertips. "There. I said it."

"I think every pregnant woman does at least once, right?"

"Probably. I'll be a terrible mother, eating Snickers bars and fish sticks. Our daughter's life is ruined."

"At least we'll know what caused it."

She laughed again. "I'm glad you're praying about the dreams and figuring them out. But I think my extra-sensitive, pregnant feelings are still a little bruised."

"Let's go check in, and I'll apologize over and over and over again."

***

The room was divine, with its soft turquoise walls, whitewashed wicker furniture, and textured seashell pillows. The weather, perfect. Laurie couldn't have asked for better.

In dazzling morning light they strolled along a shore left bare by the outgoing tide.

At midday, when hot storms rolled in to wash the heavy sea breeze farther inland, they fixed sandwiches in their kitchenette and ate in their room, where they laughed, and talked to Hope, and made love.

By early evening, after dozing and whispering sweet plans against each other's skin, they wandered to the water again. They strolled through the sand to Okey's On the Water restaurant, and enjoyed a nightly seafood buffet with fried hushpuppies. Laurie ate them like candy.

Since the classic movie channel featured Jerry Lewis all week, they got dessert to go, scurried back to the room like anxious teenagers, and ate gooey wedges of chocolate-chocolate-chip cake topped with warm fudge icing. They laughed at the absurd antics in *Cinderfella* and *The Disorderly Orderly*. They made love again and drifted to sleep without setting the alarm.

A vacation from life, Laurie thought more than once. No pastoral responsibilities or doctor appointments, no constant reminders of John, Luther, and the distressing first few months of her pregnancy. They simply had fun.

On the fourth night, she pulled Pierce's arm around her as she always did.

God, thank You for this. We needed this. I needed this.

"Pierce?"

"Yes," he whispered against her neck.

"I'll be asleep in two seconds. I love you. If we can stay close like this, I'll be as happy as I could ever be."

He kissed her shoulder. "Me, too, baby. Me, too."

Later, Laurie woke in darkness, her mind registering a little insistent pinch like school children give each other on St. Patrick's Day. Something was wrong.

Then she felt the dampness between her legs.

She yanked back the covers, flipped on the bedside table lamp, and saw the dark red stain where her hips had been.

Pierce's eyes were still closed, lips smiling as he asked, "You okay?"

She couldn't hold back the tears as her heart and mouth sputtered.

"I'm bleeding."

***

The small, local hospital stood only a few miles away, but Pierce couldn't get there fast enough. He drove through the gray streets, passing rows of street lamps, watching for signs and swallowing bile. Laurie lay helplessly in the back seat. No matter what, he *would* be strong for her.

He knew she was crying, praying, and willing their child to live. As he reached over the seat for her hand, he did the same.

He pulled right into the emergency room's ambulance bay, screeched to a stop. "Don't move. I'll get somebody." He ignored the No Admittance signs on the double doors, barreled through and into a human wall of security officers.

"Sir, you can't park there."

"My wife. She's pregnant. She's bleeding." He grabbed a nearby wheelchair.

One of the officers called back over his shoulder. "Mary Rae, we got a mama in trouble!" The ensuing flurry of activity was incredible. Last time Pierce had taken her to an ER, he'd carried her bleeding body inside, begging for help as he went. This time he was shoved aside and could only watch.

"What's your name?"

"Laurie Crane."

"Mrs. Crane, an OB is on the way. How far along are you? When did the bleeding start? Are you having any contractions?"

They whisked her away. Mary Rae, a bustling drill sergeant of a nurse, ordered Pierce to sit in the chair directly in front of her desk. He sat and couldn't help rocking himself. *Oh, God. Oh, Jesus.*

Shivering from stress and adrenaline, he strained to hear Laurie, her voice, her cries, anything to reassure him that she and his child were still alive.

***

Laurie hugged her belly, hugged her baby as they lifted her onto the bed.

"Hope," she begged as they stripped off her clothes. "Please save my Hope." Tears streamed, filled her ears as she lay flat while nurses prodded.

"Pressure 130 over 90."

"Lift your hips, Mrs. Crane. We need to get this monitoring belt on you."

The doctor burst in. "Mrs. Crane, when did the bleeding start?"

"It woke me less than an hour ago."

"You were asleep?"

She'd been dreaming of the baby. Holding the baby. Nursing the baby.

God, I will love this baby if she has special needs, if she's handi-capped, just let her live. This can't be another miscarriage. Can't be just like Annabelle. Please, Heavenly Father.

"Mrs. Crane, were you asleep?"

"Yes."

"Any cramping or contractions?" He ran his gloved hands over her belly.

"I don't think so."

"Is this your first pregnancy?"

"No." She told them about the previous miscarriage.

A nurse secured a wide, black belt around her. "Fetal heart rate normal, sir."

"Okay. Let's check her urine for amniotic fluid."

"What does that mean? Am I in labor?"

"I need to do an exam, Mrs. Crane."

She nodded fiercely. "Yes. Anything. Please."

He completed the task, peeled off his gloves. The door opened and three more bodies in scrubs entered the room. Strangers surrounded her—a dozen hands touched her—but they didn't speak to her, only to each other.

"Please, someone tell me what's happening."

A round woman with a raspy, colonel's voice closed the door and cleared her throat. The mouths in the room hushed, bodies parted like the Red Sea. With hands on her hips she marched to Laurie's side.

"Mrs. Crane, I'm Mary Rae, ER Charge Nurse. Your exam was normal." She threw a scathing glance at the doctor, turned on him. "Wasn't it, doctor?"

"There's no indication she's in labor."

"Here's a pinch," a voice said.

Laurie winced as a nurse started an IV. "Please, where's my husband?"

Mary Rae answered. "He's by my desk." She smiled at Laurie, then lasered the doctor with her eyes. "And we're going to explain everything that's happening so you'll know what's going on." Her voice became prim, and she batted her eyes at the physician. "Doctor, are you going to do a sonogram now? Check the placenta's position?"

The doctor was clearly perturbed at Mary Rae's interference, but submitted to it. He leaned directly over Laurie, so close his breath touched her face. "Why are you so scared, Mrs. Crane? Have you had any other complications?"

"Not this time. But like I said, I miscarried over a year ago. And, my husband's mother bled to death while having her second child."

He turned his back on Mary Rae. "You're no longer bleeding, Mrs. Crane." He sighed and yawned wearily. "Listen. Let me do a sonogram, and we'll set your mind at ease. Okay?"

"And that's your baby's heartbeat." Mary Rae waved her hand, indicating the soft whirring sound that Laurie could now hear. "Do you know if it's a boy or girl?"

Laurie gave a watery smile as her tears subsided. "A girl. We're naming her Hope."

"Well, you'll get to see how Hope's growing and you'll feel better. Now take deep breaths for me, try to calm yourself. You're fine, your baby's fine. You're not contracting, this is not early labor, the bleeding's stopped, and Hope's heartbeat is strong. We couldn't ask for better. Right, doctor?"

The physician grumbled, barked at another nurse to watch where she stepped.

Mary Rae huffed loudly. "Right, doctor?"

"Correct."

"Good boy," Mary Rae said and leaned down to Laurie's ear. "Guess who just quit smoking and switched to decaffeinated coffee?"

Laurie half-smiled at her. "My baby's really okay?"

Mary Rae nodded.

"Thank you," Laurie said. "Will you please tell my husband?"

***

Pierce sat shaking. Mary Rae came by every few minutes, once with a warmed blanket, to give him updates on Laurie's condition. Then she disappeared down halls and around corners through the maze of rooms. After several round trips, she returned and took his hand. "Mr. Crane, everything's going to be all right. Come sit with your wife while she rests." She patted his shoulder as she ushered him into a dull, quiet room.

He followed her instructions, and sat beside the hospital bed where Laurie drifted in and out of sleep. He brought her hand to his cheek and pressed it there.

God, this is too much. The bloodstain on the bed in their hotel room—just like the night his mother died.

They're not the same.

No, but his mother *had* died.

That's what I said. They're not the same.

The toothpick-thin security guard who had first called for help, walked in and handed him a foam cup.

"Mary Rae said to bring you some coffee."

Pierce tried to smile. "Thanks."

"It's black, it's hot. Not much more. Name's Ed. First baby?"

Pierce took a scalding sip. "Kinda."

Ed's eyes flicked to Laurie. "Don't get many couples in here like you two. Plain to see you love her."

Was love a big enough word? "She's my life."

"Good. Just like me and my Mary Rae. Though God never blessed us with children. Do you know who's giving you this baby, son?"

Pierce almost laughed. "Yes, I do." He jerked a thumb in the direction of the nurse's desk. "Does she boss you around at home?"

"I let her think she does. Besides, she's really cute in that old-timey nurse's hat, ain't she?" Ed opened the door. "Here comes the Doc."

They kept Laurie for observation, and tended Pierce like he was a patient, too.

Mary Rae told Ed to bring a cot into Laurie's room; he did.

She told everyone else not to disturb them; they didn't.

So Pierce let Mary Rae tuck him in like a child, then he reached up for Laurie's hand, and let the swish-swish lullaby of his daughter's heartbeat ease him into sleep.

He woke to the sound of muffled voices passing in the hall. Laurie slept on. He stepped out, closed the door behind him, and walked the long hall toward the nurse's station, where Ed leaned against Mary Rae's desk.

Ed straightened. "Get a nap, young man?"

"Yes, I did."

261

"She still asleep?" Mary Rae asked.

"She is."

Mary Rae stood and walked around to him, gave him a motherly pat and rub on his shoulder. "Stop worrying, Daddy. Ed, fill him in while I go check on our patient."

"Are they going to admit her?"

"Naw. She's gonna be fine, you just need to get that girl home." Ed smacked his lips. "Mary Rae's got you all fixed up. I've done been and picked up your stuff. My bride's cousin works at your hotel and is married to the manager. One call got your belongings packed. I went off shift about an hour ago, scooted out and picked 'em up." He pointed behind him with his thumb. "Everything's in the security office. After she's discharged, you can give me your key and hit the road."

Pierce looked away, humbled at the blatant kindness. "That's quite a miracle you performed. How can I thank everyone?"

"Send us a picture of that baby girl when she comes."

Pierce extended his hand. "I'll do that."

Ed motioned with his head. "You better get back in there. Mary Rae'll give you some orders about taking care of your bride."

He returned to the room, listened to Mary Rae's instructions, then helped Laurie dress.

In short order they had Laurie seated in a wheelchair for discharge. Pierce pulled their car up at a covered portico.

"You take care of her and yourself." Ed loaded their luggage into the trunk.

"I sincerely appreciate all your help," Pierce said.

Laurie slid into the back seat and lay down.

He drove away, toward their home and to Laurie's doctor, his brother.

CHAPTER TWENTY-SIX

"Pierce, everything's okay. I'm fine. Hope's fine." Laurie tried to reassure her husband as he drove. His technique oscillated between that of a near-sighted eighty-year-old, and a NASCAR driver.

He answered with a grunt.

The baby's fine, she repeated to herself. "Did they get my earrings? My mom's earrings? I left them on the nightstand."

"Mary Rae's cousin found them. They're wrapped in tissues, in a little plastic bag in our suitcase. Ed told me twice and had me say it back to him, because Mary Rae said she'd skin him if he didn't."

She lifted her arm, reached over the back of the front seat to caress his neck while he drove. "Pierce. I really am okay. The baby, too. You saw the sonogram they did this morning. They're just being careful."

Careful. She immediately regretted saying the word she'd used to describe Luther and Annabelle's relationship after Pierce's birth, when Luther avoided having more children.

"The baby and I aren't really in danger."

He shifted in the seat, as if uncomfortable with her light touch. "Laurie, I know what you're trying to do. Just give me some time."

She thought she heard him whisper, "All that blood."

"What? Pierce, what did you say?"

"I said I love you. Now please rest and let me drive. I can't talk about this anymore right now."

***

In the global scheme of things, details like this didn't normally affect Pierce. But this time, as he pulled into their driveway, he was certain

God was laughing hysterically. Or at least winking in his direction.

Their house had been painted. Green.

It was a beautiful shade, if one could call the color green beautiful. Somewhere between olive and forest, much like the foliage of the woods where he so often walked and prayed. A richer, darker hue, covered the shutters, a soft cream accented the trim and porch. Their home now resembled a quaint, carefully tended dollhouse.

Laurie met his eyes over the hood of their car. "How lovely. A little ironic, but very pretty."

Daniel and Kay descended the front porch steps and handed Pierce a note.

"It's from the church board." Kay wrapped an arm around Laurie. "Let's get you inside."

Daniel patted his shoulder. "They've got nothing but love for you, Pierce. Nothing but love."

He opened the note, read it for himself, then laughed derisively. "They want us to know that after much deliberation and discussion, the youth group settled on this color. It's fade resistant, mildew resistant, liquid siding with a twenty-five year warranty, lovingly applied with an industrial sprayer by Gilbert and Angus Mann." Pierce raised his head to meet Laurie's laughing gaze. "We should never have to paint again."

They went inside. After much convincing, his parents finally went home. Laurie left him to take a quick shower, but only after he promised to call John, as he was on call.

He sat on the couch, cell phone in hand.

He had to do this. He had to make himself call his brother and get an appointment in the morning for Laurie. It was the one thing she had asked him to do. The one thing he could do.

He dialed. And got voicemail.

"This is Dr. John Bridges. Please leave a complete message including your phone number. Remember, the beep is delayed. Thanks."

He listened and waited. Five seconds, ten.

Beep.

"John, it's Pierce. Laurie and I have been at the beach, she had a little, um, complication. She needs to see you first thing in the morning. Please call our home or my cell as soon as you get this message, even if it's late. Thanks."

Ten minutes later, as Pierce sat on the couch with Laurie's head in his lap, the doorbell rang. Then someone pounded on the front door.

"Pierce! Pierce!"

He opened the door and saw his brother. Hair disheveled, shirt unbuttoned and un-tucked, lipstick on his neck. And a hickey?

"I'm here. What happened?" John rushed to Laurie. He dropped to his knees by the couch, felt his pockets. "I don't have anything with me. Pierce, go tell Rebecca to bring my bag."

Okay.

"No. Yell out to the car for Rebecca to bring my bag. It's better that way." He winked at Laurie.

Rebecca didn't hear Pierce the first time. Or the second.

He tried waving his arms to get her attention, knowing he made quite a sight for the neighbors, standing on the porch directly under the light, waving his arms and yelling like a fool. What else could he do?

His display roused the area dogs. Pretty soon every canine within five miles joined in. Oh, yes, the neighbors *loved* him.

He had just stepped to the edge of the porch when Rebecca managed to open the passenger door and yell "Here!" She quickly tossed a standard doctor's black bag onto the grass. Pierce walked briskly to the bag, staring fixedly at the ground.

"Sorry, my zipper's stuck," Rebecca said through the open door. "Tell John I'll wait here."

"Okay."

Pierce returned in time to hear Laurie invite John and Rebecca for dinner soon, then he passed John the bag.

"Rebecca said she'll wait in the car. She's having trouble with her zipper."

***

For Laurie, time had all but stopped.

To be extra safe, John put her on partial bed-rest, which meant she was only allowed on her feet for a few short intervals each day. As long as she had no further bleeding, no contractions, didn't start dilating, and her water didn't break—so many things could go wrong—she and the baby would be fine.

But she and Pierce couldn't have sex—they couldn't take the chance of starting her labor early—which left her worrying about maintaining their closeness.

Hadn't that been a fun conversation to have with John their first night back from the beach, considering Pierce's call had obviously interrupted John and Rebecca's date.

One client with whom she'd had an initial consultation had opted to sell rather than renovate, and the other possible client was still considering her designs.

She was bored, working to hold off fear, and couldn't help counting days. Nightly leg cramps interrupted her sleep. Though Kay offered to visit often, Laurie found she preferred solitude.

During the second week of bed rest, Laurie had a private phone appointment with Dr. Goodnight.

She lay on the couch, waiting for Eric's call, trying to ignore the voices in her head spouting lists of unfinished tasks around her home. Good thing she hadn't started working right away after moving to Rowe City. Between Pierce's crisis and her pregnancy issues, she'd have been forced to resign.

The phone rang.

"Hello?"

"Laurie? It's Eric Goodnight. How are you feeling?"

"Physically I'm all right. I'm taking precautions, as you know, to keep the baby safe. So far those adjustments seem to be working."

"That's good to hear. You've got a delicate balance to maintain. Yes, you need to be emotionally available for Pierce, but you also have to take care of yourself and the baby. Is he still as afraid as he was before your detour to the ER?"

"He doesn't seem to be. He drove me there, of course. He stayed in the ER, not knowing what was happening while they worked on me. And he stayed in the room with me during the night." That marked progress, didn't it?

"As I said in the beginning, one of the biggest challenges for you during this time is you can't make a plan to fix the problem. Healing from trauma such as your husband's often happens in stages. You're still at the mercy of however God chooses to reveal the rest of his memories."

"How will I know if Pierce is healed?"

"You probably won't, Laurie. Not until you actually go into labor."

She'd let herself think they neared the end of the process. Somehow her mind had conjured a happy ending for Pierce, which coincided with her delivery. But what if that wasn't the case?

"Laurie? Are you still there?"

"Yes, Dr. Goodnight, I'm here," she said.

"Laurie, I hear your distress."

"I'm more afraid for the baby the closer I get to term. Before now, maybe my concern for Pierce overshadowed that." She wrapped an arm across her stomach. Hope kicked and pushed. "I worry that the stress is bad for our baby."

"Then you should speak with your doctor about that."

"I had such a different picture in my head of what these months would be like, happy and fun."

"Laurie, I know this is really tough for you. Having this experience during a pregnancy isn't normal. The question you need to ask is: why does that bother you so much?"

"I . . . I don't know. Maybe because we'd spent years dreaming and planning. I guess I had a list in my head for this, too."

She pondered his question long after the call ended, but wasn't sure she'd figured out the root cause.

***

Pierce walked home through the woods that night after work. Mid-October's burnished colors popped in the trees above him and throughout the countryside. The familiar smells from Pierce's childhood, of harvested fields comforted him. But they also brought to mind his father's farm. He pictured his father digging near the old pig shed, trying to find his mother. How could Luther have forgotten where he buried her?

That night, he snuggled up to Laurie in bed.

"I'm not trying to be a nag, but I wish we'd already built the shelves."

"We'll get it done. Maybe this weekend I'll start."

"I wish I could help. I wish I could *do* things."

"I wish I could make love with you." Loving her, giving her pleasure, had become one of his greatest joys.

"Me, too," she said. "I'm missing you right now. But if you hold me and we fall asleep, at least my heart can almost feel the same as if we were together."

He stayed beside her. Closed his eyes and let his mind wander as he slid into sleep.

Mama laughed as Daddy stood behind her at the sink. She shushed him before he pinched her bottom and grabbed his hat. Then Mama shook her head and smiled, as she looked through the window and watched Daddy walk to the fields.

Later, Pierce woke needing to go to the outhouse. He reached Mama's doorway and heard whispers. Mama sounded happy. Daddy didn't.

He stood in the hall, blind from the darkness, and listened.

"How far, Annabelle? How much time do we have left?"

"It's not like that."

"How far? You know what could happen. I should never have—"

"Shh. I'll be fine. I'm only two or three months."

"In the morning I'm taking you to the doctor."

"I don't need a doctor. It'll be a waste of money. Mrs. Taylor and me did fine with Pierce, and she got me the birth certificate. She can help me with this one, too. We'll give 'em part of a pig like we did last time."

"Belle, I'll sell my right arm if I have to."

"Mama?"

She leaned over Daddy. "You need to go?" She threw back the covers, padded to the door, and brushed her fingers through his hair. "Go on, I'll stand on the porch."

He hurried. Glimmering moonlight let him see, so he ran to and from the outhouse.

"Can I stay by you? On the rug?"

"I'll get your blanket."

She covered him. He lay in the dark, perfectly still yet determined to stay awake in case they whispered again. It felt like forever. Then Mama reached down and placed her hand on his back. His eyes grew heavy, heavier, so he let them close while he strained to listen.

The bed creaked. A soft smooch. "Hold me, Belle. Hold me through the night."

Mama's hand left him. "Shh. I'll be fine."

Pierce woke as his heart cramped in his chest. Mama hadn't been fine.

"Laurie. Are you awake?"

He heard her sharp intake of breath. "I can be."

"Are you all right?"

"Yeah. I'm okay."

"I didn't leave the bed this time." The baby kicked the arm he had wrapped around Laurie. "How do you sleep through that?"

"Right now I'm not."

"Sorry."

"Pierce, just tell me what you need. We're married. Neither of us should suffer alone."

"Daddy asked Mama to hold him, the night she told him she was pregnant with John."

"Scoot back."

He pulled away. In the dark, she rolled with a moan, rested their baby against his side, and draped a leg over his thigh, an arm across his chest.

"Best I can do with a basketball between us."

"It's great," he said. "It's perfect."

CHAPTER TWENTY-SEVEN

John had the wipers on his truck working at full speed. The rain pounded down in heavy sheets, blocking visibility and soaking the terrain. But he was too worried about his dad to turn back. Dad seemed to dig more during bad weather.

Thunder roared and lighting slashed. He turned off the highway and slowed. The lane was a swirling mass of mud. He inched forward, careful to stay on the path. As he inched close to the house, an abnormal eerie glow met him. He tried to see through the windshield to determine its source, but the raging storm prevented clear sight.

He had no jacket with him. His un-tucked dress shirt and jeans would offer little protection. He parked, left the truck running, and pulled off his boots and socks. No way was he ruining a favorite pair of cowboy boots. He rolled up his pants and exited on the passenger side, away from the hissing wind.

He bolted to the farmhouse. Stopped on the porch to sling excess water off his limbs and face. The house stood silent, and the light seemed to come from near the squealing pigs.

No. *No!*

John hurried down the steps and toward the light. Lightning flashed as he caught his foot on something. The orange extension cord. Dad had pulled the lamp outside and run the cord so he could see to dig.

"Dad!" He ran the last several steps, mud squishing between his toes.

A gas lantern sat in the mud, the lamp lay smashed a couple yards away.

"Dad!" He yelled again, but the rain and screaming pigs drowned out his voice.

Rain poured over his body while he quickly surveyed his father's work. What had probably been a dozen holes dotted the ground, but the rain had filled them in until each bled into the next forming a long trench.

Standing ankle deep in the muck, Dad raised the shovel. John surged forward, stopping it mid-swing.

"Dad! You'll have pneumonia in about a minute if you don't have it already!"

"I have to find her. I'm coming, Annabelle! I'm coming!"

"You can't do this now, Dad." He jerked away the shovel. "Now come inside." He turned toward the house. "I mean it, Dad. Get out of this weather."

John slung the shovel at the porch. If his dad couldn't find it, his dad couldn't dig.

He heard a smack in the mud and looked back. Dad had fallen to his hands and knees and crawled away. Cool wind plastered his soaked long johns against his skin, tossed mud and pig manure at his face and chest.

And he was digging with his hands.

"Annabelle! I'm so sorry, 'Belle!" Dad landed facedown in pig waste.

John lunged. The pen's fence posts leaned, the corner post tilted. Lighting and thunder exploded overhead. The swine squealed in terror, broke through and scurried out, trampling his dad as they ran.

He hiked through the mud, knelt to see if his father lived, and tried not to vomit at the stench.

"I'm sorry," his father whispered. "I'm so sorry."

CHAPTER TWENTY-EIGHT

Thirty-eight weeks and three days. Laurie was practically counting down the minutes to November 2.

God, thank You. Thank You for helping me get this far.

She couldn't keep from smiling with relief as she and Pierce waited in an exam room at Dr. Nate's clinic. Her pregnancy was far from what she'd imagined, her marriage unlike anything she'd ever expected. Yet in a few weeks give-or-take, she'd finally have her baby. She didn't care if she delivered in the back of a pick-up driving through town during rush hour. She simply wanted the next phase of life to begin. For herself. For Pierce. For their daughter.

"I hope John lets me start doing things." She lay back and twirled a pearl earring.

"We're going to do whatever he tells us," Pierce said. "For however long he tells us to do it."

She waved her hand, shooing away his words. "I know. But I have all this energy. The baby shower's tomorrow. We still have to hang the border and build the shelves."

"We'll get it all done, Laurie."

"We've only got a few days." These last days would pass quickly, or so everyone said.

Deb Jordan breezed in. "Did I hear someone say baby shower?"

"Tomorrow. Did you get the invitation?"

"I'll be there," Deb said. "Are you finished with the Lamaze DVDs?"

"I've got one more to go. I'll watch it tonight, give them back to you tomorrow. Am I really ready to do this?"

Deb laughed. "Sweetie, you'll have this baby whether you feel ready or not."

"I guess that's good news," Laurie said. At least, she hoped it was good news.

***

When John arrived, Pierce shook his hand. His hands hardly sweat anymore, as he was used to seeing his brother now. All patients saw both docs, an attempt to help the patient be comfortable no matter who assisted in delivery.

"So, the week's been uneventful?" John flipped through Laurie's chart. "You're feeling good?"

"I feel great, and there's so much to do." Excitement bubbled through her answer. "Can I be normal now?"

John winked at Laurie and wiggled his brow at Pierce. "Well, Pastor, you ready to be normal again?"

Pierce's ears were on fire. They might incinerate along with his face.

And Laurie was giggling. Blushing, but giggling. "That's not exactly what I meant."

John snapped the chart closed. "Ten more days, you two. Then you can have at it. Deb, get the pastor here a brochure on safe sex."

Pierce couldn't help but laugh.

Laurie raised to her elbows. "I meant the baby shower is tomorrow and the nursery isn't ready."

"Let me finish," John added. "Light activity for you. No lifting, bending, heavy housework like vacuuming. But you can be on your feet for short intervals during the day, as long as you rest more than you're up." He patted Pierce's arm. "Harp on Casanova here to finish the nursery."

"Yes!" Laurie reached for Pierce's hand. "Help me up."

John stood. "Do you two have a minute?"

The simple request filled Pierce with dread. His eyes met his brother's, then John looked away and paced.

Laurie spoke first. "What is it, John?"

It's all right, Pierce thought. Her compassionate heart is one reason he married her.

"I found Dad digging in the yard Sunday evening. I think he had been out there for a while."

Pierce had to ask. "The night of the storm?"

"Yeah." John lowered his head. "He's going to kill himself looking for our mother. If you know where she is—"

"She's by the pig shed." Pierce stepped to the window, stood with feet spread, arms crossed. He did *not* want to talk about this. "It's the nastiest, worst place possible."

"He's looked there," John said. "I've looked there. The smell is unbearable."

Pierce knew. "Worse than anything you've ever smelled, right?"

"Frankly, yes."

He didn't turn, but spoke over his shoulder. "The stench is in layers. The farther down you go, the worse it is. So the more you dig, the worse the smell."

God, help me. Help *me. I'm facing my grief, my childhood, but I'm not ready for this part.*

Laurie's arms slipped around him. She pressed herself against his back, then turned him around to face her. "I'm here. It's okay. I'm here."

He took her hands in his.

He cared about his mother's grave. He even cared about John. He didn't want to care about Luther, but a part of him already did.

John sat again, ran a hand through his hair. "I don't know what to do."

"Why?" Laurie asked.

"The farm will probably be gone within the year. Developers

have been trying to buy out Dad since before I came back. He's refused to sell. But now . . ."

"Now, what? He's the one who put her there almost thirty years ago. It never mattered to him before."

"Pierce," said Laurie.

"No, Laurie. No."

This was it. This was when his head would actually explode, like he had always thought it would.

"Pierce, it's not John's fault."

His stomach churned. His whole body tensed, poised like a spring. No, he thought. Never again would he mistreat others because of his past.

"Pierce."

Let your light shine before men, that they may see your good deeds and praise your Father in heaven.

"Pierce, please."

Laurie was right, John wasn't at fault. She was right about a lot of things. John hadn't known about him. John didn't *have* a mother. John hadn't grown up in a loving home. John didn't know God.

Laurie's expression encouraged him to reach out to his brother. Pierce looked John square in the face. "I'm sorry. Please forgive me. I'm not angry at you."

Laurie turned to John. "John, what's changed?"

"Dad owes back taxes and doesn't want me to pay them. The county's threatening to seize the property. Sunday, when I found him, he was digging in the rain. The pigs trampled him. He has a fractured tibia—a broken leg—bruises, lacerations. He's in the intensive care unit now, sedated. He has double pneumonia and a seriously infected wound on his arm that's resistant to antibiotics."

Guilt slapped Pierce. "He's been in the hospital for three days, and you didn't tell us because of me."

"I didn't know what to say." John looked at Laurie then back to

Pierce. "How do I ask my brother to dig up our mother?"

**

That evening, Pierce tried to pay attention as he and Laurie watched the last Lamaze DVD. But the images on the screen somehow didn't seem real. Or not real enough.

Could a woman really smile during labor? Possibly with the right pain medication. In the perfect place. Under the best circumstances.

Certainly not in a dark room, with a husband who offered no help, enduring terrible pain, and bleeding to death.

Were the memories driving Luther insane? Was that why he dug constantly? Or was he now aware that if he didn't find her, she could be lost forever. Or worse yet, coldly moved to an unmarked, pauper's grave, or unwittingly covered by new construction.

John still had trouble believing Luther had buried their mother on the farm. But he had contacted county officials since Luther's hospitalization. He knew how to legally have the body exhumed and prepared for a proper burial. Laurie had suggested Annabelle be moved to the church cemetery. John said Luther was stable enough to discuss that option, but had refused to do so even when told the county wouldn't allow Annabelle's remains to be left on site if the land were sold at auction.

Which meant Pierce needed to find his mother's grave, soon. What a gruesome thought.

He just wasn't ready. Could he ever be ready?

As awful as it sounded, at least Luther's condition precluded Pierce's having to decide whether or not to visit him. Pierce wasn't ready for that, either.

"Pierce, what do you think?"

"What?"

"I'll have the epidural as quickly as possible and forget all this natural childbirth stuff. I'll practice the breathing, but I don't want to feel anything I don't have to."

"I think that's the perfect plan."

"Will you hang the border for me tomorrow morning, before the baby shower?"

"Sure. Laurie?" He couldn't get a certain picture out of his mind. "What is it?"

"Did you see the holes around the farmhouse? Is the pig pen by the tree?"

She paused the DVD, waddled to the kitchen. He heard her open and close drawers. Then he smelled popcorn, heard the microwave beep. She returned with a bowl in one hand, a notebook in the other, and a bright pink pen between her teeth.

She gave him the bowl, shoved popcorn in his mouth, then clicked her pen. "I'll draw it for you."

***

Laurie was pushing. Panting and pushing. Sweating and groaning but making no progress. The baby wouldn't come—

Pain woke Laurie from a dead sleep. Both calves had cramped. "Ow. Ow."

Pierce awakened and turned on the bedside lamp. "What is it? You're not bleeding again."

"No. Help me." She reached in vain for her feet. "I have cramps in both legs."

He scrambled off the end of the bed, knelt on the floor, and gently pushed on her toes.

"Easy. Oh. Ow."

"Your potassium's probably low. I'll rub them and get you some Gatorade."

The sadistic twist brought tears to her eyes. Laurie imagined her muscles wrenching, tearing themselves apart from the inside out.

Is this how labor would feel? Except she'd be trying to push a baby into the world?

The cramps finally subsided. Pierce hurried to the kitchen, returned with a large glass for her. He was being so sweet, so supportive, despite his struggles. She didn't want to add to it, but . . .

God, if I tell him what I'm feeling, what I dreamed, it may set him back.

"Will you hold me?" she asked.

He climbed across the bed toward her. "Finish your drink."

She did. He set the cup aside.

"Hold me." She clung to him, bit her lip.

The two become one.

"I have to tell you," she said. "I don't want to, but God won't let me not tell you."

"Shh. It's okay."

But his grip on her tightened, his breath quickened, his heartbeat increased against hers.

"I don't want to worsen your struggle. But I'm so afraid right now." She buried her face in his neck. "I dreamed I was in labor. And I was afraid. I couldn't push the baby out and the contractions were immense, and you were there and I needed you there, but you were so scared and I hated asking you to stay. Please, just hold me."

For long minutes she rested in his arms. "I wasn't going to tell you."

"I wake you when I have nightmares," he said. "It's okay. If we hold onto each other, we'll be okay."

She hoped he was right.

***

They descended on Pierce's home like a swarm of perfumed bees. His living room held every woman Pierce knew in Rowe City. They moved in different directions, each performed a different task. It was coordinated chaos, complete with laughter, hugs, and all things pink. Pink

279

cups, plates, napkins, even pink finger-sandwiches.

He didn't dare touch those.

Between refilling cups of punch and wiping counters in the kitchen, he avoided hearing most of the labor stories. He allowed himself brief periods of leaning against the doorjamb to watch Laurie, his beautiful, sweet wife, whose eyes occasionally locked on his, transmitting love. Then she'd receive another gift, and the squealing and aah-ing would crescendo again. Several times he noticed her touch a fingertip to the pearl studs in her ears. The action had become such a habit, she didn't seem to realize she was doing it. Joy filled him—although more than once he yearned for silence—because Laurie was having the time of her life.

As the last car pulled away, Kay hugged him. "How are you holding up, Daddy?"

"I'm good."

Laurie sank onto the couch, extended her arms. "Look at all of this. Will it fit in the room?"

Kay shook a finger at Laurie. "Don't you overdo, putting it all away."

Daniel came through the front door, went straight to Laurie. "There's my girl. Son, you still alive?"

"I survived."

Kay hugged Pierce again. "He was wonderful. He finished the border in the nursery this morning. Everyone thinks it's beautiful. He served and cleaned. The kitchen's spotless, and there's nothing more for me to do." They kissed him and Laurie goodbye.

"I want to start putting things away, but I'm too tired," Laurie said.

"That's why we're going to bed."

"It's barely seven."

He led her to their room, helped her undress and slipped a nightgown over her head, feeding her arms through the short, soft sleeves.

Then he stripped to his boxers and turned out the light. With a gentle nudge, he coaxed her head onto her pillow and settled against her.

"I'll help you put the gifts away tomorrow, that way I'll know where things are, too."

He patted Hope, and they went to sleep.

***

The strange land Pierce found himself in the next day contained diapers no bigger than napkins, diaper bags that looked like purses, and a portable breast pump that looked like a torture device from a horror movie.

Thank God he was a man.

Laurie picked a drawer for the bibs. Changed her mind.

Pierce bundled the socks like she wanted, stocked them in the basket she gave him. She moved those, too.

More than once, she changed her mind then switched it back. Sometimes while laughing, sometimes while fighting tears. He didn't understand, and it didn't matter that he didn't understand. He simply blamed her behavior on pregnancy, and prayed she'd regain her sanity after delivery.

"What about this little guy?" He lifted the fluffy teddy bear from the bag of gifts his parents had given.

"Lay it in the crib. It'll be there waiting when we bring Hope home."

He did so, then set the bag aside.

"Wait," she said. "Look in the bottom. There's a Bible. I think we should leave it out, maybe displayed on the dresser or a shelf."

"A Bible's one of the first things they ever gave me."

"Really? You never told me that."

"Didn't think about it." He shrugged. "I guess not all memories are bad, huh?"

"And we're making happy ones now, so you'll have even more."

She looked around the room. "I think we have almost everything. But I still need receiving blankets."

"Receiving blankets?"

"You know, little, soft blankets to wrap the baby in when she's small. Babies chill easily. I have one your parents got us, but that's all."

"Oh."

"Look at these." She held up the tiniest pink dress he had ever seen, along with a doll-sized matching bonnet. "Don't you just love it?"

"Will she be that small?"

"Of course she will. Probably between six and eight pounds."

Six and eight pounds? Like, a gallon of milk or water? Was she kidding?

"But I'm all thumbs. How will I dress her?"

She smiled at him. "You'll practice."

"What about diapers?"

"You'll practice that, too. The tapes always fasten in the front." She laughed at him. "Or you'll give her to me."

He grinned. "I'm a tough guy. I can handle messy diapers."

Her voice grew tight. "Can you handle me in labor?"

He searched her face, oscillating between being ashamed and being offended. After all the changes he had made, did she think he wouldn't be there for her when the time came?

"I did okay when I took you to the ER."

She closed her eyes as if to shield herself. Tears squeezed free at the corners and her voice lowered to a whisper. "Yes. And we haven't talked about it. You took care of me, but—"

"I've changed, Laurie. Don't you know that?"

"I'm not saying you haven't. I just need to hear it."

Two will become one. Talk to her, so she'll know.

He took her hands, kissed them, and placed them on his heart. "Feel that?"

She nodded, her eyes still bright with unshed tears.

"It beats for you."

"Oh, Pierce."

"It beats for you and Hope. I will always be wherever you need me, wherever she needs me. No matter what.

"I admit, I was scared before. Partly because of my memories, partly because of my ignorance, and partly because I forgot that wherever God leads us and wherever you are, that's where I want to be."

Her tears flowed freely now, but this time they were the happy tears he had always loved.

He pressed his forehead to hers. "I love you. And I *can* handle messy diapers." He kissed her. "Now where can we buy blankets for Hope?"

Chapter Twenty-nine

Laurie knew she would always carry this memory close to her heart. And laugh about it for the rest of her life.

Pierce. Measuring and re-measuring, running in and out of the house, trying to use the table saw that Angus had sent by way of Gilbert, which now sat outside the back door. Discovering he'd cut a board too long. Cutting again, and finding the board too short.

"It's okay," he said. "I'll get it this time. I bought plenty of wood. I can do this."

She stored the freshly washed blankets and other baby items they'd bought while shopping with Daniel and Kay. Sweet bibs, tiny tights. Shiny black dress shoes that looked like they belonged on a baby doll.

She draped old sheets over the readied crib and other furniture to protect them, and was glad she did. In less than an hour sawdust coated Pierce like he'd walked through a cloud of coarse flour. Two boards had been installed, and the pile of discarded, partially destroyed planks grew outside the nursery window. If he finished the shelves before she delivered, it'd be a miracle.

She sat, rocking in the chair in the corner. The quiet creaks marked the passing seconds with a gentle rhythm like a lazy nursery rhyme. She let herself relax and nap, her sleep occasionally interrupted by Pierce's trips in and out of the room. Hope kicked, and Laurie awoke.

"You surprise me," she said dreamily, watching Pierce assemble the shelves on the nursery floor.

He threw her a grin. "Because I figured this out?"

285

"No."

What words should she use? How could she say he'd become everything she had ever wanted, ever needed, without sounding like she was throwing his past struggles in his face?

Whatever is true.

Hope kicked again, stretched and rolled. Soon, it wouldn't be just her and Pierce. Her dreams were coming true.

Gratitude bubbled up inside her. "Remember when I told you that every dream I have depends on you?"

Pierce lowered the drill, looked at her. "Yeah. I was in Florida, missing you like crazy. Why are you crying?"

"Because I'm so thankful. That wasn't very long ago; so much has happened since then. But you never stopped trying."

"You expected me to, didn't you?"

"I don't know if expected is the right word. I was scared you would walk away from our life, our dreams, away from me and our child."

"So, you're surprised I stayed."

"I'm surprised by how much you love me and our baby. It's more than I ever hoped for, more than I ever dreamed."

"I can do this, Laurie. I know God can help me be there when you deliver. I won't miss it. I won't."

She stood. Hope kicked again, hard and low. Laurie jerked. Something had just happened.

He grabbed her shoulders and held her away. "What is it? Don't you believe me?"

She laughed. She raised both hands to her face and laughed while tears streamed down.

"What?" he asked. She could hear the indignation in his words. "Tell me what's so funny. I can do it, Laurie. I'll stay with you. I'll be there for you like my father never was for my mother—."

She grabbed his dust-covered face and kissed him.

"My water just broke. Three days early, but I'll take it!"

***

To Laurie, the next moments were like being in a live episode of *The Three Stooges.*

She stood still while Pierce ran to get a towel, came back with six, and sopped up the puddle on the floor. "It doesn't matter," he said. "I'll replace the wood flooring if I have to."

He grabbed the soiled towels and dashed back down the hall. He started the washing machine, then flew back into the nursery with a jug of laundry soap in his hand.

"Pierce."

"It's okay. I'll just cover the saw and unplug it. Then it won't matter if rain comes."

"Okay, but—"

He was gone again.

She walked slowly to their room to change her pants. She'd simply toss the dirty pair in the washer with the towels.

"Pierce?" The back door slammed; she put on clean jeans.

Pierce raced into their bedroom. "Give me the pants." He yanked the wet pair out of her hand.

She heard the washing machine lid slam, saw Pierce dart straight to the bathroom. She lifted the overnight bag she'd packed upon returning from the beach, just in case. She set it on the bed, slipped her feet into her loafers, and heard a panic-filled, "Okay."

She peeked into the bathroom. Pierce stood in the shower, peeling off his clothes as the water pounded him clean and drenched the floor. In his haste he hadn't closed the shower curtain. He was moving so fast, he looked like he had eight arms and legs.

"I'm hurrying." He yelled over his shoulder without looking. "Laurie, just sit and breathe. I'll be ready in five minutes. Three. Just sit and breathe. We'll leave in three minutes."

She laughed at him, tossed a towel on the puddled floor. Then she leaned against the doorframe to enjoy the rest of the show as he lathered the soap, scrubbed with his bare hands, and mistakenly squeezed her conditioner onto his head.

"You won't be able to rinse that out in three minutes!" She yelled above the thrumming water.

"Yes. Yes, I will. Just breathe, Laurie." His hands stilled. He opened his eyes, looked with horror at his spread fingers. "What *is* this stuff?"

She giggled. "It's my super-hydrating conditioner."

His eyes widened with accusation. "It's like runny mashed potatoes."

"Rinse out what you can, then wash twice." She laughed again, turned to leave. "I'll be in the car. Breathing."

***

Once again Pierce drove Laurie to the hospital. His sweating hands strangled the steering wheel, as he repeatedly hit the brakes to avoid breaking the sound barrier—or getting a hefty speeding ticket. Laurie called his parents, and as previously instructed, she called John, who was already on duty; he met them at the doors of Labor and Delivery.

"Are you having contractions?" John motioned her toward a waiting wheelchair.

Laurie grimaced as she sat. "Maybe. Mostly pressure."

"She wants an epidural right away," Pierce said.

"I know. She reminded me when she called." John pushed her down the hall. "Laurie—"

"Her water broke an hour ago." Pierce jogged alongside. "Don't you need to call the anesthesiologist? She took a nap earlier, but hasn't had anything to eat or drink since breakfast. She might be dehydrated."

John stopped abruptly outside an unoccupied delivery room. "Pierce. This isn't my first delivery, but I *do* understand that it is *your* first delivery. More importantly, it's Laurie's. Let me do my job."

Pierce grabbed John's arm. "I need to know everything that's going on. I need to know what to do to help her."

"Pierce. I get it. I do. I'll double-check, triple-check everything, and then tell you everything, okay? This is a good hospital and I'm a fairly decent doctor."

"Can I lie down in that bed now?" Laurie panted. "This is starting to get uncomfortable."

John hit the intercom button. "I need a nurse in room nine, please—relax brother. And smile. In less than twenty-four hours, you'll be a father."

"Twenty-four hours?" he asked.

Then he heard a scream. A shout from the hallway: "I need whole blood. Now!"

He turned, looked out into the hall only a few strides away. A nurse, whose uniform was covered in blood, ran toward the room and stopped in the doorway facing him. "I paged Dr. Trent *Stat!* but he hasn't responded." She looked at John, frantic. "Can you come?"

A voice sounded from the overhead speaker. "Code 100. Code 100. Any anesthesiologist to Labor and Delivery."

John ran past Pierce, but Pierce felt compelled to follow.

"Pierce? Where are you going?" Laurie's voice fluttered with uncertainty.

He stepped into the hall as a host of medical personnel hurried past and into the next room. He pressed back against the wall, his heart raced, his vision tunneled. His knees shook, and he lowered himself to the ground.

"Pierce?" Laurie called with a shaky voice.

A hand touched his shoulder. Pierce looked up into his parents' faces.

"I'll go in with Laurie," his mom said.

Pierce simply nodded.

"Where's John?" Daniel asked.

The door of the next room slammed shut. Still, clipped voices and sharp commands echoed into the hall. Pierce stood. "He's in there. Dad, I thought I could do this. But now, I don't know."

Another nurse walked past him and into Laurie's room. She left the door open, but slid a curtain closed. "Mrs. Crane, right? Laurie?"

"I'm Laurie Crane," his wife said. He could almost hear her heart breaking. She cleared her throat. "Mom, would you see if Pierce and Dad are still in the hall?"

His mom edged around the curtain and came to him. "I don't mind staying with Laurie, Pierce. I consider it a privilege. But it's you she wants and needs most."

Beyond the curtain, the nurse murmured to Laurie, who answered back quietly. But Pierce knew that tone; he'd heard it after the miscarriage, on the phone while he was in Florida, and every other time she tried to hide her disappointment.

Dear God, I thought I had my fear under control. Why does walking into that room and staying there now seem impossible?

He looked at his parents. "Can we just stand here for a minute?"

Dad dug in his pocket, offered Pierce a stick of Juicy Fruit then took one himself. Cheers sounded from the next room; its door opened, and John exited, sweaty and smiling. He looked at Daniel.

"Hello, sir. Thanks for visiting my dad yesterday."

"You're welcome. How is he?"

"Not as good as the mother and baby behind me," he said, and entered Laurie's room.

Flanked by his parents, Pierce followed and stopped a few feet away from the bed as the nurse spoke to John.

"She isn't having contractions. The baby's turned, and her head is blocking further leakage of amniotic fluid."

"All right. If nothing changes, we'll let her rest tonight and have Dr. Nate induce her labor in the morning."

Dad popped his gum. "I think she needs a hamburger. Or a donut. A woman's got to have her strength when she's about to have a baby."

John winked at Laurie. "Sorry, Grandpa Crane," he said. "We're doing this one by the book. Clear liquids, maybe Jell-O. Dr. Nate will be here at six a.m."

"To induce me."

"Yes."

Pierce looked at his brother. "But I thought you'd be delivering Hope."

"If the baby came tonight, yes. But my shift ends at six tomorrow morning."

They all fell silent, but Pierce's heart thundered in his chest. He was supposed to do something. He knew he was. But what?

"John. Tell me about our dad."

His brother hesitated, looked from him to Laurie, then back to him again.

"Are you sure you want to talk about this now?" He paced then stopped, stared straight at Pierce. "The day I drove Dad to church, did you see him in the back, weeping?"

Pierce had seen him. And heard him. Probably everyone near Luther had. "Yes." If Pierce hadn't seen it with his own eyes, he probably wouldn't have believed it. "But I didn't recognize him."

"That's the second time in my life I have seen him cry. The first time was before that—the day he told me about burying our mother in the yard and giving you away. He cried all the way home that Sunday. He sat in my truck, shrinking right before my eyes, and quietly wept buckets." He sniffed. "The only other time was when he met Laurie, that morning at the farm."

Pierce met Laurie's gaze. She nodded, and John continued.

"Dad, our dad," he said, gesturing between the two of them, "gave me orders and chores when I was a child. He told me not to get

291

into trouble when I went away to college. He refuses to let me pay the back taxes on the farm. He barely let me install an air conditioner in the living room. He never asked me for anything, Pierce." John looked at him again. "Until the day he told me about you."

He will bring to light what is hidden in darkness.

John continued. "He told me, 'She died because I loved her.'"

Which was exactly what Laurie had suggested. Luther viewed Annabelle's second pregnancy as a death sentence.

"He believes he killed her by getting her pregnant with me." John spread his fingers, stretched them toward Pierce. "You should have seen his hands when I found him. His fingers were ripped to shreds. He'd been digging with his *hands*. Hate him if you have to—"

"I don't hate him. I thought I did, but, no."

Pierce could hear his father's frantic whispers.

"How far, Annabelle? How far?"

His father's fear.

"I never should have . . ."

He saw his daddy. Crying in the truck. Then going into the house and holding Mama.

"Don't leave me, Annabelle. Please, don't go."

Then you shall know the truth, and the truth will set you free.

Pierce knew exactly what John was going to ask. And this time he had all the power to relieve his brother's and his father's anguish.

Or he could turn his back, fold his arms, and walk away. But would that cost him more?

"There's no legal will, and Dad's fading fast," John said. "Please, Pierce. If she's really there, before Dad dies and the farm is gone, help me find Mama's grave. It's the only thing he ever asked me. I can't stand the thought of careless strangers digging her up or building on top of her."

Pierce glanced at his watch. 11:42 p.m. Just over six hours until Dr. Nate would start Laurie's labor. "How many patients do you have in labor right now?"

"Laurie's my only patient so far. Of course, two more are scheduled for induction tomorrow morning when Dr. Nate arrives."

God, I know this is right. Help me, and protect Laurie and our baby.

"Can you leave for a while?"

"Now?"

"Yeah."

"Maybe. Yeah, I can fix it."

"Pierce, what are you doing?" Laurie's voice was filled with trepidation.

He took her hand, kissed it. He could see her questioning, processing. "Do you trust me?"

"Do you have . . . to do this . . . right now?"

"Trust me, Laurie."

"I want to."

The unspoken "but" cut him, yet he understood it.

"Pierce, we don't have to do this tonight," John said.

He looked at his brother. "I do. I know it doesn't make sense, but I know God wants me to do this right now."

John shook his head. "If you say so."

The monitor showed Laurie's heart rate increasing. "You promised me."

"I'm not breaking my promise. I'm not leaving you because I'm afraid to stay." He kept her hand in his, closed his eyes to concentrate. *God, help me say this right.* "John. She isn't having contractions, right?"

"Right."

Laurie pulled her hand away.

Pierce opened his eyes; she was trying to sit up. Gently he sat on the edge of the bed, faced her, but spoke over his shoulder to John.

"Right now, Laurie's not in labor, right?"

"Technically that's correct, but we can't leave the baby exposed to infection once the amniotic sac has been compromised. That's why we have to induce her labor."

"Which takes place tomorrow morning."

"Unless she starts having contractions on her own."

Laurie stared at the hospital blanket across her lap.

"Honey. Look at me."

"You're asking a lot of me, Pierce."

"Please, Laurie. Look in my eyes."

Finally she did. Hers were filled with dread and resignation. He pressed his forehead to hers. "This isn't me running away."

"Prove it," she whispered.

Pierce caressed her blanket-covered belly. "This is the right thing to do."

Her gaze again fell to her lap. "I'm not going anywhere."

"I'll hurry. I'll call you soon."

He kissed her. He called Gilbert, who agreed to meet them at the farm, and ran with Daniel to the parking lot.

***

She couldn't believe he'd left her. Not begging him to stay, not shaming him into staying with her, had taken every ounce of strength and will-power Laurie had. And now she was alone again.

Yes, Kay was there, trying to get comfortable in a hospital recliner that flattened to a bed. But Laurie felt alone, in her core. In the part of her that had dreamed of sharing a pregnancy and birth with Pierce. She touched fingertips to her mother's earrings—she was determined to wear them during delivery. If only her mom were here.

12:14 a.m. *God, I am teetering on the edge. One foot over, and I'll be so far into a canyon of resentment I don't know how I'll climb out.*

She tried to stay calm and gazed around the birthing suite while Kay slept. Wished she could appreciate the sweet teddy bear wallpaper borders in primary colors.

She closed her eyes, concentrated on the monitor beeping beside her. *The baby's fine.*

Laurie opened her eyes. 1:06 a.m.

God, if Pierce breaks his promise . . .

She didn't want to think this way. She hated being afraid, hated she was contemplating calling Pierce and begging him to return right now.

"Having this experience during a pregnancy isn't normal," Dr. Goodnight had said. *"The question you need to ask is: why does that bother you so much?"*

She'd not had an answer. Not during their conversation, not in the days and weeks that followed.

But lying here, in this room, if she closed her eyes and blocked out the hospital sounds, she felt . . . alone.

She'd been alone when she sold her parents' home. Alone when she went to college. She'd stayed on campus year-round rather than living alone in an apartment. When she'd met Pierce, there'd been no family to tell. When she'd fallen in love, gotten engaged, other than a couple of girlfriends, she'd celebrated alone, dreamed alone. She'd planned her wedding alone, walked down the aisle, alone.

Getting pregnant, having this baby, was the first adult dream she'd hadn't carried alone. Together she and Pierce had planned and—

She'd assumed if they could dream it, it would happen. Anything less couldn't possibly be God's plan for their lives.

The nurse returned, took her temperature and other vital signs. "Mrs. Crane. I'll be more than happy to close your door. Why don't you turn off your overhead light and get some sleep? You have a big day tomorrow."

"Closing the door will be fine, but I think I prefer the light on."

Kay roused. "Laurie, I can feel your struggle all the way over here. The air around you is vibrating with it." Kay rose and came close. "Can I get you more ice chips? Bathe your face with a cool rag?"

"No, thanks."

"Is there anything I can do for you?"

"Not right now."

Kay sat again. The nurse left, but Laurie couldn't go back to sleep.

How could she sleep, when every expectation she'd had about these precious moments was being shattered? When she didn't know if she'd ever be able to forgive Pierce if he missed their daughter's delivery.

When she knew Pierce was on his way to mark his mother's grave.

He was probably pulling into that sad yard right now, a place he never wanted to see again. Walking up the rotted steps, facing every memory from his childhood—

Why? Because . . . because he believed it was the right thing to do.

She smiled with relief, then closed her eyes in shame. He was out there, right now, doing the hard thing because it was necessary. Just like taking her to Isaac and Ella's after the miscarriage, and moving their belongings himself so she needn't return to the place she'd experienced such loss.

His decision affected her, but it wasn't about her. He hadn't left her, he was being obedient to God.

The only One who could heal Pierce's heart.

Not her. Not being loved by her. Not being with her during their child's delivery, nor even their child.

Oh, God, forgive me for insisting every detail be how I'd dreamed and envisioned them. You're here. You are right in the middle of our lives, and even though Pierce isn't here I'm not alone. I have You, just like Pierce does.

CHAPTER THIRTY

The moon hung behind a mist, as it had the night his mother died. He'd never forget that moon.

Silence hung over the farm like that of an empty church. How both John and Gilbert arrived before he and Dad did, Pierce couldn't guess.

Gilbert walked around the front yard, using his cell. "John's inside. I'm talking with my dad. I'll be right there."

John stood on the front porch holding a metal flashlight. "I asked Old Man Dawkins to take the pigs and the cow after Dad's accident."

Pierce paused at the steps, then walked up. "Where's the pig pen?"

"Gone. Collapsed in the storm while Dad was digging. But I can show you."

Pierce looked at Daniel. "Dad, I need to go in the house."

"There's a shovel in the barn," John said. "We need to hurry, Pierce. It's almost two a.m. and I have to be back by four a.m."

"I know, but Laurie drew me a picture of where things are, and it's not right. I need to look out from the inside."

Which meant facing all the rest. Every last *why* behind the fear and rejection.

Pierce stood beside John and pointed. "That was Mama's chair."

His brother's face filled with wonder. "Yeah?"

"She sat in it every day."

He saw that night again. How he awoke needing to go to the outhouse, heard Mama crying, looked through the keyhole and watched her suffer. How the blood seeped under the door toward his toes.

"Pierce! You still there? Run next door and get Mrs. Taylor!" Daddy yelled. "Do it, boy!"

Pierce ran to the porch and skidded to a stop. He could hear the pigs, and looking toward the Taylors' farm, he could see the outline of his own outhouse and barn. Everything was still, like life had stopped. Behind him, Mama's groans grew louder.

Beyond the barn lay the acres of fields separating their farm and the Taylors. If he hurried, if he ran as fast as he could shouting for Mrs. Taylor to come, she'd come. Then Mama would be all right.

He jumped from the porch. Ran toward the light he knew shone from a tall pole in the Taylors' yard, yelling as his lungs heaved.

Growls and barks answered him. The Taylors' German Shepherds were loose and roaming the fields.

He stopped. "Mrs. Taylor! Mrs. Taylor! Please come! Mrs. Taylor!"

But the dogs came instead. Black shapes bounded toward him, growling like they planned to eat him alive.

Terror-stricken, he raced home, hoping the dogs would stop as usual at their own property line. He vaulted the steps and jumped in Mama's spindle chair. Wrapped his quivering arms around his legs. Rocked himself and wiped tears. Listened for Mama. But Mama's cries had stopped.

"Pierce? Are you back yet? Did you get Mrs. Taylor?" Daddy called.

Pierce went back to the bedroom door and again peered through the keyhole. Daddy jerked it open and Pierce fell.

"Move," Daddy said, and carried a screaming baby out into the night.

Pierce swallowed. "You're pretty sure you know why Mom died."

John looked at him. "Yes. But I don't know what that has to do with where she's buried."

"I thought it was my fault," he said. "I remember now. Dad sent me to get Mrs. Taylor, but I was too scared of their big dogs to do what he said. After, I thought she died because I didn't bring help. And

I figured that's why he sent me away. I was the reason she died, so he didn't want me anymore."

"But I told you and Laurie why she died." John rubbed a hand over his face. "Pierce. Dad sent you for help because he knew I was early, not because Mom could be saved."

Pierce stepped to the chair, wrapped his fingers around the worn frame and squeezed.

Then you will know the truth, and the truth will set you free.

"I blamed myself for her death. I blamed myself, and I didn't even know, because I didn't remember."

Dear God, You knew all along. This is what was hidden in darkness, hidden in my memory.

The crippling, dry-up-the-spit-in-your-mouth fear hadn't been about being with Laurie during delivery—that's why he couldn't reason around it, couldn't conquer it himself by gritting his teeth and making himself stay with her. No, his terror was grounded in the lie that Mama died because of something he didn't do. All this time, in the pit of his gut, hadn't there been questions lingering in the dark? *What if Laurie needs something and I can't be there for her?* If the worst happened—like the miscarriage—it would be his fault.

He hadn't understood, hadn't recognized the voice of guilt inside him which had been whispering since the miscarriage, *stay away, stay away—if anything goes wrong, it'll be your fault.*

Relief turned his knees to water. He stumbled back against the house and raised both hands to heaven.

"Holy, holy God. Thank You for bringing me back to this place. For pushing me to discover the truth so I can heal. I trust You with Laurie and our child and all that I am."

John was staring into the distance, his hands in his pockets, a befuddled look on his face. "Maybe later you can explain what just happened here?"

Pierce looked at his brother. "I will. I promise. Now, let's finish this."

He pulled open the screened door; it squeaked the same as it always had. John turned on the kitchen light, throwing shadows to the same living room furniture and the same gapped floor.

"Did he ever put a bathroom inside? Laurie's picture didn't show an outhouse."

"There's one down the hall. It was there when I came here to live, when I was four. There never was an outhouse."

"Yes, there was."

Pierce scanned the small living room, the short hall and dingy kitchen. How large the space had seemed when he'd lived here. Now, he could easily cross the rooms in ten, twelve steps.

"Pierce," John said, clearly struggling with frustration. "I'm sorry, but I don't understand why we're in here when our mom is buried out there."

"Just stand there, okay? Just stand there, and give me a minute." His legs were now like stiff timber, his arms flimsy like rubber bands.

God, help me. The old me doesn't want to do this. But the new me, the me that just realized the truth wants Your will, Father. Your plan.

Surely I am with you always.

Mama hadn't always been there. Mama was gone.

I am with you always.

Daddy had given him away, but that's how God had given him Daniel and Kay.

I am with you.

A few steps brought him to his old room, which had been converted to a bathroom. Three more strides and the earthy scent of his father hit him full force from an open doorway. Mama and Daddy's room. It held the same bed, the same everything. Luther had changed nothing.

In the near darkness, Pierce's hands trembled first, then tremors passed through his body. Memories again kicked him in the chest. He grabbed the doorway to keep from falling and took a fortifying breath.

"It wasn't my fault," he said aloud again, to himself, to John. "It wasn't my fault."

Then you will know the truth, and the truth will set you free.

Pierce pulled his phone from his pocket, dialed direct to Laurie's room. She answered on the second ring. "Laurie. Are you all right?"

"I can't sleep thinking about what you're doing."

"I have so much to tell you. I'll be there soon. And I'll stay with you, I promise."

"Pierce, don't promise. If you don't make it back, or if you have to sit in the waiting area while I have our baby, that's okay with me. Truly. I'll be all right."

"Laurie, that will not happen. I love you. I'll be there soon. Trust me." He hung up.

"How's she doing?" John asked. He gave a bewildered look, then reached in the bedroom and flicked on the light. "Couldn't you find the switch?"

Pierce froze.

The view was the same he had seen that night, and the next morning. The view from the doorway, across the bed, and out the window to the big tree.

But, he wasn't the same. He was no longer a child, and now he knew the truth.

"Pierce!" Gilbert called, he and Daniel ran inside.

Pierce pointed straight out and turned to John. "Is that where our dad has been digging?"

"No." John motioned with his left hand. "The pig pen was opposite the barn."

"Not when I lived here."

"Pierce," Gilbert said, "I just talked to my dad. Remember that tornado, the one that ripped apart our fort when we were kids?"

301

"Yeah."

"It leveled the old pig shed. My dad built Mr. Bridges a new one on the other side of the house. He didn't think it mattered."

Which was why Luther hadn't found Annabelle's grave. He'd been searching for his wife in the wrong place.

Pierce took one last look at the room where his mother died. "Dad, move a car, shine the headlights on the trunk of that old tree. We'll mark the grave, and I can get back to Laurie."

***

Laurie bore down as hard as she could, as Pierce and the nurse counted to ten.

"Good," said Dr. Nate. "Almost there."

Pierce pulled his hand free of hers and shook it. "You almost broke my thumb."

"Yeah? You want to try doing this?"

Dr. Nate laughed. "Don't answer that, Pastor."

"I wasn't planning on it."

"Nurse Wilson, call the nursery, will you? Let them know we'll have a baby in about three minutes. Lie back and rest, Laurie. The next push should do it."

Gratefully, she rested a moment on the pillows, catching her breath. Pierce wiped her face with the cool rag and spooned ice chips into her mouth.

"Thank God for the epidural," she told him. "This is hard enough work without the pain." She smiled so big she thought her face might split open. "I can't wait to see her. I just can't wait."

"You won't have to wait," said Dr. Nate. "Here we go, Laurie. Now, take your deepest breath, and push."

Inside, the baby shifted. There was pressure, so much pressure. "I want to see," she gasped. "Can someone move the mirror?"

She took another quick breath, and bore down again, exactly

302

as Dr. Nate had told her to do, for another count of ten. She saw the doctor grab Pierce's arm.

"Here she comes. Okay, Pastor. Got your gloves on?"

Her husband's brilliant eyes focused between her legs, then shot to hers—a thousand words of love passed between them—and back to the doctor again.

"Gently, right here. Stop pushing Laurie, hold on, I've got to unwrap the cord."

Her body wanted to move, she wanted so badly to move her legs.

Hope screamed. It was one of the most beautiful sounds a mother could ever hear.

Laurie's tears came like rain. Fresh, drenching rain that promised spring flowers and new life.

Pierce cut the cord, another milestone.

Then Dr. Nate lay Hope—a pink, wailing baby—on Laurie's stomach and in her arms.

"Oh, you're so beautiful. Look at you. Look at her, Pierce, I think she has your eyes!" Laurie kissed the tiny, angry face. "She's perfect, Pierce. It's all just perfect. Kiss me. Kiss me quick."

Nurse Wilson walked over and reached for Hope, who finally stopped screaming. "Let's see how much you weigh."

Pierce stiffened. "Why are they taking her?"

"They'll bring her right back."

"They're making her cry again."

"So that's how it's going to be. You'll be the fun parent, and I'll be the one who tells her *no* and disciplines her."

Laurie watched as the nurse weighed and measured Hope, as she took Hope's footprints. Then the nurse cleaned her up and brought her back for Laurie to hold. Pierce intercepted.

"Are you going to let me hold her?"

"In a minute."

"You're going to kiss her to death."

"She's my daughter to kiss. She's soft and pink and beautiful. She tastes sweet like icing."

"But don't you want to invite your parents and John in now?"

"No, I want one more minute of sitting here with you and holding her, all to myself." He leaned down to kiss her cheek. "Laurie—"

"Wait. Don't say anything. Just, let me look into your eyes. How I love your eyes." She ran a hand through his hair. "You're my life, Pierce. Sharing this with you, knowing how hard you worked to be here for me. It means everything."

EPILOGUE

"Laurie, you were right. This is right."

Pierce breathed a huge sigh of relief as the last scoops of dirt fell onto Annabelle and Luther's fresh, side-by-side graves in the corner of the church cemetery.

Laurie slipped her arm through his. "Every spring we'll plant flowers by them. Roses maybe. They'll wind over the double headstone."

Daniel closed his Bible. "They belong here."

"He never asked to talk to me. I didn't see him before he died," said Pierce.

John wiped his own eyes. "I knew he was just holding on until after we found Mama's grave. What you did was better than going to see him. Besides, he might not have spoken to you, let alone offered an apology."

But the little boy inside Pierce, the one who'd begged—*Please, Daddy, please let me stay*—had wanted one.

You don't need his apology. You can have my healing. Every day.

Cool streams flowed. One from Pierce's brain, head knowledge; the other from his spirit, heart knowledge. The waters rushed toward each other—roaring, racing floods—and crashed together with such force the spray shot into the sky of his life and drenched him with joy. A new beginning, with a new family, for a new year.

"I love you all. Thanks for being here with me." He nudged his brother. "John, stay as long as you like. You're welcome to visit them any time and attend any service."

"Won't the roof fall in?"

Daniel patted John's back. "If it does, we'll fix it."

"One day if you have time, maybe we could talk about her. Our mother," John said.

Pierce cleared his throat. "Sure." And maybe one day with God's help, he'd be brave enough to ask for details about their father.

Pierce took Hope from his mother.

"She's just so sweet," Kay said. "I don't want to let her go."

"I know what you mean." He stood at the foot of his parents' graves, holding his daughter, in perfect peace.

Laurie kissed him on the cheek. "Her eyes are droopy. We should go home, put her down for a nap."

"I can hold her while she sleeps."

"I know that," she whispered in his ear. "But I'd rather you hold *me* while she sleeps."

Always. Every night for the rest of his life.

"See y'all later," he said to those around him. He wrapped his arm around Laurie and walked his family home through the woods.

***

Within minutes they entered through the back door into the kitchen.

"Put her in her crib for a nap," Laurie said. "Then come to the back bedroom. I have something to show you."

She hoped she'd done the right thing. Keeping her little project a secret had been quite a challenge, not to mention she had a newborn to take care of. But she'd been determined to give Pierce back one more piece of his mother.

She stood in the corner, her hand on the sheet-covered item, then touched fingertips to both pearl earrings and thought of her own mother. Finally Pierce found her.

She smiled at him. "Took you long enough."

"I like to watch her sleep."

"I know you do. Close your eyes."

He balked.

"Just close your eyes." He complied, and she lifted the sheet. "Okay, open them." She watched recognition dawn—he must've noted the chair was missing a spindle—and his blue eyes met hers.

"That's no ordinary chair, is it?"

She couldn't read his expression. "No, it isn't."

"It's Mama's chair."

Her heart thudded in her chest. "Yes. It is."

"How? Where did you, how did you get it?"

"John gave it to me." She took a deep breath and straightened her shoulders. "I told him how much I thought having it would mean to you."

"Mama's chair."

She waited, bunched the sheet in her hands as he slowly moved through the open doorway and grasped the smooth top rail of the chair.

"Did you, um, refinish it as well?"

She'd loved the feeling of working with her hands, of making something old look almost new, even more so when it was a gift for Pierce. "I did. For you."

He shook his head. "But you've got the baby."

"I did it because I love you."

She took a step away to allow him his space, and to give him time to be wholly there, in that moment, with the chair and his mama's memory.

He closed his eyes. Eased himself down until he reached the seat. When it creaked under his weight, he opened his eyes and smiled at her. Finally his face showed both surprise and joy.

She smiled in return. How wonderful that God let her play a part in helping Pierce.

"Come here." He reached for her.

She dropped the sheet and laced her fingers with his. Let him turn her and ease her down until she sat securely in his lap, their hands

307

clasped under her heart. The chair creaked again, this time in protest. Startled, they looked at each other and burst out laughing.

"You better let me go," she said, her eyes widening. "We don't want to break it."

He pressed his forehead against her shoulder. "I'm never letting you go."

DISCUSSION QUESTIONS FOR THE SPINDLE CHAIR

1. As the story begins, Pierce and Laurie have a stable and close marriage. They want the same things in life. How does the miscarriage bind them together? In what ways does it begin to tear them apart? Discuss how a tragedy can become a "marker" in one's life—marking a date, a place, an experience which greatly influences our lives. Has tragedy shaped part of your life? Your faith? Your marriage?

2. Laurie has always sensed a deep sadness in Pierce. What does she believe will heal Pierce's heart? Discuss how one can have good intentions, yet our actions might worsen someone's pain. Can Laurie really do anything to help Pierce heal? Why, or why not?

3. God first speaks to Pierce about his strange reactions and anxiety by reminding him of scripture. Why do you think God uses this method? Pierce responds by asking God to return his and Laurie's life to the way it was before the miscarriage, as he assumes the pain and stress he is experiencing indicate something "bad" is happening to him. Discuss why we sometimes assume discomfort and unease are incompatible with God's work in our lives. How has God used struggle to improve your life and faith?

4. Neither Pierce nor Laurie realizes the many expectations, hurt, and baggage they each brought into their marriage. Where do Laurie's expectations about becoming a mother, and pregnancy, come from? Initially, Laurie and Pierce dream together about their future. What hurts does Laurie bring with her into her second pregnancy process, and what new hurts does she experience when Pierce begins pulling away from her? Pierce doesn't know why he feels and reacts the way he does after the miscarriage and second pregnancy. Discuss how old wounds can influence and/or

control us, even if we are unaware of those wounds.

5. As God reveals Pierce's past, Pierce's level of panic rises. What kind of impact does this process have on Pierce's spiritual life? On his marriage? With Laurie's pregnancy, God is actually answering Pierce's prayer and giving Laurie the desire of her heart. When have you experienced a situation in which the best thing that could happen for someone else was the worst thing that could happen for you? What was your response at the time? Did your perspective of that situation change as time passed? How?

6. While Laurie struggles with anger and hurt, she still endeavors to listen to God and be proactive instead of reactive. She wants to do things that will prepare her for reconciliation and healing in her marriage. What actions does Laurie take? Notice that Laurie continues to pray for Pierce. What requests does she make when praying for Pierce? If you were in Pierce's place, what prayer requests would you want your spouse to make on your behalf? Discuss how we often experience grief and joy simultaneously, i.e., Laurie's pregnancy coincides with Pierce's struggles and marital conflict. How does one find spiritual equilibrium during those seasons?

7. Kay encourages Laurie to ask Pierce for what she needs from him, such as praying for their baby, keeping his promises, etc., even though he had previously refused other requests. Would their relationship have healed in the same ways if Laurie stopped asking for what she needed? Why, or why not? Is there an important relationship in your life that could potentially be strengthened if you shared your needs? How can you pray for the other person, as Laurie did for Pierce, while you wait for God to do a work in them?

8. At first, Laurie lets pride or self-consciousness—she is a pastor's wife—keep her from seeking help and support from others. From whom does Laurie eventually seek help as she works to rebuild her marriage and help Pierce face his past? Are these good choices for her? Why, or why not? Daniel and Kay have direct influence on Pierce throughout the story. Give an example of good advice or help they give Pierce and Laurie. Discuss the

difference between telling someone a difficult truth versus being judgmental. How do Daniel and Kay continue to show their love and support of Pierce and Laurie?

9. At times it appears Pierce is preaching both *about* himself and *to* himself. Share a time when God ministered to you as you prayed for, helped, or spoke truth to someone else. Discuss how God can still use us to touch others, even when we are injured or hurting. Do you think you are more or less sensitive to God during times of personal struggle? Why, or why not?

10. As Pierce remembers and reveals his past, Laurie realizes she doesn't know as much as she thought she did about Pierce. How does that make Laurie feel? Are her feelings warranted? Why, or why not? Discuss how important it is for a married couple to continue learning about each other. What benefits and/or risks arise from being open to discovery about each other? How does God fit into those benefits and risks?

11. The revelation of John's identity and Luther's whereabouts is a pivotal moment for Pierce. List reasons why it is so difficult for Pierce to befriend his brother. Discuss how these reasons affect his struggle as a pastor. A husband and son. A Christian. A future father.

12. Several times God speaks to Laurie about her expectations for her marriage. In her mind, the approaching delivery of their child equals a time limit for Pierce to be completely healed of his emotional pain. What is your reaction to the perspective God offers? Think of a current issue in a relationship with a spouse, family member, or friend. How can adopting God's perspective affect how you feel and what you do? Which aspects of the relationship might become more difficult or more manageable because of your expectations? Because of God's perspective?

13. Even after Pierce determines to do whatever it takes to save his marriage, even after he repents, he still has a lot of work to do. In fact, that's when the real work begins. Discuss the various "steps" that Pierce takes as he attempts to obey God. Which step do you think is most challenging for Pierce? Why? To which challenge

do you most relate? Why?

14. Early in the story, we see how much Pierce admires Laurie's ten-
    der heart and compassionate qualities—they are part of what at-
    tracted him to her in the first place. Discuss whether Pierce tries
    to use that quality against Laurie when suggesting she ask Kay to
    be her labor coach. Does Laurie maintain a sense of compassion
    for Pierce? Why, or why not? Later, Pierce has moments he relies
    on, and moments he fights resenting those qualities in Laurie.
    How do the conflicts within Pierce precipitate these feelings? Are
    his actions understandable? Are they *right*? Discuss a character
    trait in someone close to you that you once found appealing, but
    now is a source of irritation. What can you learn from Pierce's
    experience?

15. As mentioned before, meeting John and having John be an
    instant part of his life are uncomfortable experiences for Pierce.
    Why is meeting John a critical part of Pierce's healing process?
    What does Laurie contribute? What responsibilities rest fully on
    Pierce? Discuss the fact that Pierce never sees Luther alive again,
    nor does he receive an apology from him. Can Pierce experience
    emotional healing despite Luther's absence? Why?

16. By the end of the story, Laurie realizes her desire for Pierce to
    be with her during delivery has nothing to do with her dreams
    and everything to do with the pain she still carries from her
    parents' death. Discuss the similarities between Pierce and
    Laurie's emotional pain. How are their responses similar? How
    are they different? Memory repression and suppression are fairly
    common responses to trauma. Even more common is when one
    remembers a trauma or loss (as Laurie does) but doesn't realize
    the impact that loss has on daily life. Discuss that God's plan is
    to heal both Laurie and Pierce, even when it seems the worst is
    happening in their marriage. How does God healing the individ-
    ual affect the marriage? What do you think Laurie and Pierce's
    marriage looks like after the Epilogue?

17. The exposure of truth and the idea of truth versus lies are contin-
    ual threads throughout the story. God loves us too much to let
    us continue to lie to ourselves and to others. How is experiencing

emotional healing dependent on you being honest with yourself? Honest with God? Honest with others? Share, as a prayer request, what you need from God to begin this process.

18. Seldom do life's challenges line up single-file, especially within a marriage. They overlap, intertwine and affect each other—both the highs and lows—exposing a husband and wife's strengths and weaknesses. How do Pierce's and Laurie's strengths and weaknesses impact their journey? Analyze your own and your mate's strengths and weaknesses. What do you need from God to maximize the benefit of your strengths and minimize the impact of your weaknesses?

* If you or someone you love wants information or instruction to receive emotional healing, please visit my website www.shelliearnold.com. Check out the YOUR MARRIAGE resources seminars *Rise to Freedom* and *Intimacy Barriers.*

Made in the USA
Middletown, DE
25 January 2016